I0678098

NEXUS

ZIVA PAYVAN BOOK 2

EJ FISCH

Transcendence
Publishing

NEXUS

Copyright © 2014 E.J. Fisch

All rights reserved. No part of this publication may be reproduced, distributed, or transmitted in any form or by any means, including photocopying, recording, or other electronic or mechanical methods, without the prior written permission of the author or publisher, except in the case of brief quotations embodied in critical reviews and certain other noncommercial uses permitted by copyright law.

First edition: December 2014

If you would like to use material from the book, prior written permission must be obtained by contacting the publisher at transcendence.publishing@gmail.com.

The Transcendence Publishing name, imprint, and logo are trademarks of Transcendence Publishing.

Publisher's note: This is a work of fiction. Names, characters, places, and incidents are a product of the author's imagination or are used fictitiously. Any resemblance to actual people, living or dead, or to businesses, companies, events, institutions, or locales is completely coincidental.

ISBN-13: 978-0692312223
ISBN-10: 0692312226

THE
ZIVA PAYVAN
SERIES

A full dramatis personae and glossary of series terms

can be found at

www.ejfisch.com/glossary

NEXUS

· 1 ·

RESIDENTIAL SECTOR
NORO, HAPHEZ

The interior of the house was dark, but working in the dark was one of her specialties. All the windows had already been set to maximum tint when she'd arrived, which was a bit of a relief. Even though she wore gloves, it was one less thing she had to worry about touching. And in this situation, the less she had to worry about, the better.

She'd been there for close to an hour now. Much of that time had been spent standing motionless in the center of a room, taking in every detail in order to ensure nothing looked any different when it was time to leave. It was something she'd made a habit of doing whenever she was somewhere she wasn't supposed to be. It made for a slow search process though; each and every movement was carefully calculated, and she felt as though she'd spent more time focused on covering her tracks than on the actual hunt.

After searching the living room and kitchen, she had found nothing of value. There were plenty of items that were valuable monetarily, sure, but she never dealt in anything so petty. She searched only for information. It would have been more efficient to simply bug the house or install a hidden cam somewhere, but she knew the owner—an experienced and respected agent with the Haphezian Special Police—would discover such a device in no time. She would no doubt be suspected immediately, and all her efforts toward remaining invisible would be rendered futile.

Guided by the dim red light of the single glow stick she carried, she turned and crept down the short hallway toward the bedroom and personal office space. If there was anything interesting to be found, she guessed that was where it would be. When a visual sweep of the room yielded nothing of consequence, she went to work at the communications console, carefully picking her way into the call logs. She wasn't particularly surprised to find they had all been erased, but she cursed her poor luck regardless. She should have known better than to think a veteran HSP agent would leave such information—work-related *or* personal—in a place where it could so easily fall into the wrong hands.

She moved on to a shelf beside the wardrobe, shuffling through a stack of data pads and taking care to lay each one back down at the appropriate angle as she finished. None of them seemed to contain anything useful. A quick but cautious search through the wardrobe itself also produced no results. She was starting to consider calling it quits when she opened the last drawer. Rather than pull out, the front of the drawer simply folded down, revealing two smaller drawers behind it. She tugged on the upper one and found several high-powered pistols encased in protective gel. The bottom one wouldn't budge. *Hello there,* she thought.

Shutting the gun drawer, she bent down to take a closer look at the locked compartment. It was equipped with a biometric scanner as well as a small cavity that appeared to be for some sort of coded key. She knew she could eventually breach such security measures, but at the moment, she lacked the equipment to do so. She checked the time; the owner would be returning home from work any minute.

She carefully lifted the false drawer cover back into place and retreated from the room. Everything in the house looked exactly as it had been when she'd entered, and she was confident the odor-masking spray she wore would successfully conceal any scent she left behind. It was disappointing to be leaving empty-handed, but she believed she'd found what she was looking for. And she'd be back for it.

· 2 ·
GARDEN BRIDGE
PALACE OF THE ROYAL OFFICER
HAPHOR, HAPHEZ

The rain had finally reduced itself to a mere drizzle, though thunder still rumbled and some nearby sarmi trees continued to hiss as the wind rushed through their leaves. Lightning illuminated the courtyard for only an instant every few seconds, bathing the walkway and garden in brilliant white light. The raindrops could be heard pattering on the stone path and splattering into the puddles that had formed in the grass and flowerbeds. Excess water from the roof cascaded down from the gutter, making a mess as it hammered into the ground and painted everything within two meters with a thick layer of dark mud.

Kade Shevin pivoted on his left heel and spun his rigid body around, turning back in the direction from which he had just come. After pausing a moment, he began to take slow, even strides back across the footbridge that spanned the courtyard and connected the Royal Officer's private estate to his office building.

It wasn't that the disciplined movements were regulation, and it certainly wasn't that Kade was standing at attention for anyone. He was freezing, soaked to the skin through his uniform, and he could find no other way to help pass the time than to pretend he was actually doing something of consequence—not that protecting Officer Ikaro Tachi wasn't of consequence....

Forty paces across the bridge one way, eighty total. He'd lost track of how many rounds he'd made already, but the cramps in his legs told him it was a few too many. When he reached the end again, he turned, walked back several steps, and took a moment to stop and lean against the metal railing that ran the length of the bridge. There was nothing to see there in the dark except for the occasional blink-and-you-miss-it view of the garden whenever the lighting came. In the absence of lightning, a few small illumination bots hovered in the area below him, but the dim halos of light around them did next to nothing to penetrate the night.

The wad of govino gum rolling around in his mouth had long since lost its flavor, so he removed it and lobbed it out over the side of the bridge. At twenty-five years old, he was a fresh addition to the Haphezian Special Police's Royal Guard, having spent the last four years working spaceport security after a year in the military. He had a beautiful wife of almost two years and a newborn daughter. They were his pride and joy, the reason he now found himself standing out in the rain while the majority of the security detail got to stay inside closer to the party. He hadn't been with the Royal Guard long enough to earn such a privilege yet, but he was willing to fight his way up the ranks if it meant supporting his family.

Kade wasn't overly tall as far as HSP agents went, standing a bit shy of two meters. He was strong and just as good with a gun as any RG officer, but his mind was his weapon of choice. Problem solving and perseverance were his strong suits, and as such, he'd never meshed well with his colleagues who took more pride in how much weight they could lift or what their target shooting scores were. His work ethic made up for his mediocrity in other areas, and his superiors were finally starting to take notice; maybe it wouldn't be long before he too could stay inside out of the rain.

Music and laughter from the party trickled out of the main audience hall and reached Kade's ears. This gala had commanded the Royal Guard's attention for weeks. Officer Tachi was hosting it for every dignitary on the planet short of the king himself and was due to present some sort of award to the Prime Director of HSP, Kade believed. Saying security was high was like saying the galaxy was big.

With a sigh, he stood up and resumed his pacing, wishing he hadn't spit out the gum. He blinked the water out of his eyes and looked down at his boots to shield his face as the rain started pouring hard again. His brown hair was soaked black and he reached up to brush away a lock that had become plastered to his forehead. The surface of the bridge appeared to be covered in tiny crawling creatures as the huge raindrops pelted it and splashed onto him. He was about to check on how much time was left in his shift when he glanced down into the darkness just as a jagged bolt of lightning brought the courtyard into view.

Kade tensed, the sensation of the pounding rain fading into the back of his mind, and rushed back to lean over the railing. He'd seen something down there, the unmistakable shape of a crouching person, highlighted against the solid white wall that surrounded the palace and offices. It had only been for a second, but that second had been enough. He held perfectly still, staring into the darkness as he waited for another lightning strike. Even with keen Haphezian eyesight, it was impossible to see anything through the rain. When the flash finally came, the figure was gone, but a thin black cord dangled from the top of the wall, wriggling in the wind.

Instinctively, he placed a finger on the communicator in his ear, ready to alert someone, but something held him back. He squinted into the black void a bit longer, trying to see where the intruder had gone. Two more lightning flashes came and went. Still nothing.

"Bridge to ballroom," he said slowly, barely able to hear himself over the roar of the rain.

"Copy, bridge," crackled the voice of Luko Zona, his commanding officer. "What's the problem?"

"I think I saw someone," Kade answered, "in the garden."

"It was probably a guest out for some fresh air," his superior suggested after a brief hesitation. "Believe me, there are a few who've hit the open bar pretty hard."

Out of habit, Kade shook his head, though he wasn't speaking to Zona face to face. "It wasn't a guest. I closed this area off to civilians." He glanced around quickly as another lightning bolt ripped through the clouds. "Get someone up here, will you?"

He could hear the exasperation in Zona's sigh. "You sure, kid?"

"Yes!"

"I'll have someone clear the garden. Sit tight."

Kade sensed movement to his right and whirled. "Hello?" he called into the rain. He removed the spotlight from his belt and activated it, but his cold and trembling fingers failed to grasp it tightly and it slipped out over the side of the bridge. "*Sheyss.*"

He felt silly talking to someone when he didn't even know if they were really there, and he was beginning to wonder if he'd simply been seeing things. With a slippery hand, he drew his pistol and strode forward, shielding his face with his free hand. The opposite end of the bridge was shrouded in darkness that anyone or anything could be lurking in.

Gritting his teeth, he pressed forward into the shadows. "HSP! Whoever is there, come out with your hands where I can see them!"

Surely nobody would actually come out—if they were even there in the first place. He suddenly felt very afraid, and his mind wandered to Veya and Jernie who were waiting up for him at home. Assuming this was nothing, he'd have quite the tale to tell when he finally made it back to them. And if there *was* an intruder, he would still have a good story...if he lived long enough to tell it.

Something moved ahead of him, a more defined shadow that hadn't been there a moment before. It was without doubt a person, roughly the same height as himself, standing several meters in front of him. It was still too dark to make out any distinguishing features, much less tell if it was male or female. It stood there watching him, unmoving.

Despite his soaked clothes, he could feel himself start to sweat profusely. He grasped his pistol with both hands to steady it and took another step forward. "HSP," he repeated. "Show yourself, now!"

The figure ducked away without warning, and Kade considered firing at it. "Stop!" he ordered, rushing deeper into the shadows. Boots scuffled behind him and he whirled, thrusting his pistol into the darkness toward the unseen enemy.

A brilliant white flash tore through his vision, once when something heavy struck him headlong in the face and a second time when his skull met the surface of the bridge. He lay there, fluttering his eyelids, catching a blurry image of the intruder as it entered the palace. Blackness crept inward from the edges of his eyes, and he finally closed them to dull the throbbing pain.

· 3 ·

MAIN HALL
PALACE OF THE ROYAL OFFICER
HAPHOR, HAPHEZ

Skeet Duvo, sergeant of HSP's Alpha special operations team, shook his head and tugged at the collar of his tunic shirt with two fingers. Not only was it insanely itchy, but it also felt like it was restricting his air supply. His stiff, unblemished jacket hugged his muscular frame, limiting the range of motion in his shoulders. This current ensemble was probably the nicest thing he owned, other than his HSP dress uniform, but he had only worn it two or three times in his life. Such formal occasions made him feel entirely out of place, despite the fact that everyone around him was dressed in a similar fashion.

He let out a long sigh and brushed his hand over his greased hair, still unaccustomed to the fact that it wasn't sticking out everywhere like he usually wore it. He'd done his hair and dressed up for this just like he'd been told, but he'd taken a risk and left the multiple piercings in his ears, small tokens that made him feel like he was still himself.

He was suddenly aware of someone about his height standing beside him. Rather than turn or even move, he smiled to himself and continued to scan the crowd. "Remind me again what we're doing here?"

Ziva Payvan—the Alpha team's lieutenant, his boss, and the woman he respected more than anyone else in the galaxy—scoffed and crossed her arms. "Someone's got to be on protection detail for the director. Don't ask me how they decided it was our turn. Trust me, there are hundreds of things I'd rather be doing right now instead of standing around here looking like an idiot."

This made Skeet smile again. After eight years of camaraderie, they had begun to think alike. He turned to face Ziva and was rendered temporarily speechless by how stunning she looked in her evening-wear. She wore a modest but elegant floor-length black dress that draped over one shoulder, curved across her chest, and disappeared under her opposite arm. The tattoos visible on her back and upper arms seemed a bit out of place at this event, but in Skeet's opinion, they complemented the dress quite nicely. Her black and red-streaked hair was woven and folded into a braid-like style against the back of her head.

"Well," he said, turning his attention back to the party guests milling about in Officer Tachi's ballroom, "you look like anything but an idiot."

She shook her head and rolled her eyes. "Thanks," she muttered. "Where's Zinni?"

"I didn't know when you'd get here, so I stationed her by the side entrance," he replied. "What took you so long, anyway?"

"Just had a few things to take care of," Ziva answered, refraining from elaborating any further. She unfolded her arms and slid her hands down to rest on her hips. Even in the formal dress, she looked formidable enough to make anyone think twice about approaching her in the wrong way.

The vagueness of her response told Skeet not to push the matter. They may have faced life-and-death situations together on a daily basis, but their personal lives were a different matter. Ziva especially had always been a very private person, and while it sometimes drove him crazy, he respected that privacy. He reminded himself that, if it was anything important, she certainly would have shared.

He kept his eyes on HSP Director Emeri Arion as the man mingled with the other guests. While the place was already crawling with security detail from every organization represented, the Alpha team had been sent along in plainclothes to provide expertise and a few extra sets of eyes. All three of them were packing, but to any onlookers, they were just three more partygoers.

The Royal Officer had yet to make an appearance at his own gala.

He was due to present several awards in—Skeet checked the time—about ten minutes, one in particular to Director Arion for some miniscule thing he had no doubt already received similar awards for. Still, this was one of the biggest events of the year among the Haphezian dignitaries, whether it was because they were being commended or because they were looking for a good time. Skeet could honestly say he'd be enjoying himself if not for the clothes he was wearing. He gave his collar another tug and squirmed in his jacket.

"You, on the other hand, might look like an idiot, the way you keep fidgeting like that," Ziva said in a motherly tone. The corners of her mouth turned upward ever so slightly. It wasn't often that something so insignificant could make her smile—she was clearly in a better mood than Skeet would have expected of her on an assignment like this.

"Not everyone cleans up as nice as you do, Z."

"I didn't say you don't look nice," she said. "Just try not to look like you're dying."

"You two look like you're having way too much fun."

They both turned to find Intelligence Officer Zinnarana Vax moving up to stand beside them. She too wore a long black dress, this one strapless. The glittering blue sash around her waist did a fantastic job of bringing out the brilliant cerulean in her eyes and hair, which she had left down. Zinni was much smaller than either of them, but what she lacked in size she made up for in attitude and brains. If they were smart, people treaded just as lightly around her as they did around Ziva. She was tough and intelligent but wasn't nearly as callous as the lieutenant. The two of them balanced each other out, and Skeet couldn't have asked for a better pair of teammates.

"You know we are," Ziva replied, crossing her arms again. "See anything out of place?"

"Not a thing," Zinni said. "We've been here for close to an hour, and everything seems normal."

"Except that," Skeet muttered, perking up. He stepped away from the women, eyes fixed on three uniformed HSP agents as they rushed from the hall. He turned to his left to see another pair listening intently to their earpieces before they too hurried off.

Ziva and Zinni strode forward as well, with Ziva brushing past him and stopping a step in front of him. "This can't be good."

Nearby guests had noticed the commotion and were chattering amongst themselves. Some were beginning to cluster at the bottom of the grand staircase, peering up in the direction the agents had gone. Whatever had them so intrigued was happening on the second floor of Tachi's palace.

· 4 ·

MAIN HALL
PALACE OF THE ROYAL OFFICER
HAPHOR, HAPHEZ

The moment she heard the distant shouting coming from upstairs, Ziva Payvan removed her pistol from where it had been strapped to her upper ankle, well concealed under the flowing dress. Those around her scattered upon seeing the weapon, giving her plenty of space to press forward with Skeet and Zinni directly behind her.

The remaining agents she could see from her current vantage point had also drawn their sidearms and were doing their best to round up the VIPs and lead them to safety. Ziva wished desperately for an earpiece or some other form of communication that would allow her to find out what had transpired upstairs.

"Hey!" she barked at a pair of armor-clad HSP agents as they hustled Emeri Arion out of the room. "Lieutenant Payvan, HSP. What's going on?"

For a moment, the agents responded with looks of shock and Ziva was afraid they would treat her as a threat, but the director quickly intervened. "They just found Tachi in his private quarters," he said, lowering his voice as he drew closer. "He's dead."

Her eyes darted toward the stairs. A trio of Royal Guard agents remained halfway up the flight of steps, hands extended in an attempt to calm the nervous onlookers and keep them at bay. She'd never cared for Tachi—had every reason to hate him, in fact—but now, standing in the building where the head of all Haphezian domestic law enforcement had just been murdered seemed...surreal. She swallowed and glanced toward the dining hall where the VIPs were being corralled. In such a situation, it was now her team's duty to escort the director off the premises and to safety, no matter what became of the other dignitaries.

She took Emeri's arm and faced the two agents, who were growing antsy. "We'll take it from here, gentlemen."

· 5 ·

RESIDENTIAL WING
PALACE OF THE ROYAL OFFICER
HAPHOR, HAPHEZ

K ade sat on a chair someone had set up for him, surrounded by several of his peers. His shoulders sagged as he held a medi-pac to the lump on his head and pressed a cloth to his gushing nose. His left eye was swollen shut from the blow to his face. The culprit: a rock half the size of his head that the intruder had apparently taken from the garden.

The last thing he remembered before being discovered by a fellow agent was an image of the intruder entering the palace. He had no inkling of how long he'd been unconscious and thus no idea how long the figure had been inside, but according to Zona, it had been long enough to kill the Royal Officer with a professionally placed shot to the head.

"And you never saw a face?" the supervisory agent said, the fifth time he'd asked that question or one like it.

"No!" Kade exclaimed, the same way he'd responded to every instance of the question. His voice was somewhat muffled by the compress over his nose. "All I saw was that it was someone about my height, maybe a little taller. It was so dark, and they had to have been wearing all black."

"He never spoke to you?"

This time Kade resorted to a simple shake of his head so he didn't have to taste the blood leaking down his face. It bothered him that Zona kept referring to the intruder as a male, though there had been no way to tell one way or the other. Whoever it was, however, was well trained in stealth and infiltration, had the signature of a professional killer, and was determined enough to proceed with their mission even after they'd heard Kade call for backup.

He tilted his head back long enough to rearrange the cloth over his face; it was so saturated with blood he couldn't even tell whether his nose was still bleeding. "I don't know what else you want to hear— I've told you everything I know. I was out there, saw the intruder in the courtyard, went to investigate, and got hit in the head. Haven't you found anything else to go on?"

Zona sighed and wiped a gloved hand across his forehead. He was an experienced investigator in his mid-forties, but the gray stripes running through his brown hair sometimes made him look older. They certainly did now as he took a moment to rub his tired eyes. The day had been long to begin with, but the unexpected developments had pushed everyone to the end of their ropes.

"He made it over the wall using a magnetic hook and grappling cable, all the while avoiding detection by any agents or security bots. There were plenty of tracks in the mud, but by the time we got someone out there, the rain had done a fantastic job of washing away any distinctive tread marks. At this point, it would be difficult to even get an accurate boot size out of them."

Kade shifted in the chair, arms tired from putting pressure on his wounds. "Any idea how he got up onto the bridge without me hearing?"

Zona shot him a disgusted look, and Kade wished he hadn't made it sound like it was his fault any more than it already was.

"There was no evidence of a second grappling hook or other tool," the senior agent responded, "but someone in decent physical condition would have been able to jump up and pull themselves over the railing. It would be quiet and wouldn't leave any distinguishing scratches or marks."

"Fingerprints?" Kade ventured.

Zona snorted. "Anyone with a brain stem would have been wearing gloves. We checked though and came up with several sets that match Tachi, his family, and the agents who discovered the body. There are a couple of partials we're still trying to match, but chances are we won't find anything of use."

Kade was crushed, both by the stares of his associates and by his own emotions. Not only was it his fault that the intruder had gained access to the palace in the first place, but this person had also managed to kill the Royal Officer and escape without leaving any evidence of their presence. He couldn't help but have a secret respect for their skill, though he didn't dare admit any such thing to Zona.

"I'm sorry," was all he could say.

Zona sighed yet again and pocketed the gloves he'd been wearing. He extended a hand and helped Kade stand up. "Come on, kid. You could use some medical attention."

The hallway tilted for a moment as Kade searched for his footing. He was readjusting the cloth on his nose, which had nearly stopped bleeding, when he heard someone shout from the direction of Tachi's private quarters.

"Special Agent Zona! You'd better come see this!"

The agents around him took off at a dead run, leaving Kade to stumble along behind them on tired legs. He entered Tachi's room to find them gathered around a technician kneeling beside a trash receptacle built into the wall.

"The only reason I found it was because I saw the gloves," he said, indicating a pair of black gloves on the floor. "It was buried under some other garbage."

The item he referred to was a black stealth suit he had draped across his arms as if he were advertising it in a market. It was still damp from the rain and rumpled from being stuffed into the small compactor. There was no doubt in Kade's mind that it had belonged to his assailant.

"The cut is what I find most interesting," the technician said, holding the suit up so everyone could get a better look. The other forensics techs swarmed him, taking photos and gathering data.

"The killer is a woman," Zona observed after studying the garment for a moment.

"Or a very oddly-shaped man," one of the other young investigators quipped. He bowed his head and stepped away after receiving scolding looks from the rest of the agents.

"Now the question is how she escaped the building without anyone seeing," Zona said, stroking his chin with his thumb and forefinger. "Unless…"

"Sir!" another technician exclaimed, waving a compact fingerprint scanner through the air. "We have a hit on one of the partials!"

He handed it to Zona, who studied it intently with a look of disappointment on his face. He held the device up for everyone to see, displaying the HSP operations insignia and redacted profile on the screen. Whether he was finishing his last thought or announcing it for the others to hear, he cleared his throat and continued, "…she's one of us."

· 6 ·
HSP HEADQUARTERS
NORO, HAPHEZ

The Royal Guard, in all its illusive grandeur, was determined to keep any details of Tachi's assassination to itself. It was a separate division of HSP after all, with its own procedures, responsibilities, and chain of command, but the agents had always been very open to receiving assistance from the rest of the parent agency. This secrecy was unusual and was thus becoming a topic of argument among the agency's higher-ups; the last thing anyone had heard was that a crucial piece of evidence had been discovered, but what it was and what it pointed to remained a mystery.

Ziva sat at one of the workstations in her team's bullpen, watching the terminal as if information would magically appear the longer and harder she stared. It wasn't that the Royal Guard had blocked access to its findings—Zinni would have taken care of that long ago—but they had never even entered any data that could be retrieved. Anything they had discovered was being stored somewhere other than the main HSP databases, purposely out of the reach of anyone outside a very small, tight circle.

The flight back to the spaceport city of Noro had lasted well into the night, and though she had been sent home on the director's orders, Ziva had only been able to catch a couple hours of sleep before resolving to come in to Headquarters. Now it was mid-morning, and the entire agency was hard at work searching for details regarding the assassination. But there was frustration in the air as resources and ideas gradually dwindled. Emeri himself had been busy on comm since arriving home from Haphor, speaking to the Royal Guard's powers-that-be from behind the closed doors of his office.

Ziva cursed the RG under her breath and allowed an exasperated growl to escape her throat. This wasn't working. Lack of sleep and lack of information didn't mix. Heaving a sigh, she logged out of her secure account and opted to head upstairs to see if the director had been able to squeeze any reports out of their counterparts in Haphor.

As she moved across the floor, she took a moment to observe all the people glued to their stations. It was rare to have so many spec ops agents sitting idly at their desks. The majority of their time was spent out in the field, and even when they were present on the HSP campus, they could most likely be found at the canteen or shooting range—*anywhere* but their offices. But today wasn't like other days; all hands were on deck, so to speak. The thought bolstered her resolve a bit as she slipped her access key out and waved it over the scanner to summon the elevator car.

Lost in thought, it took her a moment to realize the scanner was unresponsive to her key. Cursing the defective technology under her breath, she swiped it again. This time, after a short hesitation, the scanner buzzed and flashed an angry red light at her. Again, she tried, then a fourth time, drawing the same results.

She stole a glance over her shoulder, realizing she had attracted the attention of several nearby agents. They watched her warily, and she couldn't help but wonder if they were taking secret delight in watching the great Ziva Payvan struggle with such a simple piece of equipment. She swore and slammed her palm against the elevator door.

After one last futile attempt and another sharp warning from the scanner, she conceded and headed for the stairwell, settling on the idea that she could use the extra walking time to do some more thinking. The Royal Guard couldn't hold out forever. It would only take one meddling news reporter to start a chain reaction that would spread across the planet in a matter of minutes. She hoped she wouldn't have to wait that long, and anyhow she preferred gaining intel from more reliable sources.

Despite her decision to take the stairs, the chime of the elevator bell still caught her attention just as she entered the stairwell. Out of habit and maybe out of spite, she turned back to look just as three armed agents in full body armor stepped out of the car. They scanned the area until their eyes fell upon her and one of them gestured at her.

More footsteps thundered up the stairs toward her, and she spotted yet another trio of guards emerging on the far side of the squad floor. The realization that her access key had been intentionally deactivated hit her at the same time the rest of the agents reached her.

"Hands on your head, Payvan!" one of them ordered. He held a stun baton in his hand, though he kept it lowered as he approached. "Slowly."

She complied, not wanting to cause more of a problem than there apparently already was. As soon as her arms were at a ninety-degree angle to her body, two of the agents rushed forward to disarm her and pat her down for further weapons.

"What's this about?" she demanded, wishing that fighting all of them off would do something other than make matters worse.

"If you know what's good for you Payvan, you'll be quiet." She turned to find the director himself approaching, flanked by two more armed men. "Put her in Interrogation Four, please, gentlemen."

Her arms were yanked down from her head and cold handcuffs were slapped over her wrists. She felt a faint shockwave run through her skin as the glittering purple energy reinforcement on the cuffs was activated. "Emeri! What is the meaning of this?" she growled, wrestling out of the agents' grasp.

The director watched her with a grim face. "Ziva, please. I don't even need to tell you that anything you say is *going* to be used against you in court. Just be quiet—don't make this more difficult than it needs to be."

Furious, utterly confused, and embarrassed, she shrugged away from the rough hands on her shoulders. "Don't touch me," she muttered. She knew better than to protest any further at this point; whatever was going on was big enough for them to come pick her up instead of simply calling her somewhere to talk. "I'm going, I'm going."

She walked toward the stairs and went down instead of up like she had originally planned. The agents formed a tight circle around her, though they respectfully kept their distance, and marched her down to the detention level. Ziva was quite familiar with Interrogation Four, having questioned numerous prisoners in that particular room, and she wondered why Emeri had chosen it for her. Perhaps he would try to use her own experiences against her now, for whatever the elusive reason was.

The door of the interrogation room was opened remotely as the group approached, and she walked inside of her own accord. Nothing seemed any different than it had in the countless other times she'd been there, so she stood quietly and listened to the door shut behind her. The sound of the locking mechanism sliding home sent a jolt through her head that made her cringe.

The room's only furnishings were a cold metal table with a single chair on each side and a viewscreen embedded in one wall. A small cam peeked at her from up in the corner, feeding footage into the dark room on the other side of the one-way window.

Sighing, she stooped down, scooted her bound hands under her backside, and stepped through her arms. She paused and examined the purple force field that enveloped the cuffs. With a little work, she would be able to get out of them, but right now, she was more interested in finding out what she was doing there than escaping. *Guilty until proven innocent—that's just how it goes around here...but guilty of what?*

Rubbing her hands together, she walked to one of the chairs, eyeing the cam as it tracked her movements across the room. She sat down with one leg crossed over the other and her hands resting on the table. Her reflection stared back at her from the window, and she wondered how many other sets of eyes were watching from the dark room. They no doubt wanted her to have some kind of incriminating reaction to the situation, but she was determined that they wouldn't get one. With another sigh, she closed her eyes and waited.

· 7 ·

ROYAL GUARD HEADQUARTERS
HAPHOR, HAPHEZ

"**I** don't think I have enough concrete evidence on which I could base an accusation like that," Kade protested as he strode through the Royal Guard Headquarters alongside Luko Zona.

"DNA doesn't lie, Shevin," the commanding officer replied. "What more 'concrete evidence' could you possibly want?"

Kade watched his own feet moving along the ground. "I know, I know, I get it. I guess part of me simply doesn't want to believe one of our own people would do something like this."

Zona stopped and placed both of his hands on Kade's shoulders, his smoky gray eyes full of more wisdom than the young agent could ever wish for. "None of us want to believe it, kid. I understand where you're coming from, but a high-ranking government official was killed here. The rest of the agency wants answers, the Royal House wants answers, the *public* wants answers. We have enough physical evidence to give them some, and it's our duty to present the information to them and not keep them guessing. Now, you've seen the dossier on the agent Director Arion matched that print to. The DNA from the suit is a match, she fits the profile, and although he didn't share details, the director says there may even be a plausible motive. Understand?"

"Yes, but—"

"Listen, Shevin. We can discuss this again later if you're really interested. Right now, the press is all set up in the conference room waiting for you to give an official witness statement. You're going to go in there and tell them exactly what you know."

"I understand," Kade said. "What became of the evidence found in Tachi's room? I'd like to take another look at it, if possible."

"Not possible. The suit, the gloves, data on the fingerprints, all of it was sent off to Noro late last night. Headquarters has been studying it all morning, double-checking everything. The director didn't want to believe it, but he has confirmed it's all genuine."

Part of Kade's heart sank at the news; the other part was pounding tremendously at the thought of going before the media with a story he didn't want to tell. It bothered him that nobody had actually seen anyone enter the palace—even he couldn't be completely sure about who or what he'd seen out on the bridge. But Zona was right. DNA *didn't* lie, and the information Director Arion had provided them with seemed solid enough. He sighed as the two of them stopped in front of the conference room door.

Zona's communicator beeped and he snatched it from his belt. "Zona here."

"We've got her in custody," a voice announced on the other end.

"Very well. Thank you." He replaced the device and jerked his head toward the conference room. "Get in there, kid."

· 8 ·
HSP HEADQUARTERS
NORO, HAPHEZ

Zinni Vax burst into HSP's employee canteen and spotted Skeet's wild orange hair within a split second. She strode toward the table where he sat reading over a data pad and sipping casually at a hot drink. He caught sight of her approaching and waved her toward the empty seat across from him.

"Morning. I hope you're more rested than I am."

She doubted it. "Have you seen Ziva?" she asked, ignoring his invitation to join him.

"Not for an hour or so. She was headed up to the bullpen to do some research." Skeet finished off the last of his drink. "Why?"

"I have someone who wants to speak with her about a potential job, says it's urgent," Zinni replied. "I've spent a good twenty minutes looking for her and I haven't been able to raise her on comm."

"Maybe she left," Skeet suggested.

"She's still logged into the system."

The sergeant shook his head and shrugged. "I don't think it's something you need to get worked up about. She's on campus somewhere."

Now Zinni went ahead and slid into the chair, one leg folded under her. She reached across the table and turned off Skeet's data pad, leaning forward to ensure she had his attention. "I can't help but think something is wrong. I've been up to the squad floor. The place is crawling with agents and bots, and they've got a section of workstations—

including ours—completely cordoned off. Nobody's talking. Now, according to you, the squad floor is the last place Ziva was headed."

Skeet's eyebrows dropped into a scowl. "But surely we would have heard of—" His focus shifted toward a sudden commotion at the door. "Uh-oh."

Zinni followed his gaze and found four agents entering the canteen, all of whom rushed forward upon seeing the two of them. She tensed up and reached for her pistol, but at the slightest movement of her hand, the four of them had their own weapons drawn and trained on the table.

"Officer Vax, we don't want any trouble," one of them said, waving the canteen's other occupants away. "The director just has some questions, and we need both of you to come with us right now."

"We're not going anywhere until you tell us what this is about," Skeet protested as the agents relieved the two of them of their weapons.

The officers glanced among themselves for a moment, unsure what to say, then one of them nodded. "Lieutenant Payvan has been placed under arrest and is currently in custody," he explained gruffly.

"What?" Zinni exclaimed, leaping out of her seat.

Another agent caught her shoulder and forced her back into the chair. "Director Arion doesn't believe either of you are involved as of yet. He's hoping you can shed some light on the situation, but if you refuse, you'll be implicated and I'm sure we can find something good to charge you with."

"Implicated in what?" Zinni demanded, pounding a fist on the table. She closed her eyes to suppress her frustration, reminding herself that now was certainly not the time to let emotions take control.

"Come on," one of the men said, hauling her rather roughly to her feet. "You can finish this conversation in interrogation."

·9·
HSP Headquarters
Noro, Haphez

The only things Ziva allowed to move when the door finally opened were her eyes. It had been nearly an hour since she'd been locked in, and she'd spent the majority of that time meditating, something she had not done for a long time. She felt at ease, at least more so than she normally might have been while sitting in an interrogation room in restraints.

She watched with her peripherals as the director entered, leaving two agents outside the door, and set a good-sized shipping container on the table before her. Remaining motionless, she looked him squarely in the eye as he took a stance opposite her with his arms crossed. He eyed her curiously for a moment before sighing and dipping his head in disappointment.

"As you might imagine, Payvan, I have better things to do than stand here having a staring contest with you. So why don't you start by telling me what the hell you were thinking."

She nodded thoughtfully and ran her tongue across her teeth. "How about *you* start by telling me what I'm doing here." She'd spent some of her time in custody formulating several theories about what was going on, but she wanted to play her cards wisely in this puzzling game and hoped she could coax the first move out of someone else.

"Don't do this, Ziva—it never works. You know good and well why you're here, and pretending is going to waste your time as much as it will mine."

"Refresh my memory then!" she snapped.

Nearly as frustrated as she was, Emeri revealed a tiny remote that had been clenched within his fist and activated the viewscreen on the wall. A previously recorded news report began playing, a press conference that had been held right around the time she'd been apprehended. A man in his mid-twenties was just stepping up to the podium to speak—Royal Guard Agent Kade Shevin, according to the banner that scrolled across the bottom of the screen in a variety of languages.

Shevin cleared his throat and gazed for a moment at the cluster of eager reporters standing before him. "Ladies and gentlemen," he said before clearing his throat a second time. "What you are about to hear is an official statement regarding the events that occurred last night at the residence of Royal Officer Ikaro Tachi."

"Unbelievable," Ziva muttered, so quietly her lips barely moved. This Kade Shevin character was a complete mess. The entire left side of his face was swollen from a blow that had also crushed the cartilage in the bridge of his nose, and he spoke as if he were reading from a prompter. His voice was devoid of any emotion or fervor, making her wonder if he even believed what he was saying.

"Naturally I drew my weapon and ordered Payvan to show herself," Shevin was saying, "but she was unresponsive. That's when I approached."

"Did she ever speak to you?" one of the reporters cried, thrusting a recorder at him.

"No. I ended up losing track of her in the dark, having lost my light source in the rain. She got past me and rendered me unconscious with a rock before I could react. She was then able to get inside uncontested to murder the Royal Officer."

The press began barking more questions, but now an older man— Supervisory Special Agent Luko Zona, the banner said—stepped up to the podium and replaced Shevin. Emeri disabled the audio but allowed the recording to continue playing.

"Remember now?"

Ziva set her jaw. "Can't say I do."

With a sigh, he reached under the table and switched off the interrogation room's sound recorder. He leaned over the table, arms locked, graying eyebrows furrowed, and looked her directly in the eye.

"Listen to me very carefully, Ziva. You're my best agent and I do not want to lose you, so I'm willing to give you a chance here. As of this moment, I still haven't told anybody about your little secret. You come clean right now—make me understand why you did this—and that will *remain* a secret, plus I'll do my best to get you out of yet another execution. If you refuse, however, you'll spend the last days of your miserable life in the Haphor Facility and the entire galaxy will know you're a Nosti."

A momentary tingle of panic coursed through Ziva's body at the mention of the Haphor Facility, though she was careful not to show it. She'd never had the glorious privilege of being admitted to the Facility, an HSP-run establishment often regarded as the most ruthless torture prison in the Fringe Systems. She blinked away a sudden image of herself chained up in a dark room with long burn marks covering her body.

Wondering how much difference it would make if anyone knew of her Nostia, especially if she were locked away in the Haphor prison, she raised her eyebrows and shook her head. "I'm not going to confess to something I didn't do."

Emeri slapped the table. "All right," he growled. His turquoise eyes turned to ice as he switched the recorder back on and went to the door. He gave it two gentle raps with his knuckles and resumed his position in front of her as it opened. To Ziva's surprise, the guards didn't come in to drag her away to Haphor as she had expected. Instead, a single man entered, carrying a small data pad which he placed on the table beside the container the director had brought in.

She looked up into the merciless black eyes of Diago Dasaro, one of Emeri's favorite taskmasters as well as the captain who happened to oversee her unit. Dasaro was a hulking man with a shaved head and a dark *emilan* complexion. He was one of the only captains she knew who ever spent any time in the field, and he had always been her primary competition in terms of solo assignments and black ops—'playing time' as Emeri liked to call it.

She'd beaten him out of much of this so-called playing time over the years and Dasaro had always resented her for it. She was the better shot and was more agile, but when it came to brute strength, he was on top. He was several years older than her and had been the spec ops division's top dog until the 'little girl' had come along and bested him at nearly every aspect of his job.

Dasaro regarded her silently, taunting her without having to speak a word. He stood at ease just to Emeri's left, no doubt reveling in the fact that he was currently favored by the director.

Ziva surveyed the items on the table then shifted her focus back to the two men before her. "Let's say I did kill Tachi. Any chance you could remind me exactly how I pulled it off? My memory's a little fuzzy."

Emeri muttered what sounded like a curse under his breath. "I don't have time for your games, Payvan!"

"I'll handle this, Director," Dasaro said, extending a hand to calm the man. "I'm in the mood for a good game."

Ziva sat back in her chair and scoffed, wishing the cuffs would allow her to cross her arms. "I don't recall asking you, Diago."

Dasaro ignored her and lifted the lid on the container, revealing a long black stealth suit that was rather wrinkled and covered with splotches of mud. He spread it out on the table and folded his arms across his chest. "Look familiar?"

"No. Should it?"

"You were wearing it last night when you scaled the wall surrounding Tachi's courtyard," the captain continued, treating her remarks with more patience than Ziva might have expected from him. "You were seen briefly by Kade Shevin as you made your way across the garden to the bridge. There you were able to hoist yourself up and render Shevin unconscious before he could meet with the backup he'd called for. From there, you entered the palace and were able to infiltrate Tachi's private quarters, where you killed him with a suppressed projectile weapon." He brought up a photo of the entry wound on the data pad. "You use a projectile pistol these days, don't you?"

"So do a lot of people," Ziva replied. "They've been more effective against the anti-plasma shields everyone is using."

"Right. I carry one myself. Witnesses downstairs said you drew a weapon matching that description when the lockdown began. The bullet that killed Tachi was a frag round so ballistic fingerprinting is out of the question, but we found the same type of ammunition in the pistol that was recovered from your personal locker this morning. Quite frankly, however, I'm more interested in how you got back down to the party without anyone seeing you."

"It could be that—I don't know—I was *already downstairs.*"

Dasaro flashed a wry grin, clearly enjoying himself. "The system doesn't put you on site until a few moments before Tachi's body was discovered. Based on the full forensic examination that took place after the party, investigators estimated he'd been dead for close to twenty minutes at the time he was found. That leaves quite the window of time where you're unaccounted for."

After hearing Shevin's story on the news and then sitting through Dasaro's narration, Ziva was beginning to form the opinion that this entire case was based on assumptions. "How about you explain *this* to me then?" she snapped, growing impatient. She gestured at the stealth suit with her bound hands.

Dasaro's smile grew as he fed off her anger. "This was found in a trash receptacle in the Royal Officer's chambers, along with a pair of gloves. Traces of your sweat were found on both." He switched to another photo on the data pad, this time a scan of a partial fingerprint. "This was also found on another piece of garbage, no doubt left when you ditched the garments."

"Do you take me for a complete fool?" she exclaimed.

"No Ziva, I don't. I wouldn't mind leaving evidence at the scene of a crime if I knew it would be wiped away when the trash was transferred to the incinerator. But I guess you weren't counting on every system in the palace being shut down upon the discovery of the body, garbage included."

"And I suppose I had my formalwear stashed somewhere in the room so it would just be a matter of *freshening up* before heading downstairs. Or did I already have the dress on, stuffed into that suit?"

The captain was far too amused by the entire situation and laughed out loud. "Only you would know, Payvan," he chuckled.

Ziva gnawed at the inside of her lip, mulling over the information in search of an inconsistency she could grab and run with. "Give me one reason I would want to kill Tachi." She fought away another brief image of herself dangling by the arms with her body covered in scars. Dasaro clicked his tongue. "Oh Ziva, I think we all know exactly why you'd want him dead."

· 10 ·
HSP Headquarters
Noro, Haphez

"What reason did Lieutenant Payvan have to assassinate Tachi?"

The question originated from Nejdra Venn, another captain who'd been recruited by Emeri and Dasaro to assist with the investigation. Like her counterpart, she was *emilan* Haphezian, with close-cropped hair and eerie silvery-white eyes that contrasted greatly with her dark skin. She was tall like Ziva but more slender and wiry. The woman sat beside Kyron Hoxie, yet another unit captain and former Grand Army officer, and together they stared Skeet and Zinni down, waiting for an answer.

"She didn't kill him," Skeet said. "I already told you she was downstairs with me."

"You also admitted she didn't arrive until nearly an hour after the party began," Nejdra pointed out. "Did she seem agitated, on edge, anything out of the ordinary?"

Skeet shook his head. "With respect, Captain, Ziva never says or does anything you might consider 'ordinary'."

"Cute, Sergeant Duvo. If I didn't know any better, I'd think you were stalling."

"We're not stalling," Zinni protested. "There's nothing more to say because we don't know anything else."

"I asked Ziva where she'd been when she finally showed up," Skeet said. "All she told me was that she'd been taking care of something. There was nothing out of the ordinary about it, and we left it at that."

The two captains surveyed the information on their data pads for a moment before Nejdra addressed them again. "Has Lieutenant Payvan been secretive lately, hiding information she might usually share?"

"No."

"You sure?"

"Yes!"

"Let's go back to the original question," Nejdra said. "You told us before that your boss never does anything unless she has a specific reason. That means we're looking for a considerable motive here, and you two of all people should be able to tell me what it is."

"I don't know!" Skeet said. Then, under his breath, "This is ridiculous."

"Let's try something else," Hoxie spoke up for the first time since the interrogation had begun. "Tell us why Payvan would have any reason to *hate* the Royal Officer."

"Bear in mind that whether you speak or not, Ziva is still going to spend her final days in the Haphor Facility," Nejdra added. "However, if you tell us what we want to know, you two will be off the hook and any collaboration charges against you will be dropped."

Skeet swallowed. He felt frozen, suspended helplessly between the two ideas suddenly yanking him in opposite directions. As much as it pained him to essentially betray his friend by testifying, he realized that in the grand scheme of things, it might be best. He slid his hand under the table and gently tapped Zinni's leg, trusting her to understand he had things under control. He only hoped he would one day have the chance to explain his actions to Ziva herself.

"It sounds like you're trying to put words in my mouth," he replied to Hoxie.

"Just answer the question, Duvo."

"You know as well as I do why Ziva hated Tachi."

"We need to hear it anyway."

Skeet tilted his head. "My statements are already on record from the initial debriefing."

"And they need to be on record for this case, too," Nejdra stated. "Start talking, Sergeant."

· 11 ·

3 YEARS AGO
SMUGGLERS' COMPOUND
COBI

T he concrete walls of the hallway were grimy and covered in months' worth of fungus and other growth. This corridor looked like every other in the abandoned bunker—dark and dusty. Water dripped from somewhere above, and a chilly draft swept past the agents as they crept forward.

Dust swirled in front of Skeet's face as he exhaled, highlighted by the beam of the spotlight mounted on his rifle. The dust that wasn't swirling was adhering to his sweaty face, making him feel like he fit right in down here in this filthy hole. His wide eyes strained to see into the darkness at the end of the corridor, and he took a moment to wipe away the sticky muck gathering on his forehead. The rest of the bunker had already been cleared; they'd found all but one of the agents from the missing infiltration team scattered throughout the building, all dead, obviously tortured. One final door loomed ahead, and Skeet's blood ran cold at the thought of what might be beyond it. If she wasn't in there, he wasn't sure what he was going to do.

He and the five agents behind him pulled up a few meters from the door. An old control panel built into the wall caught his attention, and he moved over to examine it. Any plant life or fungus had been cleared from it, giving him the impression it had been used recently. He tapped at the screen out of curiosity, praying it was still functional.

TERMINAL OFFLINE.

"Sheyss." He put a finger on his earpiece and took another look

around the edges of the door with his light. "Zinni, we've got a console down here that's supposed to open this last room."

"I'm picking it up," the intelligence officer replied from her station on the HSP cruiser orbiting somewhere above them. "It looks like the entire system has been deactivated. You won't be able to get in from there."

Skeet cursed again and glanced over the bunker's schematics on a viewscreen one of the agents carried. "This door is the only access to that room," he growled, fighting away the sense of panic that had been lurking in the back of his mind for the past ten minutes. "We need to get in there now!"

"There are other ways to open doors," Zinni retorted, her voice just as edgy as his own.

He understood her hint immediately and removed the single Malesium-core thermal grenade from his utility belt. It was smaller than the military-grade Class A grenades but otherwise virtually identical, cylindrical in shape with a narrow primer switch. The charge was petite enough to fit cleanly in the palm of his hand, and unlike its counterpart, it only had a blast radius of about four meters. It was beyond ideal in such a place as this.

"Move back," Skeet ordered the agents around him, though they had already begun retreating upon seeing him with the grenade in hand. He moved with them, stopping to crouch down once they had reached a suitable distance from the door.

"Stand by," he said. He drew his arm back and flicked the primer switch before lobbing the device into the darkness. It skidded across the floor and magnetically adhered to the door with a metallic *clink*. He put a cautious hand up to shield his face and waited.

A sharp crack echoed through the tunnel as the device detonated. Yellow fire seeped through the cloud of dust and debris and a large portion of the sealed door crumbled and fell inward.

Skeet had his rifle up and was pressing forward before the cloud had even settled. He ducked through the hole that had been blown in the door and began sweeping his light around the room. It was long and narrow, with old pipes and power cables lining the ceiling. Several containers lay on their sides in the corner, empty and abandoned. The last occupants of this place had left in a hurry.

He swung the light around until it settled on a pale, naked figure that stood out against the darkness of the room. The person was strung up by the arms with a thick chain looped over two of the pipes against the ceiling, just as all the others had been. Frozen in place, Skeet watched with bated breath as gravity slowly turned the figure's face toward the beam of his light.

It was Ziva. She wasn't moving.

She hung just high enough that she might barely be able to support herself on her tiptoes given the opportunity. Her arms were hooked over a narrow pole at the elbows, and her head lolled to one side, resting limply against her shoulder. Long, jagged slashes marred her abdomen and thighs, and it appeared her feet had been stabbed or cut to the point that even if she could stand, it would be unbearably painful.

Smaller cuts and black scorch marks littered the tender flesh on her chest and the underside of her arms. Both of her eyes were swollen shut, and a thick stripe of dry, cracked blood ran from her nose over her slack mouth and down her chin. The majority of her hair remained pulled back as it had been when Skeet had last seen her, though it was frizzy and frayed as if she had been electrocuted numerous times. That would explain the scorching on her skin, he thought.

Without realizing it, his feet were moving, racing toward his lifeless lieutenant. With hasty but true aim, he fired two rounds into the chain, successfully severing it, and caught her limp form before she could fall into a puddle of her own dried vomit and excrement.

"She's still alive!" he screamed, half to the agents with him and half to Zinni over the comm. "Get a medical unit in here now!" Supporting Ziva on one knee, he yanked the pole out from between her arms and removed his field jacket, placing it over her cold body. "Repeat, we need a medic in here now!"

He slung the rifle strap over his shoulder and scooped her up in his arms, struggling against the weight of her muscular frame. The other agents stepped aside, following him out the door and shining their own lights ahead to give him a clear path. He moved as quickly as possible down the bunker's narrow corridors, dodging more members of the rescue team who were busy recovering the bodies of the other dead HSP agents.

"Where the hell is my medic?" he shouted.

He could feel slight wafts of breath where Ziva's face rested against his neck, giving him a glimmer of hope. He adjusted his hand to keep her head from snapping back and his fingers found her hair matted with dry blood. "I promise you those bastards will pay for this."

12

HSP HEADQUARTERS
NORO, HAPHEZ

Ziva sat quietly, waiting for either Emeri or Dasaro to comment further or ask her more questions. She could still feel the sensation of the searing irons and blades against her skin after merely recalling those horrid days she'd spent in captivity. A tremendous chill washed over her at the memory of being left to die in that place, completely helpless and alone. Never again had she allowed herself to fall into such a vulnerable state.

"Tachi withdrew the rest of the ground forces, leaving your strike team stranded," Dasaro confirmed.

"I refused to quit without completing the mission," she explained. "My team had my back, but we were ambushed and overwhelmed before we had a chance to act. We couldn't have turned back if we'd wanted to."

"And what compelled the smugglers to take you captive to begin with?"

She didn't care much for his tone. "They were Cobian pirates, Diago. You know how they are. They didn't need a reason other than the fact that we were foreign government agents who could provide them with a few days' worth of entertainment."

"And you blamed Tachi for all of that and not your own weakness or rash decisions?"

"I was in that hell hole for a week before anyone came for me," she snapped, refraining from leaping to her feet. "Even then, it was only because Skeet had the audacity to ignore spec ops regulations and take another team back out there. My 'weakness' had nothing to do with *anything.*"

Emeri cleared his throat. "I will not have this turn into a popularity contest between the two of you, Captain. Continue with your questions or let's be done here."

Dasaro's smug expression eased a bit, though the amount that remained was still plenty to work Ziva over. "Would it be safe to say you were unhappy with the Royal Officer after this incident?"

"There were a lot of people who were unhappy with him."

"Answer the question, Payvan," Emeri growled.

"And you were one of them, Director!" Ziva shot them each a scornful glare, fighting away a shiver as she remembered how the pirates had used her body to snuff out their cigars after spending an hour blowing the smoke in her face. They'd beaten and kicked her and hit her with the butts of their rifles, all the while keeping her pumped full of enough drugs to render her helpless. One of them had even had his way with her while she was too sedated to fight back, though she mercifully remembered little of the experience. But the real scars came from the amount of time she'd spent in that dungeon feeling utterly abandoned by those who were meant to back her up.

"Allow me to pose a question now," she said quietly before either of the men could speak again. "It has been *three* long years—almost to the exact date—since this happened. Explain to me why I would have waited all this time to take my petty revenge on Tachi."

"You tell me, Payvan," Dasaro said.

A knot descended into the pit of Ziva's stomach as it dawned on her that she didn't know what to do. She was disgusted at herself for allowing simple thoughts to cloud her judgment like this, but at the same time, she could not allow them to take her to Haphor so she could relive those agonizing days. Images from that bunker burned through her memory, and she squeezed her eyes shut in a vain attempt at fending them off. She took a deep breath and tried to return herself to a meditative state.

Somewhere in the back of her mind, she heard Dasaro asking

again why she had been late to Tachi's gala, heard him conversing briefly with the director. Their voices were muffled, trapped behind the thickening cloud of pain swirling through her mind. She shuddered, much to her chagrin and no doubt Dasaro's delight.

"That's it," Emeri said, his voice cutting through the haze in her head. "Get her out of here."

The door hissed open without further ado and something sharp pierced the skin on her neck. She didn't even have time to register what it was before the room started to spin and her mind went blank.

13

HSP HEADQUARTERS
NORO, HAPHEZ

Zinni felt as though she had somehow been transported back to three years earlier and was reliving the countless debriefing sessions, disturbing images, and sleepless nights she had endured then. She followed Skeet out of the holding room in a fog, attempting to process and sort out the load of information she'd just been buried under. Everyone, including herself, had done their best to shut out any memories of the incident on Cobi after Ziva had been found and the other agents' bodies were recovered, but now it was clear that it was somehow far from over.

Skeet stopped a short distance from the door and let out a deep breath as he ran a hand through his rumpled hair, a nervous habit he had developed over the years. If there was any language besides native Haphezian Zinni was perfectly fluent in, it was his body language. Right now, he was doing the same thing she was: sorting out his overloaded mind. His recollection of what happened to Ziva had been as difficult for him to speak of as it had been for Zinni to listen to. She gave him a few moments to regain his composure.

"Please tell me that little love pat meant you have some sort of plan," she finally said, arms crossed. She'd been patient for the duration of the interrogation, mostly because she didn't know anything, but Skeet's actions had greatly intrigued her.

Skeet ruffled his hair again and refrained from answering until a pair of agents had walked by and cleared the vicinity. "I think I do."

"Good. I'd like to think you wouldn't betray Ziva just to save yourself."

Skeet's eyes grew wide. "You know I would never do that," he snapped. He looked around to see if the two of them were arousing suspicion, then took Zinni by the arm and led her into a nearby alcove.

"Telling Dasaro's people what they wanted to hear was the only way I could see to help Ziva," he continued, voice still hushed. "If we'd refused, we'd be in just as much trouble and she would be completely on her own. I'm not saying they won't still have eyes on us, but this way, the probability that we can be of some assistance is a lot higher. She'll get her week-long grace period just like any other criminal, and nobody else seems to be on her side so it's up to us to be her sponsors. If we work fast, we might be able to put an end to this...or at least get some closure."

Zinni understood perfectly but was still less than thrilled with the entire situation. "You can bet they're going to tell her what you've done, if for no other reason than to mess with her head. Nejdra will no doubt put the fact that you testified on record for all to see."

"I did not 'testify'," he retorted. "You heard the questions they were asking in there—they were clearly setting us up to say exactly what they wanted. Besides, I doubt Ziva will mind too much how we solve this problem as long as we get the job done. The end will justify the means."

She nodded and massaged her temples as she pondered the situation. "You ever wonder if she actually did it? I want to believe she's innocent, but...the evidence..."

Surprisingly, Skeet didn't chastise her for concocting such a negative idea. "I've thought about it," he said after a brief silence. "She's certainly capable of it, but it would be completely unlike her to have waited all this time. I like to think I would have known if she had something planned. And why would she have left that Shevin kid alive?" He scoffed. "I don't know—there's something very screwed up about all of this, regardless of whether she's guilty."

"Agreed," Zinni said. "We can't let them take her back to Haphor."

"Even if she killed Tachi, I think I'd shoot her myself before letting her endure all of that again."

Once again, Zinni agreed, though she said nothing. The idea was unbearable, but after reading reports and seeing Ziva in the med center after that fiasco three years earlier, she hoped someone would be gracious enough to put her out of her misery if she were ever in her friend's position.

"Well," she said, "if they had her in custody before us, she could very well be on her way to Haphor already. Let's go."

· 14 ·

HAPHOR–NORO TRAFFIC LANE

TASMIN FOREST, HAPHEZ

Ziva's surroundings shuddered and her head rolled forward, jarring her awake from a very poor excuse for sleep. Somewhere around her, a man swore, and her world tilted downward. She blinked several times and twisted her head from side to side in a futile attempt to alleviate the crick in her neck. The view in front of her slowly came into focus, and she realized she was riding in the back of an HSP aircar.

The car bounced again, jostled by a powerful gust of wind which accompanied the clouds and rain that had carried over from the previous night. The agent piloting the craft brought the car out of its dive just above the treetops, and they resumed their journey at a lower altitude where the wind was less violent.

Ziva peered out through the tinted window and recognized the Haphor-Noro traffic lane amid the foliage off to their right; the service road that ran parallel to it was almost directly under them. Traffic on the little bypass was minimal compared to the hustle and bustle of the main lane, no doubt the reason they were taking this route. It was impossible to know exactly how long she'd been sedated, and thus she had no idea how far into the trip they were. Drawing a deep breath, she redirected all her energy to focusing on what she *did* know.

She shared the car with a two-agent escort...odd, considering what a high-priority prisoner she was. Her gaze dropped to her restraints. Rather than shackles linked with a chain, her wrists were secured by clasps fixed to the seat on either side of her. A layer of blue energy reinforcement pulsed over the metal and made her skin tingle. The cuffs were fitted to her as tightly as possible, locked so firmly she could barely make out the seam where they were fastened. Her arms wouldn't budge when she tugged on them, and the metal was beginning to rub her skin raw. Even if she could somehow release the clasps, the thin force field prevented them from opening fully, and any attempt at disabling the field from where she sat would trigger an alarm on the car's control panel. Another force field separated her from the agents in the front, an extra security measure they'd implemented in case she somehow got loose. She wasn't entirely sure what would happen if she touched it, and she had no intention of finding out.

A voice up front derailed her train of thought. "Transport to Checkpoint Fourteen," the agent in the passenger seat called over the comm. "We are approaching your position."

For a moment, the only sound that could be heard was the thunder of the rain pelting the car's roof and windshield. Then the comm crackled. "Copy that, Transport. Status report?"

The piloting agent eyed Ziva in the rear cam. "Everything's under control up here," he said, waving to the agents on the ground as they passed over. "She just woke up."

"Roger that. Next check-in in fifteen minutes."

Checkpoints. So Emeri had them using a staggered security system rather than a convoy. They would check in with patrols placed strategically on the ground, and if they failed to make contact at the appointed time, agents would be dispatched into the forest to find them. It was a procedure the agency had sanctioned for special circumstances, usually when a prisoner transfer was in danger of being interrupted by a third party. Ziva doubted the public was happy about Tachi's death, and it was guaranteed that someone somewhere would want her dead. A single, unmarked transport was much less likely to attract attention than a whole procession of HSP vehicles; the agency was essentially protecting her for the sake of being able to punish her themselves.

Her fogbound mind struggled to do the math as she tried to calculate her precise location. The trip from Noro to Haphor took roughly four hours. If the checkpoints were equally spaced like they were supposed to be, and the next one was fifteen minutes away...*four hours divided into fifteen-minute intervals...that's sixteen.* Her eyes grew wide. The Haphor Facility itself would represent Checkpoint Sixteen. Only one more checkpoint remained before they entered the city.

She stopped and closed her eyes, slipping into her state of deep concentration before the panic could set in. Letting her emotions take control like she had in the interrogation room certainly wouldn't help matters, and dwelling on that experience would only drag her down farther. If there was ever a time she needed to be thinking clearly, it was now.

Though the mountains still commanded much of the view outside, the first signs of civilization could be seen in the distance. She normally found the capital to be a beautiful and peaceful place—at least compared to a rough city like Noro—but now the idea of going there sent a chill down her spine. She *couldn't* go there.

Once they entered the city, there was absolutely no turning back; any sort of escape attempt would have to happen right after they cleared the final forest checkpoint, and it was also guaranteed to result in injury. She took a moment to study the design of the car. The windshield was large, extending up over the edge of the roof and giving the pilot a clear view of the environment both around and above him. The seat where she sat was built into what would probably be the cargo space if the vehicle were for public use. The back of the car was more enclosed; she had a small window on each side of her, but there was a solid roof over her head and no rear viewport.

You know these agents will probably die if you try something.

She shook her head and shut her eyes again. *Not my problem.*

Your fight isn't with them. They're only doing their jobs.

That was true, after all, and the last thing she wanted to do after being falsely accused of murder was actually kill someone. But she was desperate, and a decision needed to be made. In the event of an... *accident,* she'd be more protected in the back of the car than the two men in the front. Going to the Haphor Facility was not an option, and thus escape was a requirement. Consequently, the injury or death of these agents was inevitable.

My life is currently more valuable than yours, she thought, convincing herself there was still a chance they'd survive. *It's nothing personal.*

Now for an actual plan. "What do you guys think about all of this?" she asked, leaning forward under the pretense of carrying on a conversation. She peered through the shimmering wall of translucent blue energy and examined the switches that controlled the force fields and clasps, careful not to stare for too long.

The pilot watched her in the rear cam for a moment and she shifted her gaze up to meet his. "I'm not going to get involved with this, Payvan," he muttered. "Sit there and be quiet. You've done a good job of it so far." Then, under his breath, "Damn sedative couldn't have just lasted another half hour."

The second agent turned his head and watched her in his peripherals. "To be honest, Lieutenant, I'm sorry things have to end like this. I know you've been a great asset to the agency."

"Shut up, Spence!" the pilot ordered. "Don't get mixed up in this."

Both agents returned their attention to the front of the craft and Ziva continued her discreet study of the control panel. An idea hit her, and she stole another peek into the front seat. If the agent called Spence was armed, his holster was on his right side, blocked from view by the seat. The pilot, however, had his sidearm strapped to his near leg. It appeared to be a standard HSP-issue plasma pistol, and at the right angle.... She looked over the switches again. *That might work.*

She leaned back in her seat and drew in a deep breath, releasing it over a count of eight and flexing her stiff fingers a bit. The jungle trees below them were thinning to make way for the ground traffic lanes and structures that became more numerous as they approached the city. She shut her eyes and remained perfectly silent as she listened for the first signs of an incoming transmission.

A lifetime passed before the comm system crackled to life. She had just begun to feel panic encroaching when she heard the voice of one of the agents on the ground: "Checkpoint Fifteen to Transport. How goes the journey?"

The same brief exchange ensued, and Ziva watched as the aircar passed over the checkpoint. She swallowed against the metallic taste in the back of her mouth and closed her eyes once more, taking one last deep breath in preparation for the events that were about to come.

"All right," said the voice on the comm. "You have fifteen minutes to reach the Facility before a patrol is sent out to look for you."

"Shouldn't be a problem," Spence replied. "I'm looking forward to getting this trip over with."

"Checkpoint out."

Eyes closed once again, Ziva silently began counting down the seconds until they would be a suitable distance away from the ground patrol. The car rushed along, only meters above the tops of the massive trees. Any landing at this point would be rough, but it would have to do.

A rush of energy surged down her spine precisely a minute later, and when her eyes opened, she focused directly on the pilot's gun. It suddenly flew from its holster, pulled by the invisible hand of her Nostia. Pain shot through the back of her head as she used her mind to hurl the weapon at the control panel, successfully striking the switches and disabling the force field. The car's safety harnesses unlocked and retracted, and the clasps around her wrists sprang open. She lunged forward, bringing her elbow around against the unsuspecting pilot's head. She seized the controls and threw them forward, sending the car plunging into the trees.

Spence swore and hollered something about the force field. He quickly established a firm grip on her arm, attempting to wrestle her out of the cockpit. She fought him off with her other hand, her sore wrists protesting angrily as she slammed his face into the control panel.

The craft ricocheted off an enormous tree branch, throwing her into the back seat. They were descending headfirst at one moment, but the next collision with a tree flipped the aircar onto its side and propelled it off in a new direction. Before she knew it, they were upside down—her head snapped back as she hit the car's ceiling. Indicator lights sparkled across the control panels and emergency alarms wailed as branches tore at the exterior and ripped through the windshield.

Dizzy and disoriented, she braced her arms and legs against the wall just as the craft finally met the ground.

Upon impact, her body bounced against the ceiling with a dull *thump*. She lay there for several long seconds with her head pounding, listening to the gentle creaking in the car's frame and the alarms that had all morphed into a single, multi-toned screech. She blinked several times as her vision began to right itself and wiped at a trickle of blood oozing toward her eye. Her neck ached as she twisted her head to look out the window, but she found that it was so cracked and plastered with mud that her view of anything outside was completely obscured.

Coughing, she worked her body around to face the front of the battered craft. She could feel more blood seeping into her hair thanks to a cut somewhere on her scalp, and a throbbing ache rendered her left shoulder and elbow numb. In the grand scheme of things, she remained relatively unscathed, and after testing the mobility of her legs, she was reasonably sure she could walk or even run. By the looks of it, however, the other two passengers hadn't been so lucky. She wormed her way between the two front seats to get a better look.

The pilot was crumpled against the ground, his full body weight bearing down on a neck that was quite obviously broken. She checked for a pulse anyway, and, finding none, turned her attention to Spence. The other agent was in a similar position, though farther on his side. He stared out through the open space where the windshield had been, eyes frantic, taking in raspy breaths through the bloody saliva filling his mouth. His chest was stained a dark crimson where a long shard of glass had embedded itself in his flesh.

She eased herself back into the rear of the car, this time facing the opposite direction, and began to deliver powerful kicks to one of the windows. Pain pulsed through her ankle as her foot broke through, separating the entire pane of reinforced glass from the car's frame. Cool, clean air rushed in; she gladly accepted it, allowing herself the luxury of a couple deep breaths before wriggling out into the leaves and mud.

It had quit raining, but a damp mist rose from the drenched earth and underbrush. She couldn't see anyone around, but she could hear the occasional vehicle pass by on the service road a short distance away. The crash had carried them far enough that they were safely out of sight of anyone traveling by, though she doubted it would take long for someone to come looking for them. A good chunk of their fifteen minutes had already been spent, and who knew what sort of distress signal could have been automatically sent out during the crash.

Ziva worked her way to her feet and staggered around to the front of the aircar, forcing her sore ankle to bear her body weight. She knelt and examined the windshield. It was almost entirely broken out, and she could see Spence inside; he appeared to be watching her, but his eyes were out of focus.

"Hang in there," she said, wondering if he was even coherent enough to hear her. She got down on her stomach and crawled under the nose of the craft that jutted out over the windshield frame, clearing as much of the broken glass out of the way as possible. Her head and shoulders entered the vehicle, and she pulled her arms along until they were in front of her.

She gritted her teeth against the pain in her shoulder as she reached in and slid her hands under Spence's arms. Digging into the mud with her knees and feet, she began to tug him out centimeter by centimeter. He squeezed his eyes shut and assisted her by pushing against the seat with his legs.

Once the upper half of his body had cleared the window, she slid out from under the nose and regained her footing, then pulled him the rest of the way out from a standing position. She dragged him across the ground and propped him up against a nearby tree, where she took a moment to survey his wounds. The shard of glass had by far caused the most damage, but it appeared he would remain stable at least until someone found him.

He stared up at her, struggling to focus, and clutched at his chest with an unsteady hand. He closed his other one around her forearm. "Y-y-you—"

Ziva pried his fingers off and placed his hand firmly in his lap. "Hold on, agent," she said, rising. "Just hold on, and know that I didn't do whatever they said I did."

She paused for a moment and listened as a flood of garbled transmissions came through on the aircar's damaged comm system. Someone somewhere had no doubt seen the craft go down and reported it, or worse yet, they'd been picked up on HSP's scanners and a squad of agents was already closing in.

Taking one last look around, Ziva stooped down and gathered up Spence's pistol and communicator. She tucked the gun into her pants at the small of her back and jogged over to the bushes on the edge of the service road, chucking the comm unit into the back of a shipping rig as it rattled by. Hoping the mobile comm signal might distract the agency for at least a few minutes, she moved away into the trees and took off as fast as she could back in the direction of Noro.

· 15 ·
HSP HEADQUARTERS
NORO, HAPHEZ

Emeri Arion stood on the comm pad in front of his conference table with his hands clasped behind his back. Surrounding him were the translucent, silvery-blue projections of HSP's six regional directors, as well as Luko Zona of the Royal Guard and the Royal General himself, Njo Jaroon. It seemed odd to have a military man like Jaroon taking part in a police conference, but with Tachi out of the picture, he was currently representing the Royal House in both a military and law enforcement capacity.

Emeri sighed and rubbed a hand over his face. He had spent a good portion of the afternoon waiting for the opportunity to meet with all these men together, and now that the chance had arrived, they could do little more than argue.

"Listen, gentlemen," he said, breaking up yet another dispute between Jaroon and Brychon Zinck, the regional HSP director in Haphor. "I'm expecting an update at any moment. Last we heard, they had cleared the final checkpoint and were making their approach into the capital. For now, I believe we should keep our focus on making a smooth transition into the Facility, not on what may or may not happen a week from now."

He received murmurs of agreement from everyone but the three men in Haphor. Zona remained silent, listening to the outburst Emeri's words had drawn from his superiors.

"While you make a valid point, Director," Jaroon growled, "I'm not sure if I completely understand why you're so intent on incarcerating Payvan in the first place. Treat her like the bloodthirsty murderer she is and execute her *now!*"

"Sir, under normal circumstances, you know we would release her and have a Cleaner assigned to her pending the results of the hearing at the end of the week. However, I don't think we can consider any circumstances regarding Lieutenant Payvan as being 'normal.' As skilled as she is, it would be far too easy for her to fall off the radar, resulting in a vast amount of wasted time for all of us. Keeping her detained is the most logical way to prevent that from happening."

Jaroon crossed his arms, his eyes dark in the shadow cast by his furrowed eyebrows. "Still, why bother keeping her alive at all? She's clearly guilty, so why wait?"

Emeri had never been able to fathom how Njo could view his own stepdaughter in such a harsh way, and Ziva had never elaborated on her complicated family background. He knew her biological father had been killed by Sardons in the Fringe War and that she had run away from Haphor as a child, but nothing more. "You know the laws of due process, General. In the grace period before they are convicted and executed, a capital criminal has the right to petition associates for help in building a case that could prove their innocence. It's only fair that we give Ziva the same chance, even if it's while she's rotting in that prison."

"I know this looks bad, Emeri," said the director from the Mairo office, "but are you sure you want to execute Payvan? She's done a lot for this agency over the past eight years. What if she could somehow be proven innocent?"

"Then that information will be presented at her hearing," Luko Zona reminded them, as calm and collected as ever.

"*Regardless* of whether she's guilty or innocent, I'm not going to make any exceptions to the law, not even for Ziva," Emeri said. "For now, she'll be given the death penalty, just like anyone else who has done what she's accused of. Innocent people sometimes lose their lives, and that's unfortunate." His mind wandered briefly to the incident with Soren Tarbic two years earlier. "But it's the price we pay for peace here, and everyone realizes that. You've all seen the crime rate statistics from the past few decades. An intelligent person isn't going to commit a capital crime if they know they'll be killed for it, and they'll take care to steer clear of any situations in which they might be falsely implicated. If we were to give Ziva any special treatment, what kind of example would we be setting?"

"Why are we even discussing the possibility that she could be innocent?" Jaroon protested, his voice becoming louder and more abrasive as the conversation progressed. "You saw the evidence—we *all* saw the evidence! Fingerprints and DNA don't lie, Director. As a high-ranking member of your precious spec ops division, she has the skills to back it up. If you ask me, that makes for an indestructible case against her."

Emeri was growing weary of the Royal General's personal opinions. He suddenly felt a small need to defend Ziva, at least a little, if for no other reason than to agitate Njo. "That doesn't mean she isn't entitled to her rights."

"I agree with the General," Director Zinck piped in. "If Payvan is as good as everyone makes her out to be, what's to keep her from breaking out of the prison? By bringing her to Haphor, we're presenting a danger to everyone in the city, including myself and General Jaroon. Think of the king!"

"We will take every precaution to make sure nothing like that happens," Emeri reassured them. "I don't think we're dealing with any sort of psychotic break here. She hasn't come completely unhinged."

"You never know, Director," one of the other regional directors said. "You know as well as I do that it isn't unheard of for spec ops agents to snap and begin spree-killing. It wouldn't be the first time it has happened."

The discussion was getting out of hand. "This isn't about—" Emeri stopped when his office door opened. He turned to find Diago Dasaro waiting just inside the doorway, his demeanor calm but his eyes frantic. Grateful for the interruption, he looked back to the holograms around the table. "Gentlemen, if you'll excuse me for a moment."

He stepped off the comm pad and moved toward Dasaro, who

approached simultaneously. He noticed the captain was carrying a communicator, and his face was grim as if he had come bearing bad news. The thought occurred to him that he might have preferred to continue his conference.

"This had better be good," he muttered.

"You're going to want to hear this," Dasaro replied, handing him the communicator. "Payvan escaped."

· 16 ·
CHECKPOINT FIFTEEN
TASMIN FOREST, HAPHEZ

Over an hour passed before Ziva found herself within earshot of what remained of Checkpoint Fifteen. She was surprised anyone was still there; the fact that she'd escaped was no doubt old news by now, and she wondered why these agents weren't out combing the forest for her.

She crept closer to the checkpoint and took cover behind a large patch of brush, taking the time to spread a thin layer of black mud over her pale face that contrasted so starkly with the dark forest. It wouldn't take too long for someone to catch up to her. Hoping to throw off any of her pursuers' calculations regarding time and foot speed, she had made a point to start out traveling as fast as possible and in irregular patterns. Still, any decent tracker would be able to trace her movements over the wet ground easily, and she needed a new mode of transportation before they could do so.

There were more agents at the checkpoint than there had been when the aircar had passed over, giving her the impression reinforcements had been brought in to assist with the search. That was exactly the case, according to what she could hear of a conversation going on nearby. Similar camps were being set up within ten kilometers of the crash site and agents would soon be dispatched into the forest to try to box her in.

She was exhausted and soaked to the bone with sweat and rain, but she was relieved her strategy seemed to have worked. She slipped behind a nearby tree and began to move around the perimeter of the camp, watching as portable tracking equipment and supply caches were set up in the clearing. Several groundcars and hoverbikes were parked unattended on the far side, and she decided that would be her destination.

A holoprojector table like those in HSP's situation rooms was being set up under a cover to protect it from the weather. Once they got it operational, they might be able to hunt her down via one of the infrared probes hovering in the Haphezian atmosphere, assuming there'd been any in the area. Unless one of them had been pointed in exactly the right direction at exactly the right time, the chances were slim that they'd picked her up at the crash site. Even if HSP did manage to trace her to this place, she liked to think she'd be safely away by then.

She made up her mind then and there that taking out any of these agents would draw far too much attention. Still, she knew walking up to one of the bikes and riding off on it wasn't exactly subtle, either. She would have to come up with an appropriate combination of the two.

"It was a stupid idea in the first place," one agent was saying as he and a colleague carried a cargo container nearby. "I understand where they're coming from, but they know better than to send a spec ops agent off with such little security. Did they really expect things to end well?" He grunted as they set the container down.

The second agent nodded in agreement and the two of them began unloading equipment. "If it were up to me, she should have been shot the moment she was apprehended. Keeping her alive was just an invitation for her to escape again."

She took their remarks as compliments and continued moving. The process was slow, and several times she was forced to move away from the camp in order to stay adequately concealed. Twenty long, tedious minutes later, she found herself within several strides of the cluster of cars and bikes. There were seven vehicles in all, and one particular bike on the outer edge beckoned to her. It would do nicely.

Ziva cautiously picked her way across a more open area, careful to avoid detection by a few nearby officers who had their backs turned. A large stack of empty storage containers hid her from view as she knelt down among the cars and began to formulate a plan.

None of the vehicles had their ignition keys in them, a smart move on the part of these agents. But finding any keys in the camp—all the while avoiding being caught—would be close to impossible. Hotwiring was always an option, but it would take time she wasn't sure she had. For now, however, it was the best choice she had. She began to fiddle with the control panel on the bike she had chosen.

Not ten seconds after she'd started, she ducked down behind the machine to avoid being seen by an agent who suddenly appeared on the edge of the camp. He wore a full riding suit and had a matching helmet tucked up under one arm. A key dangled from his other hand.

"I'll check in when I get there," he hollered back into the camp. He shook his head as if he were glad to be getting away and mounted the bike on the other side of the car beside Ziva's.

She saw the opportunity and made her move. Staying low, she crept around the bike and car and came up behind the unsuspecting agent as he started his bike's engine. She came within a meter of him as he leaned over and took up the helmet from where it had been balancing on the handlebars. With her footsteps drowned out by the hum of the engine, she leaped onto the seat behind him and hooked her elbow around his throat just as he slid the helmet over his head.

The young officer was too stunned to do anything other than flail his arms at her and claw at the helmet visor that had fallen down over his face. By the time he mustered up some semblance of a reaction, Ziva could already feel the sleeper hold taking effect. She tightened her grip, gradually cutting off the blood supply to his brain. The agent slowly quit fighting and slumped back against her, unconscious.

She slid off the bike, moved the body to the rear of the seat, then jumped onto the front with his limp form leaning against her back. Yanking the steering column around, she took the bike into a sharp turn, spraying mud over the vehicles around her with the repulsors. She steered it out into the forest and away from the camp, keeping the officer's body between herself and any agents who happened to look up at the departing vehicle. By the time anyone realized the man and his bike weren't coming back, she would be long gone.

· 17 ·

ABANDONED RELAY STATION
OUTSKIRTS OF HAPHOR, HAPHEZ

Two hours later, she stepped off the hoverbike outside an old relay station no longer in use. The building sat at the base of a tall comm tower; both structures were positioned on top of a hill that rose up between a small river and a road connecting Haphor to some outlying towns. The route was seldom used anymore due to the more powerful relay stations that had been built farther away from the city.

Thick foliage concealed the area well, but from where she stood now, Ziva had a decent view of the road below and could also see several different air traffic lanes from a distance. She looked down the other side of the hill to the little river. It rushed along at the bottom of a crevice it had worn over the years, with steep banks on either side. The edges of the bed were lined with boulders and pebbles of all sizes that had been washed smooth by the water that rushed faithfully toward Haphor and the Tranyi River. It would provide the perfect means of escape if the need arose.

She now donned the riding suit the young agent had been wearing. It was a bit baggy, but that was fine, she concluded; it would allow her to remain androgynous and faceless in just about any setting. The suit was dark gray in color and had a reinforced fiber mesh chest plate of a slightly lighter shade. It was moderately comfortable, and the matching helmet, gloves, and her own rugged boots made up the rest of the ensemble.

As for the unconscious agent who had accompanied her on part of her journey, nobody would be hearing from him for a while. After leaving the checkpoint, they had ridden deeper into the forest to the north, successfully escaping HSP's perimeter before it had risen to full strength. She'd stopped briefly to disable the agent's comm locator and the bike's nav computer, and at that point had to hit the helpless officer over the head to keep him from waking up. They'd continued for another fifty kilometers or so until they reached yet another old forest road, which were prevalent in the area. Here, she had relieved the agent of his suit, weapons, and supply belt before leaving him lying in the bushes a good distance from the road. She'd taken off to the west from there, carefully working her way back toward Haphor until she'd discovered the relay station.

Ziva walked the bike up to the side of the little building and left it there, taking the time to cover it partially with large fronds from a nearby bush. She stood at the front door, studying it, tunneling into it with her mind. The lock was strong, though not nearly as sophisticated as some she had seen recently. She closed her eyes and reached into the lock with her thoughts just as she might with any tangible tool she normally used. The headache set in almost immediately and she winced, struggling to focus. The locking mechanism rattled inside the door for a moment before the bolt fell back into position.

She sighed and massaged her temples. With as little as she exercised her Nostia, it was easy to forget how badly it was failing. Under any other circumstances, she'd be content to rely solely on her physical skills and let her special abilities remain dormant. But right now, she needed any edge she could get, and it was disheartening to realize she couldn't count on the one thing that had always given her that edge. She needed to rest, to focus. Focus and concentration seemed to be the key to eking out what little Nostia she had left.

Frustrated, she drew her pistol and shielded her face, then threw the butt of the weapon against the nearest window. The impact sent a fresh bout of pain shooting up into her shoulder, and she took a moment to test its mobility before clearing away the broken glass and crawling inside.

Lighting panels activated via a motion detector when she entered the shack, but they were old and flickering, leaving the light dim at best. Judging by the lack of severe dust buildup inside, it hadn't been long since someone had been there. Nearly everything had been cleared out, with the exception of the original control panels. There were three workstations to her left with terminals that had been shut down indefinitely. Thick cables ran from the dead terminals up the wall and through the ceiling, presumably connecting somehow to the large tower outside.

The area to her right was even more vacant. The floor was wide open as if a sofa or some other large piece of furniture had once been positioned there. An empty gun rack hung on the wall beside a metal cabinet whose doors stood open to reveal unoccupied shelves. Aside from that, the only other thing of note was a cramped lavatory with an old-fashioned sink, which she wandered over and twisted the handle— yes, still worked. She let the chilly water trickle over her fingers then splashed a little over her face.

She wiped away the excess water with a sleeve and surveyed her surroundings again. First things first—the automatic lights would be a problem once it got dark. She went to the control panel and used the utility knife from the stolen supply belt to pry the cover off, taking a moment to examine the mass of wires within before choosing a select few to cut. The lights flickered a final time before shutting off, casting the interior of the station in shadows. The darkness would be unfortunate, but she didn't plan on staying long and anything was better than having the place lit up like a beacon for all to see once night fell.

The lack of sleep the night before and the long trek that day were beginning to take their toll. Thoroughly exhausted, she leaned against the wall and undid the clasps on the riding jacket, grimacing when her hand brushed over a sore spot on her side that had begun plaguing her not long after the prison transport crashed. She peeled her sweat-soaked shirt back and examined the area in the waning light; a bruise roughly the size of her fist had formed at the base of her rib cage, and a bit of careful probing told her she'd likely fractured a rib. Her supply belt held a small storage pouch, spare plasma cell, grappling cable, stun baton, and the hoverbike's key. No caura gel or painkillers. "*Sheyss,*" she sighed.

Keeping her back flat against the wall, she sank slowly to the floor. She studied the light shining in from outside, then recovered the agent's communicator from the utility belt. She examined the locator chip again, ensuring it had indeed been destroyed, then set a timer for a few hours. Then, tilting her head back, she allowed her eyes to shut.

· 18 ·
HSP HEADQUARTERS
NORO, HAPHEZ

Zinni was just passing the doorway to the special operations situation room when a massive hand reached out of nowhere and threw her against the wall. She dropped the data pad she was holding and whirled, finding herself caught under the crushing gaze of Diago Dasaro.

He stepped out of the situation room, keeping his meaty hand clamped over her shoulder with his thumb digging harshly up under her collarbone. The man was huge, standing taller than Ziva or Skeet by several centimeters, and his shoulders were wide enough to account for two of Zinni. The arm that held her was like the trunk of a tree, and it didn't budge when she took hold of it hoping to relieve the pressure on her shoulder.

Dasaro bent down closer, drilling into her with emotionless black eyes shrouded in the shadows of the darkening room. He glanced at her hands on his arm as if he couldn't even feel them. "Where is she?" he growled.

Zinni didn't dare break eye contact for fear of revealing how terrified she was. She winced against the discomfort of his thumb pressing on her bone. "I don't know," she replied through her teeth, listening for anyone who might be nearby. It was late in the evening and many agents had already left for the day. No one seemed to be around.

"Somehow I don't believe you," Dasaro said. He adjusted his grip, shifting his thumb over to her windpipe. "I think she's got help on the inside."

Zinni clutched his arm, feeling panic beginning to set in as it became harder to breathe. She felt her feet leaving the ground as Dasaro's entire palm enveloped her throat. She clung to his arm with both hands, trying desperately to support herself.

Blackness began creeping in from the edges of her vision just as something threw Dasaro off balance, causing him to release his grip. She slid to the floor with her head pounding and rubbed her sore neck for a moment before a gentler hand took her by the arm and hauled her to her feet.

She found herself standing behind Skeet, who had positioned himself between her and Dasaro and now stood facing the captain with his arms crossed. Dasaro eyed them both maliciously, particularly Zinni, but then he directed his attention toward Skeet.

"You're lucky I don't report you for striking a commanding officer," he said with a smug grin that told Zinni his words were more of a threat than a statement.

"If you've got a problem, Dasaro, you bring it to me. Leave her alone." Skeet held his ground.

Zinni felt an immense combination of anger and embarrassment settle over her once her mind cleared. It wasn't often that she found herself as completely helpless as she had been just then, and it was humiliating. Dasaro had taken her totally by surprise, as her attention had been focused on the data pad. She stooped down and gathered the device up.

"He thinks we know where Ziva is," Zinni said, feeling rather emboldened. She placed a hand on her hip, straightening her shoulders.

Skeet regarded her without taking his eyes off the captain. "Is that it?" he muttered. "Well, we don't."

Dasaro took a step closer to the two of them. "Fine," he said, "but know this. We will get to the bottom of this, and if we find out you've been helping her, it will be the end of the line for both of you." He glared at them a final time. "Now get out of here. That's an order."

· 19 ·

PALACE OF THE ROYAL GENERAL
HAPHOR, HAPHEZ

The estate of Njo Jaroon loomed ahead, swathed in the silver light of the only two Haphezian moons that had managed to peek out from behind the dense, dark cloud cover. Ziva glanced up at what she could see of the sky through the thicket in which she was concealed. A strong wind somewhere high above kept the clouds gliding steadily across the black void beyond, causing the moons to blink in and out like lights someone was switching on and off. She shivered against a chilly breeze that carried through the damp bushes and drew a deep breath, watching the little cloud of steam diminish in front of her as she exhaled.

She sat cross-legged at the base of the thick wall surrounding Jaroon's mansion and yard, identical to the one she had allegedly climbed over to enter Tachi's palace just down the road. Directly behind her on the other side of the wall was a thoroughfare that cut straight through the Royal City, the private community in the center of Haphor in which all the dignitaries and their families lived. She had left the relay station at dusk, and it had taken her well into the night to reach her current location due to a massive boost in security. Aircraft patrolled the night sky with spotlights and there were nearly twice as many guards as normal on duty. The process of infiltrating the Royal City had been painfully slow, but now here she sat, well hidden in the shadows.

Ziva slowly released another breath, letting her eyes follow a member of the Royal Guard as he came around the corner of the estate and made his way across the yard. He was dressed in full uniform and toted a rifle as well as a service pistol, just like every other guard who had passed by in the half hour she'd been watching. Like the others, he also carried a small spotlight that bathed the grass in bright blue light as he walked. She watched until he disappeared around the side of the mansion, then focused her attention on the corner from which he had come, counting under her breath.

The next guard in the rotation appeared precisely twenty-two seconds later, flawlessly following the pattern she had been observing. If being the stepdaughter of the Royal General—however estranged—had any perks, it was that she had come to understand almost perfectly the security systems at all the palaces. Even with the boost in numbers, there was still a distinct pattern she'd been able to pick up on in just a short time.

From her vantage point, she peered up to the three balconies jutting out over the back patio, supported by several large columns. Each belonged to an apartment-style bedroom within; the one on the far right was her half-brother Jaril's, and the one in the middle had once belonged to her and was now used for who knew what. The room on the left, the one nearest to her, was the one she had her eye on.

Wincing against the pain in her side, she slowly began to move through the bushes toward the edge of the grass, working every part of her body centimeter by centimeter so as not to disturb the foliage. It took her a good ten minutes to move far enough that she could get turned around and lower herself onto her stomach. There she lay for another several minutes, allowing herself to once again become invisible in the darkness. Three more guards passed as she estimated the height of the balcony and waited until the moons had disappeared behind the clouds once more.

In a single, silent movement, she pushed up with her arms and forward with her legs, already sprinting by the time she reached an upright position. Five strides across the large lawn, she yanked the grappling hook from her belt, unraveling the sturdy cable as she moved. *Eighteen seconds.* She skidded to a stop at the edge of the patio, taking a moment to steady herself, and tossed the hook up toward the balcony railing above one of the massive columns. It caught on the first try, and she pulled the cable taut. *Fifteen seconds.*

Her arm and shoulder protested angrily as she braced her legs against the column and began to climb. The extra effort sent fire shooting through her midsection, and for the briefest of moments, she wasn't sure if she'd make it to the top. Her foot slipped as she reached for the railing, but she caught the edge of the balcony before she could fall. *Six seconds. Get up there!* Gritting her teeth, she established a grip on the railing and hauled herself over the edge, unhooking the grappling cable and collapsing to the balcony floor just as the glow from the next guard's spotlight became visible at the corner of the house.

She lay there flat on her back with the tangled cable resting on her stomach, listening to the grass crunching under the man's boots. When he paused for a moment, she turned her head and saw the beam of light extended out over the yard as if he were taking a closer look at the bushes. She held her breath until she heard him move on. Unsure if his delay had thrown off the pattern, she waited for the next guard to pass before she rolled over, got her feet under her, and slipped through the glass door into the darkness of the room within.

Thin curtains billowed slowly in the breeze that had come in through the open door, and she held them for a moment to stop the movement. She stepped aside so her silhouette wasn't visible in the recurring moonlight and began coiling up the grappling cable as her eyes adjusted to the dark.

The room was good sized, with every living accommodation short of a kitchen. Light from the hallway outside seeped in under the door directly across from her. To her left was a quaint sitting area situated around a small table. A desk and private communications grid sat in front of a picture window overlooking the side yard and the south end of the Royal City. A large, extravagant lavatory and a walk-in closet the size of the *Intrepid's* cargo hold made up the remainder of that half of the room. To the right was a more private alcove where fragile curtains like the ones at the balcony door surrounded the occupied bed. A dark form lay nestled into the white bedcovers, which had taken on a silvery hue in the moonlight.

Ziva walked forward onto the antique circle rug in the center of the room, unable to even hear her own soft footsteps. She made her way over to the bed and pushed a curtain to one side. Jada Jaroon remained motionless except for the rising and falling of her chest as she snored softly. Her face was turned away, and her long braid trailed across the pillow like a serpent attached to the back of her head. As Ziva watched her sleep, she felt a sudden pang of jealousy and wished she could be as much at peace as her young human friend.

Inching a bit closer, she rested a knee on the edge of the bed and leaned over the sleeping girl, who started to stir just as Ziva clamped a hand over her mouth. Jada was immediately awake, clawing at her arm, looking wildly about with wide eyes. She grunted behind the hand and began to lash out with her legs, but she fell still and silent as the two of them locked gazes.

Ziva slid her hand from Jada's mouth and moved away to sit on the edge of the bed as the young woman sat up. "Sorry about that," she said quietly. "I wish I could sleep as well as you do."

Jada rubbed her eyes. "How—" she began, but then thought better of it. "No, I won't even ask how you got in here. I forgot who I'm dealing with."

"Do you believe what they're saying about me?"

She was quiet for several seconds. "I believe the Ziva Payvan I know wouldn't do the things they've said," she replied, a hint of uncertainty in her voice Ziva had never heard before. "If there is another Ziva who would go so far as to kill Tachi, it's not the same one I'm talking to right now."

Her words brought little comfort to Ziva, though it was better than anything else anyone had said all day. "I hate to ask you for help, but I need it if you can give it."

A split second of silence elapsed before Jada nodded. "Of course. Anything specific I can do?"

"A little caura would be nice," Ziva replied, wiping away the perspiration that had forced its way out onto her forehead.

Jada climbed out of bed, her delicate nightclothes flowing as she glided silently across the room. Ziva remained near the bed while the young woman slipped into the lavatory and retrieved three caura treatment autoinjectors from a cabinet on the wall. "These are low dosage, not much good for anything worse than a headache. But they might help."

Ziva nodded her thanks and lifted her shirt, turning to study her bruised ribs in the moonlight. The treatment wouldn't be enough to fully mend a damaged bone, but it would help alleviate some of the pain and draw more of her body's natural healing agents to the area. She touched the first autoinjector to the skin just to the left of the bruise, feeling a measure of relief the instant the small needle penetrated her flesh. She stuck herself in the shoulder with the second, hoping to ease some of the discomfort throughout her arm. The third went into the little pouch on the supply belt; she had no doubt she'd need it later.

Already feeling better, she went over to the closet, where she found Jada rummaging through a footlocker nestled back under the hanging clothes. From it, the girl removed a fiber mesh vest, followed by a stack of credits and a handful of plasma cells. She held the vest up to Ziva, sizing it without a word, then handed it to her along with the credits.

"I don't know if any of these will fit what you're carrying," she said, displaying the four plasma cells, "but feel free to take what you want."

It didn't appear that any of them matched her stolen weapon, but Ziva selected two anyway and placed them on her belt. "Thank you, Jada. Your help means a lot."

"I only wish I could do more. Do you have a plan?"

Ziva pocketed the money before removing the riding jacket and pulling the vest on over her soiled clothing. It was a bit snug, but enduring the slight discomfort was better than getting shot. "This should be enough to get me back to Noro," she replied. "Once I'm able to leave the planet, things will get easier."

Jada crossed her arms, her eyes filled with the same strange uncertainty her voice had possessed earlier. "And just how do you plan on doing that?"

In all reality, Ziva still wasn't quite sure. "For your own sake, I'm not going to tell you any more than I already have. HSP's net isn't as tight as they think it is, and if anyone has the advantage here, it's me. I know how they operate, I know their procedures. They're not going to bring me down."

"This is big, Ziva. There are a lot of people after you."

That was it. "Jada, I don't like your tone," she hissed. "Now what's the matter?"

"All of this is just incredibly taxing," the human girl said, voice shaky. "I don't know who to believe, and even if I did, I wouldn't know *what* to believe. Ziva, what if they find out you were here? What will happen to me?"

"That's not *going* to happen," Ziva replied, feeling her cheeks start to flush with anger. "I wouldn't have come here if I thought it would incriminate you."

Jada nodded and rubbed away a tear that had escaped her eye. "Just be safe, okay? I don't know how all of this started, but it seems to me like you're the only one who can stop it."

Ziva moved back to the balcony door and brushed the curtains aside, peering out over the yard and watching as the spotlight on a distant aircar swept over the structures of the Royal City. "Believe me, Jada. Someone out there chose the wrong person to start this fight with, and it will have been the last mistake they ever made."

Without another word, she slipped through the door and disappeared into the night.

· 20 ·
HSP Headquarters
Noro, Haphez

Noro was just beginning to rise over the crest of the hills surrounding the city of the same name. Diago Dasaro turned away from the window, interested in anything but the sunrise, and watched Nejdra Venn and Kyron Hoxie enter the situation room. Judging by the two captains' general demeanor, they'd had little or no rest overnight and the hunt for Payvan hadn't yielded any results. After dragging through a sleepless night himself, Dasaro's patience was running thinner than ever and he let out a deep breath in the form of a growl.

"Nothing!" Nejdra exclaimed as she came to a standstill at the table. "It's unbelievable. Absolutely nothing!"

"The trail is still cold at the checkpoint," Hoxie said, elaborating on his associate's outburst. "The homing beacon on the missing bike has been effectively disabled, and there's still no sign of the officer it was registered to. We've been unable to pick up a signal from his comms."

Nejdra rested her hands on her hips, her face twisted with fury. "You're sure we're not just dealing with a deserter there? Do we know for sure Payvan even *took* the bike?"

"There were footprints found around the camp that matched those discovered at the crash site," Hoxie explained.

"And what of the crash survivor?" Dasaro's attention shifted in Nejdra's direction. She'd been responsible for that sphere of the investigation. "Agent Spence."

"He was released from the Severe Cases Center in Haphor late last night," the woman replied. "They've got him under observation at a local med center now, and they say he'll be ready for questioning later this morning. But get this—he's already claiming *Payvan* is the one who pulled him out of that car."

"Well," Dasaro muttered, "we can't have that now, can we?"

"It's probably true," she said with a shrug. "And if it is, she saved the man's life. With that injury, he wouldn't have lasted long in the position he was in."

Dasaro eyed her warily. "It still needs to be dealt with."

"We'll head over there soon and take care of it," Hoxie said.

Dasaro looked out the window again and blinked against the sun, which was by now casting golden light across the sprawling city. "Tracking Payvan down is going to take time. Until then, we can't let her have anything." He looked up at the other two captains. "Ruin her."

· 21 ·
RESIDENTIAL SECTOR
NORO, HAPHEZ

Dust swirled around her with each breath she took. The window of the abandoned house was covered in such a thick layer of grime Ziva could barely see out of it. More importantly, no one outside could see her concealed in the shadows within. She didn't need a crystal-clear picture of the street, either—only a general view of the shapes that passed by, particularly any that entered or exited the house across the way.

The first light of dawn had been visible by the time she'd made it back to her hoverbike at the relay station. She'd pushed the machine to its limits, reaching Noro in a bit less time than it had taken the prisoner transport to travel to Haphor. Upon arriving in the city, she'd gone immediately to a street bazaar, where she'd purchased an unregistered communicator and a new pair of boots from behind the cover of her helmet. After dumping her old footwear and the stolen comm unit into the river, she'd maneuvered back into the residential area of the city where she'd found this house exactly as she remembered it. Energy depleted, she was grateful for the opportunity to sit down and rest after yet another miserably long night.

She noted the time. After two hours of watching and waiting, she concluded it was safe to approach. Unfolding her legs, she rose to her feet and removed her helmet from where she'd set it on what had once been a kitchen counter. She hesitated for a moment before opening the door and surveyed the trail she had left. There was a clear semi-circle on the floor where she'd been sitting, and there was an abundance of well-defined footprints coming from where she'd broken in through the back window. No matter. In the improbable case that someone searched this dilapidated little house, such marks couldn't be traced back to her.

Tugging the helmet down over her head, she opened the door and stepped out onto the street. It wasn't the most peaceful of neighborhoods, with little foot traffic and moderately busy streets. She waited for a lull between two groundcars then jogged across, using the cover of the helmet visor to keep an eye out for approaching HSP vehicles. Seeing none, she focused her attention on the door of the house, probing the locking mechanism with her mind just as she'd tried to do at the relay station. To her surprise, it was already open. Without faltering, she hopped up the two short steps and let herself in as if it were her own home.

The interior was darker than she had expected; the windows were almost fully tinted, and there was no other source of light she could immediately see. She removed the helmet and stood there blinking for several seconds, then took a step farther inside.

While she had only been in this place on one other occasion, Ziva remembered it well enough to realize something drastic had happened since then. The simple, well-kept bachelor pad had been transformed into a place that would have been better suited to a mob world like Niio or the slums on Chaiavis. Empty liquor bottles and other trash littered the kitchen table as well as the living room's center table, and the air was thick as if someone had recently been smoking govino. Other than a bizarre insect attempting to drag a piece of rotten food across the floor, there was no sign of life.

She set her helmet down on the center table and gazed at the sofa where she had sat the last time she was here. The data pads she had read were gathering dust on the shelf from which she had once taken them. She made her way into the kitchen, which was in the worst shape by far. Soiled dishes and utensils, as well as more foul food, joined the liquor bottles on the counter and in the sink. Water dripped from the leaky faucet with a steady *clink clink clink.* She went to the cooler and found it to be nearly empty except for a couple of unopened drinks and some containers of unidentifiable leftovers. She could feel the corners of her mouth turning farther and farther downward the more she discovered, and she hadn't even been down the hall.

She froze when the floor creaked somewhere in the house, ever so slightly. She held her breath and listened, picking up the sound of feet—probably bare—moving cautiously across the carpet in the hallway. She was not alone.

In one deft movement, she drew her pistol and reached the archway leading back into the living room. The footsteps stopped, their owner having no doubt heard her. She raised the pistol over her head and exhaled slowly through her nose; the person on the other side of the wall did the same.

She jumped out into the hallway at the exact moment the man came at her. The first thing she saw was his pistol leveled at her head, and she immediately went for it as he lunged toward hers. Struggling against his muscular arm, she managed to angle his weapon upward just as it discharged. She flung his arms across each other and pivoted, catching him hard in the face with the back of her head before leaping backward and sending him staggering back against the wall. She whirled, pinning him there with one hand closed around his throat and the other pressing her pistol to his forehead. He held his hands up in surrender and let his gun fall to the floor.

"That wasn't much of a welcome," she said.

Aroska Tarbic turned his head away from the barrel of her pistol, squinting at her in the dim light. "Ziva?" he muttered. "What the hell are you doing here?"

She released him and took a step back. "I've been good, thanks for asking, but I don't think I can say the same about you." She took a moment to survey the mess around her again. "What happened here?"

He recovered his pistol and went to set it on the dining table. The first thing that came to her mind was that he looked like one of the Solaris junkies he'd worked with during his stint in the SCU. Dark circles enveloped his drooping eyes, and he had an all-around greasy look to him as if he hadn't bathed in at least a few days. His shaggy black hair was loose from the neat ponytail she remembered him wearing, and a very unshaven face completed his ragged appearance. A stale scent hung about him, confirming her suspicion he'd been smoking.

"Can't a man have a few drinks?" he retorted.

She crossed her arms. "I think there's a little more to it than that."

"I doubt you came here to criticize my personal habits. What do you want?"

"It seems I'm in a bit of trouble."

"Oh? I wouldn't know—viewscreen's been down for two weeks."

She filled him in on the basics, which at this point mainly consisted of being wanted for murder and escaping. He appeared to be listening for the most part, but he was clearly hung over, still smashed, maybe high, or perhaps a vicious combination of the three. She'd caught glimpses of his peculiar drinking and drug habits before, but this was extreme; she couldn't begin to fathom what had caused the severe change in lifestyle. The two of them had neither seen nor spoken to each other since he had come to her home over two months earlier to inform her that Emeri Arion had revoked the order to terminate her life.

"Now, tell me what's going on with you," she said again when she had finished.

"It's not your problem."

"It *is* my problem if you're going to be helping me."

He scoffed. "Who said anything about helping you?" He cringed at his own abruptness and took a moment to compose himself before trying again. "Why come to me?"

"Aroska, you know I'm not one to ask for help, and you know *you're* probably one of the last people in this galaxy I would ever ask for help. The fact that I'm here now has to tell you *something*."

He shook his head. "You of all people should have more than enough resources for a time like this. What can I do that no one else can?"

As Ziva searched for a place to even begin, the stench and grittiness of her skin and clothing suddenly overtook her. "You can start by letting me use your shower."

· 22 ·
TARBIC RESIDENCE
NORO, HAPHEZ

Z iva slid the lavatory door shut and made sure the lock was securely engaged. Slipping out of her newly acquired boots, she stepped into the shower fully clothed. One by one, she peeled the filthy garments off and watched the muddy water swirl down the drain. She took the time to scrub and rinse each item before throwing them over the shower wall to dry.

The warm water felt heavenly compared to the chilly rain she'd grown accustomed to over the past day and night, and for a moment, she closed her eyes. Never in a million years had she imagined she'd ever be present in Aroska Tarbic's home again, much less bathing of all things. Even seeing him again seemed odd—they'd parted on what had seemed like civil terms but had both allowed each other to fade into the background. She thought back to the moment she had offered him a special ops position as the two of them stood in her home. In all reality, she didn't know what she would have done if he'd accepted—the suggestion had been more of a filler for a conversation that had been growing rather...delicate.

Life had virtually returned to normal after that day. She'd endured a couple weeks of unpaid disciplinary probation, during which she'd been able to rest and allow her wounds to heal. The fall of Dakiti and Dane Bothum had crippled Solaris to the point that HSP's clean-up crews hadn't had much work to do when it came to permanently disbanding the radical group. She had seen Aroska's name listed on agency bulletins as a primary contributor to the effort, and there'd been a short internal investigation into his relationship with the treacherous Saun Zaid, but nothing more. The only other thing she knew was that he was still receiving a paycheck from HSP.

She couldn't help but feel that his newly discovered alcohol and drug problems were somehow her fault, but she dismissed the thought as foolish and continued picking leaves and twigs out of her hair. She wasn't about to let anyone blame her for anything else at this point.

While exploring her scalp, her fingers encountered the gash she had sustained when the aircar crashed. The hair around it was caked with dried blood, which she carefully began to rinse away. The wound stung when the water contacted it, as did the rest of the small scrapes and cuts that were the result of broken glass and hours of climbing and crawling through the forest. On the bright side, the warm water helped alleviate some of the discomfort in her shoulder, and the caura she'd injected the previous night seemed to be doing its job on her ribs. She scrubbed at the tender area gently, unable to differentiate between the dirt and the bruising. Mud and gunk had found its way into every possible nook and cranny, so she spent another couple of minutes doing a thorough rinse before allowing herself a few moments to just stand still under the scalding water.

Had HSP really thought it would be so easy to take her down, or was she missing something? It would benefit her to know what they knew, what direction the investigation was headed. Contacting her team was out of the question; hell, contacting *anybody* was out of the question. She needed someone she could send in to gather the facts, someone who wouldn't be recognized as her emissary. A sudden thought struck her.

Wishing she didn't have to return to reality, Ziva reluctantly shut the water off and stepped out. Steam swirled around her as she dried quickly and pulled on the clothes Aroska had put out for her, a set of loose-fitting loungewear that had apparently belonged to a former girlfriend. She wondered briefly if the garments had belonged to Saun, though she doubted he would have kept them if that were the case. Regardless of whose they were, she was grateful for something clean and dry to wear. Aside from her undergarments, the only item of her own that she took was the therapeutic knee sleeve she'd been forced to wear since Aroska himself had shot her. She wrung it out and pulled it on.

When she ventured out into the hall, she was pleasantly surprised to find that the windows had been brightened and some of the old bottles had been cleared away. The rug still felt grimy under her bare feet, but she was pleased to already be seeing improvements.

She found Aroska in the kitchen, scrubbing weeks' worth of slime from the table. The trash compactor was standing open, full to the brim with old bottles and dishes that had probably been ruined by spoiled food. The only item occupying the counter now was a small tray holding a stick of govino. A fine column of smoke rose from the end that glowed orange.

Ziva took another few moments to study the man as she took up a position against the wall where she'd stood the first time they'd officially talked. Aroska continued cleaning, aware he was under observation but apparently not caring. He was still a large man, but he had lost a noticeable amount of weight, no doubt due to this depression he seemed to have fallen into. When combined with the changes in his hair and face, he was hardly the same person she had come to know two months earlier.

Presently, he finished cleaning and tossed the cloth into the sink. He pulled out one of the dining chairs and motioned for her to take a seat before sliding around to the other side of the table. "I suppose we have a lot to talk about."

She took the chair and watched as he transferred the little tray over to the table. He lifted the half-smoked govino stick to his lips and took a long drag from it, holding the smoke in his mouth for a moment before turning slightly and exhaling it through his nose. He gazed at her through the cloud of smoke, waiting for her to begin.

First things first—she held out her hand. "Let me see that."

He glanced quizzically from her palm to the govino stick then handed it over, placing it between her middle and forefinger. For a moment, she was tempted to take a puff herself, but instead she flipped it over and snuffed it out on the table before snapping the remainder of the stick in half.

Tarbic's only reaction was a wag of his head as he leaned back in the chair and drummed his fingers on the table. "You have to make this as difficult as possible, don't you?"

She shrugged and drew one leg up against her, casually wrapping her arms around her knee. "I think you'll find that when someone chooses to make my life miserable, I can't help but return the favor to anyone unfortunate enough to be nearby."

"That's an interesting strategy when it comes to asking someone for help."

"Put yourself in my shoes, Aroska. How would you feel if the one person you could ask for help was too strung out and screwed up to do anything?"

"Why me, then?" he demanded.

"For starters, you know my secret."

He sighed and hung his head, combing his fingers through his stringy hair. After a moment, he placed his hands on the table and eyed her with bloodshot eyes. "Start from the beginning."

· 23 ·
TARBIC RESIDENCE
NORO, HAPHEZ

Aroska listened patiently to her story in its entirety, though he struggled to keep his mind from wandering. He forced himself to pay attention by watching her mouth move as she spoke. It was amazing that so much had happened in the past forty hours. He'd been telling the truth when he said his viewscreen wasn't working—Tachi's death, Ziva's escape, it was all news to him. When he got to thinking about it, he wasn't sure how much he would have cared about any of it if the woman wasn't sitting there in front of him now.

He studied her intently as she continued regaling him with the events of the past two days. He had to laugh to himself—the borrowed clothes fit her rather awkwardly, but she seemed comfortable enough, and she certainly smelled better than she had when she'd first come in. He would see to it that, if anything, the rest of her belongings received a proper cleansing before she left.

"She gave me a few credits to get by on until I can make it off-world," she was saying, speaking of Jada and her experience in her stepfather's palace the night before. "I came straight here after leaving there early this morning."

There had always been something fascinating about her face he couldn't put his finger on. It wasn't just her eyes, the feature that had so effectively captured his attention the first time he'd caught sight of her. Though her countenance often appeared to be carved out of stone, she was still one of the most striking women he knew. She had a rather narrow jaw and high, sharp cheekbones, but the wisdom and experience spoken by her eyes helped counter the severity of her other features. Her hair had taken on a wavy form while damp, and it hung loose like a black frame around her pale face, giving her a very innocent air that was totally foreign to him. He realized he hardly noticed her scar anymore.

He was suddenly aware she had stopped talking, and he looked up to find her staring him down through slightly narrowed eyes. Her jaw was set, and she looked altogether unhappy, but at the same time, he could tell her mind was elsewhere. Judging by her appearance and body language, the woman was exhausted and trying hard not to show it. Despite the fact that he'd only known her for a short time, the way she shut others out and tried to do everything herself still drove him mad. The behavior posed too many unnecessary risks for his taste.

"Are you going to do this or not?" she demanded.

"That depends."

She scowled. "On what?"

"On whether or not you killed Tachi," he replied. "So, did you do it?"

She shook her head in disgust and made no move to respond. For a moment, Aroska couldn't tell if she was looking at him, but he concluded that she was looking past him at nothing in particular while the wheels inside her head spun. She gnawed at the inside of her bottom lip, her eyes once again narrowed slightly.

Her hesitation made his stomach flop over and he suddenly felt very wary. "Ziva?"

"No," she snapped, her eyes shifting back over to meet his. "The galaxy knows I would have liked to." She shook her head again.

He lifted an eyebrow. "Sounds like there's an interesting story there."

"*Later.*"

He sighed and placed a hand on the little ashtray, wishing desperately for his govino stick as he pushed it around and listened to it scrape against the table. "I'm still not sure I understand what exactly you want me to do."

Ziva let her leg down and scooted her chair in, leaning forward a bit with her hands folded. "I have a plan," she said, "and I doubt you're going to like it."

Aroska wanted to laugh out loud, but he resorted to a short snicker and nodded slowly. As much as he was tempted to refuse, there was something in her eyes that went to work on him, just as it had when his hand had been the only thing keeping her from plunging over a cliff to her death. He wondered briefly if she always got people to do her bidding just by looking at them.

"Let's hear it, then," he said with a shrug.

"You want to know why I came to you. It's because you're my only resource. Trying to contact anyone on the inside—Skeet, Zinni, even Adin and his team—would be suicide on my part, not to mention the other party would probably be imprisoned or fired at the least. What I need is someone I can send inside, someone who can get close enough to Dasaro to monitor the progress of the investigation. It has to be someone they wouldn't suspect."

Now Aroska did laugh. "You want me to be your mole inside HSP."

She nodded but said nothing, keeping her hands folded in front of her mouth as her crimson gaze continued to bore into him.

"You're crazy," he said. "That's insane. I don't work for HSP any-more."

"You were still on the payroll last time I checked. What do they have you out on? Medical leave? *Psych* leave?"

He sat up straight and leaned toward her. "I told you before, that's none of your business."

Ziva glared at him for a moment before sitting back in her chair with one leg crossed over the other. She folded her arms, and any shred of innocence vanished from her face. "Fine," she muttered, "whatever helps you sleep at night. But you can't deny that you have a problem."

"I'm not denying anything!" he exclaimed, fighting away a sudden wave of nausea as it coursed through his stomach. A good portion of the bottles he had just cleaned up were from the previous night, and some were even from early that morning.

She stood up and approached him, perching on the edge of the table just to his right. Her arms were still crossed as she bent down closer to him, eyes ablaze. "You're going to help me," she growled. "The fact that I'm the one asking should be reason enough."

Aroska was too focused on the churning in his stomach to pay much attention to what she was saying, let alone come up with a snappy response. He felt his intestines cramp violently and managed to lean away from her just as he spewed vomit all over himself and the table.

She merely sighed and stared forward, unfazed. Neither of them said anything for several awkward moments, and the only sound to be heard was the soft gurgling in Aroska's belly.

Finally, she rose to her feet, leaning down to whisper in his ear before walking away. "I once put someone through a thirty-hour detox," she said. "It almost killed him. I hope you can handle it better."

Queasy and thoroughly embarrassed, Aroska groaned and let his pounding head come to rest on the table.

· 24 ·
CAPITAL MEDICAL CENTER
HAPHOR, HAPHEZ

W hen Kade stepped out of the med center elevator, he immediately directed his attention to a nearby workstation where a cluster of nurses were going over some files on a large viewscreen. Feeling rather self-conscious with his face still bruised, he made his way toward them, dodging a medical bot as it zipped past him carrying a tray of surgical tools.

One of them, a heavier-set woman wearing brightly colored eye makeup, looked up as he approached. The shock was apparent in her face as she assessed his injuries.

"Can I help you, son?" she asked, eyes wide and eyebrows arched.

Kade flashed his HSP identification halfheartedly. "Agent Shevin, Royal Guard," he introduced himself. "I'm looking for an HSP agent who was brought in yesterday."

The woman shrugged and placed her hands on her hips. "You'll have to be more specific than that. Thanks to some 'domestic disputes' that got out of hand last night, we've got twelve of your friends in here."

"The name is Spence. He was the survivor of a crash involving a prisoner transport."

"Oh yes," one of the younger nurses piped up, shooting an irritated glance at her associate. "Follow me, please."

She gave him a flirtatious once-over as she slipped around the counter and began moving down the hall. Kade strode along behind her, desperately trying to come up with something he could say to Spence.

Reports said the man had suffered some mild brain trauma in the crash. By now, they'd all heard about the ludicrous claim he was making, but so far nobody seemed to believe him. Questioning him again seemed futile, and for a moment, Kade wondered if there was even any point in being here. The thought occurred to him that Zona might have given him this assignment for no other reason than to get him out of the agency's hair.

After a minute of walking and weaving around busy bots and medical personnel, the young nurse stopped in front of a room with an open door.

"He's in here, Agent Shevin," she said, leaning up against the door frame with an appreciative smirk. She looked like she couldn't have been more than a year his elder, if not his age. "You know, maybe you should let me take a look at that eye of yours." She reached out to touch his bruised face.

Appalled, Kade gently brushed her hand away and took a slight step back. "Thanks, but they cleared me yesterday," he said. "And..." he held up his left hand, displaying the fragile silver band—hardly more than a wire—that adorned his middle finger. It was identical to the one he had given Veya when they were married two years before.

"Oh," the nurse muttered, sounding more annoyed than apologetic. "It never fails." She pivoted and stormed back in the direction from which they had come.

More than relieved, Kade stepped into the room and let his eyes adjust to the dim yellowish light cast by the panels surrounding the base of the bed. Agent Spence lay there dressed in a comfortable hospital tunic and pants. His chest was thick as if it was heavily bandaged under the clothing, and he wore a sturdy brace around his neck. An IV line ran into his left arm, but other than the oxygen mask over his face, he seemed to be in incredibly good shape considering what he'd been through. He turned his head to look when Kade entered.

"Damn," he muttered, his voice muffled through the mask. "How many more of you are they going to send?"

Again, Kade displayed his HSP credentials. "Royal Guard," he said. "My name is Kade Shevin. I understand it's been a long couple of days, but would you mind answering a few questions?"

Spence mumbled another curse and pulled himself into a more upright position. According to the report, he was in his late thirties, having worked in HSP's field ops division for the past sixteen years. His dirty blonde hair was streaked with vivid yellow stripes that matched his eyes and were accentuated by the lighting in the room. He gasped a bit and placed a hand on his wounded chest before sighing and easing back against the pillows.

"Sorry kid, that was a little harsh," he said after pulling his mask down. "You can't blame a man, though, not after the day I've had. It's hard to feel up to being debriefed by everyone on the Fringe when all you want to do is overdose on painkillers and catch some much-needed shut-eye."

It suddenly struck Kade how much the two of them had in common. "I couldn't agree with you more," he said, pulling up a chair a comfortable distance from the bed.

Spence nodded up at him, eyeing his purple face and his crushed nose. "What's your story?"

"I had my own run-in with Payvan," he responded as he took a seat and examined the data pad of notes Zona had sent with him.

"That's right," Spence said. "You were the guy who got flattened outside Tachi's palace. I saw you on the news—looked like you wanted to be anywhere but that press conference."

After two nights and a full day of listening to such statements, Kade was growing weary of the conversation. "Agent Spence, if you don't mind, I'm here to talk about *you*."

"Right," Spence said, placing the mask back over his mouth for a few seconds. "We were fine until we cleared the final checkpoint, then all hell broke loose. One second, I'm staring out the window, just wishing the trip was over, and suddenly the car is going down and I'm trying to wrestle Payvan off me."

Kade reviewed the information on the data pad. "First responders reportedly found the force field control switch in the 'off' position. Same can be said for the switch that released Payvan's cuffs. Even if she wasn't cuffed, she obviously couldn't have reached through that field to mess with the switches. Any idea what happened?"

"Don't tell me you think I had something to do with her escape!" Spence exclaimed. "I swear I didn't touch anything! Everything was working fine. The energy shield was activated, the switches were on, but…maybe they got moved when Gerrit's service weapon came loose from his holster."

"The gun 'came loose' from the holster? This was before the car started to go down?"

"I…I think…that doesn't make any sense. Everything happened so fast, I can't be sure. There was some turbulence—we were dealing with wind gusts the whole way to Haphor. Maybe that knocked it loose."

Kade sighed, beginning to wonder himself if the man was delusional or not. "Okay," he said, jotting down some notes with the data pad's stylus. "Let's move on."

"I remember hitting my head," Spence continued, "but I must have blacked out after that because the next thing I knew, we were on the ground. I could hear Payvan moving around in the back, and once she broke out, I figured she was long gone. When I saw her come around to the front of the car, I thought for sure she was going to kill me. Instead, she took the time to pull me out of there when she could have been making a run for it." Spence shook his head, and unless it was Kade's imagination, his chin wobbled a bit. "The doctors say I probably wouldn't have made it if she'd just left me."

Intrigued, Kade wrote faster. What business did Payvan have saving the life of a man who was transporting her to prison after she'd assassinated the Royal Officer? The story excited him, but at the same time, it contradicted everything he'd been made to believe about the woman.

"Did she ever say anything to you?"

Steam clouded the inside of Spence's mask as he took another breath from it. "She said something right before she pulled me out, but I was having trouble focusing. I think she told me to hang on. All I wanted was to get out of there, so I let her drag me out. I figured if I was going to die, I might as well let her put me out of my misery instead of drowning in my own blood. She sat me up against a tree and took my weapon and my comm. She told me to hold on again, help was coming."

Spence paused and placed a hand on his chest, staring vacantly ahead. "I know there was something else," he murmured. "My ears were ringing, and I could barely understand her." He closed his eyes. "They say I suffered some head trauma, and I...I'm sorry, Shevin. I honestly can't remember."

For a while, Kade said nothing. His gaze remained fixed on the data pad, though he realized he was neither reading nor retaining any of the information it displayed. He let his mind race, lost in the rhythmic beeping of the machine pumping oxygen through Spence's mask. So many questions had yet to be answered.

"I know it sounds crazy. Everyone seems to think I've lost my mind, but I know what happened. Please tell me you believe me, Shevin."

Kade sat forward in the chair, rubbing his tired eyes before bringing his elbows down to rest on his knees. "Let's put it this way: I don't *not* believe you. But there's too much going on and too many different stories floating around for me to figure out exactly what I *do* believe."

Spence nodded in agreement. "Before that crash yesterday, I felt pretty sure of things. All the evidence seemed solid, and your witness statement backed it all up. But it doesn't make any sense. What would have compelled Payvan to stick around and risk being captured again just so she could rescue me?"

"My thoughts exactly," Kade said. "And why wouldn't she have finished me off before breaking into the palace? What good did it do to keep me—a witness—alive? I suppose the obvious answer is that she wasn't planning on getting caught, but something isn't right there, either. What veteran operator would leave evidence of their presence even if it would theoretically be destroyed? I know I wouldn't."

Spence scoffed. "Do they really expect everyone to believe all of this?"

"I don't know," Kade replied, "but people do believe it, and anyone who dares to ask a question gets shot down. If I didn't know any better, I'd think someone is covering something up. Personally, I can't wait to get to the bottom of this." He stood up and pocketed the stylus. "Thank you for your time, Spence. Is there anything I can do for you while I'm here?"

The agent thought a moment then nodded toward an empty water container on the bedside table. "I'll take another round." He managed a weak smile.

Kade smiled as well at the attempted humor and set the data pad down in the chair, taking up the bottle. Across the room, the door to a small lavatory stood halfway open, and he angled toward it.

"I didn't do what they said I did."

Kade spun around, puzzled. "Come again?"

"That's the other thing she said. Payvan." He replaced the mask once again.

Feeling rather overwhelmed, Kade gestured his thanks with his free hand. "I appreciate it, Spence. Even if it does nothing to further the investigation, it will still help me."

He continued into the little lavatory, lost in thought. After a moment of fiddling with the bottle's lid, he set the faucet to cold and stood there waiting for the container to fill.

Ziva Payvan had now spared his life as well as someone else's. Zona's argument had been that perhaps she *thought* she'd killed Kade out on the bridge. Out of respect, he had agreed, though it didn't stop him from reflecting on how he truly felt. No HSP agent in their right mind, whatever rank, would ever walk away assuming an enemy was dead, especially if that enemy was a potential witness to a capital crime. Then there was the theory that Payvan had been emotionally compromised by her quest to kill Tachi, resulting in her carelessness, but again, he refused to believe it. This was an operative who killed for a living, and her very survival hinged on her ability to remain level-headed. Even if the assassination had been emotionally driven, he doubted she would have allowed herself to get sloppy.

On the other hand, perhaps the others were right. Maybe Payvan had indeed left him for dead and would now come back to finish him off after discovering he had survived. Someone had suggested that she'd only pulled Spence out of the car in a futile attempt at atonement. The thought made Kade shudder; in the back of his mind, he'd been giving her the benefit of the doubt all along, and he dreaded to think of all the time and energy he'd wasted should he turn out to be wrong.

He was suddenly drawn back to the present by the realization that the bottle had overflowed and water was running out over his hand. Startled, he transferred it to his other hand and snatched a folded cloth from the shelf above the sink, wiping away the excess water. Fumbling for the controls, he shut the faucet off and returned to the room, where he found the hefty nurse from the workstation waiting in the doorway.

"Agent Shevin, would you mind answering a few procedural questions regarding the care of the other agents we have here? Since you're here now, I thought it would be more efficient than having to call in to the agency."

Kade nodded and handed the water bottle to Spence before following the woman out the door. "I'll see what I can do."

She led him down the long hallway to a larger room that housed multiple beds, each occupied by one of the HSP officers involved in the—how had she put it—*domestic disputes* from the previous evening. A large viewscreen displayed all their vitals on the wall outside, saving the medical staff a trip into the room to check them all individually. She began to give him a quick rundown of what some of the readings meant, but he was too preoccupied by the sight down the hall to pay much attention.

Two plainclothes HSP agents—at least they struck him as being HSP agents—had materialized from the far stairwell and were making their way into Spence's room. One was a tall *emilan* woman, about his same height, and the other was an *avilon* man with a long scar cutting through the thick brown hair on the back of his head. If the agency was really sending this many people to ask questions and get statements, it was no wonder Spence had been irritated by his arrival.

"...so then does this data need to be added to the agents' personnel files, or just their medical records?"

Kade shifted his attention back to what was in front of him and stared at the viewscreen for a moment as he tried to process what the nurse had asked. "Assuming the Haphor field office follows the same procedures as the Royal Guard, you'd only add this data to the medical records. Med reports are directly linked to each agent's profile, so entering it in both places would give us redundant data." He gave her a friendly smile and shrugged. "Then someone like me has to go in and normalize everything."

The nurse began to ask another question, and again Kade found he had trouble focusing on her. He felt even more useless standing there answering tech questions than he had coming to talk to Spence in the first place—he refused to let himself be relegated to a mere errand boy. His mind was on the story the wounded man had told about Payvan, and all of *that* was above his pay grade.

"Just enter the data like it is, and the agency will take care of the rest," he said, not entirely sure what the question had even been.

"Thanks, I think that's everything. Have a good day, Agent Shevin."

Kade bowed his head and continued down the hall toward the workstation and elevator where he'd come in, keeping a leery eye out for the young nurse who had taken so much interest in him. Spence's statements had seemed sincere enough, but the head trauma he'd sustained could render his testimony inadmissible in any sort of legal setting. He could rant about Payvan saving his life all he wanted; adding that detail to the incident report was just futile at this point. At any rate, it wasn't the rescue itself that bothered Kade—it was the escape. *The gun came loose from the holster?* That was no doubt the reason everyone was so quick to dismiss the story. No ops agent would carry their weapon unsecured, and even if it had slipped out, the chances of it striking the control panel in exactly the right place were minimal.

With a sigh, he slipped into the elevator and began the journey down to the parking bay. Part of him still wondered if Spence had indeed had a hand in Payvan's escape and had fabricated the whole story. Maybe that explained why he'd survived and the pilot hadn't. Had Payvan blackmailed him and forced him to help her break out, granting him his life as a reward? Or had he let her go because he too believed she was somehow innocent? On the other hand, maybe everything had happened exactly as Spence had said, as far-fetched as it all seemed. Kade looked forward to sitting down and taking another long look at his notes and—

His notes. "*Sheyss,*" he grumbled, punching the control panel and sending the elevator car back up the shaft. He thought he recalled setting the data pad in the chair before going in to fill Spence's water bottle.

When the elevator door opened onto the recovery floor, Kade found himself in the middle of a war zone. Alarms blared at the nurses' station, and he was forced to leap out of the way as a team of medical personnel sprinted by with a crash cart hovering on repulsors. Startled by the sudden change in atmosphere, he regained his footing and glanced up at the readings on the monitor that had triggered the alarm. He recognized the room number immediately.

Within a split second, Kade was hot on the nurses' heels, jogging along behind the crash cart. He pulled up short when he reached Spence's room, stunned by the din created by the wailing machines and shouting doctors within. A voice in the back of his mind commanded him to retrieve his data pad before it got broken or lost, so he moved forward and snatched it up out of the chair moments before it was shoved out of the way to make room for the crash cart.

"He's in v-fib!" someone shouted just as Kade opened his mouth to ask what was happening.

A firm hand took hold of his arm, and he looked over to see the young nurse gazing up at him, all signs of her playful behavior gone. "Agent Shevin, we need you to move out of this area."

"What's wrong with him?"

"He's gone into cardiac arrest," she said, cut off by a high-pitched screeching before she could elaborate further. "Please, you need to move away."

Kade complied, eyes fixed on the flat line spanning Spence's heart rate monitor as he shuffled toward the door. Based on what little he could see through the crowd of staff and medical bots, the man wasn't responding to any of their interventional procedures. According to the incident reports, the shard of glass from the windshield had been lodged dangerously close to his heart, but his surgery had been successful, and he'd seemed fine while Kade visited with him. He wondered how stable he'd been while the other agents questioned him, and he was stricken with the realization that neither of them were currently present.

The hairs on the back of his neck stood on end as he ventured out into the hallway and swept his gaze from side to side, searching for any sign of the two agents he'd seen arriving at Spence's room only minutes before. They were nowhere in sight, but the knowledge that they were the last people to have seen Spence alive sent Kade racing toward the back stairs they'd come up earlier. He burst through the door and paused to listen. The echo of faint footsteps carried up from the bottom of the stairwell; whose they were remained a mystery, but it was a mystery he intended to solve.

Moving as fast as possible, he began the seemingly endless trek down the ten flights of stairs, pausing to peer over the edge of the railing every so often. A door at the bottom dumped him out into a small docking bay for med center staff. He shielded his face from a light rain that was falling and darted to the right, sprinting along the edge of the building and glancing about for any signs of life. There didn't seem to be anyone around at all, much less the two agents he searched for. He pulled up when he reached the corner and found himself staring out at the busy street and the towering structures of central Haphor.

Cursing under his breath, he turned and made his way back toward the door. Whoever these mysterious visitors were, Kade was reasonably sure they'd just murdered Spence. And whoever they were, they were long gone.

· 25 ·
Tarbic Residence
Noro, Haphez

Ziva had already taken the liberty of putting her clothes and the riding suit through Aroska's laundry system and was glad to once again be wearing her own things. She'd risked a brief trip out of the house, disguised in the suit, and had traveled down the street to a market on the corner that had seen better days. There, she had carefully selected some specific herbs and supplements, as well as a few general grocery items to stock Aroska's cooler. She had barely eaten in the past thirty hours, and if she was going to be staying in his house, she wanted something other than the unidentifiable slime she'd discovered during her earlier investigating.

Now, after returning to the house and making herself at home again, she stood in the kitchen and finished crushing up one of the plants she had purchased. She scraped the depleted leaves into the trash compactor and dumped the juices into the bowl containing the rest of the solution she'd already created. It had taken on a reddish-brown tint, and it made her eyes smart as she mixed in the new ingredients. She'd learned the recipe from Marshay but had never been brave enough to try the stuff herself—the word was it could work miracles on anyone in need of a complete system cleanse. The smell alone told her it worked.

She finished stirring and poured some of the chunky mixture into a glass, placing the remainder in the cooler. She carried the glass gingerly down the hall to the lavatory, where she found Aroska exactly as she had left him: secured to a chair within the walls of the shower, head drooping, clothes still stained with vomit and sweat.

His head bobbed gently from side to side, and he murmured something unintelligible under his breath. When he didn't react to Ziva's presence, she passed the glass under his nose. For a moment, he stopped moving, then he turned away to escape the stench. Finally, he came to his senses and gazed up at her with furrowed eyebrows and still-bloodshot eyes.

"What the hell is that?" he muttered.

"It's what you're going to drink in the next five seconds unless you want me to force it down your throat."

He eyed the gritty substance and started to stand up before realizing he was tied to the chair. He swore. "What are you doing to me?"

"I told you I'm putting you through detox," she said. "Or were you too wasted to pay attention?"

"I'm fine," he protested.

"You spent an hour wallowing in your own vomit, and you just spent another hour tied to a chair in your shower without even knowing it. You're not fine. Now drink this."

He began to refuse, but she was already too impatient to allow him the luxury. She shoved his chair backward, tipping it against the shower wall and tilting his head back. Taking his jaw in her left hand, she pried his mouth open and held the glass to his lips. He hollered like a child—or perhaps an old man refusing medication—and bit down on her fingers, drawing blood as the disgusting herbal mixture fell in. When the glass was empty, Ziva let it drop to the floor and ripped her hand from his mouth. She moved it up to the top of his head and placed the other under his chin, holding his jaw shut.

"Swallow it!" she hissed in his ear.

Tarbic struggled against her, but his restraints held him fast. He sputtered and coughed, enabling some of the concoction to escape out over his chin. Finally, he clamped his eyes shut and allowed the contents of his mouth to drain down his throat.

She released him and cursed under her breath as she shook her sore fingers. She stepped back and crossed her arms, bracing herself for the barrage of verbal attacks she expected from the man.

He swore again. "What was *that*?" he exclaimed, still sputtering. He spit down into the shower drain.

"It contains herbs and laxatives that will go to work on your system," she said. "You might want to make yourself comfortable in here. By tonight there won't be anything left inside you."

"Why are you doing this?"

"You just can't get it through your head, can you? I'm counting on you to help me. What happened to the charming Aroska Tarbic who used to jump at the opportunity to help a damsel in distress?"

"I would hardly consider you a damsel in distress, Ziva. You killed my brother."

She laughed out loud. "Oh, where did that come from?"

"I told you I'd never be able to forgive you."

"Right. I think this is the hangover talking."

Aroska shook his head. "Why should I help you? What would I get in return?"

"You help me, and I'll help you get clean."

"What if I'm not interested in getting 'clean'?"

"Look at yourself, Aroska," she said. "This isn't you. This isn't the field ops lieutenant I knew two months ago. That's the man I came to for support, not the one sitting in front of me right now. The way I see it, you should be flattered that I was even willing to seek you out." She knelt and began loosening his restraints. "Now sit tight. We've both got a long way to go, but you're going to have to take the first step."

She left him there.

· 26 ·
ROYAL GUARD HEADQUARTERS
HAPHOR, HAPHEZ

Supervisory Special Agent Luko Zona looked up from his work when he heard a gentle rap on the frame of his office door. There stood Kade Shevin, pale as a ghost, looking deeply troubled. The fact that something was on his mind was as clear as it would have been if the words were tattooed on his forehead. Zona was growing weary of listening to the young agent's opinions about the Payvan case, but nevertheless he motioned toward the empty chair on the other side of his desk.

"Shevin," he greeted. "Back already?" He had hoped the errand to the med center would have kept him out of the office a bit longer—the kid needed some fresh air.

When Kade made no move to respond, Zona saved his work and logged out of his terminal, guessing the young man was there to discuss the events of the past two days. He had, after all, promised to speak further with Kade about the assassination, though he wasn't entirely sure what more there was to talk about.

"You got a statement from Spence?" he asked, hoping to coax some signs of life out of Shevin.

"I did," Kade responded, his voice dry as if he hadn't spoken or even opened his mouth for some time.

Zona shrugged and leaned back in his chair, lifting his feet up to rest on the surface of the desk. "And?"

The instant Shevin glanced nervously to the door, Zona knew

something wasn't right. A disconcerting air suddenly settled over the office, and he was overcome by the urge to pull his feet back down.

"Shevin?" he said. "What happened?"

"Did we have any more of our people scheduled to go question Spence today?" Kade finally asked.

"No one else from the RG," Zona answered. "The Agency might be sending someone out." He paused, troubled by the question. "Why?"

Kade all but leaped to his feet and ran to the door, pounding the controls with a fist. He spun around as it slid shut, eyes crazed. "Sir, Spence is *dead*! The med center just confirmed it."

Zona wasn't sure what he was hearing. "He didn't make it? I thought you said—"

"You don't understand, sir. I'm almost positive he was murdered."

Of course something like this had to happen on *his* watch. Zona placed his hands in his hair and leaned forward with his elbows on his desk, letting out a deep breath. "Okay Shevin, slow down. What the hell are you talking about?"

Kade began relaying the events—in meticulous detail, Zona observed—starting from the time he'd left RG Headquarters. He presented the data pad bearing Spence's statements at the appropriate time, but at this point, Zona was more interested in hearing the rest of the story than reading it.

"They must not have known I saw them go in," Kade concluded after another few moments of explanation. "Spence was fine when I saw him. When I came back, he was dying, and those agents were gone. They were the only common factor."

Zona rubbed his hands over his face and left them there until his mind stopped racing. Shevin was renowned throughout the RG office for forming his own ideas and theories about cases, so this situation was nothing new. The young man tried hard, so very hard, and Zona had never known him to be dishonest. He had, in a sense, taken the kid under his wing upon his arrival at the Royal Guard, recognizing both his skill as an agent and his work ethic. It was times like this that made him question his decision to bring Kade along so quickly, but there was always something inside him that prompted him to give the young agent a second chance no matter how ludicrous his beliefs were. But this was probably his fifth or sixth chance. Zona had lost count.

Still, it was troubling to think of what was going on behind the scenes if the story checked out. "How do you know Spence's heart didn't fail because of his injuries? Are you saying these people killed him *with* cardiac arrest?"

"It's possible, isn't it? They could have given him something. We'll know for sure after the autopsy."

"What makes you so sure they were HSP?"

Shevin leaned forward in his chair, shifting his thumbs around and swallowing hard. "It was one of those things you just know, you know? Something about them, the way they moved, the weapons they carried...I just knew."

"They were dirty HSP agents and not private contractors?"

"Please, sir," Kade said, his indigo eyes insistent. "No matter who they were, they killed one of our people. Don't you think we should at least find out why? Did they not want him talking?"

Zona agreed wholeheartedly, or *almost*. The problem at this point was the fact that Emeri Arion and the mother agency in Noro were set on the decisions they had made and questioning them in any way would be looked upon with suspicion. Ziva Payvan had murdered Officer Tachi, the evidence confirmed it, and a person would have to be crazy to believe otherwise. He was already worried about what would happen to Kade if he kept up this game he was playing. He didn't need his own head on the chopping block when he was supposed to be running an investigation.

He leaned over his desk again and looked the young man squarely in the eyes. "Tell you what, Shevin. You go and look through surveillance feeds from the med center and see what you can find. Get me a positive ID on these people, and then we'll talk."

· 27 ·
ROYAL GUARD HEADQUARTERS
HAPHOR, HAPHEZ

Both emboldened and discouraged by Zona's words, Kade nodded respectfully and left his commanding officer's office. He knew good and well why the man was leery about his approach to the entire matter, and he couldn't blame him for being hesitant. The Royal Guard was looked upon as the spoiled little brother in the grand scheme of things, and he was well aware of how the rest of HSP would handle a feeble RG agent if they showed signs of treachery. Ordinarily, asking questions wouldn't have been such an issue. After all, Payvan was legally entitled to have someone try to build a case for her throughout this week; his behavior should be considered normal. But after the appearance—and subsequent *disappearance*—of the strangers in the med center, Kade was convinced there was more going on than met the eye. The situation was anything *but* normal.

The wheels in his head were spinning so fast that when he arrived at his workstation, he couldn't recall how he had gotten there. He couldn't shake the feeling that Payvan was being set up, but there was no logical explanation for the evidence brought against her. Everything seemed almost *too* airtight. He blinked into the fiery orange light streaming through the window as Noro began to sink below the city skyline. With a heavy sigh, he sat down in his chair, all too eager to get to the bottom of things, one way or another.

· 28 ·

TARBIC RESIDENCE

NORO, HAPHEZ

A bright, undefined light shone through the blurry film over Aroska's eyes when his eyelids finally parted. He immediately closed them again, wincing against the pain shooting through his head. He ran his tongue over his crusty lips—his mouth felt like someone had stuffed fiber mesh into it and left it there overnight. Drawing a deep breath, he fluttered his heavy eyelids again and now realized he was looking into the warm yellow light of dawn as it poured in through the window. He turned his head lazily to one side and squinted into the sunlight that had managed to break through the clouds for the first time in days. A thick layer of condensation coated the glass, the result of all the warm moisture suddenly rising from the ground.

Unable to discern exactly what time it was, he groaned and flopped over onto his stomach. He could feel that he was indeed wearing his pajama pants, but he was lying uncovered on top of his made bed. The sour stench of vomit filled the bedroom, and he vaguely remembered stumbling in, changing out of his soiled clothes, and collapsing onto the bed without so much as a second thought.

His head seemed to weigh a ton, but he felt oddly coherent considering the amount of alcohol he had to have consumed to be in this condition. He lay perfectly still for a moment, straining to remember what had happened. The realization that this was no ordinary hangover hit him when he felt his stomach rumble with hunger. Everything came rushing back to him at that exact moment as if he had just awakened from a long and puzzling dream. Ziva had come, she had used his shower, they had talked, and she had forced him to drink that awful concoction. He thought he could still taste the stuff in the back of his mouth.

Groaning again, he sat up and swung his legs over the side of the bed, feeling the carpet between his toes as he placed the heels of his hands in his eye sockets and held them there for a moment before rubbing the sleep out of his eyes. He could feel his arms trembling involuntarily, no doubt the result of low blood sugar. Ziva had been right when she'd explained the consequences of drinking her mysterious mixture—he had no desire to relive his experiences in the lavatory the previous night.

He stood up, feeling a bit light-headed but otherwise better than he had in a long time. As he went to his wardrobe, he recalled the conversation he'd had with Skeet Duvo two months earlier, the conversation that had taught him what he now considered one of the most important lessons he'd ever learned: Ziva was always right. As much as he hated to acknowledge it, the lesson had continued to manifest itself every time he'd been near the woman, and now that she was back, here it was again.

Aroska selected a lightweight shirt and pulled it over his head, adjusting his deceased brother's military tags which hung on a chain around his neck. He'd often wondered what Soren would think if he knew his brother had forged a friendship with the sniper who'd shot him. He hesitated a moment—no, at this point, he wouldn't consider himself friends with Ziva. The two of them were in a better place than they'd been when they'd started, but he had a lot of frustration built up inside him, and she was the perfect person to take that frustration out on. He pictured it as giving her a taste of her own medicine. At any rate, their current predicament could safely be considered the second chance the two of them had agreed upon the last time they'd met.

When he opened his bedroom door, the rest of the house was silent. Haze from his govino habit lingered in the living room, swirling lazily through the shaft of light shining in through the window. He stood at the end of the hall, watching for any signs of Ziva. Perhaps she had already gone? He knew that was just wishful thinking. She wouldn't have bothered going through the trouble of getting him sober or even coming to find him if she was just going to turn around and leave. Half of him saw her arrival as a sign—of what, he wasn't quite sure—but the other half wasn't ready for another round of dealing with her just yet.

He continued silently down the hall with all his energy devoted to listening, just as he had the previous day when he'd first heard someone enter his house. When he broke out into the living room, the sight of her lying on the couch startled him out of his skin. She was flat on her back with her head propped up against the armrest, arms folded across her chest, legs crossed at the ankles. She still wore her boots and her pistol lay on the center table, which had been pulled to within arm's reach. He couldn't imagine she could possibly be comfortable, much less asleep, but for the duration of the time he stood observing her, she didn't move. Her eyes remained closed, and he could hear her breathing quietly.

Once again caught off guard by how innocent and peaceful she was capable of looking, Aroska continued across the room and peered into the kitchen. To his surprise, he found the dining table neatly set and an assortment of food spread across the kitchen counter. Puzzled, he turned back toward the sofa and found Ziva looking at him, crimson eyes dark in the shadows of the room.

"Feel any better?" she asked. Other than her tilted head, she remained motionless.

The sound of her voice made his skin crawl for a reason he couldn't explain. He nodded, raking his fingers through his tangled hair. "I do, actually," he replied. "Thanks, I guess."

She rose fluidly into a sitting position and leaned forward, studying him with her elbows resting on her knees. "Good," she said, "but you're not in the clear just yet."

"You've got to be kidding me," he muttered, hoping that didn't mean he still wasn't allowed to eat. His stomach was roaring now and had cramped up to the point that he was afraid he might throw up again.

"One more day," she explained, waving a single finger. "You can get started early and get to feeling better by tonight. We've got a lot of planning to do before tomorrow."

Oh yes—he had almost forgotten he would be infiltrating HSP on her behalf. At this point, he doubted refusal would be an option. His chance for that had been blown the moment he'd spewed his guts all over the table the day before. He doubted, however, that any performance he gave HSP would be convincing with the shape he was currently in, yet another instance of Ziva being right even when her actions seemed so cold and merciless. She had also been accurate when she'd told him the fact that she was asking for help should be reason enough for him to comply. There had been a time when he might have jumped at the opportunity to help her, for no other reason than that she could be such a *shouka* when it came to cooperating with anyone. Now, though, he just felt…maybe *jaded* was the word, though he could think of no reasonable explanation for feeling so.

Aroska watched her watch him for another several seconds before he shifted his eyes down to her folded hands. Her body wasn't much more than a silhouette against the morning light shining through the tinted window, but he was still able to make out the white medical tape binding the index and middle fingers on her left hand. Another bout of regret and embarrassment smacked him in the face.

"I'm sorry I bit you," he said.

Ziva glanced down at the bandages. "You've done worse."

For a brief moment, he found himself standing on the boarding ramp of her ship, staring at the mass of burned flesh and clothing surrounding the hole he'd just blown through her right kneecap. He shook off the memory, not wanting to relive any more of his mistakes than he would have to whenever she forced him to sit down and talk. He had a feeling the time was not far.

"I'm sorry for that, too. Did I ever tell you that?"

"No. Did I ever tell you how I feel about people apologizing to me?"

He chuckled. "No."

Ziva stood up, face grim, and placed her hands on her hips. "For the price of helping me, I thought I would at least make breakfast. Why don't you eat something? I could hear your stomach from the other end of the house."

So she'd been awake after all. "Ziva, hold on," he said, stepping to one side to block her entrance into the kitchen. "I'm sorry for the way I was acting yesterday. You were right, that wasn't me."

He stopped when she held her hand up for silence. "Did you not hear what I just said?"

"Yes, but I—"

"Made an ass of yourself is what you did."

He had to smile a little—there she was again, brutally honest but totally accurate. "Yeah."

"Now go eat something. Purging again won't be any fun, but we need to keep your blood sugar up to control withdrawal symptoms. I'm sure it's all cold by now, with how long you stayed in bed."

"Excuse me, but I think you would have been exhausted too after the night I had. I can't remember the last time I felt that *sheyssen.*"

"If I had to guess, I'd say it hasn't been that long judging by all those empty bottles you had piling up around here. Can you even remember the last time you woke up without a hangover?"

Again, Aroska had to admit he felt good, though it killed him to think of drinking any more of Ziva's concoction. Still, he imagined it would all be worth it later, judging by how rejuvenated he felt after a single round.

He sat down at the table and looked over the different dishes as she set them out, remembering the leftover warco stew he'd tasted during dinner at her house. "Pardon me for not picturing you as a cook," he said, filling his plate.

She slid in across from him and did the same. "Something constructive to do with my spare time," she replied. "You're not the only one who finds it hard to believe. I have to laugh about it myself sometimes."

"Pardon me for not picturing you laughing, either."

"Figure of speech," she retorted, stuffing a bite of food into her mouth.

Aroska stabbed a piece of meat with his fork but hesitated with it in front of his mouth. "Smile," he said.

"What?"

"*Smile.*"

Flames might as well have been bursting from her eyes. "Why?"

"Because you just look so pissed all the time."

She glared at him for a moment before shifting her attention back to her plate and taking another bite. "And I usually have good reason to be."

Aroska snickered and shook his head. Working Ziva over was almost *too* easy, and her attempts at remaining the hardened spec ops assassin never ceased to entertain him. He'd seen that little shard of a heart she had buried inside of her, perhaps more times than any other living being thanks to his previous experiences with her. The fact that he—or anyone, for that matter—could sit and carry on a civilized conversation with her was evidence enough that she wasn't as bad as she made herself out to be. He had to admire her focus, but the further she locked herself away, the more compelled he felt to fight his way in.

The two of them continued eating in silence, she no doubt contemplating the situation and he respecting her wishes for quiet. It seemed that was what the would-be partnership consisted of: Ziva taking center stage while he followed her lead like a lobotomized guhr hound. He wasn't so sure he would allow it to stay that way this time around.

Aroska scraped the remaining food from his plate and let his fork clatter to the table, releasing a contented sigh. He had to hand it to Ziva—the woman was as talented a chef as she was a killer. He leaned back in his chair and placed his hands behind his head, allowing a chuckle to escape his throat. The assassin who had murdered his brother before his eyes had just cooked him breakfast.

Ziva swallowed the last of her own meal and gazed at him quizzically. "I hope you're not going to irritate me this much for the next few days."

He was tempted to make a comment about how much pleasure he took in it but thought better of it. "Is there any being in this galaxy who doesn't irritate you?"

She ignored him and picked up the empty serving bowls, taking them to the sink. *Ziva Payvan, the housekeeper,* Aroska thought. She was a peculiar one, she was, and he doubted he would ever fully understand her. That was why she was so good at everything she did—nobody could comprehend how her mind worked.

She resumed her position across from him, drilling into him in much the same way as she had during their conversation the day before. "I think it would benefit us both if you just tell me everything right now. I'm in no mood to interrogate you, and I doubt you'd enjoy being interrogated if I'm not in the mood."

He couldn't help himself. "Would I enjoy it any more if you *were* in the mood?"

She stared at him, unblinking.

Aroska brought his arms down and crossed them. "Why is my story so important to you?"

"Because I want to know what caused *this*—" she extended her hands toward him "—so I can keep it from happening again."

"And why do you care so much about what happens to me?"

"Damn it, Tarbic! Were you paying attention to a word I said yesterday?"

Aroska blinked. Even if he could have come up with a reply, it would have been cut off by an insistent rap on the front door.

· 29 ·
TARBIC RESIDENCE
NORO, HAPHEZ

A hot, prickly sensation surged through Ziva's nerves, causing every hair on her body to stand on end. She was up and out of her seat, pistol in hand, before the visitor even stopped knocking. Skeet had often told her she reminded him of a wild animal—tame while in the right company, deadly and vicious when threatened. She certainly felt like an animal now, backed into the corner that was Aroska's house with little choice but to fight her way out.

Tarbic got to his feet as well, though his movements remained slow and calm. The two of them stood with eyes fixed on the door, listening, calculating. The pounding came again, this time louder, more adamant, and accompanied by a male voice.

"HSP! Open up!"

In that instant, both Ziva and Aroska were at the door, she with her back flat against the wall, arm and pistol extended at a ninety-degree angle to her body. Tarbic stood still for a moment, then mussed up his shaggy hair and rumpled his clothes a bit before hitting the controls.

She held her breath and gripped the gun tighter as the door hissed open. Aroska was a tall man, and she watched as he lifted his own eyes to meet the gaze of the agent outside. She caught a whiff of a familiar scent, and her heart immediately leaped into her throat. Even without seeing him, she knew exactly who the caller was.

His voice confirmed it. "Aroska Tarbic?" he demanded.

"Yes?"

"Captain Diago Dasaro, special operations. I'd like to ask you a few questions."

Crossing his arms, Aroska took up a casual stance with his left shoulder against the doorframe, blocking Dasaro's view of Ziva if he happened to move too close. "Sure," he said, adding a respectful dip of his head. "What would you like to know?"

"Lieutenant, I think it would be best if I came inside."

Ziva took her cue and began to move away from the door, edging along the wall and keeping her pistol trained in Aroska's direction.

"Is that really necessary?" he asked, buying her just enough time to bolt across the living room on silent feet. She slipped into the kitchen and again pressed her back to the wall, gripping the gun with white knuckles.

"If you don't willingly let me in, I can have you detained for impeding an ongoing investigation."

"It's that serious, huh?" Ziva heard the floor creak as Aroska stepped aside to allow Dasaro's entry. The door closed behind him.

The desire to simply step in and put a single plasma bolt through the man's brain was overwhelming. However, if Dasaro had followed protocol in this instance and had brought backup—which he likely had—she would have at least three other agents to deal with, and a firefight in a residential neighborhood wouldn't exactly be subtle. As much as she hated to sneak around and run from danger rather than just confront the problem, she felt that on this occasion it would be the wiser choice. Fuming, she slowed her breathing and focused on the two men in the other room.

Dasaro coughed briefly against the smoky haze lingering in the air. "Picked up govino, have you?" he asked, an icy edge to his voice.

"It's a nasty habit," Aroska replied.

"Yes, well, that sort of thing happens to someone in your line of work. If that's what it takes to get close to a target or gain an informant's trust and gather intel, then so be it. I would commend you for it."

"You've been doing your research on me," Aroska said. "So what brings you out here?"

"I understand you once worked closely with Ziva Payvan," Dasaro answered. "You are aware that she is wanted for murder and is currently at large on the planet?"

"I've heard something to that effect, but I haven't followed the story too closely. My viewscreen isn't working, and I haven't been feeling well the last few days."

If Ziva hadn't been hiding, she would have laughed out loud. The only reason the man could even stand on his own two feet right now was because she had showed up to save the day—in the nick of time, too. She pictured this conversation going on about twenty-four hours earlier and knew Aroska probably would have given her up from a sheer lack of control over his mental faculties.

"Tell me about your relationship with Payvan."

"I met her for the first time a little over two months ago," Aroska replied. "Even then, we only worked together for about a week. We managed to drive each other crazy most of the time—you could say we didn't see eye to eye on a lot of things. That woman ended up saving my life two different times, but when the Dakiti mission was over, we parted company. I've neither seen nor spoken to her since then."

Three, Ziva thought. She'd saved him *three* times, though they'd agreed to call things even. She remembered everything as if it had happened the day before. The Sardons, the hybrid soldiers, Saun....

Her heart skipped a beat when her gaze drifted to the dining table and the two place settings that remained there. A fresh bout of the prickly sensation coursed through her and she shuddered violently, hoping for Aroska's sake that Dasaro couldn't see into the kitchen. She held so still it felt as though her blood had stopped pumping. As far as she could tell, Dasaro was on the far side of the room, facing the kitchen. Aroska's voice was closer, and she knew he was between her and the captain.

Slowly, as if disturbing even the air would alert Dasaro to her presence, she lifted her hand and concentrated as hard as she could on the dish, ignoring the pain in her head and holding her breath as it began to quiver slightly. It finally rose a few millimeters, suspended in mid-air by only her thoughts, and with a slight flick of her hand, she sent it floating away parallel to the table's surface. She didn't breathe until the dish was resting on a shelf out of sight.

"Is there any chance Payvan would come here seeking help?" Dasaro asked.

"It's unlikely," Aroska responded after a thoughtful moment and a short grunt. "I think if she was going to come, she would have already. Besides, she never struck me as the type who would put her trust in someone she knew for a week. We may have gotten the job done together once, but it's been a while now and a lot has happened since then." He was silent for several seconds. "You're certain she's still on the planet?"

"We've had an airtight blockade in place since the night of the assassination," Dasaro answered. "No ship can even leave the system without being searched inside and out. It's not the most efficient method for netting Payvan, and it's wreaking havoc on trade, but keeping her trapped on the ground is better than having her running loose somewhere out in the galaxy."

Ziva expected as much. She'd spent most of the night lying awake formulating several tentative plans, all of which depended almost wholly on whether Aroska could gain Dasaro's trust and secure an advantageous position within HSP. Having to depend so strongly on someone else sickened her, but if Dasaro's blockade was as strong as he claimed it was, it would be virtually impossible for her to get away on her own.

"If you're in need of an extra gun, I'd be glad to assist in the search," Aroska offered. "I could provide insight, though a limited amount. I'm sure you're aware Payvan killed my brother, and I'd be more than happy to finally see her brought to justice."

Her skin crawled as she waited for Dasaro's response. The offer had been too quick—Aroska should have waited until the end of the conversation. Surely the captain would grow suspicious now and all her plans would be wasted. But perhaps she was jumping to conclusions. Again, she held her breath until he spoke.

"I would be much obliged, Lieutenant. I could use a man with your knowledge and skills."

There was a slight smack of skin on skin as the two men clasped hands and shook. "Great," Aroska said. "I'll check in first thing in the morning, if that works."

"I'd rather you started this afternoon. The sooner we find Payvan, the sooner our troubles are over." Then he added coldly, "If that works."

"Sure, sure," Aroska stammered, making Ziva wince. "Give me a couple of hours to get cleaned up, and I'll be in as soon as possible."

They were silent as their footsteps moved across the floor and the front door opened. "Good day, Lieutenant," Dasaro said.

"Good day, sir."

Then the door closed again, leaving the house as silent as Ziva had found it the day before. She relaxed her grip on the pistol but refused to move otherwise, picturing herself waltzing out into the living room to discover that Dasaro was somehow still there, lying in wait. She stood perfectly still, listening to her own blood rushing through her ears until Aroska appeared in the kitchen doorway. He nodded that things were all clear.

"Does this mean I'm off the hook for the rest of my so-called treatment?" he asked, flashing a playful smirk.

She stepped away from the wall and holstered her weapon. "You're going to have to be more careful around Dasaro if you want to keep him convinced of anything for more than two minutes," she sighed, brushing a hand back over her head and leaving it there. "Did he know? Could you tell?"

"If he did, he did a good job of not showing it," Aroska replied. "Something tells me if he knew, he would have just put a round between my eyes then and there. I don't think he saw you, and I doubt he could smell you with the smoke in the air. I know I couldn't."

She raised an eyebrow. "I don't know whether to be relieved by that or disturbed that you were trying."

"So am I ready or not?"

"You're going to have to be. Dasaro's a tough one to impress, but you can start by taking some initiative and showing integrity." She gave him a once-over. "You're a complete mess, but at least you're sober. Now hurry and clean up. You don't want to keep him waiting."

· 30 ·
RESIDENTIAL SECTOR
NORO, HAPHEZ

Diago Dasaro waved his fingers and the three agents accompanying him materialized from the shadows around Tarbic's house and fell into stride behind him. He waited a moment before crossing to the other side of the street, where the four of them piled into the parked HSP-issue groundcar without a word. He was fed up with everything—the case, the people around him, *everything*. How Payvan could have evaded all the checkpoints and infrared probes was completely beyond him. He was confident she was indeed still on the planet, but it was impossible to know if she was still running around in the forest or hiding out somewhere in one of the cities. What they really needed were more checkpoints on the ground, but at this point, tightening the net would only create holes elsewhere that Ziva would take advantage of at first opportunity.

Dasaro pulled the car out and joined the flow of mid-morning traffic. He looked forward to bringing Tarbic on board. He'd heard good things about the man; his excellent work ethic, investigative skills, and his experiences with Payvan would prove to be invaluable. The only thing that made him uneasy was the fact that the lieutenant had been away from the agency on leave for over a month. According to the director, it was nothing more than accumulated vacation time, although it had escalated from some personal time awarded to him after the Solaris group had been disbanded.

He maneuvered the car into a busier traffic lane and began

weaving back toward downtown Noro and HSP Headquarters. Once they settled down to a steady speed, he reached over and activated the mobile comm system on the car's control panel.

"She hasn't been at Tarbic's place," he said when Nejdra Venn answered the transmission.

The woman swore. "We're running out of ideas and time."

"That doesn't mean we stop trying," Dasaro snapped. "I'm bringing in another resource. Tarbic volunteered his services—says he thinks he can help us find her. I think he'll be a valuable asset."

"Whatever you say."

"Gather up the information we have and make a copy of the files so we're ready to brief him when he arrives. We're about twenty minutes out."

· 31 ·
TARBIC RESIDENCE
NORO, HAPHEZ

"Nejdra," Ziva corrected. "Nejdra Venn. The woman is a complete *shouka*. I guarantee she's going to hate you the moment you walk through the door, so don't do anything that'll dig you deeper into the hole. She'll eat you alive."

"Nejdra," Aroska repeated from behind the closed door of his bedroom. "Nejdra, Kyron and Diago."

Ziva leaned against the wall at the end of the hallway, arms crossed, and had been since she'd heard him emerge from the lavatory. "Don't bother getting on a first name basis with them," she said. "They won't be friendly enough to do so with you—hold your ground."

There was a thump as a footlocker closed, followed by some rustling. "Venn, Hoxie, and Dasaro, then," Aroska said, his voice muffled as if his head were inside a piece of clothing.

She looked down and watched his shadow shifting around under the door, listening as he moved across the floor to the closet and began going through it. She felt like a mother waiting on her dawdling son. After nearly two hours, she was beginning to wonder if there was another man in the galaxy capable of taking so long to get ready. Considering the condition he'd been in, however, she was grateful he'd taken the time to do a thorough clean-up job. Not only would it allow him to fit in at HSP as if he'd never left, but she wasn't sure how much longer she could have put up with being around him before he showered.

She stepped out of the way when she heard him come back to the door and stop. The door slid open slowly and light from the bedroom poured out into the dark hallway. She strode out into the living room with him hot on her heels and snatched up her communicator from her meager pile of belongings.

"What do you want me to do if I see Skeet or Zinni?"

Ziva turned back to face him in the better light, startled by what she saw. She suppressed her shock by coming up with a speedy reply. "Tell them everything except where I am. I don't need them getting in trouble for knowing too much."

She hoped her mouth hadn't hung open as long as it felt like it had. The man standing before her was neither the Aroska Tarbic from two months ago nor the one who had locked himself away in the lav two hours earlier. She studied him for another microsecond. The warm amber eyes and the kind face belonged to the man she had known, the one who had helped her bring down Dakiti and the Sardons. However, his familiar shoulder-length hair had disappeared entirely—it had been replaced by a close-cropped cut he had styled into a short ridge on top of his head. He had also done a careful job shaving, masterfully resurrecting the thin black goatee she remembered. In addition, he had successfully gotten rid of the musty alcohol stench that had been hanging around him. He'd donned a set of clean clothes and wore the same black field jacket he had always worn.

He shrugged, and the corners of his lips quirked upward. "Do you approve?"

Ziva placed her hands on her hips and nodded, allowing a slight smirk of her own. She wagged her head. "I have to say I'm impressed," she said, eyebrows raised. "Much better."

Aroska shrugged again and scraped his fingers against the short, bristly hair on the back of his head. "So what is this, the second or third time I've ever done anything right by you?"

"What's that supposed to mean?"

"Maybe I've got some points in your book. Maybe it's time to stop treating me like I'm totally incompetent."

"Oh, so this is all a game and we're keeping score now?"

"I think you know that's not what I meant."

"*I* think you should learn that there are times for joking and now is not one of them."

"*And I think* you need to lighten up a little."

Heat flooded her face as she ventured a step closer to him. "Damn it Aroska, what will it take for you to figure this out? You want to get shot? How about tortured? Maybe then you would understand why I take everything I do so seriously. The more you focus now, the faster we can get this all over with. Then—*then*—I might 'lighten up a little'."

She stared him down for a moment, giving her words ample time to sink in. Then, after turning over the communicator in her hand and tossing it into the air once, she offered it to him.

Aroska took it and glanced at the tiny screen before pocketing the device. He opened his mouth to speak but looked away, wisely choosing to remain quiet and allow her to give him further instructions.

"I'll contact you on that by early evening," she explained. "Ignore the transmission if you're not in a position to talk. And by all means, do *not* let Dasaro know you have it."

"I have a comm," he said, raising a cynical eyebrow.

"You can bet Dasaro will have yours bugged. It's a standard part of his initiation process—everyone under his command has been through it at some point, including me."

He shuffled his feet and glanced toward the door. "If you're in such a hurry to get this over with, then I suggest we get this show on the road."

Ziva caught his arm with a firm hand as he turned to go. "Be smart, Tarbic."

"You know me."

"Exactly—that's why I'm worried."

· 32 ·
HSP Headquarters
Noro, Haphez

When Skeet glanced up idly from his work, the last person he expected to see emerging from the elevator was Aroska Tarbic. At first, the man's identity hadn't registered—he'd just happened to be looking in that particular direction at the exact moment he'd stepped out onto the squad floor. The faded black jacket was what he had recognized initially, and then he'd realized who he was looking at. The changes in Tarbic's hair had been enough to throw Skeet off, but now his eyes were glued to the man as he moved across the floor.

He unwrapped a fresh chunk of govino gum and popped it into his mouth, savoring the fruity juices as they swirled over his tongue. Zinni sat just to his left, absorbed in her computer, so he nudged her shoulder and nodded in the direction Tarbic was headed with a single agent escort. "Hey," he said, shifting the govino around in his mouth.

She glanced up quickly, startled and blinking as if she had been jolted awake from a dream. "*Sheyss*, Skeet," she muttered, rubbing her eyes. "What?"

"Check this out." He gestured toward Aroska again. The sight of the man stirred up an odd jumble of feelings within him. The last time he'd seen him, the team had been dangling by grappling cables in the Dakiti building's primary elevator shaft. All Skeet remembered was an image of Aroska and Ziva climbing out of the shaft in full tactical gear before he and Zinni had gone on to complete their part of the mission.

The next thing he'd known, both lieutenants had been captured and the Grand Army had arrived with ground support. Helpless and frustrated, he'd been ordered to depart Sardonis and return to Noro, where he, Zinni, and the Tantali prince Jayden Saiffe had been held under observation at a med center.

"Aroska?" Zinni said after studying the man for a moment. She stood halfway up and peered over the wall of the bullpen. "What the hell?"

Skeet hadn't even heard Tarbic's name mentioned for the past two months. One moment, he had shot and arrested Ziva—after she'd risked her life to get him out of Dakiti—for a reason that remained a mystery. Then the next thing he knew, Emeri Arion had reversed the death sentence rendered on Ziva and she had been free to go. When prompted later, she'd refused to discuss what had transpired. He'd left the matter alone, though it was still eating at him to this day. He couldn't help but think Aroska had somehow had a hand in the sentence reversal, though it made no sense when compared to what he had only *just* done to Ziva.

Empowered by a fresh bout of curiosity and anger, Skeet locked his terminal and pushed his chair in so forcefully that it hit the desk and bounced back to nearly the exact position it had been in.

"Skeet, what are you doing?"

Zinni called after him again, but he ignored her and began jogging across the massive room. He wound through the maze of cubicles and workstations, blind to everything except that which was directly in front of him. Somewhere in the back of his mind, he could hear Zinni's hurried footsteps running to catch up to him, but they were little more than an echo.

Skeet broke out into the aisle and turned right, having missed the interception by about six meters. Not breaking stride, he took one last set of jogging steps to close the distance between him and Aroska. "Hey Tarbic!"

Aroska pivoted, looking around for the source of the voice. His eyes brightened when they fell on Skeet and he turned fully, offering a hand. The word 'hello' hadn't quite escaped his lips when Skeet's fist collided with his jaw.

"No, Skeet!" Zinni called out as she leaped at his arm and restrained him from lashing out again. The guard escort did likewise with Tarbic, whose face was twisted in shock and disbelief as he rubbed his jaw.

"That's for what you did to Ziva," Skeet said, shrugging away from Zinni and thrusting a menacing finger at Aroska. His knuckles throbbed from delivering the blow.

The field ops lieutenant stole a glance in the direction he had been headed, toward the bank of offices on the far side of the squad floor. Three of the unit captains approached, including Diago Dasaro, their attention drawn by the commotion. He turned back toward Skeet, making a show of advancing in a defensive manner. His voice was firm when he spoke, but it lacked the anger Skeet had expected. "We need to talk," he said.

Dasaro and company were now upon them, and the large man glared down at Skeet, each of his eyes a black abyss. "What's going on here?" he demanded.

Aroska kept his eyes locked with Skeet's for another few seconds before answering. "Absolutely nothing, sir," he muttered, shifting his attention to the three captains.

Dasaro eyed them all warily then dismissed the guard with a wave of his hand. "Duvo, Vax, if you're still standing here in three seconds, I'll have your badges. Tarbic, come with me."

· 33 ·
HSP Headquarters
Noro, Haphez

J aw aching, Aroska watched as Skeet and Zinni reluctantly retreated under Dasaro's threatening gaze. *Some welcoming gift,* he thought, hoping Skeet's behavior hadn't made matters any more complicated than they already were. At least the outburst had been enough to convince the captain Aroska wasn't on anybody's side. He feared, however, that getting close enough to Skeet to pass on Ziva's message would now be nigh on impossible.

"Welcome, Lieutenant," Dasaro said, initiating a handshake. "I appreciate the effort you made to get here in a timely manner. Meet captains Nejdra Venn and Kyron Hoxie."

The man and woman with him each nodded silent greetings and maintained hardened countenances. The four of them continued on to the offices, where Dasaro motioned for Aroska to pull up a chair and Nejdra handed him a data pad. He read over some of the file headings, testing the mobility of his jaw and tasting a little blood from where his teeth had cut the inside of his mouth. "This is everything you have on Payvan?" he asked.

"Everything pertaining to this investigation," Dasaro said. "To tell you the truth, there isn't much else that's not classified beyond even the scope of spec ops. Rumor has it you're aware of Lieutenant Payvan's status as one of our Black Agents."

Aroska nodded. He recalled his attempts at accessing Ziva's files after Soren's death; he had no doubt most of her information was indeed restricted, but he wasn't convinced the captain was sharing everything. Being kept in the dark was nothing new—he already felt as though he had walked into HSP without a clue what was really going on. "Is there anything specific you'd like me to get started on, sir?"

Dasaro slipped an access key across his desk. "You've been granted temporary special operations clearance until we can bring Payvan down, so you are free to go about your investigating independently. Start with a thorough go-over of that material and make sure you're familiar with our methods, and then we can discuss specifics if you still have questions. Report directly to me with anything you find. And Tarbic, if you can do this, we'll see about making this spec ops position something more than temporary."

"Yes, sir," Aroska said, fighting away the smile he felt creeping onto his face. An odd tingle of temptation numbed his mind for a split second until Ziva's words echoed gently through his memory: *"What would you think of a permanent position in special ops?"*

There were times when he wished he'd accepted her offer, but the thought of continuing in ops without Jole Imetsi and Tate Luver after going through the trouble of saving them from Dakiti had seemed absurd. Perhaps turning her down had been irrational thinking—it certainly seemed like it now, considering the mess he'd worked himself into during his time away from the agency. Still, he hadn't been convinced of the sincerity of Ziva's proposition. He'd encroached enough in her space as it was, and despite everything she'd done for him, he still hadn't felt comfortable even being around her. Both were reasons he had politely allowed her to fade into the background after he'd departed her house that day.

With a nod of Dasaro's head, Aroska was dismissed from the office. He was glad to be on such a long leash, but at the same time, he felt it would be easier to maintain Dasaro's trust if he had a definite course of action to follow. What exactly was he expected to do, wander aimlessly for the next few hours and then report to Dasaro that he'd found nothing? Lie and fabricate some findings that would throw the captain off? He fingered the communicator Ziva had sent with him and wished she would hurry and contact him with further instructions.

First things first—he needed to get matters cleared up with Skeet while he was still off Dasaro's radar. Looking in the general direction the two agents had gone, Aroska caught sight of Zinni standing in one of the bullpens on the far side of the squad floor. She was leaning down over her workstation, but her head was up and she was looking directly at him. She turned away when she realized she had been spotted. Skeet was nowhere in sight.

The thought of coming across as such a cold-blooded traitor tied a sickening knot in Aroska's stomach as he made his way toward the intelligence officer. Though he'd only spent a few days working with Ziva's squad, he'd come to trust them and rely on them to the point that he thought he could at least call them friends, if not their boss. The idea of deceiving them after they had so readily accepted him as one of their own earlier drove him insane. He needed to find Skeet and make amends, and not just for the current situation.

Zinni's attention zeroed in on him again as he neared. She glanced around, and when she saw his presence didn't seem to be drawing any scrutiny, she approached. Without a word, she took him by the arm and led him off the squad floor into the wide bridge-like corridor that connected the spec ops wing and the field ops wing. Her grip was firm; despite her size, she possessed a measure of strength that didn't fail to impress him. They stopped in a secluded area and she gazed up at him, hands on her hips and eyebrows knit.

"I don't know what you think you're trying to accomplish here," she said.

"Zinni, please trust me. This isn't what it looks like."

"I certainly hope not." Her sparkling cerulean eyes turned to ice as she glared at him. "And I'm sorry, but I don't think I *can* trust you right now."

Aroska bent down closer to eye level. "You're going to have to!" he snapped, instantly reminding himself to remain calm. He placed his hands on her shoulders. "Look, there's a lot you don't know and a lot I can't tell you, but I promise you'll hear all of it in due time. Right now, I really need to talk to Skeet."

He felt her tense muscles relax a bit and her face softened. She sighed and shook her head, sucking on her bottom lip. "You make it sound like a matter of life and death."

"It could turn into one if we don't all get on the same page right now." Perhaps that was a bit of an exaggeration, but Aroska could picture things heading downhill fast if they remained at odds.

"Do you really think you can just walk back in here and expect us to cooperate after what you did?"

"Would it help at all if I said I was sorry?"

Zinni pushed his hands off her shoulders and turned in a slow circle, muttering under her breath. Her eyes flitted back and forth between Aroska and anyone who happened to be walking by. He could tell she was curious as to what he was hiding, but considering what a little fireball she was, he doubted she would tolerate his presence in the building for another minute if he didn't start talking.

"Fine," she finally muttered. "I'll take you to Skeet, but I can't guarantee he's going to want to listen to you."

The two of them turned back down the hallway. "He'll listen," Aroska said. "Once he hears what I have to say, he'll be all ears."

· 34 ·
HSP HEADQUARTERS
NORO, HAPHEZ

Dasaro watched Tarbic exit the office, his mind focused more on Payvan than anything else. The man was a good agent—his flawless service record proved that much. It was apparent that he'd had his share of problems during the last several weeks, but it didn't bother Dasaro enough to make him question Aroska's ability to produce results. Still, there was something about all this that made him uneasy, almost as if the lieutenant were hiding something. There had been an odd scent in his house, something he'd been unable to pinpoint due to the govino smoke and stench of alcohol. He knew it was probably nothing, but he also knew he'd sleep better that night if he took the time to look into it.

"Diago?" Nejdra said, cutting into the silence. She stepped around in front of him, hands clasped behind her back. "Are we all set?"

"His personal comms have been checked?"

It was Kyron Hoxie who answered. "We've looked over both his mobile communicator and his home comm system. There was nothing out of the ordinary. In fact, there was hardly anything at all. Other than several attempted transmissions from the older brother and a couple of routine collection calls, he's had virtually no contact with anyone for at least three weeks."

"Interesting," Dasaro said, shifting the whole of his attention to the other two captains after he lost sight of Aroska in the crowd of agents and workstations. "Do we have any probes available for zone two of sector six?"

"Residential?" Nejdra asked, sliding into the chair at her own desk and quickly manipulating her computer. The infrared image on the holographic screen blurred briefly then spun, finally settling on a section of the city approximately ten by ten blocks. "Got it," she said.

"Let's see Tarbic's house."

Hoxie raised an eyebrow. "Any specific reason?"

Dasaro shook his head, eyes glued to the terminal as Nejdra entered the correct coordinates. "Just curious," he replied.

The image settled on one of the houses near the center of the neighborhood. Thin orange lines represented the walls of the structure. Heat signatures from cars and passersby moved to and fro outside, standing out against the dark gray background.

The house was empty.

"The probe is almost out of range," Nejdra said. "I'm about to lose the feed."

"That's all I needed," Dasaro said. The image was enough to satisfy him for the moment, though he hadn't achieved nearly the peace of mind he'd been hoping for. "Thank you."

· 35 ·
MARKET DISTRICT
NORO, HAPHEZ

Reciting the numbers to herself as she went, Ziva stopped in a shadowy alley and programmed the code for the comm she'd given Aroska into the one she'd just purchased. It wasn't time to contact him yet; it had barely been an hour since he'd left for HSP, and the chances that Dasaro was still nearby were high. Being kept out of the loop—no, intentionally *excluding* herself from the loop—was almost more than she could stand. It was one thing to be trapped on the planet, giving Dasaro more time to revise his strategies and close in on her. But being both trapped *and* blind was almost terrifying. Worse yet, she had no way of knowing if Aroska—her surrogate set of eyes—was even going to see anything useful.

She had opted to leave the house, at least for the majority of the day, after being stricken with the fear that she shouldn't be trusting him. She couldn't shake the memory of what had happened on the landing pad on Sardonis after she'd risked her own life to rescue him from Dakiti. Not only had she successfully gotten him out of the hostile Sardon facility before the brunt of the Grand Army's attack, but she had gone on to reveal her Nosti abilities while saving him again. What had he done? He'd turned around and arrested her—after shooting out her knee—per Emeri Arion's orders. Everything had been sorted out, of course, but sometimes she wondered why she even bothered. If all she ever received in return for her hard work and stress was betrayal, it wasn't worth it.

She sighed. Aroska's problem wasn't necessarily that he was a backstabbing bastard. Rather, it was that he seemed to have a problem doing anything that defied orders. She doubted he would turn her in just for the sake of turning her in. If he confessed to Dasaro that he'd been in contact with her, she guessed it would be because he truly believed he was doing the right thing by helping bring down a murderer. *No,* she thought, wincing. There she was again, succumbing to the lie and allowing herself to believe she was what everyone claimed she was.

Aroska hadn't given her the impression he believed she was guilty. In fact, he hadn't acted like he cared much at all. In that sense, there was no way to predict what he was going to do. She had packed up her few belongings and helped herself to his small weapons cache, making sure to dispose of the borrowed clothes and wipe down every surface she'd touched when she had finished. Her plan was to spend the afternoon with one eye on his house and one eye on the street. If all remained quiet, she would risk a transmission by early evening, and if that went well, she would return to the house.

It was midday now and the streets were crowded with shoppers, children, and tourists from some of the neighboring Fringe worlds. The clouds from the past two days had also disappeared, allowing the sun to beat down on the damp earth uncontested. Ziva was sweating profusely in the riding suit and flipped the helmet visor up for a moment, drinking in the only-slightly-less stuffy air. She wondered if the agent from the forest checkpoint had been found yet. If that were the case, she imagined she should ditch the suit. With Aroska's viewscreen down and no other source of information as of yet, it was impossible to tell. Still, a generic gray riding suit, no matter who it had belonged to, would probably be less conspicuous than her own clothes that could be seen in every mugshot planetwide. Taking one last breath of fresh air, she closed the visor again.

She stepped back out into the street, surveying the immediate area for HSP foot patrols. Seeing none, she veered left and began weaving in and out of the crowd, keeping her head down and her eyes open. The shade of the abandoned house where she'd stashed her stolen hoverbike sounded inviting at the moment, not to mention it would be a quiet place where she could observe Aroska's house. The thought struck her funny. *The things I look forward to while on the run.*

The house was another four blocks to the west. She picked up her pace a bit, free to do so as the shops gradually turned into apartments and homes and the throngs of people began to thin out. She glanced out into the street as she approached an intersection, searching for a gap in traffic.

Movement on the walkway caught her attention and she shifted her focus back to what was in front of her. She took a quick step to the side, but it was too late—her shoulder collided with that of an armor-clad HSP officer who had just come around the corner with his partner. The two of them looked nearly as startled as she was, and there was a brief hesitation where the three of them locked eyes, though hers were obscured behind the visor.

"Excuse me," said the officer who had bumped into her.

Blood roiling, she skirted around them and continued on, narrowly avoiding a passing groundcar in her haste to cross the street. She jogged on to the opposite side, slowing to a stiff walk that felt so uncomfortable she might as well have kept running. Now she was glad to be hidden within the riding suit; the helmet helped contain the sound of her panting and concealed her widened eyes. She walked for a full block without stopping, focusing on keeping her breathing slow and even. The street ended in a T-intersection, with Aroska's house several more blocks to the left. She glanced in the direction from which she had come, checking for traffic, and caught sight of the two officers following at a distance. Both had their eyes on her and one of them, the one she had collided with, was speaking into his communicator.

A fresh bout of fire shot through Ziva's nerves and she pivoted, rushing to the right instead. As soon as she was out of the agents' line of sight, she took off at a dead run, looking wildly about for somewhere to hide. The area was almost strictly residential now, which accounted for fewer crowds to blend in to and fewer alleys and dark places where she could disappear. She also realized running would only make the officers more suspicious than they otherwise might be, so once again she slowed to a brisk walk, wondering how far behind they were. Certainly they had no idea who they were dealing with, but she dreaded the thought of giving them any opportunities to find out.

Glancing quickly at any reflective surface she passed, she finally caught sight of the familiar armor. She was a good sixty meters ahead, but the street was long and straight and offered little to no cover. She considered the option of simply facing them and taking them out quietly. Either choice—killing them or merely incapacitating them—would no doubt result in a canvassing of the entire neighborhood by HSP, putting both her and Aroska in jeopardy. Once again sickened by the idea of having no choice but to run from the problem, she ducked into the first alley she came to.

The space was narrow, with tall apartments on either side. Broken glass and other trash littered the ground, crunching and rattling under her boots. She moved on light feet, eyes on a smaller passage that branched off from the one in which she now stood. She pulled up short when she reached it. *A dead end.* A drunken homeless man lay passed out on a bed of rags he had created against the far wall, the liquor bottle still in his grasp. Mind and heart both racing, she slipped back out and continued deeper into the heart of the apartment complex, able to hear the voices of the two agents out on the street as they drew nearer.

The main vein of the alley made a sharp ninety-degree turn ahead and she made a beeline for it, imagining a maintenance ladder or some such means of escape beyond. Her heart skipped a beat when all she found was a solid wall adorned with various city-operated control panels. Ripping the helmet off, she looked wildly about for any alternate route. With a little work, she could climb the pipes and cables lining the wall, but once her pursuers knew she was on the roof, she'd be fair game to any air patrols that happened to be nearby. Leaving the alley was no longer an option, either—she could now hear footsteps approaching.

Replacing the helmet, Ziva drew the pistol she had taken from Aroska's house and held it at the ready. She kept her ears focused on the alley and her eyes on the wall, where she could see the shadows of the two agents as they moved closer. They were coming as silently as possible over the filthy ground, neither chatting casually nor relaying information via comm. If they were coming into the alley alone, they more than likely hadn't called for backup. As far as she could tell, she still had the upper hand in the situation. From the shapes of their shadows, she could also see that they had not drawn their weapons. She hated having to attack two virtually innocent people, but she saw no other way out.

Her muscles tensed, her finger settled against the trigger, and she inhaled all at the exact moment one of their communicators crackled to life. She froze, as did the two officers. One of them cursed and his partner responded with a chuckle and a snide comment. "Go ahead, Central," said the first, replying to the transmission.

The dispatcher began rattling off instructions and numbers, and Ziva caught the phrase 'assault in progress' toward the end of the string. If she'd heard the address correctly, this call would take them back to the area where she had purchased the communicator. She lowered her pistol but didn't loosen her grip.

"Copy that," the agent said. "On our way."

With that, they were gone, leaving everything silent except for the hum of passing traffic. Ziva stood there in the alley for another several minutes, back flat against the wall, giving her racing heart time to settle. She wasn't sure why all of this was getting her so worked up. Maybe it was the fact that those who would normally be backing her up were now against her. There were still the select few who were on her side, though they were severely outnumbered. Realistically, this was like any other mission. The only difference was that the enemy was her own people.

Feeling as calm as she guessed she would ever be, she slid the pistol back into her pants and smoothed the jacket over it. Sighing, she established a firm grip on a thick pipe running up the wall and shinnied upward. She heaved herself over the edge of the roof and rolled to her feet, then, baking in the damp heat, she began walking.

· 36 ·
HSP Headquarters
Noro, Haphez

Skeet almost stormed away again when he noticed Aroska approaching, but he hesitated when he realized Zinni was with him. He gripped the railing surrounding the vacant landing pad on which he stood and continued staring out over the cityscape.

"Skeet," Zinni said quietly, inserting herself into the space between him and Tarbic.

He sent a fiery glare in Aroska's direction. "You'd better have a good reason for being up here," he muttered before shifting the same glare toward Zinni.

"As a matter of fact, I do," Aroska said. "I've got something important to tell you both—a couple of things, actually."

"You shot Ziva, betrayed her right after she saved your ass. Now you're here to help Dasaro catch her. Why should we give a *frou*—"

"Listen, Skeet!" Tarbic snapped. "I don't need this *sheyss* from you. I'm trying to do the right thing here."

"If this is your definition of the 'right thing'—"

"Skeet!" Zinni cut him off again, crossing her arms.

"First of all, I want to apologize to you both for selling Ziva out on Sardonis," Aroska said before anyone could speak further. "Violation of protocol or not, she had just put her life on the line to save not only me but Tate and Jole as well. Without her, the mission would have fallen apart. Hell, it never would have even existed. I thought I was doing the right thing by taking her into custody, but it didn't take me long to realize I was wrong." He hesitated a moment. "I'm the one responsible for convincing the director to drop the charges. Nobody's supposed to know."

"Have you told her all of this?" Zinni asked.

"Of course."

Skeet stood, still holding the railing, trying to decide whether to be relieved by Aroska's words or infuriated that he would wait so long to confess. The latter, he realized, was little more than an excuse to be angry about everything else that was going on. If Tarbic had taken the time to seek them out for this, he was most likely on their side. But that didn't account for the fact that he had come to Headquarters to speak with Dasaro—there was still some explaining that needed to be done.

"Any chance we'll ever get to find out what that 'violation of protocol' was?" he asked, allowing the tone of his voice to soften significantly.

Aroska shrugged. "If you do, Ziva should be the one to tell you. The only thing I'll say is that she knew the consequences, but she chose to do it anyway. She saved my life…again."

Skeet ruffled his hair and glanced at Zinni, who eyed him like a mother waiting for an apology from her child. "So is that why you're here? Decided you'd drop by and tell the truth when you had a few spare minutes?"

Aroska's face hardened a bit and he drew closer to the two of them, speaking in a hushed voice. "I'm here because Ziva sent me."

For a second, Skeet wasn't sure if he'd heard him right, then he wasn't sure if he could hear at all. All the noise around him was suddenly drowned out by a deafening…*silence* inside his head. The idea that Ziva was alive and well sent a shiver of relief down his spine.

"She's with you?" he asked, voice dry.

"She said that for your safety I shouldn't tell you where she is," Aroska replied. "She's safe, though, and we're doing everything we can to get her off the planet."

"We?" Zinni asked.

"She's probably doing more work than I am at this point," Aroska explained, "but I like to think it's a collective effort. Jada Jaroon is on board to a degree, but according to Ziva, she's afraid to do too much for fear of being implicated. My instructions were to come here and monitor the progress of the investigation, as well as to make sure the two of you were aware of what was going on."

A pang of guilt for the way he'd been acting coursed through Skeet's stomach, though he still wasn't thrilled with the choices Aroska had previously made. "And I thank you for that," he said. "How's the old girl holding up?"

"I think she's scared," Tarbic replied, "but you'd never get her to admit it. She's doing better than I imagine I would if I were in her place. She's quiet...and irritable as ever."

"I don't doubt it," Skeet said, allowing a short chuckle before sobering again. "Listen, though. I'm not sure how much you remember of that conversation we had—"

"How could I forget any of it?"

"—but you're going to have to tread extra lightly around Ziva right now. If she ever feels threatened in the slightest way, she's like an animal trapped in a corner and she won't hesitate to fight her way out. She may want to do things you don't agree with, but odds are she knows what she's doing and trying to interfere will result in bodily harm at the very least. Sound familiar?"

"Very much so. On that note, I may have to do some things you don't agree with, either. Part of 'monitoring the investigation' includes gaining the captains' trust to the point that they're willing to give me the information I need. I can't foresee what all that's going to entail."

And then there was that. However, the thought of having someone else on their side in this seemingly impossible struggle was enough to make Skeet willing to forgive both Aroska and Ziva in advance for any lengths they went to in order to get the job done. There was no question of whether things would get ugly, but he hoped this turn of events would get everything moving along faster. The sooner this was all over, the better.

All he could do was nod in agreement as Zinni responded. "Understood," she said quietly. "I suppose we would do the same if we were in your boots. Is there anything specific we can help with on our end?"

Aroska shrugged and stole a nervous glance back into the building. "Ziva says she didn't kill Tachi. The way I understand it, everyone is supposed to be doing everything they can to convict her. I would start by trying to prove her innocence."

"It won't be easy," Skeet said. "Dasaro's running this place like a mining camp on Midore. Do you think you can keep him occupied?"

"I'll do my best. Speaking of which, I should be getting back before he wonders what I'm doing."

Skeet rushed forward when Aroska turned to leave. "One more thing, Tarbic. Take care of her, will you? She's going to want to handle everything herself and she's not going to be able to."

The man grinned wide. "And yet you just finished telling me not to interfere with anything she does."

"There's a difference between interfering and looking out for her," Skeet replied. "You can help her by being there for her and backing her up on the rare occasion that she actually asks you to. Compliment her, try to keep her thinking positive." He smirked, though he doubted it did much to hide his disappointment—disappointment that he couldn't be there for his friend when it seemed she needed him most. "Keep her from wreaking more havoc than necessary."

Tarbic's eyes darted back toward the building again before he shook Skeet's hand. "Will do, Sergeant. I'd say we'll contact you, but there's no guaranteeing what will happen in the next couple of days."

"Do what you have to," Zinni said. "Be safe."

Nodding respectfully toward each of them, Aroska turned and rubbed his freshly cut hair as he walked back toward the building. Skeet watched him go, lost in the rhythmic echo of his footsteps as he crossed the landing pad. He was startled out of his trance when the man stopped and turned back to face them, eyes wide as if a sudden thought had come to mind.

"Do either of you have a spare memory stick I can borrow?"

· 37 ·
ROYAL GUARD HEADQUARTERS
HAPHOR, HAPHEZ

Ready to rip his hair out, Kade buried his face in his hands and let a growl escape his throat. Feeling the sudden urge to stand up, he did so, sending his chair skidding backward and drawing the attention of those working nearby. Only then did he realize how cramped his legs were. Upon thinking for a moment, it struck him that he had not left his workstation since arriving at the Royal Guard office six hours earlier. After staring at his computer screen for what had seemed like an eternity, his eyes felt as though they were about to ooze out of their sockets, and he was jittery after not eating anything all day.

Clearing his throat and sending apologetic glances toward his co-workers, he lowered his head and slinked into the building's main corridor, angling toward the lavatory. Upon entering, he wasted no time in going to the sink and splashing a generous amount of warm water over his face. Angry and at a loss, he lifted his eyes to meet the gaze of his reflection in the mirror and watched the drips of water as they trickled down over his chin.

What am I doing? Since the previous evening, he had been over the med center's surveillance feeds dozens of times, scouring them for any signs of the mysterious visitors who had—he was sure of it—murdered Spence. He'd checked every cam, every angle, yet he was still empty handed. It was almost as if they were ghosts, as if he had only imagined seeing them there. That, or they were good enough to recognize the placement of the cams and avoid them entirely. In a way, the less information he found, the more he was convinced someone was up to something shady.

Feeling mildly better, he dried his face and hair and returned to his desk. He wasn't sure where to even pick up the search, having the sense that he had already depleted all the possibilities. He'd even checked footage from traffic cams surrounding the med center, still to no avail. He dared not go to his superiors and colleagues and say he'd given up—there had to be a clue somewhere. He would sooner go back and question every living soul in that hospital than admit he was done.

His communicator beeped and a text-based alert appeared, informing him that the coroner's report from Spence's autopsy had just been posted. A new spark of motivation ignited inside him, and he immediately made himself comfortable in his chair. Spence may have been wounded critically, but at the time Kade had spoken to him, he'd been in no condition to just keel over unexpectedly. Surely a well-trained group of medical personnel would take that into consideration. He eagerly accessed the database and began reading over the newly posted report.

He scanned through the beginning of the text, composed mainly of surgery reports and medication logs. The anticipation was growing almost unbearable when his eyes finally fell upon the words he was looking for.

Cause of death was deemed cardiac arrest (with evidence of chemical induction), as determined following a thorough study by veteran medical examiner Eason Fromm.

Kade would have cried out if not for the fact that his heart had suddenly lodged itself in his throat. Dumbfounded, he read over the report again and then a third time, confirming he hadn't missed something. Confident that he was sure of what he was seeing, he once again leaped from his seat.

"Special Agent Zona!" he exclaimed, startling those around him. He picked up his comm receiver, changed his mind, and shouted again, louder this time. "Zona!"

Without even realizing it, he was on the move. He couldn't even tell he was running—it felt more like floating than anything else. All he could see was an image of the text in his mind as he stumbled blindly up the stairs. Aside from this discovery, nothing else mattered. "Zona!" he hollered once more.

The supervisor appeared at the top of the steps, looking as though he were responding to an emergency alarm. He caught Kade by the shoulders and held him firmly, smoky-gray eyes wide.

"*Huhren shouka souhn...*Shevin! Have you completely lost your mind?"

"Not at all, sir!" Kade replied, grinning as wide as his facial muscles would allow. "Anything but, for that matter. I've got something you need to see."

Zona shook his head and glanced around at the agents who looked on in confusion. The corners of his mouth curled downward into a frown, but Kade was certain the information he had discovered would change that. "This had better be good, Shevin," he growled.

Refraining from all-out dragging his superior officer down the stairs, Kade turned and descended quickly, ignoring the strange looks sent his way by the other RG agents. "I was never able to find any footage of our mysterious friends from the med center," he explained, "but what I *did* find does a pretty damn good job of proving my theory correct."

"I never said I didn't believe your theory," Zona said. "Is that what this is all about?"

Maybe part of it was. "Just read this, sir."

With a sigh, Zona cleared his throat and took a seat in front of Kade's screen. "What am I looking at?" he asked.

"The report from Agent Spence's autopsy. If I could direct your attention to the third paragraph..."

Zona scanned to the place Kade had indicated and cleared his throat once more. "'Cause of death'," he began, "'was deemed natural causes according to sustained injuries, as determined following a careful study'...I'm not sure if I understand what your point is, Shevin."

Kade hardly heard him as he leaned down to reexamine the report for himself. Sure enough, the text was different than it had been only moments before, now displaying the exact words Zona had just read.

Stammering, Kade reached over the man and scrolled up and down through the report, searching desperately for the one sentence that would have solved all his problems. He saw this was indeed the correct report—Zona hadn't accidentally opened a different one or some such thing—and yet it was far from correct. He stood back, one hand pressed against his sweaty forehead, heart pounding.

"Payvan must have hit him harder than we thought," the agent sitting at the next workstation snickered.

"That was uncalled for!" Zona snapped, shutting the other man up. He stood and faced Kade, locking eyes with him for a moment before putting an arm around his trembling shoulders and guiding him casually off the work floor. "If you have *any* reasonable explanation for what just happened, I'd really love to hear it," he said, tone grim.

"Sir, I can explain," Kade said quietly, feeling as though he had taken one step forward and two steps back. No, it was more like he'd taken a giant leap forward and then he'd fallen on his face, pushed by some unseen hand that seemed bent on making sure the investigation went as miserably as possible for him. "You've got to believe me when I say that's not what the report said when I read it. It was somehow changed in the time it took me to leave my desk and come find you."

He'd never seen Zona's face so cold and hard in all the time he'd known the man. "Do you have any idea how ridiculous that sounds?"

"I know!" Kade said, steadying himself against the wall as nausea began to set in. "But it's true, and it would explain why I couldn't find those agents in the med center. The coroner said Spence's heart failure was chemically induced! He was murdered, and Fromm found the evidence!"

"Tell me how it got changed, then."

"Well, the people who killed him could have done it. That's logical, right?"

"The people who don't seem to exist," Zona said. "I'll admit you piqued my curiosity, Shevin. I contacted the med center myself, but nobody remembers seeing anything out of the ordinary. You're the last logged visitor, so they know you were there near the time of death, regardless of how Spence's heart failed. Unless you're the one who killed him—and I'd like to think none of my people would be that stupid—you're out of luck."

Kade's shoulders sagged. "You think I'm crazy, don't you."

"Here's the thing, kid," Zona said, softening a bit. "This case has been tough on all of us. I've been cutting you a lot of slack lately, more slack than I usually give a rookie." He held up his hand for silence when Kade began to interject. "I like you, Shevin, and I've tried to look out for you, but you've gone way too far this time. Please don't make me regret everything I've done for you."

Kade swallowed, suddenly stricken with fear. "Yes, sir."

"Why don't you take a couple days off and get some rest. The galaxy knows you could use it. Go home, spend some time with your family, get yourself calmed down, and I'll contact you when I'm ready to have you back. And Shevin, it's not a suggestion."

"Yes, sir," Kade said again, feeling incapable of formulating any other words.

"I'm doing you a favor here." Zona clapped him hard on the back. "Say hello to the missus for me."

· 38 ·
MEMORIAL GROUNDS
ARGALL, HAPHEZ

Argall, Haphez—one of the only cities on the planet that wasn't located in the lowlands along the Tranyi River. It was situated in an atypical valley deep within the mountains over forty degrees north of the Haphezian equator, nearly four thousand kilometers from the nearest metropolis. The settlement—home to a little under a thousand people—saw few visitors other than the freighter pilots who came through periodically, and it wasn't often that the occupants went elsewhere. They didn't mind the isolation, didn't mind the quiet. They were a tight community with little concern about anything unrelated to their humble home and way of life.

The sun had already dropped behind the rocky hills, shrouding the valley and the little city in darkness. The mountains were nothing more than jagged silhouettes standing out against the fiery orange sky. Some stars were visible in the distance where the black night encroached. Evening insects squawked and chirped, unseen among the rocks, and the sounds of larger nocturnal animals could be heard as they emerged from their daytime hideouts.

Mag Reilly stood with closed eyes, taking all of it in until the fire cracked and his attention was drawn back to the funeral pyre before him. The heat stung his face and the smoke made his eyes water, but he couldn't bring himself to move away. He stuffed his hands into his pockets and stared into the fire, watching as the body of the woman gradually melted away. There was something mesmerizing about the flames that did a fair job of distracting him from the reason he was really standing there. This was the third gathering of this nature he had attended in the past two weeks, the fifth in the past month. The first had been for his neighbor, the second for the wife of his best friend. Now he stood in silence watching his own flesh and blood burn. His mother had been shot in the head two days earlier, executed at point blank range in the same manner as the other four.

But these most recent killings hardly made him bat an eye when compared to the massacre that had occurred three years earlier. *That* bloodbath had taken the lives of his father, his sister, and many others he was close to. He and his younger brother had helped form a militia to resist the mercenaries who had overrun the humble town of Argall, and they had seen moderate success until his brother had been fatally wounded and Mag himself had nearly been killed. He had resolved then to stop fighting and care for his grieving mother, but now here he stood watching the fire eat away at her body, feeling as though he had not only failed but had wasted his time as well. It was all mentally exhausting, and he wondered if he was even capable of feeling emotion anymore.

At thirty-six years old, he was the oldest child in his family, survived now only by his youngest sister who had been ostracized as an infant because of birth abnormalities. After a bit of calculating, he concluded she would be around twenty-five now, assuming she was even still alive. He wondered if, wherever she was, she had any inkling of what was transpiring at her birthplace—or if she had ever even heard of Argall.

Mag lifted his head and took a few seconds to look around at the circle of people who had gathered to pay their respects to his mother. It was the same general group who had attended the other four memorials. He knew everyone there by name and could also name the loved one each of them had lost. It seemed they were involuntarily drawn to one another, propelled by the pain, sadness, and subconscious understanding that others were experiencing the same loss.

The silence around the bonfire was suddenly broken by the rumble of approaching cars. Several people began to rush away, snapped out of the trance the fire had put them into. Most stood fast, murmuring nervously among themselves as three groundcars came barreling up the hill in a cloud of dust. They pulled up just meters from the burning pyre, their spotlights waving wildly about. Six armed men jumped out, hollering and brandishing their weapons at the fleeing mourners.

Mag slid his hands out of his pockets and found they had curled into fists. He turned from the light of the fire and looked into the glaring light from the cars, squinting but refusing to blink. As emotionally spent as he was after the crazy hyperspace trip they had all been on over the past month, the grief had transformed itself into a thick shell of anger he'd learned to use as a defense mechanism. He was jaded. One hundred percent jaded.

A familiar laugh that made his stomach flop pierced the air. The beam of one of the spotlights swung his direction and settled over his face. Past the bright white glare, he could see a pair of boots approaching.

"This is quite the party," the man said. "It looks like we're missing out."

"Nobody invited you," Mag muttered, deadpan. He knew the man only as Loric, though the other mercenaries could sometimes be heard calling him 'Sarge.' *Sergeant Loric.* Somehow Mag couldn't picture the man actually being affiliated with any organization in which he would hold such a rank.

"Mag Reilly," Loric chuckled, advancing toward him and blocking out some of the light. "Having fun out here?"

Mag didn't answer. He had exhausted his supply of sarcastic remarks during the past few weeks and couldn't muster up the energy to come up with anything new. It was probably for the best, since Loric took great delight in tearing up anything he had to say as it was. Mag was as weary of dealing with Loric as he imagined the mercenary was of dealing with him. The man had come and gone from Argall in the past three years but had played a key role in all the turmoil, being personally responsible for most of the executions that had directly affected Mag.

"What do you want, Loric?" With no one and nothing to live for but himself, Mag considered killing the man then and there, though the idea of doing it at his mother's funeral somehow seemed inappropriate.

"That's a silly question coming from such an intelligent man," the mercenary said. "I want the same thing I've wanted since I first came to this *sheyss* hole." He gestured toward the pyre. "You ever think it would be easier to just give it to me?"

Mag shifted his eyes away from the man and gazed out across the Argall valley. The memorial grounds where they currently stood were a few kilometers out of town, nestled into the foothills surrounding the basin. Past the glare of the spotlights and through the glow cast by the town's lights, he could see the location of the mining operations almost directly across from them. Bright, generator-powered lights illuminated the cave entrances, enabling workers to conduct business even at this hour.

According to geologists, the depression in which Argall sat was the remnant of an ancient volcano that had blown its top centuries before. The surrounding area was predominantly volcanic, accounting for the elaborate system of caves and old lava tubes that ate through the mountains. Those caves were home to the naturally occurring niobi crystals, which ranged from white to pink to the rarest and most expensive form, a deep crimson red. They had been dubbed 'blood crystals' due to their color, but the harmless nickname had taken on a whole new meaning in the past three years.

The crystals were the reason the mercenaries were there, the reason for all the killing. Mag knew it all had to do with power and greed. The growing and harvesting of the crystals was Argall's primary industry, so with control of the mining operations came control over the city itself. None of it would have been so bad, he reasoned, if the mercs hadn't started forcing the workers into what many considered blatant slave labor. The mining procedure had traditionally followed a strict schedule. One rotation—one trip around the valley harvesting all available crystals—had typically taken a little over four months, giving the mining specialists known as farmers ample time to grow fresh crystals to be harvested the next time around. The mercenaries had forcefully accelerated the process by demanding more work be put in, effectively shortening one rotation to about ten weeks. As a result, farmers were unable to raise enough mature crystals to meet their quota in the allotted amount of time, and thus many had been executed, Mag's father included. The shortage of crystals had sent the whole city plunging into a financial depression, and any attempts by workers to stand up and defend themselves had only led to more killing.

The fact that this was all about some stupid shiny rocks made Mag sick. It wasn't the crystals themselves that were causing all the hype; it was the ludicrous amount of money being gained by selling them on the black market. Through the years, Argall had sold a good portion of the harvest to the Haphezian military for use in weapons development. Occasionally, some had been sent off to private companies for research—only after receiving special permissions from the government—but all the remnants were kept by the city to provide the fuel and power required for everyday life. Not wanting to draw attention to what they were doing, the mercenaries had allowed the contracted number of crystals to continue being shipped to the military. The rest they had put out to the Fringe's underground markets, retaining only enough to successfully keep the mining operations thriving. Consequently, many businesses that had previously relied on niobi power had been forced to shut down, resulting in lost jobs and torn families. Anyone who wasn't in debt was barely able to afford essential supplies. Loric and his gang had the city by the throat and their grip was only getting tighter.

It didn't take a genius to realize the mercs weren't acting on their own. They were mere puppets, controlled by powerful hands from an armchair in a big office somewhere. Mag had no doubt this unseen puppet master had some form of government standing—any attempts to call for help or reveal the situation in Argall had been summarily ignored, leading him to believe they had been intercepted and manipulated by someone powerful enough to do so. At the same time, any additional incoming or outgoing transmissions had been filtered by the mercenaries and jammed accordingly, and nobody had been allowed to leave the city in months. With Argall as secluded and independent as it was, the lack of communication was hardly noticeable in the rest of the Haphezian population's eyes. No one had a clue what was really going on.

When Mag made no move to respond to the question, Loric thoughtfully examined his weapon before pulling it up and aiming it teasingly at the bystanders. Most yelped and shied away; Mag stood fast, frozen in place by a combination of fear, sorrow, and again, anger. He stared at the gun, wondering first if he would be able to grab it fast enough, and second what a plasma bolt coming head on looked like. He decided he was in no mood to find out.

"Here's the thing, Reilly," the man chuckled. "With the old lady gone, that leaves you the sole beneficiary of all her property. That includes the map to the vein of crystals your old man discovered. After three years of seeing what I'm willing to do to get a look at it, I hope you'll be more cooperative than your mother was."

Mag wanted to laugh out loud, but the knot in his throat prevented him from doing so. A thirty-year veteran farmer, his father had known the cave systems like the back of his hand. He'd stumbled upon a hidden room deep within the mountains about two years before the arrival of the mercenaries. Mag had never seen the room for himself, but the story was that it was rich with niobi growth and contained primarily crimson blood crystals. His father had insisted on keeping its location a secret, foreseeing that great conflict and tension would ensue should anyone find out where it was. He had, however, created a map that would allow him to find it again and preserve the crystals, which he'd managed to hide before his death. Not even Mag knew where it was. He imagined that was for the best, enabling him to maintain deniability whether Loric believed him or not.

"Tell you what," the merc said, motioning toward the pyre and the people around it with a faux grin on his face. "I'm feeling generous tonight, and your mother's funeral is hardly the place to kill you. You have one week to get me that map. Otherwise—"

The rifle was lifted, extended, and fired so fast that Mag hadn't even realized it was happening. The white-hot bolt sliced through the darkness and struck a nearby woman squarely in the chest. She screamed, as did those around her, and crumpled into a heap on the ground.

In that instant, Mag was shouting, cursing, allowing sheer anger to take control of his mind. He wasn't even sure what he was saying—only that it was pure hatred in the form of words and it was directed at Loric. Others behind him were shouting as well, holding him back to keep him from rushing the mercenary and getting himself killed. They were all silenced when the butt of the plasma rifle swung around and struck Mag in the face, sending him stumbling back into the arms of his friends and neighbors.

"Listen!" Loric growled. "Do you want more people to die? Give me that map!"

Mag could feel his tongue bleeding as he struggled to sit up. "Those crystals are the last hope this town has," he said. "I can't let you win."

"And you think *you* can win? Pay attention, Reilly! You surrender the map, people die. You don't, people die. The only thing you have control over anymore is *when* and *where*." Loric stared him down for another several seconds before turning to his own men and jerking his head toward the cars. "Let's go."

For the first time in recent memory, Mag felt utterly defeated. Loric couldn't possibly be right; there had to be another way out, another way to end this, but at the moment, he was drawing a blank. Mind numb, he squinted into the darkness and watched the mercenaries pile into their vehicles until he was once again blinded by one of the spotlights.

"One week, Reilly!" Loric's voice carried through the night as the cars roared away.

· 39 ·
HSP Headquarters
Noro, Haphez

It felt as though time stopped entirely when Ziva's communicator began going off. Aroska stood there listening to it chirp in his pocket, unwilling to break eye contact with Dasaro. He had spent the afternoon familiarizing himself with the case just as the captain had instructed, and now it seemed Ziva had chosen to contact him at the exact moment he'd decided to check in with his new superior. It was more than ironic.

Aroska continued relaying his thoughts regarding the information stored on the data pad, his mouth running on autopilot as his mind worked feverishly to come up with an excuse for carrying a second comm. *Idiot,* he thought. He was working himself up over nothing. For all Dasaro knew, this was his one and only communicator, the one that was supposedly bugged, and he would look foolish for not responding to the transmission. Still, he recalled Ziva's instructions to ignore the message were he in a bad situation. He decided this predicament met such criteria.

By the time he stopped talking, the early stages of a smirk were visible on Dasaro's face. "Are you going to answer that, Lieutenant?" he asked.

Trapped, Aroska shrugged sheepishly and slipped the device out of his pocket. "Yes, sorry. Excuse me." He glanced at the screen then held it to the ear on the far side of his head. "I thought I told you not to call me at work."

Ziva hesitated a moment before responding. "Is this a bad time?"

"It could be worse." Then, playing on his initial greeting, he added, "I'm sorry I didn't tell you I was going back today."

"I have an errand for you if you're free."

"I'll see what I can do."

"I need some things from my house," she said. "Go there and tell Marshay and Ryon that 'the bird has flown.' They'll know what to do."

Aroska made a show of checking the time before glancing apologetically at Dasaro. "Got it—I'll see if I can swing it."

"One more thing. There's a row of decorative tiles on my bedroom wall—the third one from the right is a pressure switch. It opens another panel in the wall that houses a hidden compartment. I need you and *only* you to bring me the contents of that compartment. Don't let anyone catch you with it. You'll know what it is."

"I'll be there. Don't wait up for me." He ended the call abruptly and slid the communicator into his pocket. "Sorry about that," he said. "Sister-in-law is making dinner plans. Anyway, I was thinking I would head out to Payvan's house and do some digging. I know there's already been a patrol out there, but considering my past experience with her, Rubin and Kittner might take more kindly to my presence. Besides, they won't have any idea I'm there on your behalf."

"Very good," Dasaro said. "Thank you again for your help, Lieutenant. My hope is that with your assistance, we can end this in a matter of hours, not days."

"No problem, sir. I'll do my best."

Aroska turned and rushed out, the feeling of finally accomplishing something fueling him with newfound energy. He located his car in the parking bay and, twenty minutes later, found himself pulling into the front drive of Ziva's house on the Tranyi River. He had almost forgotten what an elegant structure it was, but he hardly had time to admire it as he leaped out of the vehicle and bolted toward the front door.

The door opened just as he reached it, and he let his momentum carry him through without a second thought. Marshay Rubin, Ziva's kind-hearted, motherly housekeeper, stepped back quickly with her hand still on the door controls. Ryon Kittner, an old friend of the Payvan family and an uncle figure to Ziva, stood up from where he'd been sitting on the sofa, startled.

"Marshay, Ryon," Aroska greeted them, making a beeline across the living room toward the hall and Ziva's bedroom door.

"Lieutenant Tarbic!" Marshay cried. He couldn't tell if she was unhappy with his presence or merely shocked.

Ryon managed to cut him off just as he reached the hallway, extending a solid hand to stop his advance. "Slow down, son. What brings you out here?"

Aroska stopped, realizing he was moving too quickly even for his own good. He took a deep breath and stepped back, calming himself under the wary gaze of both the housekeeper and the former military officer. "Sorry," he murmured. "I'm here for some of Ziva's things."

Marshay lifted an eyebrow. "And just what do you mean by that? HSP has already been through here tearing this place apart, confiscating anything they think could possibly be related to this damn investigation. What more do you want?"

"This is different," Aroska said. He lowered his voice and took a step closer to the two of them. "Is the area secure?"

"The agency has the comms bugged, but I swept the house and it's clean," Ryon replied. He tilted his head, studying Aroska with a thoughtful expression. "Isn't that something you should know already?"

"No. I'm on Ziva's side here."

"You'll have to do better than that," Marshay snapped. "The entire agency is supposed to be on Ziva's side, and they didn't even try to defend her!" She glanced away, blinking back angry tears, muttering curses under her breath.

"Marshay, the bird has flown."

For the second time in an hour, time itself seemed to stop. For a moment, Aroska wasn't sure if he had actually spoken or if he'd simply imagined it, because neither Marshay nor Ryon moved or had any other visible reaction to his words. Finally, the housekeeper reestablished eye contact, her face full of the same unspoken gratitude he'd seen as she'd read Ziva's pardon document two months earlier.

"I'm here under the pretense that I'm interrogating the two of you," he explained. "It's a bit of a long story, but HSP currently believes I'm working against Ziva along with the rest of them."

Without a word, Marshay and Ryon were both on the move, silently rushing in and out of rooms and gathering an assortment of items until Aroska lost track of where exactly they were. Feeling rather out of the loop, he resumed his journey to the bedroom. What he found through the open door saddened him—what he remembered as the most fanatically-organized room he'd ever seen had been turned upside down by a typical HSP raid. Cords and equipment were scattered on the floor where Ziva's personal terminal and comm console had been plucked away like plants. Tools and broken objects littered the floor, destroyed beyond repair.

The tiles Ziva described were glossy and translucent, alternating between a rich black color and beautiful dark green. They had been set at about shoulder-height, creating a barrier between the white upper wall and the lower half that was colored a pale gray. He saw that they had only been placed along the far wall, suppressing his fear that they went all the way around the room and he wouldn't be able to figure out which one she had specified. He'd scoured his memory on the way over, trying to recall the layout of the room, but the one and only time he had been there, his mind had been otherwise occupied.

Aroska followed the line with his eyes and found the third one from the right positioned over what remained of Ziva's bed. He made his way over to it, climbing gingerly over the tossed bedcovers and the mattress that had been ripped from its frame. The pressure switch had been expertly installed. If not for the fact that Ziva herself had told him it was there, he would never have known. It was no doubt the reason HSP had passed it over...assuming they had.

He placed his palm flat against the tile and held his breath as he slowly began pressing against it. It gave after a few moments, collapsing into the wall about two centimeters with a soft click. He could hear mechanisms whirring within the wall and one of the adjacent tiles suddenly popped from its place, startling him. Glancing toward the door and listening for signs of Marshay and Ryon, he took hold of the tile and lifted it, finding that it folded on unseen hinges. This compartment had also been cleverly hidden, invisible to anyone who didn't know it was there. He took another look at the long line of tiles and wondered how many others might house secret compartments.

Behind the cover, Aroska found a metal strongbox, the kind designed not so much for security as for protecting against fire or water damage. There was no keypad or manual lock, just a sturdy handle and some writing in a language he wasn't familiar with. The box was as large as the tile itself, roughly thirty centimeters wide, and it appeared the compartment was equally deep. It was a hiding place whose contents were not meant to be accessed often, but when they were, it was meant to be fast. Part of him wondered what Ziva could be hiding that was so important, and part of him knew better than to bother questioning anything she did. The realization that he still barely knew the woman kept creeping to the front of his mind, and yet the fact that he was currently the only person she could trust made him feel as though they should be long-time acquaintances. The dissonance was beginning to give him a headache.

Risking another look at the door before proceeding, Aroska took hold of the handle and twisted it downward, hearing the satisfying click as the latch released. The sturdy door swung open, revealing a dark space occupied only by a stack of credits and another object he didn't recognize. Heeding Ziva's instructions to bring all the contents of the box, he stuffed the credits into his pocket then reached in for the other item.

It was narrow and cylindrical in shape, about the length of his forearm and only about four centimeters wide. He turned it over slowly, trying to wrap his mind around what exactly he was seeing. It was solid black, with a soft outer layer that enhanced his grip on it. The object weighed about a kilogram and didn't rattle at all when he gave it a gentle shake. Each end had a narrow slit cut in it, but he couldn't see inside far enough to tell what might emerge from those slits. Unable to see anything else of consequence, he held it up and took another long look at it in the light.

"For starters, you know my secret."

"Don't let anyone catch you with it. You'll know what it is."

Then, his own voice. *"You don't have one of those retractable swords, do you?"*

When Aroska realized what he was holding, he wanted to drop it. He couldn't, however, because his grip on the kytara had suddenly tightened to the point that his knuckles were white. He stood there staring at it, feeling unworthy to be holding this forbidden weapon, until something in the back of his mind reminded him he should hide it and close the compartment before Marshay or Ryon came in.

Suddenly brimming with questions, he tucked the weapon under his arm and lifted the tile back into place. It fell into position, and the pressure switch popped back out with a monstrous *click* that sounded ridiculously loud in the silence of the room. He slid backward off the mattress and managed to turn around just as Marshay appeared in the doorway.

She hesitated a moment before making eye contact, surveying the damage for herself and giving Aroska a split second to slip the kytara out of her line of sight. If anyone, he guessed Ziva would trust Marshay and Ryon to keep her secret, but he wasn't about to take a chance and screw things up. Merely holding the thing made him feel uncomfortable enough.

"HSP did this?" he asked in an attempt to keep the older woman's mind off the reason he had been snooping around in the bedroom.

"I don't know why they were so quick to turn against her," she said with a nod. "We all understand the concept of guilty-until-proven-innocent, but she's one of them. Even if she did commit the murder, they should have at least tried to defend her." She paused for several long seconds. "She didn't do it, did she?"

"I don't believe so," Aroska said, sliding the kytara up the sleeve of his jacket. "There's more to all of this than meets the eye."

Marshay nodded sadly and glanced down at the sturdy backpack she carried. "This is what you came here for," she explained. "It's a collection of items Ziva keeps for when she has to leave quickly, for when the bird has to fly. If you're familiar with that phrase, it's evident to me that she's been in contact with you. I won't bother asking where she is or where you're going. I'm sure she told you not to say, and it's probably best that we didn't know anyway. I will say this: we're on her side, and we're ready to help if she needs it. I don't know the full extent of the situation, so you two look out for each other. Bring her back in one piece."

Somehow Aroska got the feeling Ziva would be doing most of the work in that department, but he nodded respectfully and moved forward to relieve the woman of the heavy pack. "I will, but if there's anyone capable of getting herself out of a mess like this, it's definitely Ziva."

That brought a hint of a smile, and Marshay wrapped an arm around his shoulder as if he were an old family friend. "True. Now come, stay a while. The agency has a team watching the house and we don't want them to think you just came to chat. 'Interrogate' at will, Lieutenant."

· 40 ·
RESIDENTIAL SECTOR
NORO, HAPHEZ

Ziva snapped to attention when she caught sight of Aroska's car pulling back into his garage. She once again sat cross-legged in her place behind the filthy window of the abandoned house across the street, having successfully navigated her way back after the incident in the alley. She had yet to stop sweating and had been stricken by an inexplicable trembling that still wracked her body. She'd deemed the cause to be nothing more than nerves, but again had been unable to understand why she was allowing the current circumstances to affect her in such a way. She'd made it through situations ten times more difficult than this—or so she told herself—and of all the times she'd found herself in a pinch, now was when she needed to be strongest.

Hoping to relieve some of the pressure on her nerves, she had once again allowed herself to slip into a state of deep concentration, letting her mind go completely blank. She had never been a fan of meditation and the like, finding it to be a waste of time and energy, but in light of current events, she found it very soothing. At this point, with nothing more constructive to do with her time, she saw it as a way to stay on top of the game. If Emeri had not yet gone public with her Nosti abilities, he no doubt would at any moment, so she saw no harm in preparing herself for whenever that news was released. There was no guarantee that her Nostia would work at any given moment, but the meditation always seemed to help tilt the odds in her favor.

Somewhat stiff, she rose to her feet and remained there behind the window for several more minutes. Satisfied that Aroska hadn't been followed, she once more exited the little house and slinked across the street, toting her helmet under one arm. Night had fallen and traffic was scarce, allowing her to cross relatively unconcerned. She reached out with her mind and, finding the front door locked this time, carefully manipulated the internal mechanisms until it slid open.

Aroska stood in the light of the kitchen and whirled when she entered, pistol drawn. He immediately relaxed when he saw her, though his wrinkled brow told her he was displeased, and he came into the living room and turned on the light.

"It's good to know you can still be ready for a fight," she said, tossing her helmet onto the sofa. She saw her old backpack sitting in one of the dining chairs and silently thanked Marshay for sending it without fuss. If there had been a time when she'd been happier to see something that belonged to her, she couldn't remember it.

"How did you get in here?" he demanded, his perplexed gaze shifting between her and the door.

She tilted her head. "Take a wild guess."

"I thought you were just going to crash here today," he said. "Where the hell have you been?"

His voice had taken on a quality Ziva wasn't sure she liked. It was one thing to have a general concern for her well-being, but to question her actions when he knew good and well *she* was the one calling the shots? She would see to it his attitude didn't last long. "Who are you now, my father?"

She thought she saw him roll his eyes before he turned back into the kitchen. "Here's your stuff," he muttered, waving half-heartedly at the pack where it waited in the chair.

After being in the same room for thirty seconds, she already felt herself growing impatient with the man. She watched with crossed arms and knitted eyebrows as he went to the cooler and stood there with the door open as if trying to decide whether he actually wanted something to eat. Mood becoming increasingly foul, she went to her pack and opened it up. Everything seemed to be in order—she found credits, a pen light, several medipacs and caura injectors, a small toolkit, hunting knife, pistol, and even a change of clothes. The pack contained every item she had stashed around her house except...

Her heart rate quickened, and she whirled. "Where—" she said, the words 'is it' trailing away when she caught sight of her kytara. Aroska had it in his hand, balancing one end on his forefinger and shifting his arm back and forth as it teetered. He let it fall into his palm when he saw he had her attention and held it up, the corners of his lips curling upward in a slight smirk.

"Give it to me," she ordered, hands on her hips.

The smirk widened into a full smile. "Not unless you show it to me, tell me how it works."

"I don't have time for games, Tarbic," she growled. She took a quick step forward and grabbed for her weapon, but Aroska was quick as well and pulled it up just out of her reach. He cocked his head and shrugged, clearly saying *I told you so* without having to speak the words.

Not about to let him manipulate her like a puppet, Ziva took a step back and sent him a hot glare before focusing on the kytara. He held it above his head and slightly behind him, smiling down on her like a brother who had just stolen his little sister's favorite toy. She was sure he wanted her to jump up and down and throw a fit, but she was determined he would receive no such pleasure. As if the juvenile popularity contest between her and Dasaro wasn't bad enough...

With a quick jerk of her hand, she had an invisible grip on the kytara and gave it a sharp tug with her thoughts, just enough to take Aroska by surprise—which it did, judging by his wide eyes. He released it immediately and it flew into her hand. The grip was warm and soft from being held, and it formed perfectly to her palm as if it had always belonged there. She rubbed her fingers gently over the smooth surface, then, tightening the muscles in her forearm, she flicked her wrist upward.

The metallic *shink* of the blades engaging echoed through the room. Each was thin, perfectly symmetrical, and extended nearly a meter from the end of the grip. Unlike the serrated kytara she had impaled Jak Gamon with nine years earlier, hers had straight stiletto blades. She ran her thumb over one of the razor-sharp edges, drawing blood with the slightest touch. Gripping the handle with both hands, she began to pull in a way only she knew how; the weapon broke apart at a previously invisible seam, separating into two lethal short swords. She looked directly into Aroska's eyes as she fitted the two halves back together, and with another flick of her wrist, the blades retracted silently back into the handle.

"I don't know what you think this is," she said, holding it up to him with white knuckles, "but it's not a toy, got it? There's no way you could understand and you're never *going* to understand. You're lucky I don't gut you right now."

That did a sufficient job of shutting him up, though she had expected some type of challenge or smart remark. He shut the cooler door and glanced about the kitchen, reluctant to make eye contact. She caught herself when she realized she was reveling in the fear she'd clearly struck in him. Perhaps he wasn't the only one in the wrong when it came to getting along.

His shifting eyes finally settled back on hers, unsteady as if they would dart away again without warning. "So does that work on all doors?" he asked, voice dry.

Ziva turned and dug a tunnel through the items in the backpack, stuffing the kytara down into it. "No," she replied. "It only works on standard doors—homes, businesses, that sort of thing. Blast doors, security doors, the ones that use more complex locking mechanisms, those are close to impossible. If I had more experience, I could probably do it, but I don't mind using tools. It reminds me I'm not invincible."

She could tell Aroska was being eaten alive by curiosity, but also that he was trying hard to remain professional after her brief display of power. She knew she would have to share at least a portion of her story at some point, if for no other reason than to keep him quiet, though she had a feeling her abilities would come into play during their escape just as she had been contemplating earlier. There were times when part of her still regretted sacrificing her secret to save Aroska's life, but as she stood there with him now, she realized she would be completely on her own if she would have allowed him to die on Sardonis. It wasn't that she couldn't handle things on her own—it was just nice to have someone backing her up when virtually everyone she knew had either turned against her or had their hands tied.

"Is it some sort of magnetic field," he asked, "or is it more like telekinesis, mind control?"

"Look," she muttered. "We both know how much I would *love* to tell you all about it, but it will have to wait. There are a lot of important things that need to be done in the next couple of days, and it is imperative that we both stay focused. That means you don't pester me, and I will do my best to not be short with you."

"Fair enough," he said with raised eyebrows. "I take it you came up with some sort of plan?"

Ziva walked into the living room and, after confirming that the windows were sufficiently tinted, took a seat on the sofa with her legs crossed and her arms folded. "I will admit I have yet to come up with a way of actually getting off the planet, but I know what we can do to buy some time."

Aroska followed her in, bringing one of the dining chairs with him, and seated himself on the opposite side of the center table a comfortable distance from her. "This coming from the woman who keeps telling me the sooner we get this over with, the better?"

"We have no choice. We're not going anywhere with the way things are right now. What we need is a way to climb over the virtual wall Dasaro has set up, and once we're on the other side, we can move about more freely. Theoretically, my plan should bring the entire wall down, and then it will just be a matter of figuring out what to do next."

He shrugged and brought his elbows to rest on his knees. "Let's hear it, then."

"Think for a minute," she said. "How would you react if you were walking down the street and caught sight of a capital criminal even HSP's finest hadn't been able to catch?"

He appeared thoughtful for a moment, though there was a glimmer in his eyes that told her he was catching on to what she was asking. "I would approach and identify, stay out of sight. Once the identity was confirmed and I was certain they hadn't spotted me, I would call for backup and continue to follow at a distance, reporting developments as

I went. I would hope the agency would send someone to help take care of it."

"Good. Remember all of that tomorrow, but keep in mind that you're the agent in charge if Dasaro is out of the picture."

The glimmer faded instantly. "Meaning what, exactly?"

She leaned forward, making sure she had his attention. "Go to Haphor first thing in the morning and take my bag with you. Go to my stepfather's palace—I couldn't care less what you do there, but make sure Dasaro thinks you're there to question them. You'll be on your own, but that's what we want. No matter what happens around you, play along. I won't tell you any more than that because I want you to make it as realistic as possible. If all goes according to plan, the blockade will be lifted, and we can get off this rock. There's a chance we'll only have a short window of time to get away, so we're going to have to make it count."

"Hold up," he said. "What do you mean 'we'?"

"I mean *us*, Aroska. That's the thing—you're going to have to come with me. If you do any more to help me, Dasaro will come after you too and you'll have to run just as much as I will. If you want out, just say the word and I'm gone, but I need a decision right now."

There was a brief hesitation before Aroska sighed. "I'm in," he said. "Feels like it's too late for me to turn back now—you've done a good job of piquing my curiosity. Besides, I've been sitting on my ass for too long and it will do me some good to get out of the house."

Ziva fought away a smirk. "You tasted blood on the Dakiti mission, didn't you? Now you've been exposed to spec ops, and you can't help but involve yourself again. Am I right?"

He smiled slyly and shrugged. "Maybe...I trust you're speaking from experience?"

She had to admit she was, at least a little, but she was suddenly silenced as the things she had been pondering all day eased back into the front of her mind. There was something about Aroska's undisputed willingness to help her that made her entirely uncomfortable. She wasn't sure what reason he would have to turn against her, but then again, she had no inkling as to what his motives were for standing by her in the first place. He'd had plenty of opportunities to say no and make excuses, yet he'd stuck with her despite the fact that she'd given him no incentive other than empty threats.

"Why help me?" she asked.

"What?"

"There's got to be more to it than 'getting out of the house.' What reason do you have to help me when you know it will put you in just as much danger?" It felt odd asking the question. Upon thinking harder, she wasn't sure how she would answer were she in his place.

He hesitated in a manner that gave her the impression she'd caught him off-guard. "Well, you're right—Dasaro seems like a complete bastard." He stopped again, his smile dwindling when he realized she wasn't laughing. "You've been a great help to me in the past couple of days. It's the least I can do to return the favor."

She scoffed, unconvinced. "Yes, but helping someone sober up and helping someone evade the law are two entirely different things. I want a better answer than that."

Aroska shrugged again and added a wag of his head. "Well, I honestly can't give you one. Give me some time and I might be able to come up with something. How does that sound?"

She wasn't sure whether that meant he was hiding something or that he truly had no genuine motivation for helping her. Either way, she was less than thrilled with his response. "What is this, some sort of creepy Elsara life-debt thing?"

"Maybe."

"Did I ever mention how much I utterly detest the Elsara?"

For several seconds, the entire house fell completely silent as Aroska stared at the floor and Ziva stared at him. The man clearly had something on his mind he was refusing to share, but to be fair, she didn't press the matter. There were things he would discover about her in due time, and she had no doubt the learning experience would go both ways.

"Can I ask you something?" he finally asked, eyes narrowed as if he were deep in thought even as he spoke. "How do you know you can really trust someone?"

Perhaps she was letting on too much. Still, if she wasn't going to put her full confidence in him, she wanted him to be well aware of it. "You don't," she replied, "but that's the whole point of trust, isn't it."

Aroska smiled again, impressed by such a philosophical answer. He grew quiet again for a moment and glanced away. "Do you trust me?" he asked. "You asked me why I'm helping you, but I could just as easily ask why you chose to come to me."

"We've been through this, Aroska."

"Yes, but *do you trust me*?"

If there was one thing that pleased Ziva about the conversation, it was that he was cutting to the chase and asking direct questions rather than stumbling around the issues and irritating her even more. "I haven't decided yet," she replied. "I'm not sure if I can, given what happened last time I chose to trust you and risk my own skin for you. It would be impossible for me to shut you out completely at this point, but I'm being cautious. I'll admit I'm watching my back."

Aroska said nothing, though the look in his eyes spoke of utter shock and disappointment. The fact that he had taken offense to her words confused her. She wondered briefly if he had ever been betrayed by someone close to him, but when she remembered Saun Zaid, she knew part of him had to understand how she felt. She wouldn't have blamed him at all if he'd severed all relational ties and refused to open up to anyone ever again after what had happened with his former partner and lover.

"Ziva, I wouldn't do that to you again."

"I would certainly hope not," she said. "I would hope you had learned your lesson last time. I never believed you would turn me in for saving your life, regardless of how I did it. But you did, and then you came groveling back asking for a second chance. Luckily, Emeri gave you one. If you were to try something like that again, I can guarantee you won't get another chance, and neither will I. Dasaro will eat me alive the first opportunity he gets. I hope you realize that."

Aroska nodded. "You seem ungrateful that I even bothered *asking* for a second chance."

"Don't get me wrong—I'm happy to be alive. I'm just taking

everything with a grain of salt right now."

The house was again filled with the same odd silence, but this time Aroska kept his eyes locked with Ziva's. She could tell he was discouraged, though it seemed he got her point. That made the two of them even—she still possessed a certain measure of disappointment with him, despite the fact that he had risked his reputation and probably his career to get her off the hook. She couldn't remember the last time she'd willingly given someone another shot. They were both starting over on so many levels.

"I understand," he finally said. "So do you have any initial ideas for transportation off the planet?"

"I'm thinking public transport," she replied. "The *Intrepid* would attract too much attention even if the plan is executed flawlessly, and it's probably been impounded by the agency anyway. The hard part will be getting aboard, but once we do, we can travel as refugees and head to the other side of Fringe Space."

"Do you have anywhere specific in mind?"

"Where would you go if you wanted to blend in, where nobody would care that you're a wanted criminal?"

Aroska shrugged. "Niio, Chaiavis. I have a contact on Chaiavis who might be able to help us."

"Chaiavis it is, then. We'll have to steer clear of the embassy. I'm not sure how much of a threat they would be anyway, since they're usually a couple of steps behind the government here. We'll see how things go tomorrow and play this all by ear."

"That's all the planning you're going to do?" Aroska said. "Don't you think—?"

She cut him off. "I think on the move—you should remember that. We went into Dakiti with less information and still came out successful."

He scoffed. "Only after we were both captured—you multiple times—and had enough brushes with death to last a lifetime."

"If you think that mission was a brush with death, then you haven't seen anything yet," Ziva said. "Just follow my lead and I'll get us through this." She had to admit Dakiti had been a close call, but she wasn't about to confess any such thing, not now. Besides, it hadn't been *much* worse than countless other situations she'd managed to fight her way out of.

"Here, then," Aroska said, removing a small memory stick from his pocket. Ziva recognized it as one that belonged to Zinni. "This has all the information Dasaro gave me regarding your case. If I'm going to be 'following your lead,' I would prefer you knew what was going on."

She took it from him and placed it in her own pocket. "Thank you," she said indignantly, still not pleased with his attitude. "Maybe we can use this to plan some counter moves. How much do they know?"

"Not a lot," Aroska replied. "The evidence found in Tachi's palace is solid, and the whole case revolves around the fact that nobody's going to question it. That memory stick contains a copy of the personnel file they gave me on you. It doesn't go very deep, but I'll warn you now— there's some stuff on there I think I need to understand if I'm going to be helping you."

"And you should know you're not going to get any answers until we get out of here."

He nodded. "Like you said, we should stay focused on the task at hand. Now, I don't know about you, but I'm exhausted. I haven't had this much excitement in one day since Dakiti. If tomorrow is going to be as crazy as you make it out to be, I suggest you get some rest as well—you look like *sheyss.*"

Although Ziva certainly felt like it, she didn't appreciate the comment. She remained silent, however, and watched as he stood up and made it only half a stride before stopping. He hesitated there for a long time with one hand on his hip as he thoughtfully rubbed the other over his goatee. She could tell something was ripping him apart inside, and she wished he would just spit it out for both their sakes. Still, they did need to stay focused now and she imagined they would have plenty of time for catching up and filling each other in once their journey got underway.

Finally, he turned around and looked down on her with a sigh and another shrug. "I'm sorry," he said. "You know, I can sleep out here if you want to take the bed. You'll be more comfortable."

"Offer appreciated but not accepted," she said. "I doubt I could sleep if I wanted to."

"Suit yourself. Good night."

Not in an overly friendly mood, she refrained from replying and watched him wander away down the hall. The frustration was rolling off him like energy from a powerblade. It had clearly been building for some time and wasn't strictly the result of the preceding conversation, though that had certainly been a contributing factor. She would let him sleep it off—or, if he was anything like her, lie awake and dwell on it until there was nothing left to think about—and wait to bring it up again until they were well on their way to Chaiavis.

Exhausted but far from sleep, she went to her pack at the dining table and retrieved her small toolkit. Settling back into the meditative state she'd grown accustomed to over the past couple of days, she set about fixing Aroska's viewscreen.

· 41 ·
SHEVIN RESIDENCE
HAPHOR, HAPHEZ

Despite the fact that he heard the floor creak when she entered the room, Kade was still startled when Veya placed her hands on his aching shoulders and began to massage them gently. He jerked his head up from where it had been resting on his desk and rubbed his itching eyes, letting out a tired sigh. He hadn't realized he'd been dozing, and now his head hurt worse than it had when he'd first sat down at the terminal.

"Didn't mean to startle you," Veya said quietly, wrapping her arms around him and resting her head on his shoulder.

Kade sat there and let her hold him, placing a hand over hers. Her ebony hair was damp from a recent shower and tickled his face. Fragrant lotion had softened her already-flawless skin, and for a moment, he forgot all about his headache and the stress of the past several days. He was sure Veya had no idea how much comfort she was capable of bringing him. His wife was the strongest woman he had ever known— he'd always thought she would have made a fine HSP agent.

"Being startled by *you* is a refreshing change," he said, rubbing his face with his free hand. "Actually, I should thank you for waking me. I have a lot to do."

"Are you doing okay? You've been running yourself into the ground lately and it's not good for you."

"I've got a lot on my mind." Kade knew trying to avoid the question was useless. They were both young, but they knew each other like they had been best friends since birth. He'd met her one day in the spaceport, he a security guard fresh out of the academy and she a student traveling from Cual to Haphor for higher education. What had started as a simple request for directions had blossomed into an incredible friendship that had resulted in romance and finally marriage.

"Kade Shevin, answer my question."

"These last few days have been crazy for all of us, you know that," he replied. He didn't dare tell her he had nearly lost his job that very afternoon, not yet. It would only cause her to worry more than she already did, and he didn't feel much like talking about it anyway. Telling her he was afraid he was losing his mind wouldn't do any good, either, so the only solution was to say nothing. At any rate, it wasn't like there was much to tell about the case unless he actually *wanted* to lose his job.

Veya pulled away but left her hands resting on his shoulders. "All right," she said, "you win, but you do need your rest. You're taking this whole case way too personally."

"What's not to take personally?" Kade said. "I'm the one Payvan attacked."

"She would have done the same thing to anyone else."

He had to restrain himself from complaining further about the incidents with Spence and the coroner's report. He knew she would find out something wasn't right as early as the next morning when he failed to leave for work. There was always the option of spending the day hiding out in the city as he had done after Zona dismissed him that afternoon, but he wasn't sure how long that charade would last. The best option was to knuckle down and get to the bottom of matters, but that would be difficult without access to his terminal at RG Headquarters.

His train of thought ignited a tiny spark in his mind, and he turned his head to meet Veya's eyes. "By the way, Zona says hello," he said.

She tilted her head, confused by the abrupt change of subject. "That's nice of him," she said, resuming her massage. "You know, we should have him over for dinner one of these days."

At the moment, the thought made Kade shudder, but he forced a short nod of agreement nonetheless. It wasn't that Zona was a bad man by any means—Kade respected him more than anyone else in the galaxy—but with his job, his reputation, and possibly even his life hanging in the balance, he thought it best to steer clear of his boss altogether. He had a family to care for, and losing his job or getting himself killed wouldn't do anyone any good.

A wave of relief washed over him when the sound of the baby crying reached his ears. Veya sighed and brushed a lock of hair away from her face as she pulled away. She excused herself with a gentle smile, stopping one last time before disappearing down the hall. "You, sir, get some sleep. That's an order."

Kade watched her go then turned back to the terminal; it had gone into standby mode as he'd dozed. He rebooted and brought up Eason Fromm's report again, the farthest his short access leash would allow him to go while working from home. It remained the same as it had been when he'd showed it to Zona, containing the information he knew to be false. There were times when he'd wondered if what he'd read initially was merely the result of wishful thinking based on what he'd seen at the med center. It was certainly possible that he could have been hallucinating, especially after the mild head trauma he'd suffered. That combined with lack of sleep made it nearly impossible to focus on anything. After a time, however, he'd forced himself to stop second guessing—he knew what happened to Spence and that was that.

For the time being, the best way he saw to uncover the truth was to hear the story from the doctor himself. Perhaps he could be convinced to share his observations with Zona as well. Taking a quick look at the contact information listed in the report, Kade opened a direct transmission to Fromm's private comm.

· 42 ·
Palace of the Royal General
Haphor, Haphez

By the time Aroska pulled up in front of Njo Jaroon's estate in the Royal City, it was mid-morning and the rest of Haphor was bustling with life. There had been some to-do when it came to letting him through the gates—one of several negative side effects of having been away from work for a month and a half—and only after contacting the director himself had he been allowed through. Everyone else was in the same boat, it seemed. Since Tachi's murder, the security detail had been on edge and virtually the only people allowed into the Royal City were those who lived there, according to one of the gate guards. Aroska didn't blame them at all for being cautious, though he felt crushed under many a wary gaze as he exited the car and made his way up the front walkway.

It was a pleasant day, warm but overcast, and the hum of insects buzzing in the flowerbeds filled the air. The grounds surrounding the mansion were meticulously maintained, with freshly cut grass, ornate fountains, and thriving green plant life. The house itself was even more impressive. The outer walls were pure white stone, and, despite only being two stories, it had a commanding presence fit for the king himself. Why Ziva had chosen to give up life in such a place was beyond him.

A man with the look of a butler about him waited at the front door and let Aroska in without a word. The grand entry hall was still and quiet, with no signs of life in the immediate vicinity. The place reminded him of a museum—cold and delicate—so he moved forward into a pristine little sitting area and contented himself with looking rather than touching.

A massive spiral staircase rose up before him, stretching up to the second floor where he could hear faint footsteps approaching. A woman appeared at the top of the steps and hesitated for several seconds, looking down on him as if his mere existence was somehow an inconvenience. He didn't need to read his data pad or study the *gesh punti* on her face to know she was Namani Payvan-Jaroon. The woman was a spitting image of Ziva, but about twenty-five years older. She had the air of a trophy wife about her, with perfect clothes, perfect nails, perfect hair, and skin she had no doubt paid a large sum of money to maintain. Nonetheless, this was the first blood relative of Ziva's he had met to date, and it was surreal.

"My lady, my name is—"

"Lieutenant Tarbic," she interrupted, quickly descending the stairs with her head up in a pompous manner. "Your captain told us you would be coming, and I will tell you right now that you are wasting your time. I assure you that you will find nothing here, and none of us can tell you anything that will help you."

"That may be true, ma'am, but with respect, I can't leave just yet. With your permission, I'd like to just take a look around—you won't even know I'm here."

"Very well," said a male voice accompanied by heavy footfalls. "Do your work, Lieutenant, and then be done here."

Aroska turned and found himself looking into the all-knowing eyes of Njo Jaroon. He couldn't recall that he'd ever seen the man in the flesh, and now that he was seeing him face-to-face, he felt put in his place. Intimidation was probably a large factor in Jaroon's skill as a politician; he was just as tall as Aroska and as burly as Dasaro. If Ziva didn't look so much like her mother, he would have guessed Njo was the relation, not Namani.

Aroska dipped his head, still caught off guard by how impressive the Royal General was. "Yes sir, thank you sir." He suddenly felt very small and wished he was dealing with someone with whom he was more familiar—which, he realized, was only Jada. After the mere thirty seconds he had been in the presence of the Jaroons, he already thought he understood at least partially why Ziva wanted nothing to do with them. He doubted she'd be willing to tell him her family backstory, but curiosity was beginning to gnaw at him.

Jaroon's speech was dignified but his voice was gruff. "You may dispense with the pleasantries, Lieutenant. Rest assured no one in this household has seen or heard from Ziva since the assassination."

"Do either of you have any idea what would have prompted her to kill Tachi?" The question felt strange—after such a brief conversation with her about the matter, Aroska was not yet convinced Ziva was entirely innocent. At any rate, it seemed she was potentially *more* innocent than whoever else was involved, if that even made sense. *What have I gotten into?*

Njo glared at him from behind bushy black eyebrows, silently chastising him for daring to ask another question. "No," he snapped. "If anyone had any idea, it would be you and your agency."

So the mysterious incident that had sparked Ziva's hatred for Tachi wasn't known outside of HSP. That would help when it came to narrowing down exactly what it was. Reminding himself he should currently play the role of loyal investigator rather than actually *be* one, Aroska forced another abbreviated nod. "Thank you, sir. I'll be on my way."

The three parted company, with Njo and Namani exiting through an open patio door and Aroska heading up the impressive staircase. The house truly was a masterpiece, no doubt dating back to the original establishment of the Royal City. It was eerily quiet, and that combined with the fact that he didn't know what he was supposed to be doing left him frozen halfway up the steps. He had made a point to rise early in order to prepare himself for the day and had found, to his surprise, that Ziva was already gone. On second thought, it hadn't actually surprised him at all. The woman was a ghost, disappearing on a whim and affecting his mind to the point where he'd wondered if everything that was happening was just part of some insane dream. It was no wonder HSP was unable to track her down.

If it *was* a dream, he was still in it. With no way of knowing when or if he would ever wake up, he concluded it would be best to at least do something that would leave him with a sense of accomplishment when the time came. Helping an alleged capital criminal evade the authorities was accomplishing something...wasn't it?

Aroska broke out of his stupor and continued to the top of the staircase, where he found himself in a small open area with a sofa and table and a hallway on either side of him. According to the data he had gathered before leaving Headquarters that morning, there was Jada and then there were Jaril and Jazel, the Haphezian half-siblings. He preferred to not deal with the latter two if he could so help it, but at the same time, he thought he should probably try to stall in order to buy Ziva the time to do whatever the hell it was she was doing. On the other hand, he didn't want to take too long and drag out the escape process any longer than necessary. "Ziva, you owe me big time," he muttered, turning down the corridor on the left.

Several closed doors lined the wall to his right, no doubt bedrooms overlooking the back of the property. He felt odd intruding on anyone, but standing in the hallway looking lost wouldn't do any good, either. Inhaling deeply, he went to the first door and knocked, waited, and then tried the controls—the room was unlocked. The door slid open with a hiss, and he found himself looking into a large apartment-style bedroom that appeared to have been unoccupied for some time judging by the storage containers stacked about and the bare mattress in the bedframe. He ventured a few steps inside and listened for a moment before retreating back out into the hall, satisfied no one was around.

Mind wandering, he continued to the next room, this one on his left. He repeated the process of knocking and waiting and found that it too was unlocked. Inside he found a well-furnished room similar in style to the other, though this one was clearly still in use. The massive canopy bed sat unmade behind a thin pale-green veil, and a variety of clothes were strewn about the floor—all feminine, mostly undergarments, he noted. This room obviously belonged to...

Her name trailed away when her voice rang out from down the hallway. "Who the hell are you?"

Aroska turned in the direction he'd been heading to find Jazel Jaroon standing outside the lavatory door wearing only a flimsy house robe. She pulled it tighter around her scrawny body and strode toward him, face scrunched in a manner that attempted but failed to intimidate him. She was about the same height as her mother but only bore a resemblance to Ziva if he squinted a little. According to the information, she and Jaril were twenty-year-old twins, though Jazel made herself up to look several years older. In the few seconds he'd stood there studying her, it was clear that she tried way too hard, whether it was to draw the eyes of men or give her self-esteem a boost. It was typical behavior for a child in a family with a structure such as this one, nothing but an attempt to compensate for the lack of attention from royal parents. Her face was caked with powder, eyes lined with black half a centimeter thick, eyebrows plucked to the point that they were nearly nonexistent. Vanity aside, she wasn't bad-looking—if he'd had no idea who she was, he might have expressed interest.

"Hello Jazel, HSP," he said, displaying the spec ops credentials he'd been given. "Care to answer a few questions?"

The young woman smirked and leaned up against the frame of her door, no longer quite so conservative with the grip on her robe. "Are you here to interrogate me, agent?" she asked, letting her eyes flit about flirtatiously.

The girl had no shame. In any other situation, Aroska might have responded with a coy comment of his own, but considering the circumstances, he was determined not to stoop to her level. "Have you heard from Ziva recently?" he asked, refusing to indulge her.

"No," she snapped, "and I don't care to. Thanks to her, this whole city is on lockdown, and I've been stuck in this house for three days."

He lifted an eyebrow. "Sounds brutal."

"It is. If you ask me, she's getting what she deserves for what she did to Tachi, but it's unfair that the rest of us have to suffer."

"It sounds like you don't care much about what's happening to your own sister."

"*Half*-sister," she bit. "It's too bad a relation could be proven using DNA—otherwise I wouldn't claim one at all. All she's ever done is cause problems for us. She's messed up in the head."

Aroska wondered *who* exactly was messed up in the head, as well as what the definition of a 'problem' was. He couldn't fathom how she'd even had the opportunity to develop this attitude, considering he was fairly sure Ziva had done everything in her power to avoid her family during recent years. Had Namani instilled this mindset in her? Was this conflict the reason Ziva had left so many years earlier? He considered the things he'd read in Ziva's background profile, and now he was even more curious to hear her take on the situation.

A dozen points of argument spun through his skull, but Jada appeared out of thin air and prevented him from speaking his mind.

"Lieutenant Tarbic, right?" she said, gliding up to them with a distasteful eye on Jazel. "We met a couple months ago in Noro."

"Jada," he replied, hoping his relief wasn't as obvious as it felt. "Always a pleasure."

Her long brown hair was loose from the braid she had worn when they'd first been introduced, reaching two thirds of the way down her back. She seemed shorter than Aroska remembered, though he realized she was barefoot. Despite the fact that she was younger than her Haphezian counterpart, it was clear merely in the way she carried herself that she possessed wisdom and charisma beyond her years.

"If you're here about Ziva, I'd be glad to answer any questions," Jada said, turning back the way she had come with a short cough.

"Great," he said, mustering all the poise he could with Jazel still present. "I won't be long—I've got somewhere else to be and they're expecting me back in Noro soon."

Thankfully, Jazel took her cue and turned away. "If there's anything else, *Lieutenant,* I'll be in the shower." She began to strut back toward the lavatory, throwing a wink back at him as she went.

Aroska shuddered and began walking beside Jada, bewildered by the reaction Jazel had provoked in him. Ordinarily, he would have been delighted to be flirted with without having to work for it, but at the moment, it was making his stomach churn.

Jada walked like true royalty, with shoulders rolled back and head held high. Aroska wasn't sure if it was two months' worth of maturity or simply the fact that they were under the Royal General's roof, but there was definitely a more aristocratic air about her than there had been during dinner that night in Noro.

"I'm terribly sorry about that," she said, loud enough that Jazel could no doubt still hear.

"Your sister has a very...*mature* outlook on life," he scoffed, stealing a glance back toward the lavatory.

Jada led him past the staircase to the room at the far end of the hallway. "One of many side-effects of being raised in an environment like this," she replied, opening the door and stepping aside to let him through. "Don't get me wrong, living here isn't a bad thing, but unlike Jaril and Jazel, I've had enough experience with life on the outside to know I shouldn't take all of this for granted."

"A logical perspective."

"Yeah, well around here the logical thinkers are the ones who are considered narrow-minded. If they want to know who's *actually* short-sighted, all they need to do is look in a mirror." She showed him to a comfortable chair near a glass door that led out to a balcony overlooking the yard. "It's an interesting phenomenon. I'm under the impression everyone thinks I'm as crazy as Ziva the majority of the time."

Aroska took the seat and waited for Jada to sit down across from him. "Speaking of Ziva," he said, hoping to move things along as efficiently as possible.

"Speaking of Ziva," the girl sighed, her tone making it sound like some sort of agreement rather than a simple echo. She was quiet for a moment, thoughtfully rubbing her hand across her forehead with her eyes closed. Even after having only met her once, it was clear to Aroska how close Jada and Ziva were, and he respectfully gave her some time.

"I can tell merely by your voice that you have a different view on all of this than most people," she said. "I couldn't care less whose side you're on right now and I understand you're only doing your job. However, I want you to know I really appreciate the attitude you seem to have. You're not here to interrogate anyone, you're here to carry on a civilized conversation like a true professional. I think Ziva would appreciate it, too."

Aroska found himself rendered momentarily speechless, part of him happy for the compliment and part of him feeling guilty about even being a part of HSP at the moment. He reminded himself that he had yet to hear the whole story and that he should remain a neutral party for the time being. "Thanks," he replied. "Like you said, I'm only trying to do my job. Despite everything, I have a lot of respect for your sister, and I'd like to catch up to her before the rest of the agency does. I don't want to see her suffer any more than she has to."

"If I asked if you knew where she was, would you tell me?"

"Even if I *did* know, I doubt I could tell you." That much was true—he hadn't the slightest clue where Ziva was, though he imagined she might be somewhere in Haphor since she'd gone through the trouble of sending him here. He felt more and more like a pawn as the seconds passed, and the more he thought about it, he couldn't come up with a better term to describe himself. Ziva was using him to keep Dasaro and company occupied while she was running around doing the galaxy only knew what. Suddenly he wanted nothing more than to get this nonsense over with and see some action.

He shifted in his seat. "If Ziva were to come here to Haphor, where would she go?"

Jada seemed puzzled by the question but broke out into a grin. "At this point, she would probably infiltrate the Royal City in broad daylight just to prove she could." Then the smile dissolved as abruptly as it had appeared. "Honestly I don't know," she said with a sad wag of her head. "She never liked spending much time here."

And with that, Aroska felt as though he was back to square one. Ziva had neither told him what to do nor told him how to figure out what to do. Did she expect him to go sit at a bar somewhere and wait for her to make contact? That actually didn't sound like such a bad idea.

He stood up, unsure how to end the conversation. He'd been there for what, fifteen minutes? Jada watched him quizzically, her wise brown eyes telling him she was aware he was fighting some sort of internal battle. He wanted very much to tell her what he knew, though he recalled what Ziva had said about her being fearful of getting too involved. At this point, he didn't feel like he even knew enough for it to be a problem; he'd be putting himself in more danger than anyone else.

"I wasn't entirely truthful with you a minute ago," he said, resolving to at least fill her in on the basic details. "It's true that I have no idea where Ziva currently is. However—" he glanced toward the door and lowered his voice a bit "—she's been with me for the past two days. The agency does have me running point on the team assigned to track her down, but I'm doing it on her behalf."

The look on Jada's face made Aroska wonder if she believed him. She watched him through slightly narrowed eyes in a manner that reminded him of Zinni or even Ziva herself. Neither of them said anything for a while as they each contemplated what he'd just said. For a moment, he regretted saying anything at all, but after a few more seconds of studying the girl's face, he could tell a certain shadow had been lifted from it. Still, she didn't smile, and her eyes didn't change.

"Good to know, Lieutenant," she said, standing up as well, "but I ask that you don't tell me anything further. If we were in Noro, that would be one thing, but right now I'm stuck under this roof, and it would be best if I didn't know any more than I have to."

"Completely understandable," Aroska said, offering a hand. "I thought it was only fair that you be aware. I wish I would have had your good judgment when I was seventeen."

Jada shook his hand and her lips finally parted in a radiant smile. "Try eighteen."

"My mistake, my lady," he said with a sheepish dip of his head. He checked the time—he'd managed to waste a total of twenty minutes there at the Jaroon estate. Perhaps he could spend a while scoping out the streets for any signs of Ziva, though he couldn't bring himself to believe it would do much good.

"There's a little café just outside the Royal City," Jada said as he turned to leave. "I've met Ziva there maybe three times—it's the only place I know of that she ever frequents when she's over here. It might be worth it to check there. If she sent you here to ask me where to go, that's where I'd tell you."

Aroska shrugged. "Hey, at this point I'll take anything I can get." With one last nod, he was on his way out, angling toward the stairs with a cautious eye in the direction of the lavatory. There was no sign of Njo, Namani, or the butler who had let him in as he strode through the entry and broke out onto the front walkway. His groundcar sat untouched where he'd left it, though it remained under the watchful eyes of several RG agents who patrolled the area. They all hesitated when they caught sight of him, so he picked up his pace, just as uncomfortable with being scrutinized as they were with him being there.

Within a moment, he was pulling the car out into the traffic of the Royal City's main thoroughfare, which was minimal on account of the lockdown. The community was large, but the road provided a straight shot to both primary entrances as well as several secondary ones. Lost in thought, he barely noticed when he arrived back at the front gate. After a brief stop and a quick search of the car by the guards, he found himself making his way through the hustle and bustle of the main city.

Jada had neglected to specify where exactly this restaurant was, but being as most of the buildings in the vicinity seemed to be offices, he imagined it wouldn't be too hard to find. Taking his chances, he guided the car to the right, easing into place on the one-way street between two slower-moving vehicles. Before he had made it half a block, the line stopped moving altogether, held up by some unseen delay at the next intersection.

Heaving an impatient sigh, Aroska leaned back in his seat and drummed his fingers on the controls, realizing he really had nothing better to do than sit in traffic. He glanced to the walkways on either side of him, wondering what the chances were that he would actually catch sight of Ziva. Keeping an eye out for someone who didn't want to be found—especially when that someone was Lieutenant Ziva Payvan—was as close to futile as something could get. It wasn't a matter of finding her, but rather of her making herself known when she saw fit.

That was why he nearly laughed out loud when he saw her. At first, he hadn't realized who he was looking at—her hair had been released from its perpetual ponytail and she wore dark shades—but after a quick double take, he saw she was watching him. She sat on a bench, using a news hologram for cover, but her head was turned directly toward him. With her eyes obscured, it was impossible to tell if she was making eye contact, yet he could feel her gaze boring into him as if she were standing a meter away. Not wanting to draw any attention to her by staring, Aroska shifted his focus back to the street. Traffic was still frozen; Ziva had clearly inserted herself into this particular spot knowing he would be held up long enough to notice her.

When he stole another glance in her direction, she had risen to her feet and was holding the shades at her side. As soon as he reestablished eye contact, she replaced them and looked up the street. Only then did he notice the HSP-issue hoverbike parked at the curb a short distance away, no doubt the same one she had taken from the checkpoint in the forest. Using it in the middle of the city was a bold move on her part...unless she wanted to be caught.

Of course. The questions she'd asked the night before had seemed odd at the time, but as he sat there now, he understood perfectly. He sat still for another moment and watched as she moved toward the bike and boarded it. With such a small and agile vehicle, she would be able to maneuver through the heavy traffic with little effort. Feeling almost sick with adrenaline, he picked up the car's comm receiver and opened a direct transmission to Dasaro. "I've got her!" he exclaimed.

· 43 ·
CITY CENTER
HAPHOR, HAPHEZ

T here were times—but only a few—when Ziva wished she had paid more attention to the teachings of her...*master*. Jak Gamon had often told stories about Nosti who'd developed a kind of sixth sense thanks to their nostium infusions. With the right amount of concentration, they could sense the movements of enemies around them, even if those enemies were a fair distance away. The nostium may have stimulated the brain and allowed the user to manipulate their surroundings, but she'd never been able to fathom how it could produce psychic powers. She'd always just assumed the stories were Gamon's way of motivating her to focus; lost and angry, she'd had little interest in anything other than the fighting aspects of her training.

Only now, after a lengthy career at HSP, did she truly understand the advantages her quiet time and meditation gave her. She darted out into the street, wishing she possessed that fabled sixth sense, and swiftly maneuvered the hoverbike through the rest of the traffic that remained at a standstill. She was counting not only on the fact that Aroska had taken the hint and called for backup, but also that Dasaro would just send a local team after her rather than come all the way over in person. In the case of the latter, she would have plenty of time to make a break for it as he traveled, but that would mean coming up with an entirely new plan which would in turn delay departure even further. For a while, she'd considered scrapping the getaway plan entirely and remaining on the planet, but without the ability to move about freely, finding Tachi's killer and proving herself innocent would be nigh on impossible.

Finally, traffic opened up and Ziva accelerated, no longer concerned about attracting attention. It was a chilly ride without the riding suit she had come to think of as her own. The wind bit at her skin and whipped her loose hair around in front of her face, but she refrained from pulling it back. It was surprising how much of a difference it made in her appearance, and she was impressed that Aroska had been able to spot her as quickly as he had. None of the passersby had paid her any notice—half of them probably didn't even watch the news.

From her current location, it would take approximately ten minutes to reach the little relay station in the forest. Upon arriving there earlier that morning, she had stashed the riding suit and supply belt and had proceeded to walk on, breathe on, and touch everything she could in order to give the appearance that she'd been there for the duration of the investigation. After that, it had only been a matter of finding somewhere to lie low and wait for Aroska. The traffic delay had been a pleasant surprise, effectively reducing the effort needed on her part. It was good that he'd come and done what she'd asked—the majority of the plan would play out the same regardless of his presence, but he was needed in order to pull off the whole *escape* part at the end.

Haphor itself began to thin out and trees became more and more prominent. Ziva could imagine a swarm of infrared probes converging on the city, controlled by similar swarms of overly eager agents at both the Noro and Haphor HSP offices. Surely the agency wouldn't be dumb enough to follow her too closely; if the activated team followed protocol, they would monitor her via the probes and wait for the ranking agent—Aroska in this case—to arrive before proceeding. She could only imagine what Dasaro must be thinking, stuck in Noro and helpless when it came to bringing her down himself.

"Come and get me," she said aloud.

Before long, the city had given way entirely to thick foliage and she guided the bike onto the road that would take her up past the old comm tower. She hoped she was far enough ahead of her pursuers to give them the impression she was oblivious to their presence. It was almost demeaning having to play dumb to such an extent, demeaning to the point that it was increasingly hard to be convincing. But she shook away those negative thoughts; within a few hours, she would be on a transport headed for the safety of Chaiavis.

The comm tower rose above the trees dead ahead, so she turned up the little hill and brought the bike to a stop directly in front of the relay station. She left the door open when she went inside and, after taking one last look around the interior of her little hiding place, leaned against the doorframe and waited.

There were two scenarios that were most likely to go down. One, HSP would go with the quick and quiet approach and send in a small squad of elite agents commanded by Aroska. Two, it would instead be an invade-and-destroy mission where she would be boxed in by an entire division of officers, also headed up by Aroska. Both cases could be dealt with—though neither was ideal—but she found herself hoping it would be the former. She doubted Dasaro would go to such extremes as to call in an airstrike or something of the sort; he would want visual confirmation of her death and multiple witnesses. It wouldn't surprise her if he had the agents equipped with cams so he could record what went down and watch it every night before he went to bed.

She waited a good twenty minutes before she saw any signs of HSP approaching. Four groundcars tore up the road, the first belonging to Aroska and the other three being of the slick black variety used by the Royal Guard. She'd just expected the squad to be sent from HSP's Haphor field office, but this had started out as the RG's investigation anyway, so their presence made sense. She let out a deep breath and told herself that these new conditions by no means altered the playing field.

Aroska's car, which contained him and another agent, proceeded directly up the hill while the RG vehicles continued on a bit farther and came around the back of the shack, cutting off any means of escape. Aroska had relinquished the pilot's seat to the agent with him and sat peering through a spotting scope, the whole of his attention focused on the front of the little building. It was time to get moving.

Before the car had come to a complete stop, Ziva bolted from the front door and took off at a dead run across the clearing toward the trees and the creek bed. Angry shouts could be heard almost immediately, and she heard Aroska's voice distinctly: "Let me handle this!"

Heavy footsteps followed, accompanied by comm chatter and the hum of something hovering on repulsors. Pointless as it was to hide from them, Ziva ducked behind a large tree at the top of the steep riverbank and stole a peek at her pursuers. Tarbic was by far closest, perhaps twenty meters from her, and the other agents hung back a bit. They all had weapons drawn, ranging from plasma pistols to large assault rifles, and they moved steadily forward through the foliage.

Killing someone was not on the agenda today, but she realized that as much as Aroska was acting, so was she. As far as anyone else knew, he was on Dasaro's side and out for sweet revenge against the woman who had killed his brother, and she needed to play that part. Pressing her back against the tree, she drew in a deep breath and tightened her grip on her pistol. She needed to stop their advance, at least momentarily. "Make it real," she murmured.

Shifting the gun to her right hand, she leaned to her left and squeezed off a shot from behind the cover of the tree. The plasma bolt struck one of the agents squarely in the right shin just as she'd intended, and he crumpled into a heap with an agonized screech. Switching hands again, she rolled against the tree trunk and extended her left arm, firing another round that barely missed Aroska's head.

Multiple sets of feet crashed through the underbrush as the agents scrambled for cover. "Ziva!" Aroska's voice rang out. "It doesn't have to be like this! You can come peacefully with us now and we'll review your case, or I can end things right here. Take your pick!"

"You think I'm stupid, Tarbic?" she shouted back. "I know you've got orders to shoot me on sight—don't bother offering me any deals at this point."

"I just want to talk, Ziva. I'm offering you a chance to tell your side of the story and you're willing to just throw that away?"

He was doing excellent. "I thought you were on my side here, Tarbic. After everything that happened on Sardonis, are you really going to just turn around and feed me to Dasaro?"

She heard him snort. "Sardonis? You shot Soren before my eyes. Do you really think I could actually forgive you for that? The only reason I agreed to go with you to Dakiti was because I thought we could rescue Saun, and now she's dead, too."

"And you think you can change any of that by killing me?" Ziva checked the charge in her pistol. Enough energy remained for one or two more decent shots if she was lucky. That would work out perfectly...unless one of the RG agents got a little too trigger-happy. Once more, she turned to her right and fired two rounds with her left hand, the first of which struck the fallen log concealing the nearest officer. The second petered out while still in mid-air, telling her the gun was now dead.

"Look around you, Tarbic," she shouted. "The only way this will work is if you come get me, and I can guarantee that I will put all of you down before that happens."

She was legitimately startled when a leaf crunched behind her, and even more startled when the barrel of a pistol settled against the side of her head. She froze, able to see only Aroska's boot and part of his leg in her peripherals.

"Tag," he said. "You're it."

· 44 ·

ABANDONED RELAY STATION
OUTSKIRTS OF HAPHOR, HAPHEZ

For some reason that Aroska couldn't explain, the fact that he was holding Ziva at gunpoint didn't terrify him as he'd expected it to. It was probably for the best, a way to make the charade all the more convincing, but it concerned him that he was...well, *unconcerned*. He stood there just as frozen as she was, kicking himself for noticing how striking she looked with her hair down.

He nudged her with the toe of his boot. "On your feet," he growled.

Face devoid of all emotion whatsoever, she got her legs under her and rose up, maintaining constant eye contact as she did so. Just as he opened his mouth to tell her to drop her weapon, she had it up and aimed at him, a picture that had become all too familiar in the time they'd been acquainted. Keeping his own pistol steady, he extended a hand toward the RG agents, signaling for them to hold their fire.

"Now where have I seen this before?" he muttered. "You're surrounded, Ziva. What exactly do you think you're going to do?"

"What I should have done the first time." Her finger came to rest on the trigger and pulled back on it, but rather than a powerful plasma bolt, all that discharged from the pistol was a half-hearted spark that jumped a few centimeters from the barrel and melted away into the ground.

Her eyes widened for only a split second before she set her jaw and reluctantly tossed the gun down into the riverbed. She held her hands up—though the look in her eyes said she was far from sur-render—and stepped slowly backward until her heels rested on the edge of the bank. She looked away just long enough to study the positions of the other agents before sending Aroska a glare that made him feel sorry for anyone playing his part for real.

"What happens now?" she asked.

He had no idea. He'd been letting her pilot the ship, so to speak, and suddenly she'd stood up and walked out of the cockpit, leaving the controls to him. He studied her for a moment, looking for a clue, a hint, anything that would enable him to make it through the next few seconds. Out of the corner of his eye, he saw one of the two yellow hover-cams the RG had brought along, its eye recording his every movement. The second bot appeared around the tree, hovering a couple meters off the ground directly behind Ziva. He imagined those on the receiving end of the transmission were waiting intently for him to say something.

Making a mental note to ask Ziva for further improv lessons, he tightened the grip on his pistol. "Now you're going to pay...for *everything*."

She scoffed and shook her head. "Empty threats, Tarbic. If you want to show everyone what you're made of, shoot me." She tapped her abdomen and spread her arms wide, her fearlessness far from an act. "Go on, do it. You'd be doing me a favor."

Aroska clenched the muscles in his face to prevent his eyes from widening. For a brief moment, he wanted to ask if she was serious, but he realized he knew better. She stared directly into his face, and unless it was his imagination, he could almost hear her voice inside his head telling him everything would be okay.

"Can you do it?" she spat. "Or are you a coward like your boss, who has someone else do all his dirty work? Show me, Aroska. Come on, sh—"

Damn it, Ziva! He pulled the trigger.

· 45 ·

ABANDONED RELAY STATION
OUTSKIRTS OF HAPHOR, HAPHEZ

Ziva had been shot at plenty of times in her life, and hit plenty of times for that matter. But none of those occasions had ever been a double tap to the chest at point blank range. The discharge of the pistol had genuinely taken her by surprise; she'd expected Aroska to be a bit more hesitant. It was as if time had somehow been slowed by the pulling of the trigger. She'd been able to see and feel everything as it happened, right down to the muscles tightening in his hands and the change in the air as she started to fall. The first round had struck her mid-breastbone, a perfect shot to the heart if not for Jada's fiber mesh underlay. The impact had forced her backward ever so slightly, and the soft earth began to crumble under her weight. The second shot came only a split second later, hitting about a centimeter above the other. Both rounds were successfully absorbed by the vest, though she could feel and smell a bit of burnt flesh where they'd overlapped.

Upon being hit by the second bolt, the chunk of ground under her feet fell away entirely. She refrained from flailing for balance, keeping enough wits about her to realize someone who had just been shot through the heart wouldn't be capable of such a thing. The sensation of falling blindly backward was bizarre. She felt like she was floating right up until the moment her back hit the ground and the air was punched out of her lungs. Then her legs were suddenly above her head and she was tumbling, blinded by dust and unable to gather her bearings. She skidded, sharp rocks and coarse dirt tearing at her skin and clothing. The bank dropped off abruptly and she rolled over the edge, falling the remaining meter and a half into the rock-infested river bottom. Her forehead collided with a large stone, sending a burst of pain back through her skull and down her neck. Her vision began to blur and the light around her began to dim as if night was already approaching. Then it was pitch black.

· 46 ·
HSP HEADQUARTERS
NORO, HAPHEZ

Zinni felt as though she were being shot herself when Aroska's pistol discharged. Every person on the squad floor was on their feet, watching with bated breath as Ziva's body jerked and fell out of view. The live footage from the two hovercams was being broadcast over the giant viewscreen on the far side of the floor, audio and all. The sound of the pistol still echoed through her head, and it took her a moment to realize only two shots had been fired.

Both those at HSP and those in the forest outside Haphor fell completely silent, either genuinely speechless or else not wanting to say what they were thinking. Zinni placed a hand over her mouth before she could throw up all over her workstation. She cringed against the sour taste of vomit and forced it back down, unable to peel her eyes away from the screen. The lights on the squad floor had been dimmed a bit to provide everyone with a better view, so she was forced to squint into the semi-darkness to search for Skeet. He stood several meters ahead of her, having been on his way back across the floor when the bots began broadcasting, and his looming silhouette blocked a portion of the screen from her view.

The cam nearest the action floated forward, capturing the steely look on Aroska's face. The sound of his heavy breathing carried over the sound system as he holstered his weapon and ventured a look down into the riverbed, as did the bot. The picture was so clear that Zinni felt as though she was there looking down right along with him. Ziva's descent had stirred up a great cloud of dust, and as it settled, several audible gasps rose up from around the floor. The first thing that struck Zinni was how steep and high the bank actually was, making the realization that her friend had just fallen over it all the more shocking. The second was the body itself, lying face-down in the shallow standing water on the edge of the creek. One of Ziva's arms was bent grotesquely under her abdomen and her head was turned to one side; even from the bot's viewpoint, Zinni could see that the water around her face was tinted red.

The murmuring of the agents with Aroska could be heard in the background as they discussed what they had just seen and asked him what he was going to do. He said something inaudible and suddenly came into view, glancing directly into the cam's lens before lowering himself over the edge and sliding down into the riverbed. The bot descended slowly after him, watching as he straddled Ziva's body and bent down to examine it. Using two fingers, he quickly checked for a pulse then took a handful of her hair and lifted her head from the ground. The bot hovered there for several seconds, taking it all in—her eyes were closed, her jaw was slack, and diluted blood oozed from a gash on her forehead.

"She's dead," he muttered, releasing her hair and letting her head fall back into the muddy water. The bot followed him to a standing position and watched as he spoke into his communicator. "Awaiting your orders, sir."

Zinni's gaze shifted to Dasaro, who had spent the duration of the broadcast standing with crossed arms directly in front of the viewscreen. Everyone else now had eyes on him as well, waiting expectantly for some form of verdict that would somehow make the situation more final than it already was. Zinni's heart raced—something didn't feel right about the events she had just witnessed. Either Aroska had played her and Skeet to a beat and had just killed Ziva per Dasaro's orders, or the whole thing had merely been staged. She wanted desperately to believe the latter but had no idea how it could be possible.

"Dispose of the body, Lieutenant," Dasaro replied. "She will meet the same end as she would have after a week in the Haphor prison. No need for any formalities at this point."

Zinni fumed. If there was some way she could get to Haphor in the next five minutes…. After everything Ziva had done for these people, they were ready to just throw her away like a piece of trash. There had to be *someone* who would side with her and Skeet, but as she stopped and looked at the agents standing in stunned silence around her, all her hopes were dashed.

Skeet brushed by her as he stormed away, his face contorted with more anger than she had seen in a long time. She decided to let him seethe for a while, afraid any attempts to calm him at this point would only tear apart their partnership, the last thing holding them together. Besides, she figured he deserved a chance to vent after being forced to maintain composure over the past few days—she only hoped he wouldn't hurt himself or anyone else.

She stood there a while longer, eyes still glued to the screen and the image of her commanding officer lying there on the rocks. She hoped the shots had been fatal, sparing Ziva the pain of falling down the bank. The bot suddenly turned, catching sight of Aroska as he scrambled back up to the surface before it went offline. As the feed stopped and the lights came back on, the agents around her began going back to their business, leaving her standing there in stunned silence. For the first time since Ziva's arrest, she thought only of herself. And she was afraid.

· 47 ·
REILLY RESIDENCE
ARGALL, HAPHEZ

Mag Reilly had not slept a wink since encountering the mercenaries at the memorial grounds the previous evening. As tired as he was, his racing mind simply prevented his eyes from closing. At the moment, he was lying flat on his back on his mother's living room floor, staring at the patterns in the ceiling and trying to think of anything other than niobi crystals.

He was at a total loss. He'd just finished moving everything out of his parents' house—or, more accurately, everything that remained after the looters had come through. During their mad quest for power, Loric and his gang had managed to turn the citizens of Argall against each other, destroying the sense of community the town had always held. Now it was every man for himself, and in recent days it seemed the mercenaries' lack of any moral standards was beginning to rub off on those they were oppressing.

The house was empty now except for a collection of items by the front door Mag had set aside for himself. Many things had been moved three years earlier after his father's death. He'd kept an eye out for the data pad with the cave maps back then as well as since his mother's death, but after the previous night, he'd searched for it like a madman. It was his hope that the looters hadn't gotten to it first, though if they had, it would get Loric off his back. *No*, now there he was looking out only for himself and becoming one of the very people he hated. Even *hate* was such a strong word—he liked to think there was still hope for the city and that he could eventually help build it back up, but right now, he couldn't help but be pessimistic.

If the data pad wasn't on the property, he had no idea where else to look. If the data pad *was* on the property, he had no idea where else to look. He wasn't even sure what to do with it if he found it. Conducting a treasure hunt would be nearly impossible to do in secret, and even if he managed to find the crystals, he didn't know what he would do with them. He knew the basics about harvesting but he was no farmer, not to mention there was no way he could care for that many blood crystals on his own. And with all the corruption around him, he wasn't about to share his knowledge with anyone else.

Feeling useless, Mag sat up and closed his eyes until his head quit spinning. The thought crossed his mind that he had a whole week to find the map, and then he kicked himself for even thinking in such terms. There was no way he would surrender it to Loric, though he didn't know what to do with it himself. And so continued the endless cycle of thoughts as he desperately tried to decide what to do.

He hauled himself to his feet and took a moment to gaze at the empty floor around him. He'd grown up in this house. Been born in it, for that matter. The current predicament broke his heart, though the thought that currently dominated his mind was that he should be familiar with any of his father's hiding places after living there for so long. He'd checked his parents' strongbox, their bank account, even the secret compartment behind the lavatory mirror, all to no avail. Even if the data pad was still intact, there was a good chance at least some of its contents had been corrupted after sitting idle for three years.

Mag hated to acknowledge the fact that Loric was right. People were going to die whether he found the map or not. It all felt like a whirlwind of a dream, something out of one of the adventure vids he'd watched as a young man. In those tales, the heroes always managed to make the right decision or find a back door, but now that the story had come to life, he felt like anything but a hero. No, Mag Reilly of Argall had the great misfortune of being responsible for the death of an entire culture, all because he was related to someone who had once tried to do the right thing. Experiencing the outcome of that firsthand made him feel motivated to do anything *but* the right thing.

With a sigh, he went to his little pile and gathered up the items to take to his car. Regardless of what he decided to do with it, he was going to find that data pad if it killed him.

· 48 ·
City Center
Haphor, Haphez

Kade knew something wasn't right the instant he rounded the corner. He paused for a moment mid-stride, studying the scene before him with a sinking feeling in the pit of his stomach. Half a city block had been cordoned off by HSP, with his destination in the midst of the madness. Due to the numerous police vehicles and the mob of people congregated outside the barricade, he was unable to tell what all the commotion was about. The fact that it was all happening directly in front of the place he was going unnerved him.

His attempt to reach Eason Fromm the night before had been unsuccessful, but the good doctor had kindly returned his call early that morning and had offered to meet him at a place of his choosing. The idea of speaking with Fromm over comm made Kade nervous; after everything that had already happened, it would be far too easy for someone to intercept the transmission, resulting in him being either fired or killed depending on who it was. He hadn't taken the time to share his suspicions with Fromm in great detail, but he had emphasized the need for some measure of secrecy, and the coroner had agreed. They were scheduled to meet at lunch hour at the small café where Kade had spent the previous afternoon killing time before heading home for the day. Toting his portable computer and all the information he had on Spence's death, he'd been headed to the meeting with a spring in his step. Now he was frozen stiff, unable to help but fear his plans had been foiled.

196

As he stood there observing what he could, he felt the familiar surge of adrenaline rushing into his veins, the same rush he had experienced on the bridge at Tachi's palace and in the med center as he'd pursued Spence's murderers. He was beginning to recognize a pattern—if the other occasions had been prompted by unfortunate events, this one probably wasn't any different. He dreaded to think of what else could possibly go wrong. The fact that anything else *could* go wrong was inconceivable.

Kade began to venture forward step by step, straining to see anything he could while remaining as subtle as possible. He could make out the flashing lights of a medical transport over the heads of the crowd, telling him that someone had either been killed or seriously injured. Judging by the amount of time it seemed the emergency personnel had been at the scene, the former was more likely.

A man in an HSP street patrol uniform emerged from behind the barricade and began directing people back onto the walkway. He looked exhausted, as did every other agent Kade had seen in the past few days. "I'm going to need everyone to step back," he said, waving his hands. "Thank you, folks, just keep moving."

The majority of the crowd began to reluctantly comply, but when Kade didn't move, the officer veered toward him. Standing there in street clothes with his satchel over his shoulder, he looked and felt like any other curious onlooker.

"That goes for you, too, kid," the agent called, grabbing his attention. "We need everyone to move out of this area."

Snapping out of the mild daze he'd been in, Kade drew out his HSP credentials and offered them to the man. "I'm RG," he said. "What happened here?"

Unless it was his imagination, the older officer looked relieved. Without bothering to study the badge, he nodded and shook Kade's hand. "Head-on collision between two groundcars," he replied. "I don't know what the hell happened."

"Initial premise?"

The man shrugged and looked back toward the crash site, lifting a hand to shield his eyes from the sun. "As near as I can tell, one of the cars crossed into the oncoming lane, traveling well above the speed limit. The pilot was an old bot—thing must have been malfunctioning. We've got techs working on what's left of it and we'll try to locate its owner or programmer. The pilot of the other vehicle was DOA. He was actually employed by HSP, a medical examiner named Eason Fromm."

Kade wasn't sure whether he should break down in tears or laugh at this almost comical string of bad luck. No, now with the death of Fromm, he was convinced this went far beyond bad luck. He was being targeted, being toyed with. He was on the trail of someone somewhere, and that person was doing everything in their power to throw him off. Maybe it was Payvan. Maybe she really was innocent, and it was the people who had set her up. Whoever it was, Kade saw that the further he dug, the more trouble he was getting himself into.

He tried to swallow as he stared ahead at the scene, unable to formulate any words other than a choked 'thank you.' The officer watched him quizzically for several seconds before turning his attention back to the loitering bystanders. With trembling fingers, Kade adjusted the strap on his satchel and turned back the way he had come.

· 49 ·

ABANDONED RELAY STATION
OUTSKIRTS OF HAPHOR, HAPHEZ

T he first thing she was aware of was the hard surface pressing against her head, and then came the throbbing pain. The only sounds she could hear were a muffled crackling and her own pulse, but as she gained consciousness, she realized she was in fact listening to running water. One side of her face and the entire front of her body were wet—maybe there was a connection.

Ziva's heavy eyelids wouldn't budge from their closed positions, but she was content to leave them be. She smelled blood somewhere nearby, but whether it was hers or someone else's, she wasn't sure. She was alive, that much was clear. Whether she would stay that way in the next few minutes remained in question.

As she grew more and more cognizant, she became aware of a new pain: a dull pang in her chest that came and went with her heartbeat. From what she could tell, it was some sort of internal bruising, and she lay there for several more moments to give her brain a chance to catch up.

Her right eye was the first to open, the lid lifting itself involuntarily while she was still focused on her chest pain. The image was blurry and her eye began to sting immediately, and she realized it was partially submerged in water. Startled, she raised her head and closed the eye again, wincing against the fire that shot through her neck and down her spine. She realized she was lying flat on her stomach; the ground felt like it was tilting beneath her as her mind attempted to reorient itself and take in the rush of new information her senses were suddenly picking up. Little by little, the events of the previous hours crept back into her memory, and she recalled being shot by Aroska before falling over the edge of the riverbank.

She was in Haphor, at the relay station outside of Haphor to be exact. The water in which she was lying was the little river she had scoped out as a potential escape route, and in the end, it had served that exact purpose, just not quite in the way she'd imagined. The pain she felt was from the impact of the two plasma shots, which, to Aroska's credit, had been flawlessly placed. She wondered for the first time where he was, what had become of the other agents, and whether it was safe for her to get up.

Ziva realized she was shivering, having spent the galaxy only knew how long lying in the cool water, but she did her best to remain still and listen. Other than the trickling water, some forest birds, and distant traffic, there wasn't a sound to be heard in the immediate vicinity. Groaning, she managed to roll onto her side and stretch out her arm, which had cramped up from being pinned under her body. The place where she'd been lying was slick with mud and she had a thin layer of the stuff plastered over her face. Heaving herself as best she could into a sitting position, she scraped away some of the muck, and when she withdrew her hand, she found it coated in tacky, half-dried blood. She scrubbed it away with a handful of water and found its source to be a gash just below her hairline, also the epicenter of the pain still stabbing through her head.

Not wishing to remain cold and wet any longer, she drew her legs in and rose stiffly to her feet, teetering there for a moment as her surroundings spun in a slow circle. The bank where she had fallen was steep and devoid of any solid handholds, so she craned her sore neck and looked up and down the riverbed in search of an alternate means of climbing out. The solution presented itself in the form of a tree growing sideways out of the bank several meters downstream.

Head still spinning, she struggled for balance as she made her way over the rocks. She couldn't remember the last time she'd felt so disoriented, other than when she'd been drugged by the Cobian pirates. At least then it hadn't felt like someone was bashing a hammer repeatedly against her skull. With a little caura treatment and some painkillers, she would be feeling better soon enough, though she imagined she would be sore for the next couple of days.

She found the little tree to be wobbly but firmly grounded in the side of the bank. Establishing a solid grip on its narrow trunk, she began to walk up the steep incline, reaching for protruding tree roots as she went. As she neared the top, a new scent reached her nostrils: wood smoke. Taking hold of one last root, she lifted her head above the edge of the bank and took a cautious look around. She saw no signs of life, but the remains of what appeared to be a funeral pyre smoldered in the clearing below the relay station. For a moment, she wondered if she was actually awake or if it was all a dream. Nothing made any sense at all, but then again, nothing that had happened in the past four days had made much sense, either.

Her whole body complaining, Ziva scrambled up over the edge and rolled, hesitating for a moment before standing up. Everything remained still, so she began to cautiously approach the shack, stopping every few meters to listen further. She used the trees for cover until she reached the clearing, where she then darted out and ducked behind the remnants of the pyre. It was a curious thing—she could see the embers and smell the accelerant, but there was no sign of a body or anything else that had been burned. Judging by what was left of the pyre, though, she guessed she had been unconscious for at least an hour. If all had gone according to plan, she was now free to seek passage to Chaiavis.

All the cars were gone and there was no sign of her stolen bike. Satisfied there was no one around and hoping the infrared probes had dispersed by now, she stood up and began taking small strides toward the little building, eyes focused on the door and ears devoted to the sounds around her. Her boots were wet and sloshed as she walked, but other than the soft squishing, she was barely able to hear her own footsteps. If anyone was watching from inside the structure, the stealthy approach was worthless, but she imagined if anyone were around, they would have been hovering around the bank or trying to pull her out.

As she came within a few meters of the shack, Ziva watched her own shadow rise up against the front door. She stopped upon reaching it and placed her ear to it, still unable to hear any sounds coming from within. Taking one last look at the scene behind her, she hit the door controls and ducked inside.

She paused and blinked several times as she adjusted to the shadows, then turned toward the cabinet where she'd stashed her things. The sight of Aroska sitting there on the floor startled her out of her skin.

"*Sheyss*, Tarbic," she muttered, relieved that it was him and not one of the other agents.

He had one knee up and was leaning up against the wall, looking quite relaxed. He even raised his head as if he'd been napping. "Good, you're still in one piece," he said with a lazy smile as he got to his feet. "After a fall like that, I'm surprised you can even walk."

Ziva scraped a handful of mud from her shoulder and flung it away. "No kidding," she muttered. "I appreciate you coming back to see if I was okay."

He raised his hands in defense. "Hey, I checked every so often, and you should be grateful that I moved your head so you wouldn't *drown*."

"Fine, I'm grateful," she said. "Can we assume they bought it?"

"Oh, they bought it. I think Dasaro was too caught up in himself to bother looking too closely, but it was convincing nonetheless. I tracked you down, shot you, then I burned your body out there on that pyre."

Ziva noticed her backpack waiting on the floor beside the place he'd been sitting. She remembered her change of clothes and was overcome with so much relief that she shivered. "What became of the agents with you?" she asked, rummaging through the bag and picking out the clean shirt and pants.

"Dasaro himself called them off," Aroska answered with a shrug. "He said he'd leave the disposal of your body up to someone 'more trustworthy'."

She laid the garments out over the cabinet shelves and faced away from him. "What I really want to know is—turn around—how you shot me."

Aroska chuckled. "I pulled the trigger," he said, more of a question than a statement.

"You know what I mean," she scoffed, slipping out of her boots and exchanging her soaked pants for the new ones. "You did a hell of a job making it realistic, and I feel like there was more to it than the simple fact that I told you to." She peeled out of the shirt, opting to remove the soaked underlay as well, and tugged the other on. When she turned around, she was pleasantly surprised to find that Aroska had respectfully obeyed and looked away. Maybe there was hope for him yet.

"If you really want to know, I thought about Soren."

She hesitated, glad he still had his back to her and couldn't see the shadow she felt pass over her face. She shook it away and busied herself with tying her hair up into a new ponytail.

He stole a peek back at her. When he saw she was finished changing, he turned around and cleared his throat, his face a bit red. "I know we agreed to try to leave it in the past, but—"

"Well, under the circumstances, I thank you for it." Ziva stuffed the soiled clothing into her pack and lifted it to her shoulder. "But next time I think it's my turn to shoot you."

Aroska nodded. "Fair enough. Just make sure I've got an underlay, though—I have to admit you had me going there for a minute."

"As was expected. Now, where's the riding suit and the rest of my stuff? I want to get out of here in a timely manner, and the fact that I'm dead doesn't mean I can afford to be any less cautious."

"I already put it in the car around back," Aroska replied. "Unfortunately, we have to go back to Headquarters before we can leave. Dasaro is expecting me for a debriefing this afternoon, and believe it or not, I've got a payment coming."

Ziva raised an eyebrow. "Well, I guess you're a regular old bounty hunter now, aren't you."

"You said it yourself—maybe I'm developing a taste for blood," Aroska said, smiling. "So, what's the deal with your family? They're a… lively bunch."

"Do not even go there."

"Yeah, yeah, yeah." He gestured toward the door. "Now, I don't know about you, but I'm ready to blow out of here and dig up some dirt."

50

ROYAL GUARD HEADQUARTERS
HAPHOR, HAPHEZ

L uko Zona watched the happenings down on the squad floor from his usual place near the top of the stairs, hands clasped behind his back. There was something about watching his subordinates hard at work that helped him think—it was almost like living vicariously through them, feeding off their creative energy. At the moment, however, it didn't seem to be helping. He had hit a wall and had spent the majority of the afternoon wandering around the building hoping to clear his head.

Something had changed there in the RG offices since the news of Ziva Payvan's death, almost as if a cloud of stagnant air had been lifted and everyone could finally breathe. It had been the topic of many a conversation over the past couple of hours. His men had returned, having witnessed the entire incident under the command of the Noro office's Lieutenant Aroska Tarbic, and had already been debriefed. Nothing about their relation of events seemed out of place—it was the smaller background details that bothered Zona.

The fact that Payvan was even in town had been brought to his attention when Captain Diago Dasaro contacted him and informed him Tarbic had spotted her just outside the Royal City. The first thing Zona had considered odd was the captain's request for the hovercams. He understood Dasaro's desire for proof of death, especially since the man himself remained in Noro, but there'd been plenty of other agents at the scene who could provide adequate testimonies. There had been something in his tone of voice, something obsessive, desperate, that Zona didn't like. With a specialization in behavioral analysis, he wondered if the man had ulterior motives for wanting the bots, whether they were related to the case or not.

The second thing that struck him as odd was Dasaro's order to have Payvan killed on sight. Yes, she had murdered Officer Tachi, and yes, she had escaped HSP custody, but why not just escort her to the Haphor Facility until her hearing as originally planned? Perhaps Dasaro was merely bitter about losing a high-profile prisoner and didn't want to risk it happening again.

Out of curiosity, Zona had brought up Lieutenant Tarbic's file, puzzled as to Dasaro's reasons for demanding that he lead the strike team. The man's record was spotless, and it even appeared that he'd briefly been allied with Payvan two months earlier, with the exception of a vague altercation at the end of that stint. Why he'd been chosen to kill her, Zona could only guess.

Then there was Eason Fromm, the coroner who had filed the autopsy report on Agent Spence. The news of the fatal car collision had come trickling into the office amid the chaos of trying to assemble a team to accompany Tarbic to the relay station. At first, it hadn't even registered that it could have anything to do with Kade or the rest of the case, but once the dust stirred up by Dasaro had settled and Zona had gotten a chance to read over the reports, his imagination had begun to run wild. It wasn't unheard of for bots to malfunction, and people were killed in vehicle crashes every day, certainly, but under the circumstances, he felt entirely uncomfortable dismissing it as a mere coincidence. If by some miracle Shevin was right about the autopsy report being altered, it meant someone somewhere was hiding something. Only Fromm would have been able to confirm the real cause of death. Zona sighed; there was just something *off* about the whole thing, exactly as Shevin kept insisting.

If Spence had been murdered, why? Had Payvan somehow done it upon realizing he'd survived the crash? It was unlikely, especially if she'd really saved his life like he claimed. If he was vouching for Payvan, then perhaps one of her enemies wanted to silence him. Dasaro was certainly her enemy, though the term was merely relative to the situation....

Zona knew it wasn't his place to go about secretly investigating a superior officer, but Agent Shevin's theory that something else was going on seemed more and more relevant as time went on. He felt sorry for the kid and had already considered inviting him back to work more than once. He'd refrained from doing so, however, wary of being accused of playing favorites. Regional Director Zinck wouldn't be thrilled with the idea, not after having heard the rumors about Shevin's outbursts and ridiculous claims. The young man could use some time to recuperate anyway, Zona had decided, even though the whole mess with Payvan seemed to be over.

The problem with voicing his opinions was the same reason he had wanted Kade to keep quiet: HSP's powers-that-be—now determined to be this Captain Dasaro—seemed bent on conducting the hunt and investigation without question. He imagined it wouldn't hurt to do a little digging now that Payvan was dead, though if Dasaro really was up to something, there was no telling what he might do in retaliation.

Torn between staying on task and uncovering the truth, Zona concluded that there was no harm in at least looking into Dasaro and Payvan's collective past. If there was some reason he wanted her dead, some reason he'd been so obsessed with hunting her down—other than from a law enforcement standpoint, of course—maybe it would shed a little light on things and help put Zona's mind at ease.

With a sigh, he pried himself away from his observation post and began to wander back toward his office, immediately feeling as though his brain had just been unplugged from an energy source. After a couple hours of solitude and quiet, maybe he'd be able to come up with something, and maybe, just maybe, he would ask Shevin to come back to work tomorrow.

His assistant looked up from her workstation outside his door as he neared. He acknowledged her with a dip of his head as he opened the office. "Lora, please hold my calls and see to it that I am not disturbed until further notice."

"Sure," she said. "By the way, Director Zinck had all the information from the car crash sent over, as well as everything the field office has on the faulty bot. I transferred all of it into your system."

"Thank you, Lora, I appreciate it." Zona continued into the office and took a moment to adjust to the silence after having spent a good chunk of time listening to the hustle and bustle of the squad floor. His comm system's message indicator blinked red, but he ignored it as he made himself comfortable in his chair. Right now, he had some research to do.

51

NORELL PUB AND EATERY
HAPHOR, HAPHEZ

K ade glanced up for the umpteenth time when another customer entered the little bar he was holed up in. He wasn't sure
what he'd do if someone hostile actually came in, or how he'd
tell if they *were* hostile for that matter. He allowed his gaze to shift back
down to his computer screen, though he continued to steal occasional
glances over the top of it. The bar was small, but the layout was such
that he'd successfully positioned himself so he could see anyone coming through the front door but not be immediately seen by them. It was
comfortable and quiet for the most part, a good place to get some work
done.

The problem was that he wasn't getting any work done. With such
limited access to the HSP databases while he was away from the office,
he was unable to turn up any useful results as he searched for information on the most recent developments. By this time, the whole planet
was aware that Ziva Payvan had been killed—the viewscreen there in
the bar had been streaming live news reports for the past hour or so.
Still, the information was vague, and without the ability to use all of
HSP's resources at will, he was left to watch the news like all the civilians around him.

Kade sighed and powered the computer down, deciding to give
his eyes a rest. He wanted to avoid breaking the rules—his career was
on the line as it was—but he knew if he wanted answers, he would have
to resort to more desperate measures. The information he needed could

no doubt be found in the RG records, but without full access, he wasn't sure how much good checking there would do. There was always the option of hacking someone else's system, and he was confident in his abilities to do so. Out of everyone in the office, Zona would have the most access….

"Don't be ridiculous," he muttered to himself, drawing the attention of a nearby customer. People already thought he was crazy—talking to himself wasn't going to help. He reactivated the computer screen, at least pretending to be busy.

Several minutes passed as he tried to convince himself there was no way in hell he was going to hack Zona's computer. The harder he tried, however, the more appealing the idea seemed. Never in his life had he imagined himself doing such a thing, but here he was now practically chomping at the bit. It would take a little time—Zona's access level was equivalent to that of a special ops agent from the mother agency—but Kade's work had required him to hack into high-security systems on several occasions in recent months, so he felt up to the task.

The job could be done remotely from right there at the bar, but the thought of accessing Zona's computer from anywhere but Headquarters worried him. An access of that clearance level would immediately raise suspicion, and Zona would be able to verify that it hadn't been him. Assuming Kade's access key hadn't been deactivated, it would be possible to do his work from within the RG field office itself, though he would have to wait a few more hours before the office was vacant. Zona would still be able to confirm that he hadn't been there, but people were less likely to even start questioning a login if it had been from his own terminal.

Brimming with more resolve than he'd had in a long time, Kade shut down the computer for good and stuffed it into his satchel. He found his credentials and access key and, making sure they were both accessible, got up and moved toward the door. There were plenty of little places near Headquarters where he could hide out, and then it would just be a matter of waiting.

· 52 ·
HSP Headquarters
Noro, Haphez

B y the time Aroska exited the elevator and stepped out onto the squad floor, the sun was already beginning to drop down toward the hills. The trip back from Haphor had gone smoothly enough, and after leaving Ziva at his house to make departure plans, he had rushed back to HSP in hopes that the debriefing wouldn't take long. He had to remind himself he was still acting at this point; it was easy enough to remember he had supposedly shot and killed Ziva, but the fact that he was still on Dasaro's side was what needed to be put into practice.

He hesitated after only a few strides, unnerved by the sudden silence his presence seemed to have incited. All eyes were on him as he shuffled forward, almost sick to his stomach with guilt. He kept his head down and his focus forward, but as he walked, a peculiar sound reached his ears: applause. Yes, several people around the room had risen to their feet and were beginning to clap, looking on with approving gazes. Those who weren't clapping seemed to be ignoring him at all costs—they either didn't approve of what he'd done, or they didn't care.

Aroska felt his face flush and picked up his pace, eager to get out. He stole quick glances out into the clusters of workstations, hoping Skeet and Zinni weren't watching but knowing they were. Upon hearing the commotion, Dasaro emerged from his office and began to applaud in sync with everyone else. Embarrassed and angry, Aroska rushed forward and didn't stop until he was safely inside the captain's office.

"What I did doesn't make me a hero," he growled, shutting the door after Dasaro entered.

"Don't be ridiculous, Tarbic," the captain said. "You have achieved an incredible feat today. The fact that you were able to kill Payvan when no one else could just goes to show you how many mistakes she made when she allowed you to get close to her before."

Aroska shook his head. "Still, I'd appreciate it if you didn't make a big deal about it. I just killed a fellow agent, one who has saved my life before." He sighed. "But it's over now."

"Yes, it is," Dasaro said, face deadpan. "Keep up the good work, and you'll be full-time spec ops in no time."

"Maybe."

The captain turned to his desk and picked up a data pad, glancing over it before handing it over to Aroska. "Very well, Lieutenant. Here is the verification for your payment, as promised. Now, I don't know about you, but I think I've seen enough." He gestured toward the viewscreen on the wall where the recording from the hovercam played on a loop. "You've done well—let's forget about the debriefing for today, shall we?"

"Sounds good to me," Aroska replied, not quite knowing what to make of it. He didn't mind getting away early, but the captain's manner seemed rushed, and it made him feel uneasy. "Am I done here?"

"You're dismissed, Lieutenant. There's one last little mess to clean up, but we'll take care of that here."

"Thank you, sir," Aroska said. He dipped his head and spun to leave, narrowly avoiding a collision with Nejdra as she stormed into the office. He skirted around her and began to walk away, but he stopped short when he heard the two captains start to converse.

"There's still no sign of him," the woman was saying. "The more time the search takes, the more time he has to find something and start talking about it."

"You're a special ops captain, Nejdra," Dasaro said. "He's a rookie RG agent. Do the math."

Immensely curious, Aroska fished his comm out and held it to his ear, giving the impression to any onlookers that he was simply making a call. He kept his back to the door and his ears open, both confused and worried by what he was hearing.

"I know, but he knows what went down at the med center—don't ask me how. Ever since then, he's been looking into the evidence, almost like he's playing the role of Payvan's grace period sponsor. She may be dead, but it won't do us any good if someone else starts digging too deep."

"Calm yourself, Nejdra. He's a smart young man, but just like Payvan, he can't hide forever. Look for a traceable means of communication and send a team out to pick him up—use our people. You'll find him. You'd *better* find him."

Aroska lowered his communicator and continued moving, fearful that one or both of them would suddenly come out and find him lingering there. He had no idea who they were talking about, but he had a feeling this young agent was in grave danger. Everyone on the squad floor seemed to have lost interest in him, so he picked the comm back up and entered the code Ziva had used to contact him the day before.

"We've got a problem," he said when they had connected. He ducked into the elevator and waited for the door to shut before relaying to her what he'd just heard. "I don't know who this guy is, but it sounds like we should do something about it. Besides, he may have information that could benefit us."

"I think I know who it is," Ziva said, "and if I'm right, I'll find him in Haphor. I'll have to get back there before that team does."

"My neighbors are gone, but they have an old car in their garage. It's not fast, but it'll get you there."

He could hear her mobilizing even as they spoke. "Got it. I'll keep you posted."

· 53 ·

SHEVIN RESIDENCE

HAPHOR, HAPHEZ

Z iva pulled the old car up to the Shevin household in a great cloud of dust and killed the lights, throwing the street into darkness. The area was primarily residential, but the structures on either side of their little house appeared to be unoccupied. No one stirred as she jumped out of the car, pistol drawn, and strode up to the front door without hesitation.

As she'd listened to Aroska's description of the conversation he'd overheard, she had understood immediately that the captains were talking about Kade Shevin. She hadn't heard a peep from him since she'd watched the news report after being arrested, but based on his behavior during the press conference, the things he was doing and saying came as no surprise. Agent Shevin was yet another victim of whoever had started this whole mess, no doubt kept alive for the sole purpose of testifying about what he had supposedly seen at Tachi's gala...testifying against *her*. Aroska was right in that he could provide them with crucial information, especially if he really had been snooping around on his own as Dasaro said. Repeating the eight-hour round trip back to Haphor after less than an hour in Noro hadn't been the least bit appealing, but here she was now, and she wasn't leaving without Shevin.

She reached the front door and listened carefully for a moment before pounding her fist against it and pressing the buzzer. The house was already dark, meaning one of two things: she was too late and

Dasaro's team had already come and gone, or the family had simply gone to bed. It was late, but she imagined the young couple might still be awake at this hour. She remained silent for several more seconds before giving the door another couple of solid raps.

Finally, a set of very soft footsteps could be heard just inside, and there was a short pause before a woman's voice spoke over the intercom: "Who is it?"

"HSP, ma'am," Ziva replied, stepping off to one side and readying the pistol. "Open up, please."

There was another brief hesitation before the lock disengaged and the door slid open ever so slightly. The woman peered out at her, silhouetted against a dim light she'd no doubt turned on upon coming to answer the door. She squinted out into the dark for a moment before her eyes widened and her hand flew to the controls.

Ziva's arm shot out into the open doorway, startling the woman to the point that she took a step back. Forcing the door open a suitable distance, she slipped through and immediately shut it behind her. The other woman remained frozen in place, tears welling up in her eyes as she lifted her trembling hands.

"Please," she sobbed, "I have a baby girl—"

"Quiet!" Ziva snapped, holstering her weapon. "I'm looking for Kade. Who are you?"

"His wife, Veya. Please, you don't have to do this."

"Listen to me, Veya," Ziva said, lifting her own hands. "Your husband is in considerable danger, and I need to find him before some very bad people do."

Veya took a step backward. "And why should I believe you? I watched you die! Everyone's seen the footage!"

"Trust me, if I wanted to hurt Kade, he would already be dead, and I wouldn't be talking to you now. There are people hunting him who have strict orders to kill him, and I can guarantee this will be the first place they look. You're putting yourself and your child in jeopardy by not helping me out here. These same people are...*were* hunting me. I can help Kade get away, but you have to tell me where he is."

The gears were clearly turning in Veya's mind even as she shook her head. She stopped moving backward, but she was still trembling and made no move to respond.

"You've got a couple of choices," Ziva said. "You can wait around until these guys show up and kill you, or you can take a chance and assume I'm telling you the truth. Only one of those options is going to save your husband."

"I don't know where Kade is," Veya replied as tears continued streaming down her face. "He's been off work for hours. He could have stayed late, he could be out with friends—" She paused as though she were beginning to acknowledge the merit of Ziva's argument but still didn't want to admit to it. "I swear I haven't heard from him since this morning!"

"Do you have a way to contact him?"

Hands wringing, Veya went to a shelf and produced a small data pad, extending it to Ziva. "I'm not supposed to contact him on that while he's at work."

Ziva entered the code into her own data pad, initiated a trace, then took Veya's from her. "Listen to me, okay?" she said, scribbling with the stylus. "These people are going to be here any minute. I'm not saying you have to, but if you're smart, you'll take your daughter and go to this address in Noro. Two people named Marshay and Ryon will meet you there. Tell them the bird is still in flight and they'll know what to do—they'll be able to keep you safe until all of this is over."

"I can't do that," Veya said, shaking her head. "I can't just leave Kade like this."

Ziva shrugged. "That's your choice, but like I said, you'll go if you're smart. I'll be able to take care of Kade, and believe it or not, he'll be able to help me, too."

"Okay," the young woman whispered, clutching the pad.

"Most importantly, it's imperative that you don't speak to anyone but Marshay and Ryon, and that you don't tell anyone else I was here. I promise this will all be over soon."

· 54 ·

ROYAL GUARD HEADQUARTERS
HAPHOR, HAPHEZ

A metallic grinding somewhere in the building jarred Kade from his thoughts. He sat up from where he'd been resting his head on Zona's desk and listened. The last of the Royal Guard agents had left nearly an hour before, leaving him the sole occupant of the division's field office. It was well into the night, if not early morning, and the fact that someone else was entering both relieved and unnerved him.

Curious, he worked his way into the security network on the terminal and accessed the surveillance feed for the lobby of the building. His screen flickered for a moment then settled on a blank image that ranged from dark gray in the top corner to a lighter blue shade on the opposite edge. The timestamp blinked faithfully in the bottom left of the screen, telling him the feed was still live. He stared at it in puzzlement, trying to wrap his head around what exactly he was seeing. Then something moved in the lighter area—a shadow, cast by someone off screen. He swallowed and sat bolt upright. Someone had moved the cam to face the wall.

Alarmed, he took up his pistol and went to the door of Zona's office. The hall outside and the rest of the second floor seemed quiet enough, so he ventured out and headed for the bridge that passed over the work floor below. The sounds of multiple muffled voices reached his ears as he neared. They belonged to three different people, all men, though none of them sounded familiar. Still, he had never been there at this time of night and wasn't sure who frequented the office during these hours. He crouched and allowed himself a peek down onto the floor.

The three men were working their way through the maze of cubicles, carrying rifles with small spotlights mounted on the barrels. With these, they illuminated and searched every workstation they passed, whispering among themselves as they went. They wore masks and were dressed entirely in black. All three were huge.

Kade felt his heart jump into his throat and understood immediately that he was the one they were searching for, whatever the reason may be. He leaped to his feet and took off back toward the office, pumping his quivering legs as fast as they would go. The computer was exactly as he had left it, so he fumbled with his memory stick, dropped it, hit his head on the desk while recovering it, and finally managed to jam it into the proper socket. He'd found plenty of potentially useful files, but Zona had sealed them all with an encryption that would have to be dealt with later. The narrow green bar that indicated transfer progress could not have moved slower as he stood there sweating.

Impatient, he went back to the door and risked another look out into the hallway. The beams of the spotlights were visible from where he stood, playing on the walls as the men made their way up the stairs. None of them were talking now, aware Kade was on the floor if he were still in the building. Using the elevator was out of the question—he was trapped unless he could make it past them to the stairwell.

The computer emitted a triumphant beep that sent a massive chill down his spine. He ducked back into the room just as one of the lights shone on the spot where he'd been standing. TRANSFER COMPLETE flashed across the screen as he yanked the memory stick out and gathered up his satchel. He stood there for a moment, looking wildly about for a secondary means of escape. The answer presented itself in the form of a door leading into the adjoining office. He slipped through, leaving it slightly ajar to prevent any more noise than he'd already made. Footsteps entered Zona's office, and he could hear the intruders whispering among themselves as they looked over what he'd been reading on the computer.

Satisfied that they would be occupied for at least a few more precious seconds, Kade went to the office's main entry and stole into the hall. He flattened himself against the wall and did his best to still his shaking hands and slow his breathing. Zona's desk was positioned so that even if they did see him making a break for it, he would be well past the door before they could react. Mustering his strength and holding his bag against his side to keep it from flopping about, he took off for the stairwell without so much as a glance behind him.

Surprised shouts from the intruders came sooner than he would have liked. Kade slid to a stop and all but dove headfirst down the stairs, gripping the railing to keep from all-out tumbling. He managed to get his feet under him and jump down the last few steps, making a sharp turn at the bottom and darting into the building's conference room. The sound of his own heart pounding was so deafening he was barely able to hear his pursuers descending the steps just outside.

Despite having to navigate his way through the maze of workstations on the squad floor, the front door was still the nearest exit and Kade knew he would have to create another diversion in order to reach it. He shrank back behind a large cabinet and waited as the three men searched the immediate area around the stairs and shone their lights into the darkened conference room. For a moment, he considered trying to call for help. His communicator sat heavy in his jacket pocket, so he slipped his hand inside and held the device in his sweaty palm. Who could he call that would arrive soon enough to help, and how would he explain what he was even doing there and why he had broken into his commanding officer's terminal? He shuddered as it struck him that he was completely on his own. He stood there shaking, searching his racing mind for the comm extension for his own workstation.

The men began to move away from the stairs and back out onto the squad floor, so Kade followed them as far as the conference room door and watched them from the shadows. His desk was on the far side of the large room, but some of the nearer ones were only about ten meters away. If there was some way to reach one of them without being seen....

He hit the button on his communicator and held his breath until the transmission connected. The three intruders whirled at the sound of his comm system beeping, just as he had hoped. They advanced with their rifles trained on his desk and Kade dashed out behind them, clutching his bag and the precious memory stick. He hunkered down behind the nearest workstation and permitted himself a few deep breaths. He wasn't quite sure how he would reach the front door from here, and he was beginning to regret such hasty actions. Turning silently, he lifted his head until his eyes broke the plane of the desk. The men were still across the room examining his comm system.

A gloved hand clamped down over Kade's mouth and an arm pulled him back against a solid body wearing a thick riding suit. Part of him was immediately frozen with terror and another part was thankful that a third party had arrived—either way, he refrained from thrashing about. He knew better than to scream for fear of attracting the attention of his hunters, so he resorted to holding his breath for fear that the newcomer was trying to drug him. He remained still, held fast with the mysterious person's free arm across his chest. That arm slowly released its grip, though the other hand remained over his mouth, and he looked up into the face of his captor for the first time.

That face was hidden behind the heavily tinted visor of a helmet that matched the rest of the person's ensemble. It appeared they were looking down at him, though he couldn't be sure, and they held a single finger up to the place on the helmet where their mouth might be within. The hand over Kade's mouth slowly slid away and went to the person's hip, where a pistol waited in its holster.

He watched as they drew the weapon and signaled for him to begin retreating. He glanced into the darkness of the hallway, which was a bit farther than the conference room. From there, it was a straight shot to the secondary stairwell that led to the lower-level parking bay. But as much as it was for him, it was also a straight shot for his pursuers—in every sense of the phrase—should they catch on and come after him. That particular hallway offered no form of cover, one of several reasons he had originally opted to escape through the front.

The men were on the move again, proceeding forward and away from his current position. He heeded the mysterious figure's instructions and scrambled away, but halfway between the desk and the hall, his communicator let out a warning *ding* to remind him he was still connected to the system at his workstation. Kade's stomach wrenched itself into a knot and he threw himself to the floor as all three spotlights converged on him. He slid and rolled to safety behind the wall, narrowly avoiding the sizzling white plasma bolts that pierced the shadows.

Angry shouts were suddenly replaced with screams of surprise and pain when a fourth pistol with a slightly different tone joined the skirmish. Kade heard a body hit the floor as he ducked away from the bolts zinging by just centimeters from his head. Shots were still being fired when his new companion appeared from nowhere and took off down the hall, dragging him by the arm. He stumbled along, still gripping his bag, and the two of them burst into the back stairwell.

There was something about this shadowy figure's presence that brought a strange comfort to Kade—at least it appeared they weren't there to do him harm. He watched the person creep silently down the stairs ahead of him, crouching and listening with the pistol up and ready. Cool air from the parking bay drifted up and dried the sweat on his face. He shivered, more from nerves than the cold, and pulled up behind the mysterious rider where they had stopped just inside the garage.

A moment of eerie silence preceded a hail of gunfire originating from behind a car on the far side of the massive bay. Kade and his rescuer ducked away, diving for cover in opposite directions. He rolled and rose up on his knees, recovering the pistol from his bag and firing from behind the cover of a parked hoverbike. The other person did the same, using the small security booth as a shield. Kade couldn't help but notice the skill and precision in their manner of fighting, and he was very glad they had arrived when they did.

There was a lull in enemy fire as plasma cells were swapped, and the suited figure took off at a dead run toward the first bank of HSP-issue armored groundcars. Kade followed as closely as he could, looking wildly about for the shooter as he dug through the satchel in search of his master key that was coded for any car assigned to that RG office. The shooting resumed when he was just meters from one of the vehicles and he dove again, sliding into place alongside his companion.

Upon seeing the key in his hand, they snatched it from him and rose into a kneeling position, unlocking the door and remote starting the engine simultaneously. They moved back and began to provide cover fire, giving Kade time to climb into the car and slide through to the passenger side. The rider was hot on his heels and had the vehicle roaring toward the exit before the door was even sealed. Cold air blew into Kade's face as the passenger window slid open.

"Down," came a muffled command from within the helmet.

He obeyed and felt his companion's arm come to rest on his shoulder as they used it to steady their aim. Even at the speed they were moving, it only took three shots to silence the other shooter, and before he knew it, the two of them had fallen anonymously into place amid the rest of Haphor's late night traffic.

The interior of the car fell silent except for the sound of each of them breathing heavily. It remained that way for several long minutes until the traffic began to thin and they found themselves entering the forested area outside the city. Kade had no idea where they were headed and quite frankly didn't care. He was alive, at least for the time being, and that was all that currently mattered.

His companion remained quiet and still except for a slight turning of the head as they continually checked the rear cams. Kade stole several wary glances in the pilot's direction. He didn't feel threatened by this person directly, but the longer they were silent and the longer they remained shrouded by the helmet, the more uncomfortable he felt.

He cleared his throat and turned directly toward the person. "I guess I should thank you," he said.

The eyes behind the tinted visor glanced in his direction, into the rear cam, back to him, then the car slowed. The gloved hands lifted from the controls and took hold of the helmet, tugging it off slowly. When it cleared the top of the head, Kade found himself looking into the face of a dead woman.

"Don't thank me yet," she said.

· 55 ·

HAPHOR–NORO TRAFFIC LANE
TASMIN FOREST, HAPHEZ

Ziva tossed the helmet into the back seat and took up the controls again, taking a quick look at Shevin as he stared back at her with wide eyes and a gaping mouth. She had expected as much, but she hoped he would be more willing to cooperate initially than his wife had been. She saw that wasn't the case as he began digging around on the floor for his pistol.

Heaving a sigh, she drew her own weapon and pressed it against the back of his neck while he still had his head down. "Don't," she snapped. "Sit up. Now."

Shevin swallowed and lifted his hands slowly, leaning as far against the opposite door as he could. His eyes slowly shifted from the barrel of the gun up to meet hers. "Are you going to kill me?" he murmured.

"I don't know, should I?" Ziva removed the pistol and slid it back into the holster. "You've caused me a lot of trouble, Kade."

"I...I thought you were supposed to be dead!" he stammered. "Everyone did! The footage has been playing on the news all day!"

She accelerated and took one more look in each of the rear cams. "Well, I'm not dead. I've had a few close calls, all thanks to you and your initial accusations. Why the hell did you testify against me if you thought I was innocent?"

The young agent was still leaning away, though the look of shock on his face had begun to diminish. "I didn't at the time! I believed the evidence, just like everyone else. But I guess that was a mistake."

"Yes, it was, but the past is the past," Ziva said. "Right now, you've got some bad people after you, no doubt the same ones who were after me. I can help you if you'll let me, and there are innumerable ways you'll be able to help me in return. If you don't want to do this, that's fine, but I can guarantee that when these people catch up to you, they will kill you without hesitation."

"How do I know you're telling the truth?"

"Veya must take after you because she asked me the same question." She paused for a moment, taking delight in the look of alarm she had triggered on his face. "I'll give you the same answer I gave her: if I wanted to kill you, you would have been dead days ago."

The young agent sat bolt upright. "What have you done with my family?"

"Relax, kid." The term struck Ziva strange—she was only three years his elder. "I sent them far away from here and I've got people who can take care of them."

Groaning, Kade rested his head in his hands and leaned forward. "Why is this happening?"

"Because you were in the wrong place at the wrong time," she said. "You must have done something right though if you've got these guys hunting you the way they are."

"I wouldn't say I've done anything anywhere close to 'right'," he muttered. "What do these people want with me, anyway?"

"That's what you're going to help me find out. Either you know something, or they *think* you know something that could potentially hurt them. I want to know what that is and how it ties to me. We'll spend some time comparing notes and see what we come up with, but right now, you need to get some rest—we're in for a long night."

She knew it was pointless to tell any decent HSP agent to rest given the current circumstances, but the reality of it was that she just wanted him to be quiet for a while. It was important that he be filled in on all the details of what she and Aroska had experienced, but after being shot, traveling back and forth to Haphor, and taking part in a firefight, she was in no mood to chat. It was completely accurate to describe him as a rookie who'd been in the wrong place at the wrong time, but it was also true that he must possess some measure of investigative skill if Dasaro was so interested in him. He would no doubt prove to be a valuable asset, but for now, he could be most helpful by staying silent and allowing her to fly back to Noro in peace.

She knew better than to believe he would actually keep his mouth shut, but it still made her cringe when he spoke again. "I want you to tell me something before I agree to any of this," he said. "Ever since the crash, I've had myself pretty well convinced you were innocent, but I need to hear it straight from you. Did you or did you not kill Officer Tachi?"

Ziva sighed and gazed out the windshield at the lights dotting the dark landscape. "You were right," she replied. "I didn't kill him, and regardless of what you may have heard, I never would have. There were times when I would have very much liked to, but that's a different story which I may or may not tell you once we're out of here."

"How did you escape the prison transport?"

She eyed him curiously for a moment, rather unnerved by the question. Investigators had no doubt found the broken switches and the pilot's gun upon searching the wreckage. "One of the agents lost his service weapon in the middle of some turbulence," she replied. "It was by pure chance that it hit the control panel. I was lucky."

Shevin gave her an incredulous look that told her he'd heard the story before and didn't believe it any more the second time. But rather than comment further, he began to massage his tired eyes. "Where are we going, anyway?"

"I thought I told you to rest," she snapped, albeit without much enthusiasm. That successfully shut him up, and each of them stared out into the night for several seconds. She looked briefly to him, curious as to his reaction, then her focus moved to the control panel. "On second thought, see what you can do about disabling the nav computer in this thing. The last thing we need right now is someone tracking us."

· 56 ·
Tarbic Residence
Noro, Haphez

Aroska was waiting in his darkened living room when the RG groundcar slid to a stop in front of his house. He immediately tensed and tightened his grip on the pistol he held at his side, but when the transmission from Ziva came through, he went straight to the garage door and raised it far enough that she could squeeze the vehicle in beside his own car. He took a quick glance outside at the silent neighborhood then shut the door, following her and the young RG agent into the house.

She went straight to the window and made sure it was tinted fully before activating a solo lighting panel. "Someone needs to start paying me to save lives, not just to take them," she muttered.

Aroska raised an eyebrow. "Nice to see you, too." He turned to the young man and offered his hand. "So much for a formal introduction. Lieutenant Aroska Tarbic, field ops."

"Kade Shevin. You both have my sincere gratitude."

"Save it, Kade," Ziva said as she fitted a fresh plasma cell into her pistol. "I already told you—we've got too far to go for you to start thanking us yet."

"Well, you're welcome," Aroska said, "but Ziva is right. We've got a whole lot to do and not a lot of time."

"Meaning?"

"Meaning we're leaving the planet," Ziva replied. "Now that Dasaro thinks I'm dead, he will have recalled the HSP blockade, and we can get safely away. But they're not going to buy our little act forever. We only have a short window of time before they realize they've been played and come after me again. Thanks to my little side trip back to Haphor to get you, that window has been cut even shorter. For all we know, they could already be on to us."

Shevin took a bold step toward her. "Look, I'm sorry I seem to be such an inconvenience, but the last few days have been hell for me, too. So let's cut the *sheyss.*"

"Hey!" Aroska rushed forward before Ziva could muster a response. He had a headache, he was tired, and arguing was going to do anything but help matters. "Don't even start this, okay? We've all had it rough lately so let's not make a contest over whose life is more *frouchten aht.* Right now, we need to focus on getting out of here."

That seemed to do the trick. Both Kade and Ziva fell silent, but not before sending one last hot glare at each other. Aroska wondered what kind of hellish experience the ride back from Haphor had been.

Ziva turned toward him with a sigh, arms crossed, eyes tired. "What did you find in the way of transportation?"

He consulted his data pad and let his gaze flit over to the time-stamp for a moment—it would be dawn within an hour or so. "There are three intragalactic civilian transports coming through the spaceport within the next two hours. All three are scheduled to dock on Chaiavis, but only one will arrive there in the next two days. The other two are headed in the opposite direction around the Fringe and don't make it through the circuit until a week from now at the earliest."

"Let me guess," Ziva said, pinching the bridge of her nose between her thumb and forefinger, "that one transport is already docked here and scheduled to leave within the hour."

Shocked, Aroska was tempted to ask if her Nosti abilities gave her some measure of omniscience. When he remembered Kade was standing there, however, he resorted to a simple nod. "Close enough," he replied. "It hasn't docked yet, but it should be in-system within the next few minutes if it isn't already. We're going to have to move fast if we want to make it."

She sighed again and brushed a lock of loose hair from her eyes.

"I can pay for passage," she said, moving her hands down to rest on her hips, "but I can't very well just walk up and buy three boarding passes at this point."

"I'll do it," Kade put in. "People would ask questions if you two went in and bought three tickets. I have a wife and child—no one would think twice."

Aroska shook his head, stopping him cold. "We can't send you in there alone, not with Dasaro after you."

"Aroska, think about it." Ziva's voice was weary but firm. "Whatever Dasaro's problem is, he doesn't want anyone else to know about it. He's not going to have anyone outside his circle looking for Kade—spaceport security and common patrols aren't going to be an issue."

It made sense, but Aroska wasn't at all comfortable with it. "Even if we make it through security without trouble, what's to keep him from coming after us once we're underway?"

"There's no doubt in my mind he'll come after us again," she said. "The trick is to get out of here fast enough that they won't be able to figure out we're gone until we're safely to Chaiavis. From there, we can regroup. Find the higher ground, so to speak. We'll be ready for Dasaro when he finds us, and maybe we can figure out what the hell is going on while we're at it."

"I suppose it would be a waste of breath to ask if I could contact my family," Kade said.

"Yes," Aroska and Ziva said simultaneously. It was no secret that the young agent was terrified; Aroska felt unsure about things as it was. But talking to anyone was out of the question right now. On that note, he suddenly felt very eager to get underway before Dasaro realized there wasn't a body at the Haphor relay station and decided to ask him about it.

"We should head out," Ziva said just as he opened his mouth to say the same thing.

"Here goes nothing," Kade muttered.

· 57 ·
NORO INTRAGALACTIC SPACEPORT
NORO, HAPHEZ

L ess than an hour later, Shevin found himself standing in line at a bank of ticket kiosks in the heart of the massive Noro Spaceport. It was amazing how many people were making their way through the port even at this hour. Noro was apparently the city that never slept; Haphor certainly had a more set routine about it, and the sheer chaos of the larger city intimidated him.

The beady-eyed Elsara behind him chattered something he didn't understand and shoved him forward, snapping him out of the trance the throngs of people had put him into. He shook his head, taking a quick step forward to close the gap between himself and the old man in front of him. Somewhere out in the crowd, Ziva and Aroska were watching him, though he didn't dare look around for fear of drawing unwanted attention. The lieutenants had advised against looking around anyway, saying that adhering to a strict route and keeping his head down would make it harder for someone to spot him on the surveillance cams. He'd heeded their words, though he still couldn't believe he'd agreed to accompany them.

Fingering the stack of credits Payvan had provided, Kade stepped up to the booth and fed the payment into the machine. He snatched up the three pass cards it distributed, moving away quickly before the Elsara could protest again. Boarding the transport together had been deemed out of the question, so he angled toward the place that had been designated as the first drop-site: the nearest men's lavatory.

It took a good minute or two of weaving in and out of the crowd before he reached it. He felt rather silly and old fashioned for making the exchange like this, but it was both the quickest and the easiest way to get the tickets dispersed and get moving. Retaining one ticket for himself, he held the other two in a relaxed grip at his side. "Coming in," he said into his earpiece, one of several they'd found in a supply box in the RG car. The door of the room opened just as he reached it, and Aroska emerged right on cue. His hand barely brushed against Kade's, and with that, the other two pass cards were gone. Both fascinated and terrified, Kade continued into the lavatory and lingered there in front of the sink. He eyed the other travelers around him, wondering if any of them were HSP or bounty hunters who had already managed to catch up to them. While he was confident in Payvan and Tarbic's abilities to safely escape, he was also confident in the abilities of whoever was after them. They'd done a fantastic job of remaining unseen and foiling plans so far, and he felt the need to brace himself for something horrible to happen in the next few minutes.

Eager to get away, he took a deep breath and raked his fingers through his hair before turning to leave. It was a relief to know that the boarding gates for their transport were nearby, and even more so to know that even if HSP caught up to them, they had no way of knowing which ship they'd taken. The pass cards were valid on any of the three transports coming through—if they could get away quickly, the agency wouldn't know whether to follow them to Chaiavis or Midore or Duruta.

Kade fell into place again amid the throngs of travelers, head down but eyes darting wildly about. Aroska was nowhere to be found, and Ziva had been invisible since they'd arrived. It was up to each of them to reach the transport on their own, and while Kade wasn't overly comfortable with the idea, he was even less comfortable with the thought of being left behind.

He pulled up just meters short of the gate and turned his head to study a boarding schedule as a pair of security officers ambled by. It made sense that this Dasaro person wouldn't send anyone after him if he was so intent on keeping his secrets, but there was always the possibility that some trumped up charges could be brought against him so he could be picked up, only to fall right into Dasaro's hands. Wishing to be safe rather than sorry, he waited a moment until the officers were gone before continuing through the gate.

The boarding ramp was vacant with the exception of a busy cleaning bot, so Kade jogged forward and swiped his pass card over the scanner, slipping through the airlock door as it opened. The interior of the ship was ill-lit and crusty, as were the majority of these heavily used public transports. People and aliens moved back and forth through the main corridor, and the airlock opened and closed behind him as others came and went. Checking the bunk number on his ticket, he pointed himself in the right direction and began walking.

These transports were essentially mobile hotels, providing passengers with all their basic needs. Other than seating and sleeping accommodations, they were equipped with cafés, small supply shops, clubs, and other entertainment. It provided the trio with means of staying hidden or blending in, whichever they wanted or needed to do at any given moment.

Glancing at the bunk number again, Kade turned down a narrow corridor, studying room numbers as he went. He looked ahead, catching sight of Aroska as he disappeared into one of the rooms at the far end of the hallway. Peering behind him and seeing no one, Kade picked up his pace and ducked into the room as well.

It was a small space, only a couple of meters across and hardly deeper. Its only furnishings were a pair of bunk beds, one against each wall, and a small table with a single chair. Aroska had tossed his bag onto one of the top bunks and stood in the narrow space between the beds, looking exhausted. Ziva was nowhere in sight.

"She'll be here," he said, as if reading Kade's mind. "The drop was good, she's got her pass...she'll be here."

The words were barely out of his mouth when the door slid open once more and in walked the suited figure who had come to Kade's rescue at RG Headquarters. Ziva removed her helmet and tossed it onto one of the beds, taking a quick look around the tiny room before sighing and letting her eyes settle on the two men.

"It's a little early to say 'we've made it'," she said, "but we seem to be on the right track, gentlemen."

Aroska consulted the departure information on a small display beside the door. "We're scheduled to dock on Chaiavis tomorrow night."

"Good." Ziva brushed past Kade and took a seat on the bunk beside her helmet. "That gives us some time to get rested up and compare notes. We'll sleep in shifts—one person awake at all times. You've got a computer, right Shevin?"

Kade nodded and placed a hand on his satchel.

"Get it set up, put it to good use." With that, she lifted her legs onto the bunk and leaned back against the pillow, one arm draped across her face.

Aroska raised an eyebrow. "What are you doing?"

"What does it look like? Like I said, we'll sleep in shifts."

Kade wasn't sure whether to be amused or disgusted. He cleared his throat and glanced from Ziva to the bunk above her, then down to his feet.

"Go ahead," Aroska said, jerking his head toward the bunk as he took a seat in the chair.

"You sure?"

"Hurry up before I change my mind."

· 58 ·
HSP Headquarters
Noro, Haphez

S keet was startled out of his dazed stupor when the screen of his data pad cracked under the pressure of his thumb. The image he'd been looking at fizzled away as the hologram failed. He blinked, trying for a moment to process exactly what had happened. In an attempt to keep his mind off Ziva and the previous day's events, he'd been reading random news articles—in this case, about a new species of fern someone had discovered in the forest outside Seran. Somewhere along the lines, something—he couldn't even remember what—in his train of thought had sent him in a direction that ended with Ziva. It was becoming an all-too-familiar occurrence. Try as he might to keep his friend's death off his mind, the memory kept creeping back, bringing with it the subconscious rage that had resulted in his broken data pad.

He stared at the cracked screen a moment longer before looking up at Zinni, who sat across the table from him, deadpan. They'd spent the past hour or so sitting there in the spec ops employee canteen, each of them silent as they went about trying to distract themselves. This was the first time they'd even made eye contact—he'd found her there at the table and had sat down without a word. Even now, Zinni said nothing, and the dark makeup she wore didn't quite conceal the redness around her eyes.

Skeet wasn't entirely sure what they were even doing there. He'd come in that morning almost by pure reflex, one more attempt at simply going through the motions and not thinking too hard about anything. The entire special operations division had been assigned to the manhunt, and now that Ziva was gone, things had returned to business as usual. A team with only two members wouldn't be given any new assignments—they would be disbanded entirely before long thanks to the Rule of Three—so in all reality, they were wasting their time even being there. He was surprised Zinni had even shown up.

"Attention!" someone called.

He looked up to see the director himself standing in the doorway of the lounge, scanning the room as if searching for someone. He and Zinni worked their way to their feet, as did everyone else, though he found he was unable to straighten his sagging shoulders. Emeri approached when he caught sight of them, holding his hands toward the other agents as he passed.

"As you were," he said.

It was rare to see the director outside his office at all, let alone in a place like the canteen. Whatever was on his mind was important enough to bring him down from the high reaches of the spec ops wing. Skeet and Zinni sat again and watched, still silent, as Emeri took a chair from a nearby table and pulled it up to theirs.

"What the hell are you two doing here?" His voice lacked the gruff edge such a question might normally have warranted.

"I've been wondering the same thing," Skeet replied.

Emeri leaned forward and folded his hands on the surface of the table. "Look, I'm sorry it had to come to this. I know how close you both were to Lieutenant Payvan—it's one of the reasons you functioned so well as a team."

Skeet was startled when Zinni spoke. "With all due respect, sir," she said, "was there something specific you needed from us? Because if not, I think I'll be on my way."

"As a matter of fact, I was just about to *send* you on your way," Emeri said. "I'd like you two to take a few days off, at least until the dust settles. I also don't need a couple of emotionally compromised agents taking up space in my building."

"We can do our jobs, Director." Skeet felt the rage returning and looked down at his data pad to remind himself that Emeri should not be the recipient of it.

"I'd like you to take a break all the same." Emeri's turquoise eyes took on a cold gray hue as he fixed them on Skeet. "I know how it feels to lose a squadmate, and I can't even imagine what it's like under these circumstances."

His behavior seemed odd—the director had never been the chatty type, much less someone who would try to give any consolation to the friends of a dead criminal. Skeet couldn't help but be suspicious; the time for trusting anyone had ended the moment Aroska had shot Ziva after claiming he was helping her. Zinni was still in denial, clinging to the hope that it had somehow been staged, but he was convinced she was wasting her time.

Emeri leaned forward a bit more, keeping his voice low. "To be honest, it's not looking good for you two. I will try my hardest to postpone any decisions regarding either of you being reassigned. You're two of my best people and I want to keep you in ops if at all possible."

That didn't make Skeet feel any better, but he managed a respectful dip of his head. "Thank you, sir."

"For the record, I'm not thrilled with the approach Dasaro took on all of this, but what's done is done." Emeri stood and gestured for them to remain seated. "I know you probably feel as though you've been treated unfairly throughout these past few days. I thought you at least deserved to hear from me in person."

He turned abruptly and left, walking with a familiar stiff gait that had always given Skeet the impression he hated talking to anyone. All eyes were on him until he reached the door, then all attention was shifted to Skeet and Zinni. Tired of the critical looks and false sympathy, Skeet stood up and began to walk away as well.

"Where are you going?" Zinni called, the first time she'd addressed him all morning.

"Where does it look like?" Skeet growled. "You heard him—I'm leaving."

He heard footsteps as she rushed to catch up. She suddenly appeared in front of him, cutting him off just before he reached the door. "Listen Skeet!" she hissed, eyes ablaze. "I know you're pissed—so am I. But don't be like this!"

She took him by the arm and dragged him out of the canteen, stopping in a quiet area in the hallway outside. He allowed her to shove him against the wall, his willpower depleted. The director was right—they were both emotionally exhausted.

"I don't blame you for being angry, but it's not going to bring her back." Zinni maintained a firm grip on the front of his shirt, ensuring she had his undivided attention. "The best thing we can do right now is stay focused and do whatever it takes to keep our jobs and stay alive. You can leave—go ahead—but not like this, understand? Not like this!"

Skeet couldn't recall her ever speaking to him in such a way, and it instantly made him regret his actions. He knew Ziva wouldn't want them to give up, but he also knew that even if they were able to keep their positions in ops, it wouldn't be long before Dasaro concocted something that would get them kicked out for good. The captain's issues had always been with Ziva, for whatever reason, but his aggression had often carried over to Skeet and Zinni as well. The way he'd treated them since the prison transport crash hadn't come as any surprise.

Sighing, he placed his arm around Zinni's shoulder, and together they walked—once more in silence—upstairs to the squad floor. The majority of the workstations were vacant, a strange sight after seeing everyone so hard at work during the hunt for Ziva. Those still at their desks didn't so much as bat an eye as the two of them came through. It was a refreshing change from the numerous odd looks they'd been receiving as of late.

Skeet didn't keep many belongings there at work; the ones he did had all been confiscated out of his personal locker immediately following Ziva's arrest. The only two that had been returned to him—his communicator and service sidearm—were in his desk drawer where he had left them the previous day before storming out of the building.

The comm's screen was red, indicating a missed transmission. Upon checking it, he found that it was in fact eighteen missed messages, all originating from the same comm code—Ziva's home.

"Have Marshay or Ryon contacted you?" He turned to Zinni, bewildered, and held up the communicator.

She shook her head and pulled her own device out of her backpack.

"I've had it turned off since last night." She handed it to him, displaying her message logs. Seventeen missed transmissions, again from Ziva's home code. All of them had been sent within the last three hours, as had his.

Suddenly rather concerned, he led her into a more secluded area and opened a reply transmission, holding the communicator where they could both hear it. The call took what seemed like an eternity to go through, and the eerie silence made him sweat. It was Ryon who finally answered.

"Ryon, it's Skeet. I just checked my comm and saw that someone over there tried to contact me, so—"

He got no further before the other man swore and hollered something in the background. Marshay could be heard shouting in reply, and Skeet was sure something was wrong. However, the relief and excitement were evident in Ryon's voice when he spoke again.

"You're not going to believe this!" he said, still on the verge of shouting. "You two need to get over here right now!"

· 59 ·
FRINGE SYSTEMS TRANSPORT LINE
DEEP SPACE

T heir conversation ground to a halt when the serving bot appeared at the table, hovering there on a pair of repulsors while its glowing yellow photoreceptors studied them quizzically. "Can I get you folks something?" it asked in an overbearing feminine voice that gave Ziva the impression it had been in the serving business for a few too many years.

"Govinolin for me," Kade said.

Aroska signaled for the bot's attention. "Make that two."

She wasn't sure whether a couple of drinks would help or hinder their venture—the galaxy knew they could use a little rest and relaxation, but she didn't feel at all comfortable with Aroska so much as glancing at an alcoholic beverage after the things she'd seen in his home.

"Hold it," she said. "He'll have govino *juice*. So will I."

The bot acknowledged them with a squeaky tip of its rusty old head and went rushing back toward the kitchen. She watched it go and took a moment to scan the little café for the umpteenth time. All the other tables were occupied, yet nobody seemed to be paying them any mind. Still, she felt far from safe.

Her attention was drawn back to the table when she heard Aroska snort. "Really Ziva? Juice?"

"No drinking on the job." She knew good and well what he meant, but he also knew good and well what *she* meant.

"Oh, I get it. Afraid of impairing your judgment and not being able to react quickly enough when that bot comes back with a power-blade and tries to kill us, are you?"

"You're impossible," she muttered, glaring at him through narrowed eyes. "If you must know, govinolin is one of the only things that doesn't make me sick. I could hardly breathe when I first walked into your place the other day."

Aroska scoffed again. "Interesting. Ziva Payvan can kill a man with her bare hands, but she can't hold her liquor."

She found it ironic that he should mention her abilities to kill, considering he was next on her list if he kept up his attitude. The three of them sat in silence until the bot returned, Ziva staring Aroska down, Aroska humbled under her gaze, and Kade not wishing to get caught in between. Their glasses were distributed efficiently with a metallic claw, showcasing the machine's years of experience. Ziva lifted hers to her lips and took a gentle sip from it before lowering it back to the surface of the table and watching her two male companions take generous gulps from theirs. Mind wandering, she began to spin her glass in a slow circle, allowing her eyes to once again flit around the café.

Her attention was drawn back to her hand and the orange liquid sloshing around in her cup when she sensed Aroska staring at it. She glanced up and, when she saw his brow wrinkled in a perplexed manner, she cleared her throat. "What?"

"That's what it was," he murmured.

"*What?*" she said again.

"You seemed familiar the first time we met—not in the director's office, but when I first saw you outside the elevator bank."

"You mean when you were ogling me like a half-starved guhr hound?"

"Hey, I'm serious," he retorted. "I knew I recognized you from somewhere."

"I'm surprised you recognized anything with your eyes glued to my ass."

His eyes widened and his face turned bright red. He forced a nervous smile and glanced quickly from Kade back to her. "I wasn't that bad, was I?"

She tilted her head and lifted an eyebrow. "Tell me where you think you saw me."

He recovered quickly and shrugged. "It was late last year. My team and I had just wrapped up an investigation in Mairo, and we stopped for a drink at one of the spaceport bars when we got back. You were sitting at a table by yourself, spinning an empty glass around just like that. Tate and Jole headed home early, so I was just sitting there watching you and trying to decide whether or not to come introduce myself and give you my comm code. The next thing I knew, the place was crawling with security, and when I looked around again, you were gone."

Ziva remembered the day he spoke of. She'd been there at the bar surveilling an informant, a man who was supposed to take part in a drop that would give her intel for her next hit. But the drop had never taken place; the informant had been discovered by the would-be target, and she'd had to bug out before anyone traced him to her. The fact that she'd unwittingly been under surveillance herself that day made her shiver.

"I think that's more than I needed to know," she said.

"You asked." Aroska swallowed the rest of his juice. "So, were you on a job? I can't picture you hanging around in a bar by yourself just for the hell of it."

"That would be telling," she replied, taking another sip of her own drink.

The serving bot returned and refilled their drinks and they all ordered something to eat. She could feel her blood sugar dropping—she hadn't eaten since making breakfast at Aroska's house—but she was too worked up to actually be hungry. The quality of the transport's food was questionable, especially compared to what she was used to, but her brain needed the energy, and she reluctantly began to eat when their meal arrived.

Kade finished chewing a bite and cleared his throat. "Speaking of 'telling,' there's something that's been bothering me."

She wasn't the least bit comfortable with discussing anything there in a public place, but arguing in a public place was hardly an option, either. "And what would that be?"

"Correct me if I'm wrong, but we're only helping you based on your word and our own assumptions, right?"

"Sounds about right." She wondered where he was going with this.

"Statements say you didn't arrive at the gala until *after* Tachi was killed. You told me you didn't do it, and I'm inclined to believe you, but why can't you tell anyone where you were that night?"

Ziva paused and set her utensils down, feeling crushed under Kade and Aroska's collective gaze. She had expected this question to come up eventually but had pushed it to the back of her mind during the past couple of days. For a moment, it seemed like the entire café had fallen silent. Both men waited expectantly for her to answer, so she wiped the back of her hand across her mouth and cleared her throat.

"I was late to that gala because I was back in Noro following up on a case," she replied.

"That doesn't explain much," Aroska said, raising a brow.

Kade leaned forward. "What kind of case?"

"It's not exactly a case, I guess," she replied, hesitant to elaborate further. "For a while now, I've suspected Dasaro of being up to something. I broke into his place to see if I could find anything to support that theory. I may have discovered something—a locked drawer and a hidden weapons cache—but I had to leave before I could look into it."

It was the first time Aroska had shown signs of skepticism about her story. "And this theory is based on...?"

"Transmissions, unexplained funds, and a hunch...a hunch I've had for over three years now."

"You're sure it's not something related to an op he's been running?"

She didn't like his tone. "I think I'd know about it if it was agency-related."

"Hey, just asking," Kade said before Aroska had a chance to respond. "I don't understand, though. If you've had this hunch for so long, why not take it to the director?"

"I didn't want to until I had something more solid. I couldn't risk tipping Dasaro off and losing my chance to find out if there was really anything going on. Once this whole mess with Tachi started, I was screwed. If I tried to come clean about what I knew, Dasaro could just deny everything, and everyone would shrug it off as a last-ditch attempt at shifting blame."

Ziva paused a moment, running her hands over her face before resting her elbows on the table. "Not to mention I have no alibi—the whole point was to be there at his loft without anyone knowing. I did everything in my power to stay out of sight, including avoiding traffic cams when I finally headed for Haphor. Looking back on it now, taking such extreme measures seems to have done more harm than good."

"Well, if you were convinced Dasaro was up to no good," Kade said, "why not go with the flow and petition a sponsor to look into it while you spent a few days in prison? I'm sorry, but the whole escaping-and-running thing doesn't look very good if you're innocent."

"You think I don't know that, Shevin?" she snapped. At the mention of the word 'prison,' the hairs on the back of her neck stood on end and another image of herself chained up in the Cobian bunker ripped through her mind.

Both Kade and Aroska stared at her with wide eyes, startled by the harsh response. Again, she found herself regretting allowing her emotions to get the best of her; the past was the past, and she couldn't afford to let it keep haunting her at such inopportune times.

She drew a deep breath and slowly released it through her nose. "They were taking me to the Haphor Facility," she said. "It's not a matter of 'spending a few days' there—once you're in, you're probably not coming back out." She suppressed a shudder and winced as another vision flashed through her memory. "I couldn't go back there."

"Go back?" Aroska asked.

"What? No, that's not—" She restrained herself from slamming her fists onto the table and instead lowered her palms into her lap. She closed her eyes and clenched her jaw, slipping into her meditative state for the briefest of moments. "Let's get back on topic, shall we?"

Both men were quiet for a long time, with Kade nervously moving food around on his plate and Aroska giving Ziva a look that told her the conversation was far from over. She was tempted to get up and leave, but she thought better of it. A hasty departure could draw even the slightest bit of unwanted attention, and they needed to take advantage of every second they were together so as to form a plan of action.

Aroska finally spoke up. "So, you think Dasaro is behind all of this?"

"I think he's more than just the agent assigned to catch me, but I'm not sure how," Ziva replied. "I figured if he thought I was dead, he might slip up and we'd have a more definitive answer, but pretty soon he'll realize he's been played—if he hasn't already—and his guard will go back up."

"Is there anyone at all we could contact for more information?" Kade asked.

"One of the agents from the prison transport survived the crash," she said. "I'd love to hear what he has to say about all of this, but establishing contact with anyone is out of the question at this point."

Shevin's eyes grew wide. "Agent Spence is dead, Ziva."

It was all she could do to refrain from shouting. "*What?*"

"He claimed you saved his life, one of the reasons I started to question whether you were really guilty. I was sent to get a statement from him, and while I was there, they came for him. He was murdered."

"Who came, Kade?" Aroska asked.

"I don't know, but I'm pretty sure they were HSP. There was a man and a woman. She was *emilan*, tall and slender, and he had a scar on the back of his head. They gave Spence something to make his heart stop."

Ziva bowed her head and stared down at her clasped hands. "That settles it, then—Dasaro's involved. The people you saw were Nejdra Venn and Kyron Hoxie, two other spec ops captains who have been associated with him." She glanced up at Kade. "They didn't see you, did they?"

He shook his head. "I was down the hall with a nurse. I think I'm the only person who ever saw them, though. I've looked and looked and haven't been able to catch them on surveillance anywhere. If they're really HSP, they can probably access the feeds and erase any signs of their presence. The coroner found the chemical they used during his autopsy, but they even managed to edit his report to make it look like Spence died of natural causes. I went to meet with him in person to see what he had to say about all of this—now he's dead, too."

"*Sheyss*," Ziva muttered, massaging her eyes so hard she saw spots when she removed her hands. "What the hell is Dasaro doing?"

"It sounds like he doesn't want anyone questioning your guilt," Aroska suggested. "What did you do to piss him off?"

She scoffed. "I was born. He's had it in for me since I first started at the agency, but this is all much bigger than that. He wouldn't set me up like this just so he could be Emeri's pet."

"You sure about that?"

"Let's put it this way: he wouldn't set me up and then proceed to eliminate anyone who could testify to my innocence just because of something so petty. There's something much bigger going on, something that started all of this...that's the sort of thing I've been looking for during the past three years."

All was quiet for several long seconds, then Kade spoke. "Is it possible he knew you were poking around? Maybe he wants to get you off his trail before you find whatever he's hiding."

If that was the case and Dasaro was really willing to kill her to keep his secret, Ziva wanted very much to know what in the galaxy he was up to. She'd been careful in her investigating, and if he had indeed caught on, she was very interested in finding out how. He was a good agent, after all—she couldn't deny that. But she was better.

"It's possible," she replied quietly, hands folded in front of her mouth. "What have you found that's got you in his sights?"

"I don't have a clue," Shevin said. "I was there the night of the assassination but couldn't really see anything, contrary to what they wanted me to tell the media. I know his people killed Spence, but nobody believes me. At the very least, he knows I've been nosy."

"That should do the trick," Aroska said. "Judging by what I heard him telling Captain Venn, he wants to shut you up before you find something he can't cover up."

Ziva leaned toward Kade, keeping her voice low. "Have you found anything that might shed some light on what he wants?"

The young agent began to shake his head, but then he perked up as if something had come to mind. "I have some files that I found on my supervisor's computer—that's what I was doing last night when you came to get me. All the case files are there, as well as information about the accident that killed the coroner. There were a few other files that appeared to just be research, but they're all encrypted. I didn't get a chance to crack them."

"Then what are we waiting for?" Ziva said. "Let's get to work."

· 60 ·
HSP Headquarters
Noro, Haphez

Dasaro paused a moment and let his eyes adjust to the dim lighting in the conference room. A single hologram stood beside the large table, that of Special Agent Luko Zona of the RG office in Haphor. Clearing his throat, Dasaro stepped up onto the communication pad and dipped his head toward the other man.

"My apologies, Agent Zona," he said. "I've been very busy with some unfinished business this morning."

"As have I, Captain," Zona said, his voice lacking the understanding and cooperation it had possessed when they'd spoken on comm the day before. "With all due respect, I'd like to hear whatever you have to say so I can attend to matters here."

Something in his tone wasn't right. Dasaro scowled. "What's wrong?"

"All hell broke loose last night," the RG agent said. "I've got two records of unauthorized entry, three corpses on my squad floor, and another in my parking bay. My workstation was hacked, and case-related files were accessed."

Dasaro hesitated, careful not to let his face betray any outward signs of the sinking feeling in the pit of his stomach as he pondered what Zona was saying. He had no doubt these dead bodies were the men he had sent to pick up Kade Shevin, though he couldn't imagine Shevin had killed all four of them on his own. Regardless of what had transpired, the outcome was not what he'd hoped for.

"Do you have any idea what happened?"

Zona sighed and rubbed his face. "I hate to even think about it," he said. "We've got an agent over here who's been causing trouble ever since Payvan's escape. He seems to think he can solve the entire case on his own, but all he's managed to do so far is complicate things."

"You're speaking of Kade Shevin," Dasaro said.

"Ah, I see he's landed on your radar as well." Zona winced. "I finally decided to send him home for a couple of days to cool off—part of me wonders if he ever should have been released from the med center that night after the assassination. His access code is still valid, and according to the logs, he used it to enter the office last night after hours. If anyone can tell us what went down, I think it's him."

"You think Shevin is the one who hacked your system?"

"Like I said, I hate to even consider it, but honestly, nothing else makes sense. He's certainly capable of it."

"What about the unauthorized entries?"

"One was through the front door approximately two hours after Shevin logged in, and the second was through a side entrance just a few minutes after the first. Judging by the evidence, it looks like the three intruders got in through the front—we still haven't been able to identify them. The second entry remains a mystery. It looks like someone got into the security cams—mobile cams were all programmed to turn and face the walls, and the feeds from the fixed cams have all been erased. The window of time when all of this transpired is completely blank."

As much as it angered Dasaro that Kade Shevin had once again slipped through his fingers, the young man could not have possibly set himself up to look guiltier. "Those cams can only be accessed by someone with proper clearance," he said, leaving out the fact that he'd ordered Nejdra to do it. She no doubt had a copy of the feed she'd cut out, and he looked forward to seeing it and discovering the identity of whoever else had entered. "And what has become of Agent Shevin?"

"Gone," Zona replied. "His car is in the parking bay, but there's no sign of him. A transmission came through at his workstation and we were able to trace it back to his mobile comm. We haven't been able to get a fix on it, though—we can't even pick up a signal, giving me the impression it's been destroyed."

Dasaro sighed. "You might not like the sound of this, Agent Zona, but it's possible that your man may have had a hand in Tachi's death. The attack outside on the bridge that night may have been staged. He could have let Payvan into the building. Why else would she have left him alive? We also have reason to believe he is responsible for the murder of another HSP agent who survived when the prison transport crashed, and we're looking into his involvement in the death of the coroner who performed the autopsy on that agent."

"Spence and Fromm?" Zona exclaimed. "No, that's ridiculous. Shevin could never have…" His voice trailed off and he sighed, muttering under his breath.

"We don't know anything for certain," Dasaro said. "What matters is that we find Shevin and end all of this." *In more ways than one*, he thought.

Zona's hologram flickered. "Understood, sir."

"Thank you, Special Agent Zona, that will be all." Dasaro ended the transmission before the man could speak again and turned to find Nejdra Venn and Kyron Hoxie waiting in the shadows behind him. They each nodded, signaling that they had been present for the majority of the conversation.

"Anything?" he asked.

Nejdra shook her head. "Nothing at the house, either. The wife and daughter were both gone. Looks like they left in a hurry."

"Shevin's got help," Dasaro said. "You accessed the RG security cams last night—please tell me you kept a copy of the footage you erased."

Nejdra smirked and held up a small memory stick. The two men followed her to one of the room's computer terminals and watched as she brought up the recording and jumped forward to the point where their men had entered.

Dasaro crossed his arms and studied the screen intently. The four mercenaries were ex-military, provided by an old friend of Hoxie's; they were, unfortunately, more muscle than brains, and he saw now that relying on them to grab Shevin had been a mistake. The footage showed them all to be large and well-armed, however, making him wonder what kind of help Shevin had that would have allowed him to escape.

The answer presented itself after a few minutes. The view was of the squad floor, as seen from a cam positioned at the top of the stairwell. Shevin crouched behind a desk, out of sight of the mercenaries as they investigated one of the workstations across the room. A fifth figure suddenly appeared in the frame, and for a moment, Dasaro wondered if it was the last mercenary. It didn't take long for him to realize this third party was involved with HSP—the riding suit they wore was the first clue, and so was the way they effortlessly dropped the three mercs with well-placed plasma bolts. Dasaro watched as Shevin and the figure disappeared from the screen and then turned to Hoxie, who had cursed under his breath.

"Remember that hoverbike pilot who went missing from the forest checkpoint the day of the prison transport crash?" the man asked in response to Dasaro's questioning gaze. "They just found him last night, wandering in the woods, half-starved, and—" he cleared his throat "—missing his suit."

Time seemed to stop for a moment as both Dasaro and Nejdra shifted their eyes to meet Hoxie's. He swallowed and gestured at the screen. "I don't know how, but I think there's a very high probability we're looking at Ziva Payvan here."

Without even realizing it, Dasaro had his communicator out and was entering Lieutenant Tarbic's code. When no one answered, he tried again, then a third time before hurling the device across the room. "I want someone out looking for a body at that relay station, *now!*" he growled, restraining himself from outright shouting. He watched on the screen as Shevin and his companion sped out of the parking bay, taking out the fourth mercenary before disappearing into the night.

"*Sheyss.*"

· 61 ·
Payvan Residence
Noro, Haphez

When Skeet and Zinni pulled up to Ziva's house, Marshay was standing on the front step looking frazzled but grinning wide. She stepped down to meet them as they approached and greeted them both with a friendly embrace.

"I don't think you two will be looking quite so glum here in a moment," she said.

Unsure what could make the woman so excited short of seeing Ziva herself, Zinni followed her in and paused just inside the doorway, taking in the sight before her with knit eyebrows. A strange woman, perhaps a few years her junior, was seated on the sofa, gently rocking the occupied baby carriage beside her. She stopped rocking when the two of them entered and glanced nervously between Marshay and Ryon.

"Skeet Duvo and Zinni Vax, meet Veya Shevin," Ryon said.

"Hello," Zinni said, dipping her head toward the woman. She turned to Marshay, still not sure what the point was. "What is this?"

"The bird is still in flight," the housekeeper announced, clasping her hands and grinning again.

Zinni glanced quizzically at Skeet, who shook his head and shrugged. "I don't understand," he said.

"A flying bird has always been a sign of life, of freedom," Ryon explained. "When the bird flies, it's safe from its enemies on the ground. It's free."

"It's a code Ziva created for us," Marshay said. "It's a way for her to let us know she's safe, and it's our cue to prepare the resources set aside for when she's in trouble. Lieutenant Tarbic came here the day before yesterday, telling us that the bird had flown. The only way he could have heard that phrase is if Ziva told him herself."

The way Zinni saw it, nothing that happened before the previous day even mattered. The day Aroska had come to Marshay and Ryon was the same day he had come to her and Skeet, claiming to be helping Ziva and asking for their assistance. Too much had happened since then for Marshay's words to bring much comfort.

"Aroska is a traitor," Skeet said, jaw clenched. "He may have been 'helping' Ziva, but he was doing it all on Dasaro's behalf. The man killed her yesterday—how can you still believe something he said two days ago?"

"Skeet," Zinni said, placing a warning hand on his arm as something clicked within her mind.

"You're not listening, son," Ryon said, his voice firm. He looked down at Veya for a moment before turning back to the two of them. "As of zero one hundred this morning, *the bird is still in flight.*"

Zinni looked to Veya when she realized the woman's presence was directly related to what they were hearing. She took a step forward, hands resting on her hips, and looked her squarely in the eyes. "Are you telling me Ziva is still alive?" The question was directed at Veya, though she couldn't have cared less who actually gave her an answer.

The young mother nodded. "She sent me here," she replied. "She showed up at my house looking for my husband last night, and she said if I didn't leave, I would probably be killed. I was afraid *she* was the one there to kill me, but there was something in the way she spoke that told me she was telling the truth. I wasn't going to wait around and find out." She shrugged and looked to each of them in turn. "So here I am."

Both Skeet and Zinni stood in stunned silence for several seconds, letting the news sink in. The idea that Ziva was alive and well contradicted everything they had come to believe since the day before. There were no details, though—were Ziva and Aroska really working together as Tarbic originally claimed? Or had Ziva somehow escaped after being shot? Was Veya lying and somehow in league with Dasaro and Aroska?

Zinni felt compelled to ask. "You're *sure* it was Ziva Payvan?"

The incredulity was clear in Veya's face. "Are you saying you don't believe me? She came into my house, she had a gun, and she sent me here with that message. I sent her after my husband and haven't heard from either of them since then. I dropped everything to rush off into the night with my baby daughter, based on nothing but the word of a woman who killed the Royal Officer and was supposedly killed herself." She scoffed and shook her head. "I've just been to hell and back, and after all of that, you have the gall to question what I'm telling you? Do you think I'm crazy?"

"Not at all, dear," Marshay said gently.

Zinni admired her audacity, though she didn't appreciate being spoken to in such a manner. "Let's start over," she said. "Veya Shevin… your husband is Kade Shevin, the RG officer who allegedly witnessed Ziva entering Tachi's palace."

Veya nodded. "She told me there were people after him, and that they were probably the same ones hunting her. She said they could help each other."

"Why would anyone be hunting him?" Skeet asked, crossing his arms. "He gave his testimony—if anyone's still got it in for him, it should be Ziva."

"He hasn't been himself since all of this started," the young woman replied. "He's been quiet, reserved, like there's constantly something on his mind. He's been working himself into the ground, staying late at the office, sitting for hours in front of our home computer. He's become obsessed with this case, and I'm afraid he's in way over his head."

"Any idea what's driving him?" Zinni asked.

"Ever since Payvan escaped custody, he's had this idea that she's innocent, that she's being set up. I haven't argued against it, but then I have no basis for believing it, either. I'm just afraid he's going to hurt himself if someone else doesn't beat him to the task."

She paused for a moment as if struck by a sudden thought. "Oh," she said, placing her hand over her mouth. "Do you think that's why these people are after him? Did he find something they're willing to kill for?" The first signs of tears became visible in her eyes.

"It's possible," Skeet said, "and if it is the case, they would more than likely try to get to him through you. It was good of Ziva to send you here, and it was smart of you to come."

Veya wiped away a teardrop that had strayed onto her cheek. "What should we do?"

"Zinni and I will handle this," he answered. "The best thing you can do is keep your head down—if anyone finds out you're here, they'll know Ziva's alive and that she's working with Kade. She staged her death to escape from someone, and we need to make sure she stays dead as far as they know."

"You think it's Dasaro?" Zinni asked. The more details they got, the more reasonable the idea seemed.

Skeet nodded and turned toward the door, car key in hand. "I think it's high time we find out."

· 62 ·
HSP HEADQUARTERS
NORO, HAPHEZ

I f the sight on the large viewscreen hadn't rendered Dasaro completely speechless, he would have let loose a string of colorful expletives directed at Nejdra and Hoxie as well as himself. He stood instead with his eyes fixed on the screen, stroking his chin as he tried to wrap his head around what exactly he was seeing.

Not wishing to alert anyone to the situation until they were completely sure of what was going on, they'd opted to send a bot out to the Haphor relay station rather than an agent. It was there now, recording what it saw and transmitting a live feed back to the screen in Noro. It hovered in front of the pyre upon which Lieutenant Tarbic had supposedly burned Payvan's body. It was clear that something had indeed been burned there, but it was also clear that it hadn't been a corpse.

"Focus in on the pyre, please," Dasaro said into the earpiece he wore.

The bot complied, panning back and forth and giving him a closer view of the charred pile in its entirety. There were no visible bones, no clothing fragments, not so much as a tooth to tell him Ziva had been taken care of. Not wishing to believe he'd been deceived, Dasaro once again entered Tarbic's code into his comm. Again, there was no answer, and he allowed a growl to escape his throat as he returned the device to his belt.

"What are you thinking?" Hoxie asked, his smooth voice carrying through the darkness of the situation room in which the three of them were holed up.

Dasaro couldn't help but smile, almost amused by the sheer ridiculousness of it all. "Payvan's good, I'll give her that much. Tarbic had me fooled, too—I should have realized he was up to something."

"And now that they have Shevin?"

"Now that they have Shevin," Dasaro echoed, rubbing a hand over his face as he thought. "Now that they have Shevin, everything could start coming unraveled faster than we can tie it back up. The key is to keep all those knots intact."

"What do you propose we do?" Nejdra asked, pivoting in her chair to face them.

"Eliminate ways for them to untie any knots before they have a chance to try," Dasaro replied. He paused a moment and studied the computer screen Nejdra was working with, watching as a pattern recognition program searched through a seemingly endless string of surveillance feeds for the riding suit Payvan wore. They'd already spotted Shevin on one of the spaceport cams, but the angle had been bad and there was no way of knowing which transport he'd boarded. It was time to find another approach. "How many leads besides Shevin does she have? Who else has she been in contact with recently?"

Nejdra turned back to the workstation and brought up a transmission log on another screen. "No activity on the Alpha team's office comm for the past four days. The last incoming message appears to be from an intragalactic code."

"Run it," Dasaro said.

He and Hoxie stepped forward and leaned closer, watching as Nejdra began a trace on the code. The source was found after mere seconds, both startling Dasaro and piquing his curiosity.

"It's from our embassy on Chaiavis," Nejdra said. "Looks like someone used their weekly transmission to contact Payvan."

Dasaro nodded thoughtfully. By 'weekly transmission,' she referred to the allotted single message the Haphezian outcasts were allowed to send or receive per week. The government had thought it only fair that the Defectives be allowed to stay in touch with their culture of origin if they so chose, but at the same time, this method prevented too much contact. The fact that someone at the embassy had sacrificed precious communication time to contact Ziva's team intrigued him.

"Do we have any audio from the call?"

Nejdra manipulated the terminal and opened the audio file that had been saved with the transmission log. Rather than Ziva's voice, they found themselves listening to that of Officer Vax. The caller was a woman who introduced herself as someone who had heard good things about Ziva's track record and hoped to discuss a potential job offer with her. Dasaro took another look at the transmission's timestamp—the call had come through just moments after Ziva's arrest. No wonder Vax had answered.

"Tell you what," the intelligence officer said on the recording. "I'll see if I can find her, but for now, I'm going to transfer you over to someone in records where you can leave your contact information."

There were several seconds of static and random tones as the transmission was routed to a different department. The automated voice came on asking the caller to leave her name—she responded, "Kat Reilly." A short pause followed before the system prompted her for a comm code, but she ended the transmission abruptly before answering.

Nejdra had a search running before the audio file had even ended. "Kat Reilly," she said. "Age twenty-five, she was born in Argall and has lived at the Chaiavis embassy since birth due to an appearance abnormality. According to their records, she left the residential wing seven years ago. She lives on her own but stops in periodically to send a transmission or look for work."

"Reilly," Dasaro echoed as the gears in his mind began to turn. The room fell silent for several long seconds.

Nejdra pivoted in the chair to face him. "You think it's—?"

"Could this girl know something?" Hoxie asked.

"For now, it's the best lead we've got," Dasaro replied. "It looks like we'll be taking a trip to Chaiavis."

· 63 ·
CENTRAL SPACEPORT
CHAIAVIS

The Chaiavis spaceport where their transport touched down bore a striking resemblance to the one in Noro. The sense of familiarity sent a wave of relief washing over Ziva—or maybe she was just happy to be off the ship. Being in close quarters with others came with the job, but after being cooped up in a tiny room with Aroska and Kade for close to two days, the fresh air felt heavenly.

It could hardly be considered fresh, though; the port where they'd landed rested on the border of an industrial sector, and the air was thick with smoke and emissions from various nearby factories. This was the only city on the planet, situated in a temperate zone halfway between the equator and northern pole, but it was nearly the size of Haphez's Noro and Haphor Regions combined. The planet itself was a capital of sorts for many of the Fringe worlds, a political hub for the civilizations that weren't part of the Federation. Still, it rested on the edge of Federation space and thus saw heavy traffic due to the merchants, politicians, smugglers, and tourists traveling back and forth between the Fringe and the Core. If someone wanted to hide, this was the place to do it.

Night had long since fallen, casting the crowded streets in shadows, and the people in the area had an all-around grimy look to them that reminded Ziva all too much of home. She sighed and nodded to herself; this place was perfect.

Slinging her backpack over her shoulder, she moved down the ramp and through the boarding gate with her two male companions in tow. She steered them out of the heart of the crowd and paused for a moment on a street corner, familiarizing herself with the area. There were a variety of cheap hotels and flophouses in the immediate vicinity, though the thought of remaining there so close to the docks made her skin crawl.

"We need to keep moving," she said, not wanting to but also not wishing to be caught after all the trouble they'd gone through to get there. She turned to Aroska and Kade, hesitating for a moment as she studied the looks they both gave her.

"What?" she demanded, feeling even less secure loitering there in the street than she would have in one of the flophouses.

She didn't need a response to know what they were thinking. They stood with sagging shoulders and deadpan faces, telling her they were trying hard not to broadcast how exhausted they really were. They glanced briefly at each other before Aroska stepped forward, hand extended in a calming manner.

"You know we can't stay here," she exclaimed before he had a chance to say anything. "We are at *war* right now. We've got to move, regroup."

"Do you see Dasaro here?" Aroska said, his voice just as gruff. He held his arms out and looked around. "I didn't think so. *One* night."

"And how do you know he's not going to be on the next transport that docks here?"

"He won't be. We were careful—he has no way of knowing which transport we were on, and even if he *does*, he can't know where we landed. For all he knows, we could have gotten off yesterday."

Kade remained calmer as he spoke. "I vote we stop," he said. "We can rest a bit and start fresh in the morning. The way I see it, trying to press on in this condition will more likely result in mistakes, and that's when we'll get caught."

"You two have been planning this, haven't you?" Ziva placed her hands on her hips and turned back to study the docking area for a moment. Most of the travelers from the transport had dispersed by now, leaving Chaiavis's nighttime crowd to govern the streets. Sighing, she pivoted and looked over their lodging options before peering up and down the street as far as she could see.

"Fine," she said, "but I want to move out of this area."

The two men seemed pleased as the three of them secured their packs and began walking. As they moved farther from the factories, the lights became brighter and the crowd thickened. Ziva couldn't help but wonder how many of these people might recognize them from the news.

Half an hour's trek hadn't taken them as far as she would have preferred, but the feeling of being exposed in the street was beginning to take its toll on her. She paused in front of a dilapidated little hotel with a flickering sign sandwiched between two booming nightclubs, her eye on one of four rooms with windows overlooking the street. One of these would do nicely.

The three of them entered and, finding the lobby's only occupant to be a drunken man passed out in a crusty old chair, continued up the stairs. There didn't seem to be any other tenants, so they chose one of the street-view rooms whose door faced the stairs. The room was sparsely furnished, with a single bed, tiny sofa, and a faulty lighting panel that only seemed to work for ten seconds at a time. All in all, it was perfect— it was a place where nobody would be inclined to look for them, and where anyone who found them wouldn't be inclined to bother them.

Ziva made her way across to the window, coughing against the scent of cigar smoke lingering in the curtains. They had an unobstructed view of the street below and could see the majority of the ships heading to the docks. She set her bag on the floor and turned to find Aroska and Kade watching her as if they weren't sure what to do.

She gestured toward the bed and the sofa. "Well?"

Kade slid his satchel from his shoulder and placed it gingerly at the foot of the bed. "What are you going to do?"

"I'll keep watch," she replied, turning back toward the window. "I'm not tired." Several seconds of silence passed before she reassured them, "I'll wake one of you if I have to."

For a moment, she wasn't sure if they were buying such a lie. She took comfort in knowing she wouldn't be able to sleep even if she wanted to, so in a way, what she was telling them was true. Both men studied her for another beat before reluctantly moving away to their respective sleeping arrangements, Aroska taking the bed and Kade the sofa.

Ziva sighed and stretched her stiff shoulders. She parted the curtains slightly, remaining far enough back in the shadows that she had a clear view of the street but that any onlookers were unlikely to see her lurking there. She wasn't quite sure what she was looking for, short of Dasaro in the flesh. Part of her wondered if there would be bounty hunters coming after her, but another part wondered if the rest of the Haphezian population even knew she was still alive. Surely the captain and his posse had figured it out by now, but perhaps he had chosen to keep it quiet so nobody would know about his mistake...and so no one would start to question the supposed charges brought against her.

She wasn't entirely sure what she preferred. The fewer the people who knew she was alive, the lower the risk—dealing with Dasaro and the other two captains would be easy enough. On the other hand, if more people knew she lived, it could help discredit Dasaro and he would go down all the more quickly. At this point, Veya Shevin was the only person who knew. If she'd done as she was told and had gone to Noro, Marshay and Ryon would know, and if they knew, Skeet and Zinni most likely did, too. That thought coaxed a sigh of relief out of her, but the relief didn't last. All of that depended wholly on Veya, and she didn't have a lot of confidence in the young woman. Worse yet, maybe everyone else already knew her death had been staged, and Dasaro had had time to paint her and Aroska and Kade as criminals on the run.

Aroska and Kade. Surely Dasaro realized by now that Tarbic had played him. Did he know Kade was with them? How was he explaining the young agent's disappearance? Had anyone from the Royal Guard even noticed he was gone? Shevin had told her about being dismissed from the office; chances were nobody would be missing him for a couple more days. Did they realize his family was gone? What about the bodies left at RG Headquarters? And so the questions continued to spin through her mind, questions that spawned new questions and eventually led her back to where she'd started.

As her brain worked, her eyes remained on the window, taking in each individual and vehicle that passed by. Time ticked by; the crowd reached its apex and finally began to die down as the morning hours approached.

She was brought out of her trance by the sound of Aroska's heavy breathing. She turned away from the window to find him curled up in a semi-fetal position, clutching the pillow with white knuckles. The light from outside reflected off his sweaty forehead and partially illuminated a face contorted with misery. Sighing yet again, she returned her attention to the street. He'd done better than she'd expected so far in terms of withdrawals, but considering the condition he'd been in when she'd sought him out, she knew they were inevitable. He'd handled the journey here well enough, probably due to the fact that he'd snuck out for a drink two different times under the pretense of stretching his legs—she'd been able to smell it on him upon his return. The man was a fool if he thought she didn't know, but she'd allowed it for fear that he would be incapacitated by withdrawal symptoms sometime when she needed to count on him.

She eased back into her semi-conscious state, this time leaning against the window frame and looking down into the street at an angle. All the questions came flooding back within a moment, getting so tangled up in one another and vying for her attention that they all became a dull buzz in her ears. The majority of them were impossible to answer from where she stood now, yet having those answers would help her figure out what steps they needed to take. For the first time in a long time, she felt rather lost. At the moment, her plan consisted of acquiring money and some form of transportation and then seeking out Aroska's contact. Then what? Kade was getting closer to breaking the encryption on his boss's files. Perhaps that would help point them in the right direction.

It seemed like only minutes later that Ziva heard someone say her name and became aware of something cold and hard pressing against her head. More accurately, her head was pressing against the cold hard thing—she was perched in the windowsill, one leg dangling down to the floor, her face resting against the glass. What little of the horizon she could see through the forest of buildings was already pink with dawn. She snapped to attention and turned to find Aroska standing there with his hand retracted as if he'd been about to tap her shoulder.

"*Sheyss*," she muttered, rubbing the sleep out of her eyes as she got down and stretched her cramped legs. "You're terrible about letting me doze off like that."

"Come on. You know as well as I do that you could use the rest."

"Where's Shevin?"

"He went downstairs to see if anyone knows where we could find an old aircar for sale. I assume we could use one?"

"Good, good," she said, pleased someone was accomplishing something even while she was being useless. "We can use the money I have left, and once I can access one of my accounts, we'll be good to go."

"One of your accounts, huh?"

She remained deadpan. "I've made money over the years that hasn't necessarily been clean. It requires off-world accounts HSP doesn't necessarily know about."

Kade returned presently, bearing a small holographic advertisement. "The bartender at the club next door has an old car he's been trying to sell. I told him we were interested—his shift ends in twenty minutes."

"Thanks, Shevin," Ziva said, checking her pistol and tucking it back into her pants. Her fingers brushed over one end of her kytara where it dangled from its special harness under her jacket. "You stay here, hold down the fort, and we'll go get the car and find Aroska's contact. We'll keep you updated."

"Got it," Kade said with a respectful nod. "What if someone comes?"

"If anyone walks through that door?" She gestured toward the pistol resting on the sofa beside his bag. "Shoot them in the head."

· 64 ·
BOSCO'S PARTS AND REPAIR
CHAIAVIS

T he car was a rusty red thing that had to be over twenty years old. The exterior had seen better days, but after a brief inspection of the engine compartment, Ziva had deemed the machine stable. The bartender had charged them a fair price, too, and he'd seemed just as excited to be paid in cash as he had to get rid of the thing. The repulsion system needed repair, so gaining altitude had been a bit tricky, but Aroska was confident his friend could help with that.

They left the aircar parked on the small landing pad outside and walked across to the shop, which was nestled between the rest of Chaiavis's towering structures high above the level of the street. Judging by its outward appearance, it seemed to be a large, well-kept store, making Ziva wonder if Aroska knew what he was doing after all.

"You don't strike me as the type of person who would have resources like this," she said, turning in a slow circle as she followed him inside. The rest of the landing pad was clear, and nothing seemed out of the ordinary.

A motion detector emitted a friendly chime as they entered. "I've had my uses for this sort of place," Aroska replied. "Besides, Bosco is an old friend. He always seems to have exactly what I need—for a good price, too."

The interior of the shop was warm and could maybe even be described as homey. Several antique weapons and parts were on display in the foyer, on sale to any collectors fanatical enough to fork over the credits. The walls and floor were well maintained and free of clutter except for the occasional deactivated bot and an old engine someone had left for Bosco to take a look at. A long counter separated them from a warehouse-style back room lined with massive shelves stretching to the ceiling. These contained various parts and boxes of equipment, all neatly organized by brand and purpose, it appeared. If not for the fact that there was work to be done, Ziva would have liked to spend more time looking around.

"Coming, coming," bellowed a deep voice from back amid the shelves. An older Haphezian man appeared, wiping grease from his hands on a thick apron he wore around his waist. He was one of the Defectives who had been ostracized from Haphez as a child and sent to the embassy there on Chaiavis, having one blue eye, one green eye, and no hair streaks Ziva could see. His face was devoid of any *gesh punti*—he'd no doubt been exiled before he was old enough to receive them. He was a bit scruffy and had styled his close-cropped hair into short spikes that ran down the center of his head. Both ears and one eyebrow were pierced, and his forearms were enveloped in tattoos, but his eyes were kind and he beamed when he spotted Aroska.

"Aroska Tarbic!" he roared heartily, giving his own bulging belly a solid pat. "Now *there's* a face I haven't seen in far too long!" He waddled toward them, arms open wide, with a rich laugh that reminded Ziva of her father. She noticed he was walking on two prosthetic legs.

Bosco and Aroska embraced, and the older man clapped Tarbic hard on the back. "How've you been, boy? You still working for those scumbags at HSP?"

"Might I remind you that if it weren't for those 'scumbags,' *you* wouldn't be standing here talking to me right now."

Bosco chuckled again and waved a finger. "Aye, isn't that the truth." He turned to Ziva, who had been watching the situation unfold from a couple of meters away, and grinned wide. "And who's your pretty friend, here?"

The smile on Aroska's face dissolved and he looked to her, a flicker of uncertainty flashing across his eyes. "Oh, this is—"

"Ziva," she said. She crossed her arms but managed a slight dip of her head.

"Welcome, Ziva. I'm Bosco Jagger." He bowed deeply and swung his thumb back toward Aroska. "Takes a certain kind of girl to be letting this guy drag you around."

"Believe it or not, I think *she's* the one dragging *me* around," Aroska said. "I finally found one I can't handle."

By 'one,' Ziva assumed he meant a woman, and she immediately thought of several snide remarks that would make sufficient comebacks. But she remained silent and instead followed him to the counter, where the two of them took a seat on some tall stools.

"What can I do for you, son?" Bosco asked, scooting back around to the other side of the bar. "You in need of equipment?"

Aroska nodded. "I'm looking for an anti-grav stabilizer that would fit the repulsion system on an old Cording VX-2 aircar," he replied. "I can take care of any modifications myself."

"What's a hot rod like you doing flying around in a twenty-year-old hunk of junk like that?" Bosco chuckled. "Anti-grav stabilizer, huh? Sounds like you're trying to get somewhere high and get there fast."

"Something like that."

"I'll see what I can dig up for you. Anything for the lady?"

His tone made it sound like a joke. Ziva drummed her fingers on the surface of the counter, suddenly aware of an opportunity that needed to be taken advantage of. "What have you got in the way of projectile rifles?"

Bosco blinked and the friendly glimmer vanished from his eyes. He stroked his chin in an attempt to mask the change and hummed to himself. "I believe I've got an old Korberon rifle in the back somewhere. Been there for a while, though."

"That'll work. I'll also need a twelve-round mag and a barrel extension and suppressor. If you have a spare hair trigger lying around, I'll take that, too. And an empty plasma cell."

"Empty, huh?" Bosco's eyes shifted briefly toward Aroska. "What kind of ammunition?"

"I won't be needing ammunition."

"No ammunition?"

"No ammo."

The old man snorted and slapped the counter. "Who would have thought? Let me see what I can find."

He disappeared among the shelves again, whistling to himself as he went. Ziva swiveled on her stool to maintain a partial view of the front door and continued to tap her fingers on the counter. Aroska watched her with furrowed eyebrows.

"Real subtle," he muttered, shaking his head. "What do you think you're going to do with an antique rifle?"

"Probably shoot something with it."

His only response was a scoff.

"HSP confiscated all my weapons, Aroska. I need something more than a plasma pistol. Long range is my forte. They should know better than to separate a sniper and her rifle. Besides, the gravity here is comparable to that at home. If—galaxy forbid—I actually have to use it here, it won't be a problem."

Aroska shook his head again. "It just seems counterproductive."

"I'll tell you what's counterproductive: *you* handling the car repairs."

"What makes you think I can't handle them myself?"

"I didn't say you couldn't. We just need this thing running properly in a matter of hours, not days."

Aroska looked in the direction Bosco had gone then leaned a little closer. "Can you at least try to be civil for the next few minutes?"

She held her hands up in mock surrender and looked away. The two of them sat there in silence for a while, listening to the faint music carrying through the shop's comm system with a gentle beat. Ziva could hear Bosco rummaging around among the shelves; his casual whistling had ceased. Now that she had a rifle, there were a couple of other items she would need to get her hands on, but she doubted he carried what she was looking for. Despite his pleasant demeanor and the way Aroska had spoken of him, she couldn't bring herself to trust the older man. Even if he didn't betray them voluntarily, it was possible HSP could eventually track them to this shop, and she didn't need anyone knowing any more than they had to.

Bosco returned presently, toting the stabilizer in an old pack and carrying a long rifle case. He set both on the counter, his multi-colored eyes fixed on Ziva. "The other things you asked for are in here," he said, tapping the case. He spoke as if something were lodged in his throat.

She placed a stack of credits on the counter and flipped the latches on the rifle case. After a brief examination, it appeared its contents were in order, and she looked up to meet Bosco's questioning gaze.

"I don't want any trouble," he growled, though his eyes were filled with fear. "I don't spend much time at the embassy, but there are a couple of things I know—you're the one HSP was looking for, and you're supposed to be dead."

"Look, Bosco," Aroska said. "Ziva's innocent and we're doing our best to stay off the radar, okay? We didn't come here to give you any trouble, but we don't need you to give us any, either."

The old man nodded and folded his brawny arms. "I'd rather not get involved. I'll erase my surveillance feeds, but I'm going to have to ask you two to go ahead and get on out of here."

Aroska's eyebrows dropped into a scowl. "So that's it then? You're not even going to hear us out?"

"Son, I've got a business to run and other customers to take care of." Bosco held his hand out to the items on the counter. "I think I've already done my part to help you. There *is* someone else you could be talking to, though."

"Who?" Ziva asked, pulling the rifle case toward her before Bosco could change his mind.

"Name's Kat Reilly. She's one of us, a freelancer who frequents this place to buy weapons. Pretty young thing, clever as hell. You should be able to find her around the clubs in the eastern part of the Underground."

Ziva glanced to Aroska. Their pitiful little hotel, the docks where they'd landed—both were located in the heart of the Chaiavian district known as the Underground. The area was considered a haven of sorts, a place where any species could make themselves at home without affecting the city's more dignified sectors. The eastern edge of the

Underground bordered another upper-class entertainment district—there were literally hundreds of bars and clubs to choose from.

"Care to be any more specific?" she said, somewhat annoyed. Finding people was her job, but such a vague description still left a pool of thousands to comb through.

"She's what you might call a 'private' person—she won't want you asking around for her," Bosco replied. He gave a brief physical description, informing them she might bolt or even retaliate if she got spooked. "Tell her I sent you, and she should be okay."

Ziva still wasn't thrilled with what a time-consuming process it was going to be, but if it meant acquiring a new ally and gaining any sort of edge over Dasaro, she was willing to at least try.

The door alarm chimed and another customer walked in, acknowledging them with a friendly nod as he entered. She took that as their cue to leave and gathered up the rifle case. Aroska grabbed the bag with the stabilizer.

"Good luck, for what it's worth," Bosco said.

· 65 ·
NIOBI PROCESSING CENTER
ARGALL, HAPHEZ

The number of niobi crystals drifting by on the conveyor belt was indeed impressive. Granted, the mercenaries were digging deeper than ever before and, as a result, had destroyed a good portion of the landscape in order to get them. The worst part was that most of them were nothing more than weak white crystals, some nearly clear. Bent on achieving maximum financial gain—or maybe just showcasing his dominance—Loric had ordered their harvest anyway, despite the fact that they were barely mature enough to generate any power.

Mag stood there at the conveyor, data pad in hand, absentmindedly reaching in to remove the occasional rock that floated by. There weren't many at this point in the processing, but all the recent blasting had resulted in more dirt and debris than normal. The mercs had doubled the number of workers in place at the belt, thereby helping with the problem, but now it seemed as though there were too many of them. There was Mag, essentially just standing there, feeling as though he were accomplishing nothing.

The sight of the crystals themselves had also taken some getting used to. Most of Argall's population was somehow involved with the mining industry, whether they be farmers or factory workers, but Mag's time had been spent in an office away from the actual processing centers. Roles like that, anything involving money or number crunching, had been assumed by Loric's men so as to prevent the citizens from trying to contact the outside world.

Another rock came along, and Mag scooped it up and tossed it into the bin behind him. It was such a fluid movement, the reaching and tossing, that it had almost become a reflex over the past several months. A sudden vision of himself snatching up not a rock but a crystal entered his mind. Startled, he lowered his hand to his side and wiped it off on his grimy green jumpsuit, identical to the ones everyone else was wearing. He was known for his sleight of hand—so was the rest of his family, for that matter—and he had often thought about how easy it would be to swipe up a couple of crystals without being caught. There was, however, a big difference between thinking about it and actually considering it.

"*Take care of yourself,*" his mother had instructed him just prior to being shot before his eyes. Stealing crystals—crystals that were nigh on worthless, at that—didn't seem like the best way to respect her final wishes. What did he expect to accomplish by taking them, anyway? The mercs had made it abundantly clear that stealing crystals meant a plasma bolt to the brain. They'd even rigged up some scanners to detect the elemental composition of the crystals and all workers had to be inspected before leaving the factory each day. If Mag were to be caught with them, Loric wouldn't hesitate to kill him then and there, map or no map.

The map. He had managed to shut it from his mind for most of the afternoon, a relief after spending the past few days with it plaguing him constantly. After a bit more back and forth, he had finally concluded that finding it would be the best move, regardless of whether he kept it or handed it over to the mercenaries. Even if he was killed or managed to hide it, he knew Loric would continue to execute people and tear up the mountains until he found that room of crystals.

Was there somewhere he could send the map when he found it? Getting it out of the city would mean somehow avoiding the net the mercs had cast over it, something that had already been proven impossible many times by people who were now dead. He dared not trust anyone else to take it for safekeeping, and he was suddenly hit with the realization that his father wouldn't have, either.

Preoccupied with this new idea, it took Mag a moment to notice the cluster of rocks passing by him on the conveyor. He shook his head and began picking them out, wracking his brain trying to think of anyone his father had ever confided in, someone elsewhere on the planet or elsewhere in the galaxy. No one came to mind immediately, at least anyone who would be familiar with Argall and the mining system. Maybe that was the key—wherever the map was, it was somewhere far enough away that it was meaningless to anyone who saw it. Unfortunately, if that were the case, there was a good chance it was no longer in existence.

If it *was* still intact, retrieving it would mean leaving the city. He was sure the mercenaries wouldn't allow him to just walk out, and if he told them where he was going, they would more than likely want to accompany him. That left escaping undetected as his only real option, but the mercs were keeping such close tabs on him that it wouldn't take them long to realize he was gone. Once they did, Loric would gladly start killing, and all that blood would be on Mag's hands.

Three full days had passed in the week Loric had given him to find the data pad. That left him with a little over three days to somehow connect with the outside world. Figuring out who his father had been in contact with three years earlier would be tricky, albeit easier than reestablishing that contact now. Then there was the question of whether his time would be better spent doing that or trying to send for help. Either way, there wasn't a lot of time to waste.

He paused a moment, startled by the texture of one of the rocks he picked up. Turning it over in his hand, he scratched at it with a fingernail, watching as the dirt crumbled from it and drifted to the floor. The rock was, in fact, a niobi crystal, roughly two centimeters long and equally wide. How easy it would be to simply throw it into the bin with the other debris! The crystal might even be worth something; it was mostly white, but the center was just starting to ripen.

A commotion behind him startled Mag out of his thoughts. He turned, crystal still in hand, to find a group of mercenaries converging on a worker attempting to exit through one of the scanners. All of them were yelling at once, drawing the attention of everyone else nearby. The thugs had their weapons drawn and forced the man to his knees, where they began searching him. One of them recovered a handful of small crystals from his pocket, and before the man could say a word, he was silenced by a sizzling plasma bolt.

Sighing, Mag shook his head and placed the crystal back on the conveyor.

· 66 ·
UNDERGROUND DISTRICT
CHAIAVIS

"Where here do we even start?" Aroska muttered.

'From the beginning' was the first reply to enter Ziva's mind, though she remained silent. After four hours of looking around the Underground, they had come up short, so they'd ventured further into the heart of the city. With the number of people around, going on foot had proved to be more efficient than flying, though not having a quick means of escape if they needed one made her nervous.

The two of them stopped and took several seconds to just stare into the heart of Chaiavis's Endion Entertainment District. With limited habitable space for expanding outward, most of the city was built upward; despite it only being midday, the massive structures shrouded the streets in darkness and the holograms were lit up as if it were late night. People and aliens of all shapes and sizes moved about between the bars and shops, dodging the occasional hoverbike or groundcar whose pilot was brave enough to press through the gauntlet. It was loud, too—music, laughter, and a variety of languages filled the air and created a single deafening roar that was already giving Ziva a headache. She looked up to where the throngs of ships and aircars moved to and fro, feeling small with the city's towering buildings rising up on either side of her. Blue sky and sunlight were visible high above.

"Just like home, eh?" she said, clapping Aroska on the shoulder as she took the first steps forward.

They began walking. Like the Underground, Endion bore a striking resemblance to downtown Noro. The sense of familiarity once again brought her comfort, but the deeper in they travelled, the less in control she felt. Knowledge of the city and street life was certainly a plus in this situation, but if this Kat Reilly character really frequented this place as often as Bosco said, she would still have a huge advantage over them.

"You've heard the old saying, 'It takes a Haphezian to kill a Haphezian,' right?" Aroska said. "If that's true, don't you think it would be just as accurate to say it takes a Haphezian to *find* a Haphezian?"

"If that's the case, she has just as much chance of finding us as we do of finding her," Ziva responded, carefully scanning the crowds as she strode forward. "This is her turf—there's no telling how she'll react when she sees us."

They continued forward in silence, weaving in and out of the drunken club patrons, gamblers, and the occasional vendor who had ventured out into the street to advertise his wares. Here in the crowd during the daytime hours, Ziva felt safely anonymous—the order for her arrest seemed light-years away, if not nonexistent, and even if anyone nearby was aware of it, she doubted they cared. In fact, most of these people were probably trying to avoid some form of the law themselves, whether they be capital criminals or petty drug dealers.

She turned and followed Aroska into the first club they came to. The two of them hesitated in the doorway for a moment under the watchful eyes of a pair of bouncers, taking in what little they could see. The interior of the establishment was dark, lit only with deep red lighting panels, and it was nearly as crowded as it might have been during late night hours. The cloud of cigar smoke was so thick that the club's patrons were hardly more than shadows visible through the haze.

Ziva caught Aroska's arm as he stepped forward. "Who's going to stand out more, the bar rat or the off-worlders?" She released his sleeve and nodded for him to head to the right. "Be vigilant."

She turned to the left and began taking slow, even strides, sweeping her gaze back and forth with each step. On her right: the bar. All but a few of the stools were occupied by customers, some of whom were conversing with the bartender or each other but most of whom were hunched over their drinks in silence. None of these people appeared to be Kat Reilly—few were even female—so she shifted her attention to the tables on her left. Most of these were full as well with people either eating or playing cards. Some of them eyed her warily as she passed, but it only took a moment for them to return to what they were doing.

Clusters of customers stood in the center of the walkway talking, laughing, and casually sipping at drinks—they paid her little mind as she slipped by and continued around the main floor's circular path. Live music could be heard ahead, though the band itself was invisible behind a wall of dancing patrons and a collection of game tables. More tables were situated farther along the path, positioned in front of several large viewscreens streaming live feeds from various sporting events around the Fringe.

The sensation of being watched had become prevalent in the past several days, and there in the bar, it had flared up again. Ziva stopped walking and took a moment to listen, not just to the general din but to each individual sound around her. She turned in a slow circle, looking back over the things she'd already seen, searching for anything that had changed since she'd passed. Nothing seemed any different than it had the first time, but the feeling of eyes upon her hadn't faded. She turned around when a familiar scent reached her nostrils and found Aroska making his way toward her. The sensation diminished as he neared, and she breathed a sigh of relief when she realized he had probably been the source.

"Nothing," he said, continuing to glance around regardless.

"Likewise." Wondering how many more clubs they would have to search before they found something, Ziva carried on in the direction from which Aroska had come and he fell into stride beside her. They worked their way back around the bar, keeping cautious eyes on the door and anyone coming or going.

One of the bouncers, a thick-bodied human man with a shaved head, eyed them again as they exited. The other, a species Ziva didn't recognize, was speaking with an aircar pilot dressed in a full flight suit and helmet. They put their conversation on hold until Ziva and Aroska were safely past, scrutinizing them as they went.

"You really think it would be that much trouble to just ask around?" Aroska muttered, stuffing his hands into his pockets.

"You tell me," she replied. "You're the one who insisted we trust Bosco. He said she wouldn't want that kind of attention, and we don't need that kind of attention."

They pressed on, though Ziva couldn't help but feel they were wasting their time. She was confident, however, that if finding Reilly was this complicated, they would in turn be safe from Dasaro. Here they had a general idea of where Kat was located—HSP had no way of knowing where they'd even landed.

They searched three more clubs, repeating the process of entering, splitting up, finding nothing, and leaving. The feeling that someone was watching had returned, and this time Ziva was unable to trace it back to Aroska. She listened carefully for any footsteps approaching behind her and checked what little she could see of her reflection as she passed a window.

She was still focused on the peculiar feeling when Aroska stopped short and began examining the items at one of the vendor booths. He selected a cheap knock-off targeting visor and fit it over his eyes, checking himself in a small mirror before turning toward her.

"How do I look?" he asked, grinning.

"What do you think you're doing?" she demanded, crossing her arms. But as soon as the words were out of her mouth, she realized something was off. She didn't have a clear view of his eyes through the visor, but she could see enough to tell he wasn't actually looking at her.

His smile diminished and he replaced the device, taking a step toward her before speaking. "We have a tail," he said. "One-eighty— our pilot friend from the first club."

Ziva bristled. This was the presence she felt, she was sure of it. She turned, glancing over the crowd before fixing her gaze on a holographic advertisement above the street. Searching with her peripherals, she spotted the blue flight suit within seconds—the pilot who had been conversing with the club bouncers stood perhaps sixty meters directly behind them, idly looking about at the booths and passersby. The face within the helmet gradually turned in their direction but looked away when its owner realized they were looking.

They turned in perfect synchronization and began walking again, keeping their heads and voices down as they went. "I've seen him hanging around outside every club," Aroska said. "He's been back there at least ten minutes."

Ziva picked up her pace a bit, though she had no intention of trying to shake their follower. The presence she felt, the presence of this person, had her greatly curious and she placed a warning hand on Aroska's arm when she saw him reach for his pistol. "Let it play," she instructed.

"What if it's HSP?"

"It's not HSP," she replied, unsure how to elaborate further.

It was always possible that it could be a bounty hunter hired by HSP—there was no doubt in her mind that Dasaro would send someone after them. Any hired guns, however, wouldn't have shoot-to-kill orders; the captain would want that great privilege for himself. These hunters would only have instructions to relay information about her location, which the agency would no doubt act upon in no time. Suddenly everyone who appeared to be paying them a little too much attention or walking a little too close was the enemy. She moved faster.

"You want to tell me what's going on?" Aroska turned his head toward her, his eyes straining to see behind him.

Rather than respond, she shoved him down the first alley they came to. The area was dark, lit only with the dim lighting panels positioned above the back doors of all the clubs. Few people walked this path—those who did appeared to be either homeless or drunk. Smaller passages branched from the main one, leading to more shady and secretive establishments, and the hustle and bustle of the next street over could be seen far ahead.

"You're going to create a diversion," she said once they'd made it a suitable distance into the alley. "I want to have a chat with this guy."

She dodged a Durutian man who had passed out beside one of the club doors and ducked down a smaller alley on her right. Signaling for Aroska to go left, she pressed her back against the grimy building wall and fingered her kytara under her jacket. She removed it and held it down at her side, prepared to engage the blades as she listened for the stranger's approaching footsteps.

The pilot paused at the end of the alley, most likely wondering what had become of them. The person took several tentative steps forward—Ziva thought she caught a whiff of their scent as they drew closer. She waited several more seconds before signaling for Aroska to step out of his hiding place. He did so hesitantly, pulling his communicator from his belt and studying the tiny screen with a frown.

There was a brief catch in the footfalls of the approaching person as they caught sight of him. Then the steps quickened, and Ziva could picture the figure lowering his head in a futile attempt at remaining inconspicuous. She drew a deep breath as she heard him come within meters.

Aroska stepped forward, successfully attracting the pilot's attention as he flashed an innocent grin and held up his comm. "Excuse me, I'm wondering if you can tell me—"

He got no further before she leaped forward, the blade of her kytara angled for the pilot's head. A second kytara blade, slightly curved, appeared out of nowhere, crossing hers before she had a chance to grab him. Aroska retreated, startled—he drew his pistol, but he held it low and looked on with wide eyes. It was for the best, Ziva decided, shifting all her focus to her weapon and her opponent. He would only get in the way.

Caught off guard and unsure who she was dealing with, she did the only thing she could think of and mentally took herself back to a previous kytara duel. Truth be told, she was out of practice—the last time she'd fought a real opponent was the day she'd killed Gamon. It appeared, however, that the stranger was just as shocked as she was. He was a decent swordsman, though he seemed inexperienced in that he relied on sheer strength rather than the finesse and elegance that would allow him to use his Nostia to supplement his fighting skills. Still, his reflexes were good, and he continued to block her blows with little effort.

She thought she heard Aroska say something, but she ignored

him and caught the pilot's forearm with her free hand. Ducking low, she swept her leg around and caught him behind the knees, sending him to the ground and wrenching his arm around as he went. The kytara slipped from his grasp and she pulled it into her own hand, shoving him onto his back with her foot. He began trying to scoot away but fell still and held his hands up in surrender as she crossed the blades above his throat.

"Slowly," she growled, gesturing at the helmet. "Who are you?"

There was a long pause where her eyes were locked with those behind the visor. Then, gradually, keeping his gloved palms open, the pilot reached up and began tugging the helmet off. A great pile of blonde hair—so blonde it was nearly white—came cascading out, and she found herself looking into the icy blue eyes of not a man but a young woman. Like Bosco, she had no *gesh punti*, but the silver streaks in her hair were unmistakable. She held her hands up, staring fearlessly into Ziva's face and breathing hard.

Ziva retracted the kytara blades and returned her own to its holster. "Kat Reilly?"

The girl nodded and raised an eyebrow, making a half-hearted effort to sit up. "Ziva Payvan?"

Startled, Ziva offered her the kytara and helped her get to her feet.

"We need to talk," they said simultaneously.

· 67 ·
HSP Headquarters
Noro, Haphez

In the fifteen years he'd spent as Prime Director of HSP, Emeri Arion had never felt less in control of his agency. He shut the office door as quickly as he could, taking a moment to revel in the darkness and silence of the room. It seemed thinking things would return to normal once Ziva was gone had been a mistake—now everything was falling apart faster than he could put it back together.

The first issue was what had transpired at the Royal Guard office two nights earlier, the event that had perhaps sparked all this madness. The four dead men found on the premises were confirmed to be ex-military, but why they'd been there and who had shot them remained a mystery. On top of that, secure files had been compromised and Agent Shevin and his family were now missing. Emeri had spent a good portion of the morning on comm with SSA Luko Zona trying to sort everything out.

It seemed that Zona had been in contact with Captain Dasaro, who had apparently formed the theory that this missing agent was responsible for all the chaos at RG Headquarters. After hearing Zona's account of the situation, it certainly seemed as though that were the case, though Emeri had never gotten the impression Shevin was capable of such things.

Eager to hear the captain's theory for himself, he'd sought Dasaro out only to find that the man and the other two unit captains working with him had disappeared entirely. According to Zona, it had been at least a day and a half since he and Dasaro had last spoken, and since then, there was no record that he or Captains Venn and Hoxie had been present at HSP Headquarters at all. At first, it hadn't registered to Emeri that anything was wrong, though he found it rather strange that Dasaro would sever communication with the RG office after keeping in such close touch with Zona. But now, after close to thirty-six hours and not a word from any of the captains, something was clearly amiss. Upon further investigation, it appeared Lieutenant Tarbic was gone, too. That made a total of five agents missing, all gone for indefinite amounts of time and without even the slightest attempts at communication.

Sighing, Emeri played with the control panel beside the door and illuminated the office before crossing to his desk and slumping down in his chair. It was only mid-afternoon, but the realization that every-thing was out of his control exhausted him. He summoned enough energy to reach down and retrieve a glass and a bottle of liquor from one of the desk drawers, the same one he had drank from two months earlier as he'd pardoned Ziva's life.

Oh, Ziva. He'd meant it with all his heart when he said he didn't like the way things had turned out, though there had really been no other reasonable punishment for the crime she'd committed. Zona had brought up some interesting points during their conversation, how-ever—it sounded as if there was some question as to whether the late lieutenant was even guilty. It seemed most of these ideas had originated from Agent Shevin, who had turned himself into a bit of a person of interest in the case according to Dasaro. Nonetheless, with all the unex-plained occurrences and questions being raised as of late, Emeri felt compelled to go back and take a second look at things despite the fact that all the initial dust had finally settled.

There were a number of concerns that had manifested themselves since he'd begun to dig deeper. Perhaps the biggest was that he'd been unable to find Ziva's body when he'd gone to have it properly buried. The team he'd sent to Haphor had found nothing, and they'd reported signs that something—most likely a machine—had been poking around near the pyre on which she'd supposedly been burned. Taking into consideration the unique relationship between Ziva and Lieutenant Tarbic, it wouldn't have surprised Emeri if the man had elected to give her a more formal burial elsewhere rather than follow Dasaro's orders. The fact that the lieutenant wasn't around to confirm was what had him worried.

Emeri downed his glass and poured himself another before returning the bottle to the drawer and finding a more comfortable position in his chair. There were other smaller details that plagued him as well, things that didn't fit with anyone's story and made him unsure about the things they already knew. The hoverbike pilot who had been discovered in the forest, missing his suit. The missing footage from the RG's security cams from the night of the break-in. An RG groundcar, stolen that same night, had been recovered at the Noro spaceport, its supplies and weapons cache stripped clean. The only thing that comforted him was the fact that nobody else had a clue what was going on, either.

The team he'd sent to investigate the pyre hadn't had much to say, but Emeri had had them detained anyway just to be on the safe side. The last thing he needed right now was to have rumors spreading around about things he didn't know enough about to fix. In the event that Ziva was somehow still alive—the thought seemed preposterous— he thought it best to keep quiet about it. Maybe she really was innocent and he was doing it to protect her, or maybe he dreaded to think of the bad name HSP would have when the world realized it had failed to contain her. He just wasn't sure.

Did this—oh, what did they call it—*Nostia* give her some uncanny ability to survive a gunshot? Emeri had agonized over whether to go public with her secret. In the end, he had decided against it, fearful that he would get in as much trouble for hiding knowledge of her power as she would for wielding it. Once she was gone, it was like a massive burden had been lifted from his shoulders, but now that he was so uncertain about things, he found himself once again trying to decide if he should reveal what he knew.

Other than being entirely uncomfortable being around anyone who could exercise such power, Emeri wasn't exactly sure what all the fuss was about. After the Federation had retaliated against the Resistance and outlawed the use of nostium close to twenty-three years earlier, the Haphezian government had followed suit and threatened to execute all Nosti for fear of attracting a Federation presence. Emeri was by no means interested in starting a revival or some such thing—few Nosti had ever occupied Haphez as it was—but he didn't see how one person who had been careful not to reveal her abilities could possibly be an issue. It was yet another reason he had chosen to keep his mouth shut about Ziva, and why he now decided there still wasn't much point in bringing it up.

The silence of his office was suddenly shattered when his comm system came alive. He barely caught one of his aides announcing he had visitors before the door burst open and in strode Skeet Duvo and Zinni Vax, looking sleep-deprived but more driven than he'd seen them in a long time. It was a vast improvement from the two sorry people he remembered from two days earlier.

Emeri hardly had time to open his mouth before they were upon him, looming over his desk with determination in their eyes. "We need to talk, sir," Skeet said.

Somehow Emeri knew this was about Ziva and the investigation, and of all people, they were the ones he felt the most comfortable discussing such matters with. He motioned for them to be seated in the chairs opposite him and used his desk's control panel to lock the door and tint the windows.

"Believe it or not, you're just the people I wanted to see," he said, "but let's hear your story first."

It took the two of them a moment to get going, and when they did, it was slow and methodical, almost as if they'd been rehearsing what they were going to say. They each took turns filling him in on progressively important details, a technique many agents used as they gauged whether they could trust their audience. He learned they had been in contact with Veya Shevin, the missing wife of Kade Shevin, though they refrained from specifying where. He learned of their suspicions about Dasaro and how they'd started keeping tabs on him until he and the other two captains had disappeared unexpectedly. Most importantly, he learned that the bird was still in flight, a message that supposedly could have only been passed on by Ziva herself.

Emeri leaned forward, looking them each squarely in the eyes and emphasizing each syllable. "Are. You. *Sure*?"

Skeet and Zinni glanced at each other and shrugged as if there had been no point in even asking. "There doesn't seem to be any other explanation," Skeet replied. "The details don't make any sense. I mean, unless Ziva somehow reached out from the grave, there's no way Veya Shevin could have been familiar with that phrase."

"You said Lieutenant Tarbic knew it," Emeri put forth.

That brought a moment of silence as the three of them contemplated that idea. It was true that Tarbic had been in league with Dasaro and could have somehow passed on the message, but it was also clear that in order to do so, he'd had to have been in contact with Ziva at some point along the way—other than when he'd shot her, of course. Judging by Aroska's actions right there in the office two months before, he didn't strike Emeri as someone who would go through the trouble of betraying Ziva's colleagues after she was dead, even if he *had* been working with Dasaro.

It was a while before either Skeet or Zinni spoke. Their silence gave Emeri the impression that perhaps they had already considered Tarbic's involvement and had concluded that he was still on their side.

"I don't think he would do that," Zinni said, "not after making a point of coming to us the way he did."

"People can be devious, Officer Vax," Emeri said, more of an idea to keep in mind than an actual suggestion.

"Think of it this way," she continued. "Ziva's always right—you know that as well as anyone. She told Aroska to shoot her, and maybe it was for a reason. Maybe she had a plan."

"We reviewed the footage," Skeet said. "If you look at the placement of his shots and the way Ziva fell down that embankment, it's possible that she's still alive, that the two of them staged it all. And if they did, they did a hell of a job."

"And wherever she is, she's probably injured," Zinni added.

"Do you think she would trust him enough to do something like that, given their history?" Emeri asked.

Skeet paused. "I think something happened between them. I'm

not sure what it was, but I think he's one of the only people she *can* trust right now."

Emeri paused and rubbed a hand over his face. Now he was convinced there was more going on than met the eye. The players: Ziva, Dasaro, and the rest of his missing agents. Maybe Ziva was innocent, and Dasaro was hunting her for some reason they had yet to discover. Maybe she was guilty, and he was simply tracking her down like he'd been trained to. Either way, there were far too many secrets being kept and too many unanswered questions for Emeri's taste.

"I want you to bring Special Agent Luko Zona on board," he said. "Tell him everything you just told me. Between the four of us, we just might be able to get this mess cleared up."

· 68 ·
KAT'S HIDEOUT
CHAIAVIS

K at Reilly took a moment to study the three people she'd just brought into her garage. They were quite the motley crew, bruised, beaten, and exhausted. Two men and a woman, two ops agents and an RG officer. It seemed there were a hundred ways to look at it. Ziva Payvan in the flesh—Kat still couldn't believe it, especially since she was supposed to be dead. Aroska Tarbic was quite the looker, strong and handsome, but he seemed fidgety, and his mind was obviously elsewhere. Then there was the third member of their party, Kade Shevin, whom they had picked up on the way back to her place.

They'd managed to fit both her car and theirs into the small shop—parking anything on the tiny landing pad outside was bound to raise questions they didn't need. The space where she lived was one of several former mechanical shops belonging to a company that had gone bankrupt years before. Since no one else had bought the corporation after it died out, this property and others like it remained unclaimed and untouched. Up until now, no one else knew she resided there—she had a separate legitimate address where packages could be delivered and messages could be left, if necessary.

This downstairs area served as a garage, living room, and workspace, furnished with shelves of tools, a workbench, a ratty sofa, and an old heating panel that glowed a soft orange. A large overhead door and a man door separated them from the landing pad and tiny balcony outside. Upstairs was the little lavatory and the two office spaces she had converted into a crude kitchen and sleeping quarters.

Kat placed her helmet on the car's hood and took another moment to study her three visitors. "Bosco sent you, we've established that much. But that still doesn't really explain what you're doing here."

"He said you'd be able to help us," Aroska said.

How two veteran agents and a respectable RG officer expected her to help them, Kat had no idea. By now, she'd heard each of their names on the Haphezian news networks—Ziva's, mostly—enough times to deduce they were in some sort of trouble, but she couldn't fathom why Bosco would have referred them to her rather than just taking care of them himself.

"Oh he did, did he?"

"Have you ever heard the name Diago Dasaro?" Ziva asked. She went on to explain the basics of their predicament: how she had escaped HSP custody, how she'd sought Aroska out, how she'd had to go back to get Kade before the three of them made it off the planet. Much of this Kat already knew from news at the embassy, but hearing the story from Ziva's perspective helped fill the numerous gaps the reporters and HSP had left.

"So you're telling me you *didn't* kill the Royal Officer," Kat said. She'd had a hard time believing Ziva was guilty from the beginning— based on her own investigative experience, everything had seemed too clean cut in terms of the investigation and much too sloppy on the part of a professional like the lieutenant.

"That's right. This is all a setup, and we're reasonably sure Dasaro is behind it."

"I think I believe you," Kat said, perching on the edge of the car beside her helmet. "The main reason is I'm pretty sure Dasaro is dirty, too."

None of them said anything for a moment, but the reaction she'd provoked was clear. Ziva began moving slowly toward her, arms crossed, drilling into her with those intense crimson eyes. She finally paused about two meters away, and Kat's focus shifted to her scar and bruised face.

"What do you know?" she growled.

There weren't many things that made Kat squirm, but she found that Ziva was one of them. "It turns out I've been looking for you just as much as you've been looking for me," she replied, doing her best to hold her ground. "You've got quite the reputation, and I figured you'd be one of the best resources to help me with a little problem of my own. When I saw you in Endion, I couldn't believe it. I wasn't sure if my message had even gotten through, and once you were arrested, I didn't think—" She stopped when she noticed the look on Ziva's face.

"What message?" the woman asked.

Kat hesitated. "I thought maybe that was why you came to Chaiavis in the first...forget it. I contacted HSP several days ago, the morning you were taken into custody, hoping to talk to you. I spoke to someone else—Vax, I think her name was, and I disconnected after she transferred me to someone in records. Of all people, I figured you'd be able to find me even with so little information."

It was a relief to see Ziva's expression soften somewhat. "Well, I'm here now," she said. "What does Dasaro have to do with any of this?"

"I've been doing some research of my own over the past few years," Kat replied. "His name has come up a couple of times in conjunction with other information I've found, though it's never been enough to pin anything on him. That's where I hoped you'd come in."

"What kind of research are we talking about?" Ziva asked.

"It has to do with the mining operations in Argall. That's where I came from, I guess. I'd been trying to—" Once again, Kat paused when she saw the thoughtful look on Ziva's face. "What?"

Rather than respond, the woman turned to face the two men. "Argall came up during my search as well. It was only once, and it didn't make much sense, but—" she returned her attention to Kat "—if we pool our resources, we may yet be able to make some sense of all this. Give us a few minutes to get settled, and then I think we need to have a long chat."

· 69 ·
KAT'S HIDEOUT
CHAIAVIS

There wasn't much settling to do, given the space available and the amount of equipment they'd brought, or lack thereof. It was decided that the three of them would stay there with Kat rather than return to the flophouse—Ziva was glad, as it was not only safer but they would actually have some supplies at their disposal. Kade had made himself at home at the tiny kitchen table upstairs, engrossed in his computer as he closed in on decrypting the files. The rest of them remained in the garage, with Kat and Aroska exchanging small talk and a bit of harmless flirting while Ziva perused the various shelves and storage boxes.

It appeared there would be adequate tools to properly modify her newly acquired rifle, one more thing that brought her a bit of relief. There were still materials needed to create the custom ammunition for it, and certainly Kat would know the best places to find them. The weapon itself had already been laid out on the workbench and waited patiently for her to begin her work, surrounded by the other various parts Bosco had found for her. The main concern was the scope. Korberon rifles weren't known for their range capabilities, but with a little work, she would be able to increase it to her liking. Extending the range, however, would leave her with somewhat inadequate sights. It was better than nothing, though, and she'd worked with worse.

She removed a tiny blowtorch from the shelf and spent a moment examining it. "So what exactly do you do, Kat?"

"A lot of things," the young woman replied, still giggling in response to some lame joke Aroska had just told. "I've been on my own for about seven years now, and I've spent that time doing whatever odd jobs come my way. A little bounty hunting here, some errands for the embassy there. Mostly I work as a fixer, with a slight twist on the popular definition. People say I'm a mercenary, hiring myself out the way I do, but in reality, all my time is spent helping people."

Ziva set the blowtorch in the pile of other tools she thought she might make use of. "Where'd you get the kytara?"

There was silence for a moment as Kat contemplated a response. "I guess I could ask you the same thing," she said. "I got it on my very first job after I left the embassy. My client's brother was a Nosti survivor who got picked up by Federation police. I was paid to infiltrate his apartment and destroy all evidence of Resistance affiliation before the Feds searched the place. Not really sure why I decided to keep it— it was probably a stupid thing to do. I've practiced with it over the years and thought I'd gotten pretty good at it, but then you showed up and kicked my ass."

Ziva couldn't help but smirk. "I'll admit you caught me off guard. You ever been exposed to nostium?"

"Hell no," Kat replied, shaking her head. "The Feds are usually a little more lenient about kytaras. With a city the size of this one, it's not uncommon to find somebody who took one off a dead Nosti back in the day or even tried to make one of their own. But if they do a brain scan and find evidence of nostium, you're a goner. I've got enough on my plate as it is—don't want to wind up on the Federation's shit list."

Ziva nodded and continued her exploration of the shelves. "So you're a fixer."

Kat hummed an affirmative. "A friend of a friend is in trouble with a drug cartel, or maybe they've got a debt to pay and someone's not happy about it. I do my best to bail them out, or at least resolve the situation as peacefully as possible...for a price, of course." She let out a good-natured scoff. "My last job involved one of the officers from the embassy. The guy got jumped in an alley, got his service weapon stolen. He was scheduled for promotion, but if his superiors found out about the theft, he would have lost his job. He's got three little kids to support. So I tracked the gun down and got it back for him."

"Sounds like rewarding work," Aroska said.

"It is," Kat replied. "It's good pay, sure, but there's nothing better than resolving an issue and seeing a person be able to breathe again." She smiled gently, but the smile faded after a moment as she stared vacantly ahead. A flicker of some emotion Ziva couldn't pinpoint flashed across her face, but it was gone just as fast as it had appeared.

Wondering what it meant, she continued her circuit around the room and paused in front of the heating panel. The shelf mounted above it was smaller than the others and contained various items that appeared to be more sentimental than the other tools nearby. One in particular caught her eye, an older model data pad with a familiar Haphezian style to it. Odd, considering Kat hadn't set foot on the planet since birth. She picked it up and turned it over in her hand. "What's this?"

For a moment, Kat seemed almost defensive, leaping from her place on the sofa, but she carefully took the device and looked it over herself. "I'm not entirely sure," she answered. "It's from home, that's all I know. It was sent to me care of the embassy about three years ago, with no note and nothing else stored on it. I've been tempted to throw it away several times now, but I always figured if it came from home, it had to mean something."

She held the data pad out and Ziva found herself viewing what appeared to be a map—of what, she had no idea. The path was long and winding, represented by a thin yellow line against a gray background. Other than some headings indicating north and south, there were no other symbols or written instructions.

"You said you got this three years ago?" Hearing the words from her own mouth struck a chord in her mind and she took a moment to process what she'd just said. Dasaro. Argall. *Three years.*

"It has been three long years—almost to the exact date—since this happened."

She shook her head when she realized Kat was speaking. "That's when I first got curious about home," the young woman said. "Well, I'd always been 'curious,' but I'd never taken any action. I figured if they got rid of me, they probably had no interest in hearing from me."

"And suddenly someone showed interest," Aroska said.

"Exactly," Kat replied, "only I never figured out who. With such limited access to databases and records, it was hard enough finding anything out about Argall itself." She paused, forcing a scoff and adding a sad wag of her head. "I've never even been there, and after all these years, I'm still calling it home."

Personally, Ziva had always found the Haphezian excommunication rules absurd. Here was a person who, other than having different colored eyes and hair stripes, had absolutely nothing physically wrong with her. Here was a person who would have made a fine soldier in the Grand Army or a field agent at HSP. Ziva remembered the problems Skeet had had as a boy, what with the abnormal coloring pattern in his hair. The final verdict had been that since the orange was consistent with his eyes, he would be allowed to stay, though to this day there were some people who still questioned why he hadn't been sent away. Those people—the ones who held prejudices against the Defectives—vastly outnumbered those who didn't, the reason people like Kat and Bosco were still unwelcome on their homeworld. If you didn't look Haphezian, you were no better than a human or some other inferior race.

In a sense, they'd all been banished for various reasons. Kat: because of a genetic flaw that made her appearance unsatisfactory. Ziva: murder, allegedly. Kade and Aroska: in danger of returning home because of knowledge they held—knowledge of her innocence. Perhaps Kat had recognized this pattern and that was why she'd opened up to them so quickly. Perhaps, in a way, Ziva understood how Kat felt and that was why she decided then and there to trust her wholeheartedly.

"Well, you must have found something of interest if you were calling on me for help."

Kat's eyes brightened a bit, taking on the same mischievous quality Zinni's often did when she discovered a new clue. She took off up the stairs and returned so quickly Ziva wasn't sure how she could have possibly had time to retrieve the second data pad she now carried.

"I was never able to talk to anyone in Argall. I don't know if it was a problem on my end or theirs, but my transmissions would never go through. I did find these, though."

Ziva leaned in to examine the data pad and Aroska stood up to get a look for himself. The screen displayed what appeared to be a list of four death records, one of which was from only a few days earlier. Each of the deceased bore the same surname: Reilly.

"Your family?" Aroska asked.

"Apparently. Argall's not a very big place, and according to some census records I found, there's only one Reilly clan that has ever lived there. This man here must have been my father. He and the girl, my sister, were killed three years ago. One of my brothers died a few months later. And my mother? She was killed just a few days ago, around the time Tachi was assassinated."

It was all Ziva could do to formulate a sentence as the words 'three years' bounced around inside her head again. "Why do you say 'killed'?"

"I thought you would never ask," Kat said, growing more animated by the second. How someone could be excited about the deaths of family members was beyond Ziva...until she remembered she'd never met the people.

"According to these reports, they all died in a series of mine explosions that each claimed multiple other lives. Since Argall is a mining town, everyone works in the mines. Accidents happen. That sounds reasonable, right?"

Ziva and Aroska exchanged a glance, knowing better than to agree.

"If there had really been explosions in the mines, it would have stymied the flow of niobi crystals to the military and the research centers," Kat rattled on. "At no point during the past three years has that happened."

"Three years," Ziva echoed, doing her best to stay focused on the current conversation and save her own thoughts for when she actually had time to think them. "So you think we're dealing with some kind of cover-up?"

"I think they weren't really killed in mining accidents, if that answers your question," Kat replied. "And if they lied about the cause of death, there must be something happening that they don't want anyone to know about. If all my family members are dead, that leads me to believe they were specifically targeted. According to those census records, there should be one Reilly left in Argall: my oldest brother. If they've killed the rest of them, I believe he's in danger."

"And that's where I would have come in," Ziva said.

Kat nodded. "It's taken me months to gather this information. With such limited communication abilities, I just can't work fast enough, let alone actually go there. I had hoped you'd be willing to go out to Argall and look into it—you would have been compensated, of course. But now here you are with problems of your own."

Three years, three years.

"*A hunch I've had for over three years now.*"

They had each stumbled across Argall as well as Dasaro's name. By now, it was clear that the captain was somehow responsible for the turmoil they were currently facing. Had he somehow been behind the events that had occurred three years prior?

"I'm beginning to wonder if these problems are really 'my own'," Ziva replied.

"What do you mean?" Aroska asked. "You think this is all connected?"

She stopped rubbing her hand over her mouth long enough to answer. "I think it's safe to say it's more than a coincidence Dasaro's name has come up for both of us. We found information on Argall three years ago, and we're finding it again today. Now's not the time to be jumping to conclusions, though. We need facts."

As if on cue, Kade appeared on the stairs, toting the data pad Aroska had been using to review Ziva's case files. His sagging shoulders told her he had yet to conquer Special Agent Zona's encryption, but the faint glimmer in his eyes said he'd at least found something of consequence.

"I have some news about the accident that killed the medical examiner," he announced, holding up the data pad which now displayed the contents of one of the RG files.

When he had their attention, he continued down the steps, starting out with a few background details to familiarize Kat with the situation. "I managed to get into one of the smaller files," he said. "It looks like the HSP office in Haphor recovered what was left of the faulty bot pilot and had the results sent to the RG office."

"*What was left* of the bot?" Ziva repeated.

"That's right," Kade said. "According to witnesses and footage retrieved from the traffic cams, that crash wouldn't have been enough to destroy the bot the way it did. The damage was more consistent with an engine fire or an electrical malfunction, neither of which happened. The lab discovered traces of explosive material around what used to be the bot's memory core, explosives that would have to have been triggered by an outside source."

"Sounds to me like someone is trying to cover their tracks," Kat suggested. "I've dealt with my fair share of people trying to erase evidence."

"But what evidence would they be trying to erase?" Aroska said. "That they programmed the bot to target Eason Fromm's vehicle?"

Kade shrugged. "With the memory core destroyed, it's impossible to tell. And I'm sure that's exactly what they wanted."

"And they'd want him dead because he knew the truth about the man who died?" Kat asked. "Agent Spence?"

"Right," Aroska confirmed. "They killed Spence because he was starting to believe Ziva was innocent, which is why they're hunting Kade now."

As she stood there listening to them putting the pieces together, Ziva couldn't help but recognize the chain reaction she had set off. Ever since her arrest, it seemed as though anyone who had gone to the trouble of defending her was either dead or running for their lives. She hadn't meant for that to happen, and she hated to think of how they had all been dragged into this struggle against their will. It almost would have been easier if nobody believed her, enabling her to work on her own and clean up her mess without spreading the poison to everyone she came in contact with.

She suddenly wondered if her colleagues at home would be affected. Surely they would have been left alone once she was 'dead,' but if...*when* Dasaro realized she was alive, she knew he wouldn't hesitate to go after them. She pictured Skeet and Zinni being sent to the Haphor Facility, Jada being kidnapped and tortured, her house being burned down with Marshay and Ryon still inside.

"Why me?" she muttered, partially to herself and partially in response to the conversation. By now, it was clear that Dasaro was somehow behind her setup and that he had specifically targeted her, but why? Considering her predicament, Kat's story, and the details of the car crash, the situation had 'conspiracy' written all over it—someone somewhere didn't want anyone to know the truth. How did she factor in? Was it true that Dasaro knew she'd been snooping around, and he wanted to silence her before she found something? Was there something she *already* knew that would make him fixate on her? If he'd gone through the trouble of setting her up for the assassination and getting her sent to the Haphor Facility, it was obvious he wanted her dead, or permanently incapacitated at the least. With her out of the picture and the rest of HSP busy looking into Tachi's murder, the captain was free to conduct whatever business he pleased.

It suddenly struck her that, as the head of all Haphezian law enforcement, Ikaro Tachi would have been responsible for carrying out Dasaro's sentence were he to ever be convicted of anything. Perhaps, by framing her for killing Tachi, he was effectively knocking out his two biggest obstacles with one blow.

Ziva relayed her new thoughts to the others, carefully thinking over each word she spoke to ensure the theory actually made sense. There was a moment of silence as each member of the entourage considered the idea for themselves.

"We must both be in danger of knowing the same things, then," Kade said. "They continued to target me even after they thought you were dead."

"If this is truly a setup, they would have had to plant all that evidence," Kat said. "In that case, where'd they get your print and the suit with your DNA in it?"

"They could have pulled my print from anywhere," Ziva replied. "It's not that hard to plant a print. And that stealth suit? It's identical or similar to a hundred other stealth suits I've worn throughout my life.

They could have dug it out of the laundry for all I know. None of that really matters—what matters is the fact that I was *not* actually there!"

"Nobody's saying you were," Kat said, though she sounded unsure.

"So what do you think Dasaro is doing?" Aroska asked, inserting himself between the two of them.

Ziva shrugged. "We've heard of Argall several times now—there's got to be a connection there." She turned to Kade. "Keep an eye out as you search. What the hell is taking you so long, anyway?"

Stunned by her harsh words, the others fell silent for several long seconds. Kade especially looked hurt, though he did his best to maintain composure, and Ziva kicked herself for addressing him so severely. Her hunger for information was trying her patience, and there she was taking her anger out on the only people on her side.

"The encryption on the case files was weaker," he replied, hesitant to make eye contact. "Whatever Zona was looking at in those other files must be important because he's using an encryption that's stronger than anything I've ever worked with. I'm doing the best I can, all right?"

He held her gaze for a moment before shuffling back up the stairs, leaving her there under the scrutiny of Kat and Aroska. She fended them off with a hot glare then took a moment to massage her tired eyes.

It was Kat who finally spoke, breaking the silence that had begun to seem almost loud. "Tell you what," she said, returning the map to the shelf. "You people look exhausted. We should call it a day and take the rest of the evening to recuperate. Maybe you can even get a good night's sleep, and in the morning, we can make a plan of action."

Although Ziva couldn't stand the thought of sitting around getting nothing done, a little quiet time sounded more than appealing. "Fine," she said. "Where might I be able to find about a kilo of bariine alloy?"

Kat thought for a moment. "There's a swordsmith not far from here. The guy makes knock-off powerblades, cheaper than the big dealers but pretty good quality. I'm sure he's got some bariine he could sell you. I can take you there first thing tomorrow."

"Good," Ziva said. "I should be ready by then." She nodded toward the rifle.

"Well!" Kat said, clapping her hands together. Her enthusiasm nearly made Ziva flinch. "Let's see what we can find to eat around here."

Ziva watched as the younger woman headed up the stairs with Aroska hot on her heels. She could hear the two of them begin conversing with Kade as the cooler was opened and dishes were set out. Mind wandering, she followed them up and, after a bleak dinner of various leftovers, found herself back down in the garage, alone. The room was dimly lit, but a lighting panel hung down over her things on the workbench, illuminating them adequately. She adjusted it and took a deep breath, taking a moment to look over all the pieces. Reveling in the silence, she put her hands to work.

· 70 ·
RESIDENTIAL SECTOR
CHAIAVIS

It was dark by the time the little transport touched down on the landing pad behind the pitiful apartment complex. It was situated on the outskirts of Chaiavis's Government District, just a short distance from the embassies and consulates. There were no signs of life coming from the fourth apartment down, but Kat Reilly struck Dasaro as someone who would maintain a low profile.

"You sure this is it?" he said, eyes fixed on the small, darkened window of the apartment in question.

Nejdra brought up the embassy profile on the viewscreen in the cockpit. "It's out of date, but this is the last known address."

Dasaro studied the three-dimensional bust spinning in a slow circle beside Reilly's information. The image was out of date as well— she would be a couple of years older now—but those sparkling blue eyes and silvery-white hair stripes were unmistakable anywhere.

"Let's go," he said.

The two of them exited the craft and proceeded to the front of the building while Hoxie stayed behind to watch the rear entrance. There was a small keypad beside the front door, manufactured by some alien company Dasaro didn't recognize. He gave Nejdra some space and scanned the surrounding area as she knelt and began working her way into the security system. There weren't many people around, and those who were remained too far away to see them or pay them any mind.

The decryption device beeped and began to display a series of numbers as it pulled them from the keypad. After about ten seconds, it had spit out a five-digit code, and Nejdra poised her hand so as to punch in the numbers.

"We're going in, Hoxie," Dasaro said into his comm.

Nejdra's fingers flew over the keypad and the door slid open with a low hiss. The two of them burst inside, weapons up, ready to shoot the first thing that moved in the shadows within. The interior of the apartment was darker than Dasaro had expected—was it possible Reilly had known they were coming? He hit the controls on the wall, activating a set of lighting panels.

As the room was illuminated, he was rendered momentarily speechless. Aside from a bare bedframe built into the far wall, there wasn't a single piece of furniture in the place. A half wall separated the living space from a kitchen that could only be identified as such thanks to a rusty old stove and cooler that were probably bolted to the floor. A small lav was positioned across the room, its door open to reveal a sink and toilet that were in dire need of cleaning. Beside the lavatory door was the one leading out onto the landing pad where Hoxie waited. The air was musty, and a fine layer of dust had settled over the floor and walls, giving Dasaro the impression nobody had set foot in the apartment for some time.

Nejdra hovered at his side, equally stunned. "I swear this is the right place," she murmured.

"Obviously it isn't," Dasaro growled. He took one last look around before shutting off the lights and storming to the back door where they found Hoxie waiting with his pistol drawn.

"What happened?" he exclaimed.

"She's not here," Nejdra replied.

"There's *nothing* here," Dasaro said. "We've got bad information."

They walked the remaining distance to the ship in silence, careful not to attract the attention of anyone nearby. After a moment, they were all assembled in the cockpit, staring at the profile on the viewscreen and trying to decide what had gone wrong.

"This is the correct address," Dasaro said, coaxing a sigh of relief out of Nejdra.

"Then what do you propose we do?" Hoxie asked.

Dasaro massaged his temples, wishing he hadn't made the mistake of thinking everything would go the way he'd planned. "We regroup," he said. "We sit down and go over the information again. Reilly's here somewhere—we can see who she's been in contact with, find her that way."

"That will mean talking to the embassy," Nejdra said. "Then the director will know we're here."

"We may not have any other choice," Dasaro replied. "We'll start by using our own local sources—we have some old friends here who would be more than willing to help. If all else fails, we can tie this all up and hang it around Payvan's neck. Make it look like we're here wrapping up the investigation on her."

"You think anyone else knows she's alive?"

"It's doubtful," he answered. "At this point, Shevin and Tarbic are the only ones who would know for sure, and as long as HSP wants Shevin for the incident at the RG office, they're not going to show their faces. For now, we're safe."

With that, Dasaro took up the ship's controls and they disappeared into Chaiavis's night traffic.

· 71 ·
KAT'S HIDEOUT
CHAIAVIS

Night had turned to early morning by the time Aroska made his way back down to the garage. Kat had retired to her room and Kade had made himself comfortable on the floor beside his computer in case his automated program managed to break Zona's encryption during the night. Aroska hadn't heard a peep from Ziva since she'd disappeared after dinner, so he treaded lightly in case she was, by some miracle, asleep. The garage was dark except for a flickering glow originating from the area around the sofa. As he descended, a soft crackling reached his ears. There was Ziva, hunched over the workbench, meticulously working on her rifle with the tiny blowtorch she'd found earlier. Her eyes were obscured by a set of safety goggles, the lenses of which reflected the blue light from the torch as well as the orange from the heating panel. The single light above her cast odd shadows on her face, giving her an altogether eerie look.

He reached the floor and approached her slowly, feeling awkward just lurking there in the dark. Despite the mismatched parts, the rifle was shaping up nicely. He stood there watching her work for a moment, fascinated that those hands could cause so much destruction but still had the delicate touch required for creation and building.

He wasn't sure how long he'd been staring when she let out an exasperated sigh and set the torch down. "Can I help you?" she demanded, flipping the goggles up.

He only shrugged. "You've been quiet."

"And you talk too much."

Aroska slid his hands into his pockets and took a couple of steps closer. She watched him for another second before pulling the goggles back down over her eyes and resuming her work. She said nothing further, but what more was there to say? He could tell she was in pain; he'd caught a glimpse of her bruised ribs as she'd administered caura treatment during their journey, and she still sported a gash on her forehead from her fall into the riverbed. He'd also detected a slight limp, but so far, she hadn't voiced any discomfort and he hadn't asked about it. There was something else to it, an ache that went beyond the physical sense. Her mouth formed a straight line and she looked paler than normal there in the dark.

He stood there for another minute before heaving a sigh and removing his jacket. Despite being a former grease pit, the floor of the room was relatively clean, so he balled up the jacket to form a crude pillow and lowered himself down. Lying flat on his back, the side of the workbench blocked out most of the flickering light from the blowtorch.

The sparks stopped flying for a moment. "What are you doing?" Ziva growled.

"I'm being a gentleman and letting the lady have the sofa."

The soldering continued. "Aroska Tarbic, a gentleman." She snorted. "That'll be the day."

Aroska fell silent, her words striking him in a way he hadn't expected. She was right, of course. He couldn't recall more than a few courteous things he'd done since they'd met. After all, he'd wanted her head on a platter for the majority of the Dakiti mission. He still wasn't sure if he'd ever be able to forgive her for Soren's death, but at the same time, he was ashamed by the way he'd acted toward her, regardless of how he'd felt. He thought of all the things she'd done for him on that mission, despite knowing full well he hated her—coming back to get him from the harvesting room, risking her life and her secret to keep him from being crushed out on the landing pad....

And even after all that, he'd still had the audacity to be a complete jerk to her in the past few days. She'd only been trying to help, albeit in a rather unorthodox way, and in the end, she *had* helped and he was grateful for it. He couldn't pinpoint why he felt compelled to treat her so well; after all, she'd been such a *shouka* to him and everyone else around her. Perhaps he merely didn't want to stoop to her level. And maybe—just maybe—if he was kind enough to her, she would finally start to mellow out.

Aroska suddenly snapped awake—*wait, I'd been asleep?*—startled by the sensation of a thousand tiny creatures crawling over his body. He began to flail and swat at his clothes, but it took him only a moment to realize there was nothing there. A cold sweat dripped from his face, and as he turned to rearrange his jacket, he noticed he was trembling. He rolled onto his side and drew his arms and legs in tight.

It was then that he noticed Ziva wasn't on the sofa. He wasn't sure when she'd stopped working on the rifle, but all the tools sat untouched on the workbench and the lighting panel had been powered down, leaving the dim orange glow from the heater as the only source of light. He did his best to look around the room while remaining curled, straining to see past his arms and out into the darkness.

After a moment, he caught sight of her standing in front of the tiny window beside the overhead door leading out onto the landing pad. She wasn't much more than a shadow, a silhouette against the glow of the city lights outside. Even in the dark, however, he could tell she was looking at him. He watched her through the space between his arms, certain she couldn't tell he was looking back. Was she concerned? With her face obscured, it was impossible to tell—the only thing he knew for sure was that she was facing him.

The chill surging through his body was overtaken by a hot wave of shame, and he was glad the darkness concealed his red face. There he was, curled up on the floor like a small child while the woman who had come to him for help looked on expectantly. He had spent too long poisoning his body and developing dependencies on those poisons, and now there he was in such a vulnerable state when Ziva was the one in trouble. He realized then how desperately he needed to clean up his act, if for no other reason than to apologize to her for being an ass when she'd been right all along.

Curious as to what she was doing, he stole another peek out into the room. He was startled to find that she was no longer in her place at the window, but the fear that she'd know he'd been spying kept him from looking around. He wondered briefly if she had simply been a part of the hallucination, but when he saw that she still wasn't on the sofa, he knew she had to be up and about somewhere.

At one point, he thought he heard the stairs creak, but he wasn't sure if it was just another one of the strange noises ripping through his skull. He slowed his breathing as best he could to listen, and after several seconds of nothing, he settled back down against his jacket and let the trembling overtake him.

He felt sleep creeping toward him—or perhaps it was the onset of another hellish nightmare—but was startled awake again when he caught a whiff of a familiar scent and felt a change in the air as someone moved up behind him. Something warm but not particularly soft settled down over his shoulders: Ziva's riding jacket. She adjusted it a bit, so quickly and gently he couldn't even feel her touch. How she could move so silently was beyond him.

"You'll get through this," she said. Her tone wasn't particularly kind, but the words had been said nonetheless.

Her presence lingered there behind him for a few seconds longer before vanishing again, just as it had from the window. Aroska spent what seemed like hours listening for her return, but after a while, the fatigue and pain overtook him, and he drifted off again.

When he came to, morning light streamed in through the window and Kat's aircar was gone. He didn't remember hearing anyone leave, but then again, he didn't remember much at all. The only indicator that anything had happened at all during the night was Ziva's jacket, which had slid from his shoulders and now sat in a crumpled heap behind him.

He worked his way into a sitting position and took a moment to stretch his stiff shoulders. He would be sore later—he'd dreaded sleeping on the floor for exactly that reason. And then Ziva hadn't even used the sofa, rendering his chivalrous efforts futile. It went right along with the things he'd been thinking about earlier. It was hard to feel motivated to be nice to her when all he got in return was…well, a bad back.

He stood up and wandered upstairs. The only sign of life was the occasional tapping of a keypad, and he found Kade staring half-heartedly at the computer screen.

Shevin greeted him with a brief nod. "Rough night?" His tone made it sound as though he knew good and well what the answer was.

"You could say that," Aroska replied. Except for a throbbing headache, he felt much better. "Where are the women?"

"Kat was going to drop Ziva off at the swordsmith's and then go talk to Bosco. They said they wouldn't be long."

The thought of the two of them out running errands while there was so much danger to be dealt with seemed absurd, but Aroska shrugged it off and made himself busy looking through Kat's cupboards. He wasn't particularly hungry, so upon thinking harder, he wasn't exactly sure what he was looking for. When he opened the last cupboard and found it bare except for a half-empty bottle of fancy liquor, he realized what he had subconsciously been seeking. He began to sweat again and immediately slammed the door shut. Succumbing to the temptation would only make matters worse; there was a half-smoked govino stick in his bag he could use instead.

Fighting away another bout of the shakes, he filled a glass with water and seated himself at the little table across from Kade. The young man was busy rubbing the sleep out of his eyes and was no longer paying any attention to the decryption program still running on the computer. Aroska was beginning to wonder if they'd ever be able to open the locked files. He wished Zinni were there to help.

He took a sip of his water. "Are you worried about your family?" he asked.

"Of course," Kade replied without hesitation. "You have no idea how awful I feel for abandoning them the way I have. But at the same time, I know I've done the right thing by leaving them behind. Trying to bring them along would have only put them in more danger than they already were. Besides, the less my wife knows, the better—I'd hate to see her or the baby get hurt trying to help me with my own mess."

"Well," Aroska said, "if there's one thing I know about Ziva's people, it's that they'll do anything to keep your family safe."

Kade nodded and stole a glance at the computer screen. "What about you? You married?"

"Me? Hell no. I've never had much luck with women."

"Funny. You strike me as the type of guy who could get his pick of the crop."

"Who says I can't? It's the commitment part I've always had trouble with."

"So you and Ziva aren't...?"

"Oh no, no way."

Kade smiled. "Just wondering," he said.

Aroska felt his face flush and he dipped his head, forcing a nervous smile. "No, it's really not like that at all. I..." He hesitated, surprised by his own train of thought. "I *do* care for her, something I never expected to happen, but it's not like that. I owe that woman my life."

He proceeded to explain how he had come to know Ziva, how she had killed Soren, how he'd been forced to join her in the struggle against Solaris and the Sardons. It struck him how much they'd been through together given that they'd only been acquainted for a short time. "She was prepared to do whatever it took to get me out of the way," he said, altering his account of what had transpired on the Dakiti landing pad so Ziva's Nosti abilities were excluded. "I'm not sure if I'll ever understand why she chose to risk her own life for me when it would have been so much easier to let me die."

Aroska sighed and took another drink of water. "She took something from me that can never be replaced, but it hasn't been easy to stay mad at her. Every instinct I have says I should keep hating her. I *want* to. But how can I after everything she's done for me? It's like she's given me something new in return for what she stole—I'm just not quite sure what it is yet."

He paused for a moment and thought of the day she'd come barging back into his life, in the most literal sense of the phrase. *If she had come into the house a mere ten seconds later....* "She has saved me in more ways than she knows," he murmured.

"So tell her that," Kade said matter-of-factly.

"No, you don't know Ziva." *Neither do I, for that matter.* "She doesn't want to hear that, not when we're right in the middle of something as big as this. There's already something eating at her as it is—I don't want to stress her out."

Kade laughed. "Stress Ziva out? That's not very hard."

Aroska laughed a bit himself, though he felt uncomfortable doing it. Ziva had indeed been acting strange, almost as if she knew something nobody else knew. He wished she would stop being such a hypocrite, urging others to divulge their darkest secrets while she remained silent and reserved.

Shevin's smile faded when he realized Aroska was no longer laughing. He cleared his throat. "There's still something I can't figure out, and I want to know what you think. We're finding all these signs of a conspiracy—Spence and Fromm's deaths, the fact that these people want me dead—but there's nothing that *really* proves Ziva is innocent. We've heard her side of the story, but it's just...if she didn't kill Tachi, who did, and why?"

Aroska sighed and wiped his hand over his face. It was a valid point, but it sickened him to think that he'd essentially put his life on hold to help a guilty person. "I don't know what to think, kid. If she was guilty, there wouldn't be much point in her denying it anymore. She'd be defeated, she'd be caught. Besides, I doubt she would have reached out to anyone for help—she'd be long gone by now." He paused and thought of the way she'd immersed herself in his case files on the trip to Chaiavis, the way she'd snapped at Kade for taking too long with the encryption, the way she'd excused herself to work on the rifle the night before. "No, she's still fighting, searching for something. There's something driving her, and I wish I knew what it was."

Before either of them could say anything further, the computer beeped and the screen lit up in various shades of green as the decryption program finally managed to unlock Zona's files. Shevin beamed and began typing furiously, and Aroska moved his chair around to get a better look.

About half of the files pertained to the present case, and the other half were from three years prior. It appeared Zona had been busy comparing the two time periods, searching for similarities. His findings had been stored in a separate file of notes.

"This information is about Ziva and Dasaro," Kade said, eyebrows knit. "What the..." He hesitated a moment before opening the file marked CONCLUSIONS.

Aroska's eyes were on the move, eating up all the information the second it appeared on the screen. Some of it was already familiar to him, thanks to the spec ops clearance Dasaro had provided him with, but there were some things the captain had left out that immediately filled in the gaps he'd been struggling with throughout the past few days. As he read the final line of Zona's findings, everything became clear.

"*Sheyss,*" he muttered.

· 72 ·
BOSCO'S PARTS AND REPAIR
CHAIAVIS

K at was startled to find the landing pad already occupied when she arrived at Bosco's shop. It wasn't often that anyone other than locals frequented the place, so the freighter-sized vessel currently docked there seemed out of place. It had a classic Haphezian look to it, though it was nothing like the ships used by the embassy. It looked to be an older model and had no doubt been modified on several occasions.

Annoyed, she brought her aircar to rest on a neighboring shop's landing pad and got out, shielding her eyes from the mid-morning sun. She and Ziva had chosen a rendezvous where they would meet in thirty minutes after they had each completed their respective tasks. She'd refrained from saying why exactly she wished to speak to Bosco, partly because she didn't know herself. First on the agenda was to demand an explanation as to why he had chosen to send the three refugees to her. While she was glad to have crossed paths with Ziva, there were certain... *circumstances*—which Bosco was well aware of—that could potentially make it difficult for her to assist them.

But, since she already was assisting them, she thought it wise to stock up on supplies and see if the older man had any advice on how to proceed. He was the closest thing she'd ever had to a father and was the only person she'd told about the puzzle she'd been putting together over the past three years. With the new information that had come to light thanks to Ziva and her crew, a fresh set of ears might help.

She worked her way up the walkway to Bosco's landing pad, studying the strange ship as she went. The boarding ramp had been left down, indicating that the customer either didn't intend on staying long or wished to make a hasty exit.

With her attention devoted to the vessel, it took her a moment to realize the shop's open sign wasn't on. Most accurately, it was a glowing banner above the door that, when illuminated, displayed the shop's open status in a variety of Fringe languages. It sat there dead at the moment…strange, considering Bosco's shop was rarely closed, and when it was, he had always called to let her know.

The interior lights were on, so Kat concluded that the older man had simply forgotten to activate his sign. She hit the door controls and stopped short—it was locked.

"What the hell?" she muttered, trying again. She pressed her face to the small window in the door and strained to see inside. Nothing looked out of place, and somehow that made her entirely uncomfortable.

She took a step backward and glanced behind her. The strange ship still sat motionless, and it didn't appear there was anyone in the cockpit. Still, she felt as though she were somehow being watched, and she had a strong feeling she should not be there.

Even stronger, however, was the pull to find out what was going on and see if the old shopkeeper was okay. Taking one last glance through the window, she moved back and surveyed her options. The roof provided the best means of getting a look inside. The ceiling of the shop's foyer wasn't overly high, but it angled upward in the back over the warehouse and was interrupted every so often by narrow skylights.

Kat took hold of one of the reinforced cables running up the side of the shop's outer wall. These ran into fans and various fixtures on the roof, part of the ventilation system for the rest of the towering building. She began to climb, using the braces that fixed the cable to the wall as footholds, and hauled herself onto the roof. The higher part with the skylights rose up before her and stood taller than the shops on either side of it, leaving her out in the open and vulnerable should anyone with unfriendly intentions come along. She pressed on anyway.

It appeared the skylights hadn't been cleaned for some time, if they'd ever been cleaned at all. She settled down beside one and peered inside as best she could; unfortunately, anyone within the shop would be able to see her much better than she'd be able to see them. She took comfort in the fact that they weren't likely to be looking up.

Unable to see anything of interest, she picked her way down the row of skylights to the one on the far end that overlooked the rear aisle of the warehouse and the door of the little room Bosco used as an office. She lowered herself to her stomach, pressing her face as close to the filthy glass as possible.

She could hear the visitors' voices before she could see them. Wishing to be safe rather than sorry, she ducked away from the window and slowly began to scratch away some of the grime with a gloved finger. It was impossible to tell what they were saying, though one man was clearly angry. It sounded like he was directly below her, or maybe within the office.

After a moment of gentle scrubbing, Kat had a clear section of glass just big enough to see through. She rolled over onto her stomach, allowing only one half of her face to break the plane of the window. She could barely make out the figures standing below her: three men—wait, one was a woman—all speaking Haphezian. One of them, the one she guessed to be the leader, stood in the doorway of the office, addressing someone within. He was the one shouting, and she had no doubt his words were directed at Bosco.

It didn't take her long to realize she'd been holding her breath. Hot air fogged up the glass as she exhaled, obscuring her view. Fighting away panic, she rolled back over and cleared it away. Even with all the moving around, it still appeared the visitors were oblivious to her presence—the angle was just right, she concluded.

She'd barely gotten her eye settled back over the hole when an unmistakable muzzle flash pierced the darkness inside. She heard the spit of the suppressed projectile pistol as a second shot was fired, originating from the man who had been standing in the doorway. Whoever was in the office had just been shot.

Startled, she rolled away from the window and held perfectly still, listening as three sets of footsteps made their way back toward the front of the store. The echo of her own pulse sounded abnormally loud inside her head. Somewhere amid the noise, a tiny voice commanded her to move, to get to the front of the store and ascertain the identities of the three intruders.

Against her better judgment, she managed to break free from her stupor and throw herself down onto the lower part of the roof. She rolled to a stop against the ventilation duct coming up from the shop below and flattened herself out as best she could. The shop's front door opened, it seemed, at the exact moment she managed to still her breathing. Three pairs of boots exited the shop and began making their way across the landing pad, their owners silent. Heart pounding, she lifted her head just high enough to catch sight of the three of them walking up the boarding ramp of their ship. Two of them were *emilan*—the leader and the woman—and the third man had a scar running up the back of his head that parted his rich brown hair.

She ducked back down and dug her fingers into the roof's rough surface, listening as the ship's engines roared to life and the vessel lifted away from the landing pad. To her surprise and relief, it turned and took off in the opposite direction, leaving her lying there in silence.

She stayed there for a full two minutes—she counted every second—before moving. She sat up first, taking a moment to look around and make sure the area was clear. It seemed safe enough, so she climbed down onto the landing pad and paused for another few seconds before the front door. The interior still looked normal, but she forced herself to be patient and not just barge inside. One wrong move and she would be implicated in whatever had just happened.

Her hand trembled as she reached for the control panel and opened the door, which had been left unlocked. The interior was dead silent, and she took another moment to simply listen. The small security cam in the corner above the door had been moved, as had the one overlooking the counter. She couldn't help but feel that this was good. Now the authorities—and the intruders, for that matter—would never know she'd been there.

Sensing no immediate danger, Kat darted forward and slid around the bar, making a beeline for the little office on silent feet. She found the door open just as the hostiles had left it, but something kept her from entering right away—either the fear of encountering another intruder who had been left behind, or the fear of what she was going to see. She wasn't exactly sure which.

The sound of faint, raspy breathing finally drew her inside. She found Bosco slumped on the floor as if he had slid out of the chair at his desk. His eyes were closed but his chest continued to rise and fall, and he clutched at the two crimson holes that had just been blown through it.

"Bosco!" His name had been a shout inside her head, but it came out as a choked whisper. She dropped to her knees at his side, not wanting to touch him for fear of hurting him further but also not wishing to just sit by and do nothing.

His eyelids parted slightly, but the sight of her only seemed to cause him more pain. "Get out," he sputtered, clamping a blood-stained hand over her forearm. Bloody saliva oozed out over his chin as he tried to lift his head. It was all he could do to get the words out. "They came for you. Get out."

He struggled a moment longer, his fingers digging mercilessly into her arm, before he let his head fall back onto the floor. He was still staring into her eyes when he let go of her and exhaled one last time.

Stunned, Kat could only sit in silence, glancing between her friend's lifeless body and the blood he'd left on her sleeve. When she found herself upright and running back toward the front door, she couldn't remember how she had gotten there. The only thing she could process was that Bosco was dead because of her, and that if she was in danger, so was everyone else.

Underground Market District
Chaiavis

By the time Ziva made it out of the swordsmith's shop with her purchase, it was nearly time to go meet Kat at their rendezvous location. The owner hadn't been as willing to part with his bariine alloy as Kat had made him out to be. It was a pricey substance, and despite Ziva's generous offers, he had only allowed her about half a kilo of the stuff in the end. She carried the fist-sized chunk in a small sack, clutching it as if it would be torn from her hand at a moment's notice.

When combined with cheaper forms of metal, bariine created a lethal form of ammunition she had devised herself. While it was true that the popularity of projectile weapons was growing among HSP agents, bariine rounds could hardly be considered projectiles. The metal was heat-resistant, one of the only materials capable of withstanding lasers, energy shields, and the like. It made an ideal lining for powerblades.

For ammunition, she preferred projectiles that were forty percent bariine and sixty percent another soft metal, usually plain lead. When chambered in the rifle with the modified plasma cell, the round would become superheated—the soft metal took on a molten form while the bariine remained intact. As a result, the round would enter the target with the same consistency as a regular plasma bolt, burning and cauterizing whatever it touched. Once inside, however, the rapid cooling of the round would cause the bariine to become unstable and break apart, taking fragments of the soft metal with it. It not only caused internal bleeding for the victim, thus ensuring death, but it also prevented her weapon from being traced via any forensic measures.

Ziva adjusted her little parcel and began walking in the direction of the rendezvous. She only used her custom ammo on freelance missions independent of HSP and was content to use generic projectile or plasma weapons while working with her team. It wasn't that she didn't trust them with her invention. It was just that it *was* her invention, her signature—or lack thereof, considering it left no forensic trace.

Kat had given her detailed directions to where they would be meeting, and as she walked, she was able to pick out each of the structures the young woman had described in her instructions. Kat's familiarity with the area and the locals told Ziva she had spent much of her adult life exploring, and probably even while she was still at the embassy. Endion and the Underground were her stomping grounds.

As she moved up the street, she kept her eyes peeled for their rendezvous location a small square with a fountain outside one of the nicer hotels. She had been instructed to leave the swordsmith's shop and turn right, then walk straight for two of Chaiavis's large city blocks. The extra walking time would give Kat ample time to get to and from Bosco's place, though Ziva wasn't going to be surprised if she had to sit and wait a while. Kat had seemed intent on speaking to Bosco about something, something she had withheld from the rest of the group. Ziva didn't feel her secret was pertinent to the case, but she wanted to know what it was all the same.

She wasn't entirely sure how she managed to spot him—maybe she'd just been looking in the right place at the right time, or maybe she'd subconsciously picked out something familiar in this foreign environment. Either way, she found herself frozen in place, eyes glued to the humanoid creature making his way through the crowd twenty or so meters ahead of her. The tell-tale tentacles on the back of his head were bundled into a crude ponytail, and he turned his face slightly to reveal large, reddish-brown eyes that contrasted greatly with his pale green skin. A Cobian. *The* Cobian.

His name was Farag Foda, captain of a small band of Cobian

pirates that had been notorious for hitting supply vessels exporting weapons from Haphez. He was the primary target on the mission Ikaro Tachi had scrapped on Cobi, resulting in her capture. She found herself paralyzed by a fresh memory of being chained up in the pirates' bunker; Foda himself had been responsible for the torture she and her strike team were subjected to.

A tingle ran up and down her spine, caused in part by the recollection of her gruesome imprisonment. The other part was sheer anger. Foda and most of his crew had escaped before the rescue team arrived, and no one had seen or heard from them in the intervening three years. The fact that he was there on Chaiavis confused her. He appeared to be searching the crowd for something; she took a look around as well, terrified he had men nearby, but she saw no one.

She felt a certain part of herself suddenly come alive, almost like an engine mechanism on a machine that had simply been idling. It was as if a second version of herself was being activated, switched on like a light. The hairs on the back of her neck stood on end, and her heart rate began to rise. Time itself seemed to slow; she could see every detail of every face, every figure in every window, hear every engine of every ship around her. Everything but the Cobian seemed to be moving in slow motion.

This flip-of-the-switch effect was not something foreign to her. She liked to think of it as a survival mode, an autopilot of sorts that helped her focus and do what needed to be done with minimal thought or emotion. HSP's physicians had called it an adrenaline response... which it was, but to her, it was so much more.

Foda showed no signs of seeing her; his focus was devoted to whatever he was searching for. Judging by the way he moved and the way he kept glancing back and forth at the passersby, that thing was a person.

Curious, she continued forward but moved up into the shadows against the buildings, gaining a better view of Foda from the new angle. He was armed with at least one pistol, probably more. He was built like any Cobian: only about Zinni's height, but well-muscled under the thick, armor-like flesh around his shoulders.

She risked a quick glance away from him and noticed an area up ahead that appeared to be her rendezvous point. She considered ignoring the meeting plan in favor of following Foda, but there was no way of telling why he was there. His presence could be a mere coincidence, and the thought of wasting her time chasing him sickened her. It was tempting to just shoot him then and there after the things he'd done to her.

She hesitated when she saw him take a couple of shuffling steps and stop. From her vantage point under the awning over a storefront, she could see him looking intently ahead at something. She followed his gaze and found a familiar green aircar touching down beside the fountain in front of the hotel. Ziva didn't even bother to look at Kat before returning her attention to Foda and the way he was reaching for his communicator.

Something told her he wasn't calling just to chat with anyone. Without another thought, she had her own pistol drawn and was rushing into the street. At the sight of the gun, those around her began to scatter, and she successfully cleared the area when she fired a round through the back of Foda's left knee. He began to draw his own weapon, but she was upon him before he had a chance to turn and take aim. The two of them hit the street and rolled up onto the opposite walkway, out of sight of any security bots that happened to be hovering around.

Foda's gun flew from his grasp and clattered to a stop a couple of meters away. He was quick to retaliate nonetheless, and when Ziva pounced on him again, she saw he had managed to draw a sharp knife from a sheath hidden on his belt. The blade met her shoulder, slicing through her clothing and leaving a deep gash. More angry than in pain, she seized Foda's forearm and wrenched it around until he groaned and let the weapon fall from his grasp.

She heard the roar of a car pulling up behind her and was momentarily terrified the authorities had already arrived at the scene. A quick glance with her peripherals revealed it was only Kat, who had no doubt been alerted by all the commotion. The young woman reached her, armed with a pistol of her own, and together they managed to flip Foda over and pin his arms behind his back. Ziva brought her gun down against the back of his head, putting an end to his resistance.

"Nice timing," she said as she and Kat began hauling the Cobian's limp body to the car without further discussion.

"Who is he?" Kat asked. They shoved him into the back seat, and she fetched some crude restraints from the storage compartment.

Ziva climbed into the back as well and went about securing Foda's hands as they lifted off. "Let's just say if he's here, we've got a real problem."

Judging by Kat's hesitation and the strange greenish tint her skin had taken on, there was already another problem Ziva was unaware of. "Great," the young woman muttered. Her voice caught as if she were about to cry.

"What happened?"

Kat gave her an abbreviated rundown of what had transpired at Bosco's shop, emphasizing the fact that the hostiles were Haphezian but didn't appear to be local. Bosco was dead—news that would not bode well with Aroska—and his killers had been careful not to leave any evidence of their presence. Kat's account of their actions made Ziva's skin crawl, and her survival mode flared up once again as the young woman described their physical appearances.

An odd combination of fear, excitement, and anger welled up within her, leaving her paralyzed in her seat. "Kat Reilly, allow me to introduce you to Diago Dasaro."

· 74 ·
PAYVAN RESIDENCE
NORO, HAPHEZ

All Luko Zona could do as he approached Ziva Payvan's residence was wonder what he had gotten himself into. This whole case with Payvan had become far more complicated than he ever imagined it would, and whether she started it or not, she seemed to be the key to it all. Diago Dasaro must have known it, too—that explained his obsession with catching her and why he had wanted her dead. After hearing from Payvan's squadmates, it was clear the captain had been up to something beyond the investigation, and Zona felt foolish for having ever put his confidence in the man. He wasn't sure what or who he could trust now, but he knew for certain that someone somewhere was in danger, and he hoped with all his heart he hadn't made their situation worse.

He pulled his car around to the side of the house as he'd been instructed. He stepped out and unloaded his two traveling cases; one contained clothes and other necessities—the galaxy only knew how long this would take—and the other contained a portable RG computer and all the information he had regarding the case. He paused and glanced about before moving from the car. Other than the roar of the Tranyi River, there wasn't a sound to be heard, and there didn't seem to be anyone around.

When Sergeant Duvo had contacted him the previous day, he had described a short staircase leading down into the large landing bay where Payvan's ship was stored. Zona spotted the little flight of steps after a moment and carefully descended into the underground bay, stopping to listen again every couple of steps. Still nothing. The bay itself was empty, just as Duvo said it would be. Zona took one last look around and, seeing no one, he set his bags down and walked into the center of the room with his hands raised.

This was just a precaution, he reminded himself. No operators in their right minds—especially considering the circumstances—would allow him to approach without having a chance to sniff around and check him out. He preferred this overly cautious approach to getting blown away.

Somewhere around him, a door hissed open. He couldn't help but tense a bit, unable to see or hear anything further. An uncomfortable twenty seconds passed before he sensed movement on both his right and left. How long these people had been lurking there, he had no idea. He risked brief looks at each of them. The one on his left was a woman whom he recognized from Payvan's file as Zinni Vax. She was armed. The other was an older man, also armed, roughly his same age, with deep green eyes and close-cropped hair.

"Special Agent Zona?" said a voice behind him. It belonged to another man.

"Yes," Zona replied, straightening his shoulders and lifting his hands a bit higher.

Whoever stood behind him must have given some sort of signal because Vax and the other man emerged from the shadows and converged on him. The man watched him carefully from behind the barrel of his pistol while Vax gave him a quick but thorough frisking. She removed his sidearm from its holster, holding it down at her side while keeping her own trained on him.

The two of them stepped back to make way for the mysterious third member of their party. Zona recognized him as Skeet Duvo. He too was armed, but his attention remained focused on a data pad rather than his weapon. Zona caught a glimpse of his own photo on the screen along with his Royal Guard credentials.

Duvo studied it for another second or two, glancing between Zona and the screen, before holstering his pistol and motioning for his associates to do the same. "Apologies, Agent Zona," he said. "A person can never be too careful these days."

"Understood," Zona replied. "I appreciate the caution."

"I'm Sergeant Skeet Duvo," he said, offering his hand. "This is Officer Zinni Vax—"

Zinni dipped her head and handed Zona's gun back.

"—and this is Ryon Kittner, Payvan family friend."

"Pleased to meet you all," Zona said. "If you don't mind, we should get straight to business. I'd like to think I didn't come all the way from Haphor to stand around in an empty landing bay."

"Believe me sir, you didn't," Duvo said, motioning for Zona to follow as the three of them opened a door and entered a hallway running below the house. It *looked* like any other basement—the rooms that were open contained various machinery and workbenches. But the ones that were closed had complex locking mechanisms on the doors, and Zona wasn't sure if he wanted to know what they contained. A stairwell rose up at the end of the hall, leading up to the ground floor. The area around it was furnished with a sofa and exercise equipment.

"Does this have to do with Payvan or Shevin?" Zona asked as he followed them up to the living room.

"Both," Duvo replied, though Zona barely heard him as his gaze fell upon Veya Shevin standing in the kitchen with her baby. She was talking with another woman and the two of them put their conversation on hold when the agents entered.

"Mrs. Shevin!" he exclaimed. "By the five moons, I'm glad you're all right!"

Veya watched him for a moment as if she wasn't sure who she could trust, a concept that had become all too familiar during the past few days. "Special Agent Zona," she said. "Have you heard from my husband?"

"We're all in the dark, here," Sergeant Duvo said before he had a chance to respond. "The director thinks we can solve this puzzle a lot faster if we work together." He nodded toward the other woman with Veya, a heavier-set *emilan* lady with rich purple streaking her dark hair. "Marshay, if you please."

The woman nodded and took Veya by the arm. "Come on, my dear." The two of them disappeared into one of the bedrooms down the hall and were followed momentarily by Ryon.

Duvo and Vax moved into the sitting area and motioned for Zona to make himself comfortable on one of the plush sofas. Over the course of several minutes, they relayed to him a series of facts that had supposedly been given a green light by Emeri Arion himself. Zona's mind raced as he attempted to process everything—just as something began to make sense, a new detail threw a wrench into it all and he felt like they were starting from square one.

"You think Payvan is still alive?" he asked when they were finally done.

"We know she is," Vax said, "but for now, we're operating under the pretense that she's not. Either she staged her death or Tarbic actually tried to kill her. Regardless of which is true, the galaxy is supposed to think she's gone, and we need to keep it that way."

Zona nodded. "And you said she was seeking my agent?"

"According to Veya, Ziva appeared at the Shevins' home approximately eleven hours after she allegedly died," Duvo said. "She was looking for Kade, claiming someone was after him. She sent Veya and the baby here to keep them safe until this all blows over."

"And how exactly did she know someone was after him?" Zona asked, not sure what to think.

"That's where Lieutenant Tarbic comes in," Officer Vax replied. "In order to know about the bird phrase, *he* would have to have been in contact with Ziva at some point. And in order to have known Kade was in trouble, *she* would have needed someone on the inside."

"Tarbic was supposedly working with Dasaro, though he told us it was on Ziva's account," Duvo said. "For a while there, we thought he'd been lying to our faces, but now that we've heard what Veya has to say, we're more inclined to believe him."

"So you think Tarbic and Payvan are together, wherever they are," Zona confirmed. "And you haven't heard anything from my man?"

The sergeant's wild orange hair bounced around as he shook his head. "The last record anyone has of Agent Shevin's presence is from the night of the break-in at RG Headquarters."

Zona rested his chin in his hand and sighed. "I still can't believe he would have hacked into my system. I should have had his access card temporarily deactivated. I never thought he was a threat."

"Don't blame yourself," Vax said. "I don't think he *is* a threat. We just need to know what's in those files that he wanted to get his hands on."

"It was research, bits and pieces of information that had been trickling into the RG office. I'd been looking more closely at the death of the coroner, Eason Fromm." Zona dipped his head and groaned. "I'll admit Shevin's theories got me curious. I started doing a little digging of my own, hoping to get some closure, and I'd saved my findings with the rest of the current case files for easier comparison. Those were included in the files that were accessed."

"Could they be what Shevin was after?" Duvo asked.

"Sergeant, you must understand that I conducted this project with the utmost secrecy. Nobody knew about it, especially Shevin. And even if he did, those files are heavily encrypted. Kade's good with computers, but it would still take him days to get into them if he ever managed to at all."

"What did they contain?" Vax pressed.

Zona hesitated. "Information on Payvan and Dasaro," he replied. "I had a feeling there were problems between them for reasons nobody else knew about. She was captured and tortured by Cobian pirates three years ago, correct?"

The way his words affected the other two agents was unnerving. They watched him with wide eyes, their bodies rigid. "What of it?" Duvo said.

Zona told them everything.

KAT'S HIDEOUT
CHAIAVIS

Aroska and Kade stood in the garage with the overhead door open, having been summoned downstairs by an angry transmission from Ziva. They caught sight of Kat's green aircar and were startled to see three passengers in it. Ziva sat in the back seat with the stranger as Kat piloted the craft.

As they neared, Aroska recognized him as a Cobian, known as a cousin to the Haphezians despite the fact that the two species had absolutely nothing in common. Perhaps it had something to do with the fact that Cobi orbited the Noro star on the same path as Haphez. Each civilization viewed the other as a foe, though the Cobians were no match for Haphez's military presence.

He moved aside and motioned for Kade to close the door as the car entered the garage. Ziva leaped out before it had even come to a stop and tossed him a communicator that apparently belonged to the unconscious prisoner. "I want to know who the hell he was going to contact on that!" she snapped.

He only needed to glance at the outgoing code once before he gave her an answer. "This is the number Dasaro gave me when he enlisted my help in tracking you down."

"How did he find me?" Ziva spun in a circle and swore under her breath.

"He isn't looking for you!" Kat exclaimed, just as tense. "Bosco told me they were there for *me* right before he…before he…" She choked on her own words.

"Before he what?" Aroska asked, unsure if he really wanted to know.

What came next was a fast, high-decibel relation of everything that had transpired from each woman's point of view—Kat was distraught, and Ziva was just plain mad. Aroska caught the important details: Dasaro was on the planet, Bosco was dead, and Ziva had stumbled upon the Cobian pirate as he stalked Kat in the street. They'd fought, explaining her blood-soaked shoulder and why he was unconscious.

"If Dasaro is looking for Kat, this guy must have been reporting to him," Kade suggested after a rather uncomfortable silence.

"That's about all he'd be good for," Ziva growled. "He's nothing but a scout—Dasaro would want to bring us down himself if it came down to it."

The Cobian began to stir, and she seized him by the arm and dragged him out of the car with Kat's help. They shoved him to his knees on the garage floor where he sat for a moment, head drooping, struggling to gather his bearings.

Ziva grabbed a handful of his tentacles and yanked his head back, taking a moment to stare into his squinting eyes. "No," she said, her voice dropping into the same low, gravelly tone she'd used when Aroska first heard her speak in Emeri's office. "He doesn't know where Dasaro is." She bent down closer to him, her face contorted with more hatred than Aroska had ever seen. "There's nothing stopping me from killing you right now."

"I want to know why he was following me," Kat muttered.

Unless it was Aroska's imagination, Ziva looked disappointed. She glared at the Cobian for a few more seconds before releasing him and standing up. "Fine," she said, wiping her hand over the back of her shoulder. It came away bloody. "See what you can get out of him. I'll be right back."

Aroska stooped down and faced the Cobian, gesturing at Ziva as she moved away. "I don't know if you realize this, but you're about two steps away from hell itself right now."

The prisoner's only response was a grunt.

"She said his name is Farag Foda," Kat said quietly, stealing a peek back at Ziva.

Aroska glanced to Kade and jerked his head toward the computer upstairs. "See what you can find."

"Sure," Kade replied, disappearing up the steps behind Ziva.

The garage was suddenly silent, leaving Aroska and Kat to stare the man down as he glared at them in return. There was something in Ziva's case files that had bothered Aroska from the beginning, and now that this was all happening, he was reminded of it again. There had been an incident, what, three years ago? Ziva had been imprisoned and tortured in a bunker on Cobi, and it was rumored that she would have died like the rest of her squad if the rescue team hadn't arrived when they did. Most of the report had been redacted, leaving him clueless as to how she had been captured, why, and who exactly had been responsible for it. The incident was on his list of things to ask her about, but that was before they'd met Kade and Kat. As curious as he was, Ziva had seemed so miserable lately that he hadn't had the heart to bring it up.

Now, considering she knew the man's name and how much she seemed to hate him, Aroska couldn't help but wonder if Foda had somehow been involved. He sighed and took one last look up the stairs before rising to his feet and crossing his arms.

"You know Lieutenant Payvan?" he asked.

The Cobian refused to make eye contact. "Go to hell," he muttered in heavily accented Standard.

Now Kat stepped forward, her blue eyes like ice. "Why were you following me?" she demanded. "What does Dasaro want with me?"

Foda shifted his gaze, though he locked eyes with Aroska rather than Kat. Still, rather than respond, he only shook his head and smirked.

There was something about that smug face and the knowledge of how angry it made Ziva—for whatever reason—that made Aroska want to strangle him. The fact that this man was capable of evoking such a strange, emotional reaction from her confused him. Most HSP agents—operators in particular—knew better than to outwardly display emotion, especially in the presence of an enemy. Whatever happened between them had certainly been significant or she wouldn't have cared the way she did.

Kat was kneeling in front of Foda now, though the Cobian clearly wasn't interested in talking. Interrogation wasn't one of Aroska's strong points—pushing prisoners for information had been Jole Imetsi's job back when they'd worked together in field ops. He had, however, picked up on some useful techniques, and he thought himself perfectly capable of getting creative when it came to protecting Ziva and their new allies.

He rose to his feet without a word and took a grease-stained rag from a nearby shelf. He hurled it to the ground at Kat's feet and bounded up the stairs two at a time, picturing a deep water jug he had encountered while exploring the kitchen cupboards earlier.

As he passed the lavatory, he was overcome with the urge to check in on Ziva, and what he saw nearly made him forget what he'd been doing. She stood before the mirror, stripped down to a racerback compression bra, attempting to place an adhesive caura pad over the cut tracing her shoulder blade. She was turned slightly, trying to use the mirror to guide her, but she still seemed to be struggling. That angry, hateful look remained on her face, but there was something new mixed in with it: regret, unless Aroska was mistaken.

All this registered with him within half a second, but he found he was unable to take his eyes off her. It wasn't her bare shoulders, elaborate tattoos, or powerful abdominal muscles that interested him— he noticed these things, but what really caught his attention were the masses of scar tissue running down her spine and covering her lower back and stomach. Scarring on such a scale only occurred when the victim hadn't gotten caura treatment soon enough...for instance, when someone was held prisoner for a week before receiving medical attention. These injuries didn't appear to be recent, but they seemed much newer than the scar on her face. Perhaps they were about three years old.

Suddenly Aroska knew.

The four or five seconds he'd been standing there seemed like an eternity, and he felt his face flush. Ziva was looking at him now, shooting halfhearted glares his way as she continued her attempts at applying the pad.

"Need a hand?" he asked, not sure what else to say and not sure if he really wanted to help.

She didn't respond. Instead, she slapped the bandage on, content to wear it crooked, and pulled a tank top over her head.

Feeling awful, he turned and continued his trek into the kitchen. Kade sat at the computer and gave him a subtle nod, telling him he'd found something about Foda in the files. *Well, this is a fine mess.*

Aroska found the container and filled it with water from the sink. Ziva was just emerging from the lavatory, face and hair damp, as he made his way back down the stairs. He heard Kade address her clearly: "There's something you should see, and I doubt you'll like it."

· 76 ·
KAT'S HIDEOUT
CHAIAVIS

Ziva wanted nothing more than to go back downstairs and give Foda a taste of his own medicine, but the look on Kade's face piqued her curiosity. There was no harm in hearing him out, she decided. Considering he was at his computer, maybe he had found something of value.

She approached, feeling almost sick as her fresh cut continued to sting. It wasn't the pain that affected her so much as the knowledge that Foda had once more managed to hurt her, even after she'd vowed it would never happen again. And now Aroska had seen the scars...he knew, didn't he? He'd read her files but hadn't mentioned anything about her imprisonment. In turn, she'd refused to bring it up.

Kade moved aside to give her a look at the screen. He seemed nervous, fidgety, like someone who was about to bear bad news. *Great.*

"I got the rest of Zona's files open while you were out," he explained. "It turns out he was doing a little research independent of the case—I don't think he wanted anyone else to know about it. By the looks of it, he might have actually started taking everything I told him to heart."

"This is all about me," Ziva said, skimming over each of the file headings. She recognized each and every one of the incident reports and mission debriefs. Despite Zona's elevated clearance level, many of them were redacted or only partially complete, but the amount of information that remained was enough for any experienced investigator to start piecing things together.

Kade swallowed. "There seems to be one other common factor."

"Dasaro," she said. She caught his name in several of her own files, and it appeared there was a separate collection of information about him alone.

"Search queries for Argall and Farag Foda also came back positive," Kade said, sounding as though something were lodged in his throat.

"Argall," Ziva repeated, not quite a question and not quite a statement. Why would anyone else at HSP be looking into Argall, and how could anyone outside of ops have known about Foda and the incident on Cobi? She looked closer at the timestamps on each file. Some were more recent, and some were from—she did a double take—three years earlier.

Three years. *I've had this hunch for three years.*

Kat's voice: *"He and the girl were killed three years ago."*

"Three years ago is when I first found something on Argall while I was investigating Dasaro," she said. "That's when Kat's father and sister died, and judging by what Zona has collected here, it looks like he believes Dasaro was behind all those killings that took place there."

"Was that the gist you were getting back then?"

Ziva paused. "I'm not sure. There was a lot going on and I didn't have time or probable cause to search any further. All I knew was that he had some sort of operation going on outside the agency, but I never got a chance to find out what it was."

Kade lifted an eyebrow. "But did *he* know that? Here he is coming after me because he's afraid I know something I don't."

She stared at the screen, attempting to put the puzzle together and see whatever big picture Zona had seen. "Kat has encountered Dasaro's name just recently as she's searched for information about her family."

"And you've been digging again, right?" Kade said. "Three years ago, you were digging. Now, you're digging. What else has happened both times?"

Ziva remained silent for a moment, eyes fixed on the file Zona had labeled CONCLUSIONS. "No," she murmured, partly to herself and partly in response to his question, "that was completely unrelated." The harder she thought, however, the more she understood his hint. He'd no doubt already seen what was in the file.

"What do we know?" he asked, pushing her along.

"We know Dasaro is behind my set-up now," she replied, rubbing her eyes. "So, what, I'm getting a little too close, so he decides to frame me for an assassination to shut me up? You think the same thing happened three years ago?"

"It's possible, isn't it?"

She clasped her hands in front of her mouth before the trembling could set in. She was having trouble replacing the image of Foda standing before her battered body in that bunker with the one of him on his knees downstairs. It seemed clear he was working for Dasaro now, if only as an informant, so it was quite possible they could have been in league three years earlier as well. In fact, the idea made sense.

"There was no motive," she muttered.

Nobody had ever been able to figure out the exact reason behind her capture, other than the fact that she was one of the agents tasked with putting the pirates' operations to an end. During all her time in captivity, they'd never asked a single question regarding troop placement or how much HSP knew. It wasn't an interrogation—it was torture for the sake of torture, performed by someone who had been paid to take his sweet time carrying out instructions from a third party and not question his orders.

She felt her face flush with anger and mashed a button on Kade's keypad, opening the Conclusions file. The notes it contained only reinforced the theory her mind had begun to form. Three years earlier, she'd been searching for a connection between Dasaro and Argall, and the captain had arranged a seemingly unrelated circumstance to either incapacitate or kill her. Now, she'd been investigating again, and again he had arranged a way to get her off his trail. She kicked herself for having not caught on sooner, but at the moment, she was more bothered by the fact that Foda had done all those unspeakable things in that bunker under orders.

The wound on her shoulder began to seep again as her blood pressure rose. She jerked into a standing position, nearly upsetting the table and the computer equipment. Kade leaped aside to give her space as she stormed past him, descending the stairs on feet so light she could barely hear her steps over her own pulse. Once again, it seemed as though time itself had slowed when she caught sight of Foda. Kat stood behind him, holding his tentacles as she removed a dirty old rag from his face. He sputtered and coughed as water ran down his body and contributed to the puddle that had already formed on the floor. Aroska stood with the jug poised over his head, growling questions the Cobian wouldn't have answered even if he'd been able to.

Everything was still only moving at half speed when Ziva reached the bottom of the steps. Without breaking stride, she turned toward the others, sliding her pistol from its holster as she did so. She took aim for Foda's gaping mouth, the one that had sneered and spit on her as he'd tormented her. His eyes widened when he noticed the gun.

"Whoa!" Kat exclaimed, leaning forward over Foda's head.

Her sudden movements made Ziva hesitate just long enough to give Aroska time to turn and seize her forearm, but his grip was no match for the adrenaline surging through her veins. She threw her arm forward, knocking him off balance, and brought her elbow across his face. He flinched and tried to duck away, only to end up on the receiving end of a powerful left hook. Her fist met the side of his head, and the impact sent him reeling backward. If there was a time in her life when she'd hit someone harder, she couldn't remember it.

Taking advantage of the few seconds of freedom, she pivoted and leveled the gun at Foda's chest. She pulled the trigger once, twice, three times, and watched his body buck and fall backward. A stunned silence fell over the room. Kat and Aroska stared, wide-eyed, and she was vaguely aware of Kade standing on the stairs behind her.

Let them stare. There were some people who warned that revenge would never bring peace; perhaps that was true, but revenge was also sweet, wasn't it? Standing there staring at Foda's limp form, she couldn't help but be happy she'd spotted him in the street. He would've met his demise eventually, but it wouldn't have been by her choosing. This outcome was much more ideal. She stepped forward and put one last round through his head for good measure.

She wasn't sure how long she'd been standing there with the gun still aimed at him before Aroska approached her from behind and placed his hand over her own, pistol and all. "Give it to me, Ziva," he said, his voice quiet but firm.

She released the gun after a brief hesitation and let her arm fall to her side. She didn't resist when he took her by the shoulders and led her across the room to the sofa; he sat her down and knelt before her, forcing her to look him in the eye. He said nothing, but his face displayed the same qualities as it had on the landing pad outside the Dakiti facility on Sardonis—a hint of awe, but mostly fear and disappointment.

Her eyes narrowed and she shook her head. "He didn't know anything anyway."

Aroska rose to a standing position and crossed his arms, looming in much the same way as Dasaro had in the interrogation room. He was joined after a moment by Kat, who was in turn joined by Kade, and she felt smothered by their collective stare.

"I don't know what you want me to say. I'm not going to tell you I'm sorry, because I'm not."

"Nobody's asking for an apology," Aroska replied, "but we're all in this together, so I think the rest of us deserve a nice long explanation for what the hell is going on."

And there it was. All along, Ziva had known she'd have to tell her story at some point, but over time, she had found herself putting it off and hoping everyone would forget. She looked up at each of them in turn—Kat and Kade were wide-eyed and confused, and Aroska's face was stone cold. But they were all waiting expectantly.

She stood up to escape their intense stares and took one last look at Foda's body, using that time to gather her thoughts. The trembling had already set in, so she placed her hands on her hips in hopes of stilling them.

"I'm sure you all remember hearing about the series of attacks on the weapons transports three years ago," she said, keeping her gaze directed toward the dead Cobian. "I was part of a spec ops task force assigned to track the pirates down, and I ran point on a strike team that infiltrated the old base on Cobi..."

· 77 ·
3 Years Ago
Smugglers' Compound
Cobi

Ziva froze and held up her right hand, signaling for her team to halt as the garbled transmission came through her earpiece. Exasperated, she pressed her back against the wall of the outbuilding they were concealed behind and waited until the five agents with her had done the same.

"Red Leader here," she responded.

For a moment, there was nothing but static and jumbled voices as two transmissions vied for priority. She barely caught Skeet's voice: "Z, are you seeing this?"

Without turning around, she held out her hand and received a viewscreen displaying an infrared bird's-eye-view of the old military compound in which they stood. There were two other teams identical to hers, headed up by Skeet and Zinni, holding positions on the other side of the compound and represented on the screen by clusters of yellow dots. Those clusters were moving outward and away from the base's center structure, away from the target.

"What the hell?" she muttered. "Command, this is Red Leader. Why are we retreating?"

The original transmission finally got through and she found herself listening to Dasaro's voice. "Repeat, all teams fall back," he said. "New intel. I'm sending exfil coordinates to you. RTB for briefing."

"But sir!" she said, stealing a glance around the side of the building. They were so close! "My teams are all in position—if we move now, we can take the warehouse."

"Tachi's orders, Payvan," Dasaro replied. "We just received an anonymous tip—some members of Foda's gang were spotted in the city."

"But there's a high probability we'll find Foda himself here."

"An order's an order, Payvan. Pull out now!"

She handed the viewscreen back to the agent beside her and took a moment to examine each eager face as the others waited for the verdict. It had taken nearly two hours of sneaking and creeping for them to reach their current position, and she dreaded to think it had been for nothing.

"My brother worked on one of the transports that was attacked," one of the agents spoke up. "Foda's gang killed him. I'm with you all the way, Lieutenant."

"As am I," said another.

The other three nodded in agreement.

The wheels in Ziva's head began spinning. If they managed to advance another forty meters or so, they'd be past the point of no return and HSP would have to let them continue. They'd need to move fast, or an extraction team would catch up to them and blow any chance they had of bagging Foda.

She considered opening a transmission to Dasaro but decided against it for fear he would send someone after them before they had time to move. "Let's go," she said.

Two agents moved out in front of her, sweeping the area and providing cover as the rest of them darted across the grass to the next outbuilding. They froze halfway across the clearing, sending a nervous tingle through her body. She looked up to see a group of six Cobians forming a barrier across their path—all were armed and held their weapons up and ready. There was a rustling behind them, and she turned to find seven more blocking the way they had come. She was too focused on them to notice the two flash grenades rolling toward her.

Ziva tried to look away as they went off but found herself staring straight into the glare of a third one thrown by the second group. She turned, blinded by the spots and stars dancing in her eyes, and collided with one of the other agents. They fell to the ground, their feet entangled, and her rifle slipped from her grasp. Heavy footsteps thundered around her, and she was vaguely aware of shadows passing by overhead. She caught sight of her weapon—more accurately, two of her weapon. She reached for the nearest one, but her hand came away full of dead grass. Her vision began to right itself and she reached for the real gun; her fingers touched metal just as a stun baton hit the back of her neck.

· 78 ·
KAT'S HIDEOUT
CHAIAVIS

"I never saw any of the other agents again," Ziva said. "When I woke up, I was alone, strung up by a chain in a dark room. I was under the influence of something—I couldn't move, couldn't speak. Foda and some of his men showed up before long, and...."

She felt her eyes start to sting and her cheeks start to burn. She cupped her hands over her nose and mouth, blinking rapidly to keep the hot tears at bay. There were times when she could still feel the sensation of the rusty chains digging into her wrists, and this was one of them.

The only sound in the garage was the little heater as it kicked on and began to hum, causing the items around it to vibrate ever so slightly. Aroska, Kat, and Kade all stood in uncomfortable silence, unwilling to make eye contact. Ziva looked over each of them in turn, glad they seemed to regret ever asking her what her problem was. She gritted her teeth and grimaced, keeping her voice steady despite the tears that finally broke free and spilled down her face. "And then I spent the next week being cut, burned, violated, and beaten by that *huhren shouka souhn.*" She thrust a finger in Foda's direction.

It was Aroska who finally dared to look at her. His mouth formed a straight line, and the familiar teasing glimmer was absent from his eyes. "That's what you meant when you said you couldn't go back," he said. "In the café on the transport, you said you couldn't 'go back' to the Haphor Facility."

She heaved a sigh and wiped the back of her hand across her face. "Yeah, that's what I meant," she said, almost a whisper. "I think I would have shot myself before having to endure all of that again." She returned her hands to her hips and cleared her throat, taking a moment to stare up at the ceiling. "It was Skeet who finally found me. He and Zinni launched an independent rescue mission, something totally unheard of in spec ops. They say I probably wouldn't have lasted another night if that team hadn't reached me. Everyone else was already dead."

Another wave of shame threatened to drown her. "Looking back on it now, it all makes more sense!" she snarled, sweeping her hand across one of the nearby shelves and sending its contents clattering to the floor. "If Dasaro really orchestrated everything like Zona thinks, that explains how the Cobians found my squad. I was conveniently out of his hair while his men were out in Argall killing the Reilly family and dozens of others. And HSP was too focused on me and the way I'd screwed everything up to notice what he was doing. I'm sure he was hoping I'd just rot in that bunker, and I almost did thanks to his Cobian puppets."

Kade cleared his throat. "That might also explain how Foda and his crew were able to escape after that," he put in. "If Dasaro managed to cover up the situation in Argall, he could have easily arranged for them to slip through the cracks while the rest of the agency was off chasing false leads."

Ziva nodded in agreement, feeling emotionally spent and angry at herself for having not seen through Dasaro's charade. "I tried to explain to everyone that there was never even an interrogation, that it was just mindless torture, but he would always step in and remind them that *I* was the one who defied orders, it was *my* fault we were captured. Yes, I was willing to go through with the mission, but those pirates would have found us regardless of whether we'd retreated or pressed on." She shook her head again, gnawing on the inside of her lip. "Always shifting the blame back to me. And here I thought it was just because he hated my guts."

"And everyone thinks you blamed Tachi for your capture because he called off the mission?" Kat asked, staring at the floor.

"In a lot of ways, I *did* blame him. The rest of the agency saw that as a motive for murdering him. Now that we know the truth, though, I can see that his orders to retreat had nothing to do with anything that happened. For all I know, Dasaro could have fabricated this so-called tip that prompted Tachi to give the order in the first place."

Ziva paused for a moment and wiped the remaining tears from her eyes, letting a quiet growl escape her throat. She walked to the green car and took out the sack with her precious chunk of bariine, removing the little brick and running her fingers over it while staring down at Foda's body. His chest had been torn open by the three rounds she'd put into it, and the flesh on his forehead was crusted and charred around the hole she'd blasted through it. Perhaps it had been overkill, but it had felt good. She looked down at the metal in her hand. One shot was all it would take from now on.

"Somebody get rid of that *frouchten* body," she muttered, addressing no one in particular.

"What are you going to do?" Aroska asked.

She held the bariine up, estimating the number of rounds she could get out of it. "I'm going to make some new friends."

CENTRAL SPACEPORT
CHAIAVIS

The trash compactor behind the spaceport's maintenance shop wasn't the most discreet place to dump a body, but with any luck, the machine would be activated and Foda's corpse would be destroyed before anyone noticed it. Besides, this was Chaiavis, where species of all shapes and sizes roamed and where law enforcement jurisdiction was almost never clear. It was doubtful anyone would care too much about a dead Cobian.

Aroska stepped back to examine his handiwork. He selected another chunk of discarded metal and arranged it over the conspicuous body-sized package he and Kat had lifted into the compactor moments before. As satisfied as he thought he'd ever be, he found his footing and worked his way out of the machine.

Kat stood at the end of the alley keeping watch, and she came to meet him when she saw their task was complete. She took a look into the compactor and sighed. "I guess that will work."

"You sound unsure."

Without another word, she slid into the car's pilot seat and motioned for him to get in. He did so without question, and she brought the vehicle out of the alley and into traffic. They flew in silence for a minute or two until they were a suitable distance from the spaceport and the dump site. The car came to a stop, idling in mid-air behind a tall building.

He could tell there was something on Kat's mind—she sat still, gripping the controls, blue eyes staring off into the distance. The quiet was becoming uncomfortable. "What's wrong?"

She turned toward him. "Here's the thing. You said it yourself—we're all in this together. I've chosen to put my trust in you people. I've welcomed you into my home. I need to know that what just happened won't happen again. I need to know that the choices one of us makes aren't going to wind up hurting everyone else."

Aroska sighed and rubbed his hands over his face, at a total loss for words. Though extreme, he didn't blame Ziva the least bit for her actions. But at the same time, he knew Kat was right.

"I'll talk to her," he said.

"Will she listen to you?"

"Probably not."

"She's lost her mind, Tarbic," the young woman said. "I sought her out because I needed her help, and I'll be damned if all my hard work goes down the drain because she can't control her temper."

"Is that what it is, a temper?" he asked, bristling a bit. "You heard her story. How did you expect her to react when the man responsible for all of that showed up?"

"I probably would have done the same thing," Kat admitted, "but not when he could have given us information. Not if it could wind up hurting my only allies."

"Listen," Aroska said. "If you're looking for an apology, you're probably out of luck. She's on a mission right now, and the best thing we can do is stay out of her way."

"Do you always bow down to her like this?" Kat asked with a scoff. "Ever wonder what it would be like if the galaxy didn't revolve around her?"

The sharp retort caught in Aroska's throat before he could say it, and he realized he understood exactly how Kat felt. In his mind, he saw himself sitting in Ziva's living room two months earlier, asking Skeet and Zinni the very same question Kat had just asked. She had a lot of learning to do...they both did. He by no means wanted to 'bow down' and always let Ziva have her way, but neither did he want to hold her back from something toward which she was so driven. Still, if that drive resulted in her getting hurt, captured, or killed because her head wasn't in the right place, something needed to be done about it.

"Like I said, I'll talk to her."

· 80 ·
KAT'S HIDEOUT
CHAIAVIS

It was nearly an hour later that Kat and Aroska arrived back at the garage. Ziva heard the car approaching even before the overhead door began to rise—she'd left the man door open to get some air, and the familiar whine of the engine carried through.

She looked up from her work long enough to acknowledge them. The rifle itself was complete and the last batch of ammunition had just finished cooling. All that remained was to load the thing.

As her hands worked, her ears registered Kat's footsteps hurrying up the stairs and Aroska's pausing a few steps from the car. In her peripheral vision, she could see him standing there, watching her in the same manner as he had the night before. She tried not to let it bother her, but somehow, he always managed to get the best of her. She sighed and held up one of the rounds. "Have you ever seen a bariine alloy projectile?"

He shook his head and approached. "Is it like a frag round?"

Ziva nodded and handed him the bullet. It was about the length and thickness of her little finger, tapered on both ends to ensure an easy transition from the mag into the modified plasma cell and firing chamber. It was still slightly warm to the touch and had taken on a dull grayish-brown color.

"Let me show you something," she said, taking it back from him. She held it up to his forehead between her thumb and forefinger as if it were a dart she was about to throw at a target. "What you're seeing right here is going to be the last thing Dasaro sees before his miserable existence comes to an end."

The look on Aroska's face was priceless. He brushed her hand away, the shock morphing quickly into anger. "You need to calm down, Ziva."

"Calm down?" Her eyebrows immediately dropped into a scowl. "This is calm, Aroska."

He returned her scowl with one of his own. "I can see the hatred in your eyes. Your mind is running in overdrive."

"I've been doing some thinking. What's wrong with that?"

"No, you haven't. You just blew a prisoner's brains out in the middle of an interrogation. You're not thinking—you've lost your mind!"

She set her jaw and stared him down for a moment. "Believe whatever you want," she growled. "I know what I'm doing. I'm tired of running. I'm tired of all the *sheyss* I've gone through because of Dasaro. It's time to put an end to it." She began feeding the rounds into the mag.

"And you seriously think going after him like this is going to fix everything?" Aroska scoffed. "You're smarter than that, Ziva. I'm sorry about everything that's happened to you—I'd want to kill the bastard myself, but not like this. Maybe you think this is your battle, but you're not the only person he's tried to kill. Think of Kade, of Kat. They're victims just as much as you are. We've come this far as a team, so let the rest of us help you now. We can all sit down, come up with a plan. I urge you to think this through."

"I *have* thought it through!" she retorted, slamming the mag up into the rifle.

He grabbed her hand. "Then reconsider!"

"I'm not going to argue with you anymore." She wrenched her arm from his grasp. "Contrary to your belief, this *is* my battle, my business. I don't understand why you can't leave me to make my own decisions."

"It's because I'm concerned about you! You're treating this as more of a revenge trip than anything else and your personal feelings are starting to cloud your judgment. You know better than that! Someone's going to wind up getting hurt."

"Oh, so now you're going to try to teach me a life lesson, is that it? In case you haven't noticed, I've been at this a lot longer than you have."

"That doesn't mean you're not capable of making mistakes! Ziva, you're the most powerful, brilliant woman I know, but you frustrate the hell out of me. I know how skilled you are, and I know how much pride you take in that, but I cannot even *begin* to tell you what you mean to me." He stopped short and shook his head, clamping his mouth shut before he could continue.

A prickly sensation crept over Ziva's skin and the hairs on her arms stood on end. "What the hell is that supposed to mean?"

"*Sheyss,*" he muttered, turning in a slow circle and bringing his hands to rest on his hips. "A week ago, I was sitting in my bedroom with a gun in my hand trying to muster up the courage to *end it all* when I heard someone in my house. That someone happened to be you." He shrugged and let out a short snort. "That's right, Ziva. Whether you like it or not, you have once again saved my life. I'm just trying to save yours."

She was growing nearly as tired of this guilt trip of Aroska's as she was with Dasaro and his crew. Hearing of his near suicide caught her off guard and confused her, and judging by his demeanor, this was what had been plaguing him for the past several days. But now was neither the time nor the place to be discussing such matters. She picked up the modified rifle from the table and secured the strap over her shoulder. "I don't need anyone to save my life," she muttered, stepping toward the car.

She started across the floor, annoyed by the sound of his heavy footfalls as he stormed after her. Did he seriously think he was going to stop her? What was he going to do, tie her up? Render her unconscious? Shoot out her knee again? She balled up her hands, ready to deliver a blow if needed.

When he reached her, she barely had time to half-turn before he caught her face with a firm hand and pulled her to him. Before she could register what was happening, he had his lips pressed to hers, so suddenly that she couldn't even voice a protest. Her left fist hovered in mid-air, frozen halfway through the process of delivering a hard hook.

Aroska pulled away after a moment, and it was over just as quickly as it had begun.

It was almost as if he had sucked the life out of her because for what seemed like a long time, Ziva could neither breathe nor speak. Aroska was silent as well, eyes closed as he gently traced her scar with his thumb. It was all she could do to keep from shaking as she removed his hand from her face and lowered it back to his side. Still at a loss for words, she swallowed and edged closer to him, leaning up into his space and placing a hand on his chest. "Aroska," she murmured.

His only reply was a nervous "Hmm."

Her fingers curled abruptly into a fist, taking a handful of his shirt with them. "Unless you *want* me to castrate you right here and now, you will *never* try anything like that ever again. Do you understand me?"

He hung his head and looked away. "Yes."

"No, I'm not sure you do." She took hold of his jacket and forced him back against the wall, pinning him there with her forearm across his chest. "You're a good man, Tarbic, and I know you mean well, but I'm counting on you here. You're telling me my mind's not right? It's certainly not going to help if yours isn't, either. You're going to have to make a choice—either you do what I say and help me out here, or *there's* the door."

"I'm sorry, I shouldn't have. It was a stupid—"

"No!" she exclaimed, holding her hand in front of his mouth. "I don't want your apologies. What's done is done, and you're not going to bring it up ever again. Got it?"

He nodded, still reluctant to make eye contact. "Let me help you."

She released him and took a step back, placing her hands on her hips. "You're the one who shook my hand two months ago and told me we make a good team. That's what I need from you, okay? We can be a team by watching each other's backs, and right now, that means staying out of my way and letting me do this. I have tried to be as patient as possible with you, but I *swear* if you ever pull another stunt like that or try to talk me out of something again, I *will* kill you." The realization that she was serious took her by surprise.

There was a long pause where the two of them refused to look at each other. Ziva turned and stared out the door, rubbing her hand over her mouth in hopes that it would keep her jaw from trembling. In all reality, she was terrified by what had just happened, and the fact that she was terrified scared her even more. She wasn't sure what Aroska had hoped to accomplish. It had been a foolish, impulsive move, and if anything, it had destroyed whatever shred of focus she'd had.

She sighed, taking a few seconds to calm her nerves and her thundering heart. "I'm going to need a spotter," she said, turning back to look him in the eye. "Trying to take a shot from anywhere on this bloody planet is going to be hell. Do you still have the comm Foda was using?"

Aroska's face was pale as he fished the device out of his pocket and slapped it into her open palm.

She closed her fingers around his hand before he could pull away and tightened her grip, ensuring she had his full attention. His eyes flitted about just as they had in the kitchen with the kytara, settling on her for only a split second before darting away. She shook her head. "Damn it, Aroska," she muttered through clenched teeth, "what the hell were you thinking?"

He didn't give her an answer, but she hadn't wanted one. She took the comm and headed upstairs, where she found Kat and Kade sitting at the table in awkward silence. By the way they squirmed and refused to make eye contact, she guessed they had not only heard but had also witnessed everything that had just transpired downstairs. The last thing she wanted—or needed, for that matter—was for such a ridiculous incident to be affecting everyone in such a way.

"Pull it together, people," she said, placing the comm on the table beside Kade's computer. "We need to pull Dasaro's code from that and get a fix on it. Can you do that?"

He hesitated a moment before nodding. "I can." He connected the device to the computer.

Ziva leaned down over the table. "Listen—we've all got scores to settle with Dasaro. I'm doing us a favor here."

She left it at that.

· 81 ·
HAPHEZIAN EMBASSY
CHAIAVIS

T he woman behind the desk looked as though she'd spent a few too many hours there and acted as though she'd dealt with a few too many incompetent visitors. She kept a distasteful eye on the three HSP captains, and for a moment, she looked like she was considering turning them away.

"I'll need to see some identification, then," she said with a sigh.

Dasaro reluctantly pulled out his credentials, as did Nejdra and Kyron. "HSP, special operations," he said.

The woman swiveled to face the terminal at her workstation. "What's the name?" she asked, rolling her eyes down to the screen.

"Kat Reilly," Dasaro replied. "She lived here in the embassy dorms since birth and left about seven years ago. Hometown is thought to be Argall."

For a moment, the only sound that could be heard was a gentle tapping as the woman's fingers flew over the keypad. Her search queries produced the appropriate results, and she projected them via hologram so the three agents could see.

Dasaro's eyes went straight to the address listed under CURRENT RESIDENCE. "*Sheyss*," he muttered. It was the same address their search at HSP had produced, the little abandoned apartment not far from where they stood now. "This is the only residence you have listed?"

"What you see there is everything we've got."

"We've already been there. It's empty."

"Captain, I don't know what to tell you," the woman said with an exasperated sigh. "This is the last known address we have, and if she's not there, I don't know where she is."

Nejdra stepped forward. "Is there anyone we could talk to who would know?"

"Let me explain something to you. The majority of our Residentials who leave never come back. The ones who do are free to come and go as they please—quite frankly, no one really pays attention to who's hanging around because once they're of age, they're not the embassy's problem anymore. It's doubtful anyone knows where she is because they probably don't care." She deactivated the hologram and stared up at them for a moment, letting her words sink in. "Now, if there's nothing else, I've got work to do."

Dasaro sent her a hot glare, though she didn't notice with her gaze directed toward the terminal. He turned and waved Nejdra and Kyron toward the door. "Thank you for your time," he muttered.

· 82 ·
GOVERNMENT DISTRICT
CHAIAVIS

The Haphezian embassy was dwarfed by the other buildings around it, any of which would have made decent snipers' nests. Ziva settled down behind her scope, lying on her stomach with the rifle's bipod resting on the lid of a locked control panel. Aroska had assumed a similar position to her right, surveying the area through a high-powered spotting scope. The airspace around the embassy had less traffic than they'd expected, reducing the risk of accidentally hitting a vessel and therefore making the shot much easier.

Kade had successfully traced the location of Dasaro's communicator and had transferred the tracking data to a small viewscreen they'd set between them on the roof. They'd followed Dasaro and his crew there to the embassy and had performed a brief flyover—the little HSP ship hadn't been hard to spot. Then it had just been a matter of finding a vantage point with a decent line of sight. Now they waited, concealed in the shadows under a massive holoprojector displaying a glowing advertisement.

"Wind is ten kilometers per hour, north-northeast," Aroska said. "The area is clear for now."

Ziva made a slight adjustment to account for the breeze and swept her gaze over the landing area and the embassy doors. The knowledge that Dasaro was in the building brought her a twisted sense of comfort that almost made her forget about killing Foda and arguing with Aroska.

The Cobian's communicator was connected to a portable comm system beside the viewscreen.

"I know you need to do this," Aroska said, "but I don't want you to end up regretting it. Do we know for sure if Dasaro knows you're alive? Are you sure you want to risk revealing yourself?"

"Hush," Ziva hissed. A tingle of excitement surged through her at the sight of the three figures exiting the embassy. She took a deep breath and let it out through her nose, eyes unblinking as she stared through the rifle's scope. She'd been anticipating a faceoff with Dasaro for the past six days, and now that she had reached one, she was feeling almost giddy. She drew another deep breath to steady herself.

The three captains had paused on the steps outside the door and appeared to be caught up in heated conversation. Dasaro had his back to her and seemed to be yelling at Nejdra and Kyron. Judging by their faces and his antics, it was as if their day had just been ruined by whatever news they'd received within the embassy. Ziva smirked and let the crosshairs fall into place against the back of Dasaro's head—they had yet to find out what a ruined day was really like.

"Call him," she instructed.

Aroska lowered the scope and initiated the transmission, which connected through the earpiece Ziva wore. Dasaro paused his ranting long enough to look down and check his communicator. He rolled his eyes when he saw the incoming code and answered immediately. "Yes," he said.

The look on his face when he heard her voice nearly made her shudder. "By the time you're able to trace this transmission, this conversation will be over," she said. "Don't bother."

For a moment it looked as though he was going to drop the comm. "Ziva, how nice to hear your voice," he said, shooting a glare at each of the other captains. "What am I going to do with you? You just won't die."

"You should have thought of that before you set me up," she replied. "Tell me, did you really think it would be so easy to bring me down? Just ship me off to prison, maybe get me killed. Didn't matter as long as I stayed quiet, right?"

Dasaro chuckled and turned, facing in her general direction. "Oh Ziva, I give you more credit than you might think. I knew you could never be fully contained, though I must admit I had hoped things would turn out more favorably for me."

Somehow, she didn't believe him. Her finger itched to just pull the trigger, but there was information to be gained yet, and there was something just as satisfying about getting inside Dasaro's head as there was about killing him. "What do you want with Kat Reilly?" she asked.

"Curious, aren't we? I'm not sure if I see how that concerns you."

"It sure as hell concerns me. I'm not stupid, Diago. You're after her for the same reason you're after me and Kade Shevin." She paused, wondering how he'd react at the mention of Argall. At this point, his involvement was really only an educated hunch based on Zona's findings, and bringing it up was a bit of a gamble on her part. She wasn't even sure what was going on there, other than the murder of innocent people. It was, however, a risk she was willing to take. "It's because we know about Argall."

The look on Dasaro's face was just as good as it had been when he'd answered the call. He stood there with his mouth agape, obviously unaware he was being watched, and whirled around to face Nejdra and Kyron. They each approached, and Ziva heard a faint *click* as Dasaro switched the call to an open transmission so the two of them could listen in.

"You're running quite the little club, aren't you," Dasaro said. "Can I assume Lieutenant Tarbic is with you as well?"

She said nothing and brought the pad of her index finger to rest against the trigger.

"Let me tell you something, Ziva. You're talking like you've already won, but I can assure you that if the four of you think you can put an end to what I'm doing, you are sorely mistaken. It's far too late—you'd only be wasting your time."

She had to admit he had a point. Now that he knew that *they* knew, there was no telling what he might do to speed up his operation or erase evidence of his involvement.

"Maybe so," she replied, "but you're not going to stop me from trying. Just like you didn't stop me the other night. Just like you didn't stop me three years ago."

Once again, there was a short hesitation on Dasaro's end. Yes, now both of his precious secrets had been uncovered. "It was worth a try, wasn't it?" he said. "You were the only person who ever gave a guhr hound's ass what I was doing. If it makes you feel any better, you had to be eliminated because you were the only real threat."

She smirked. "You flatter me, Diago."

Through the scope, she saw Nejdra step forward to get Dasaro's attention. "We can still salvage this, Diago!" she hissed. "We can eliminate her before she has a chance to expose anything."

"You're wrong, Captain Venn," Ziva said. "You may have noticed that I'm pretty good at disappearing. And if you send anyone else after us, any more of your Cobian dogs, I'll kill them. Pretty good at that, too."

Dasaro merely chuckled, and the sight of his content smile made her sick. "Stand down, Payvan. You can do whatever you want—run, hide, fight—but you can't win, not at this point."

"We'll see about that." She paused, adjusting her sights ever so slightly as a new thought came to mind. "Do you know how long it takes a bariine round to travel eight hundred meters?"

· 83 ·
HAPHEZIAN EMBASSY
CHAIAVIS

It struck Dasaro as a rather odd question. The words were barely out of Ziva's mouth when he heard a moist *thump* and warm blood splashed across his face. Nejdra crumpled into a deformed heap at his feet, a jagged exit wound marring what remained of the side of her head.

"That's how long." Ziva's voice carried through the comm.

The transmission ended abruptly.

· 84 ·

GOVERNMENT DISTRICT

CHAIAVIS

She had the rifle up and was shrinking back onto the roof before the transmission was even cut. She scrambled to her feet and slung the weapon's strap over her shoulder, sprinting for the car. Aroska was hot on her heels, clutching the comm equipment and the viewscreen. He leaped into the pilot's seat and had the car moving in seconds.

"What the hell was that?" he exclaimed. It wasn't quite a demand—his voice was filled with surprise and confusion, maybe even relief.

She remained silent, unable to decide for herself what had prompted the sudden change of plans. "Just get us out of range," she said, massaging her forehead.

Aroska scoffed. "Oh, don't worry, I think it will take Dasaro a while to figure out we were beyond eight hundred meters. And that'll only be after he cleans the *sheyss* out of his pants."

The corners of her lips twitched upward briefly. Perhaps that had been her line of thought as well. Her quest for revenge, however, had been a mistake. Getting inside people's heads had always been her specialty, and after allowing Dasaro to beat her at her own game, all she'd wanted was to take the reins back from him, show him that he was no longer in control. To her credit, it had worked—the fact that she'd done it all under the influence of her emotions was where she'd gone wrong.

There was no time to waste now that Dasaro knew she was on the planet, knew she was on to him. Things could always be worse, but thanks to her, they were now more complicated than they needed to be.

If she'd just killed Dasaro, they might never have had the opportunity to find out what he was planning. Alerting him to her presence, however, could wind up costing hundreds of people their lives. Heat flooded her face and she slammed her hands against the car's dash, allowing her stinging palms to command her attention for a few moments.

Aroska pushed the vehicle to its top speed, weaving in and out of the busy afternoon traffic. "I hope you're happy," he muttered in the same accusatory tone he'd used during their confrontation in the garage.

"I screwed up," she growled, clenching her hand into a fist to keep from tearing her hair out. *I blew it. I was wrong. I hope* you're *happy.*

"I won't disagree with that," he said. "Let's make up for it by catching up to Dasaro before he has a chance to finish what he started." When she didn't respond, he turned toward her and nudged her shoulder. "We'll fix this, okay?"

Ziva shook her head and turned to look behind them, keeping her eyes peeled for any signs of HSP or Dasaro's ship. "This has never happened before," she murmured. "I've never lost control like this."

He remained silent, knuckles white as he steered the car, no doubt kicking himself for his actions in the garage earlier. At least she hoped that was the case. It was tempting to blame him for her lack of focus, and in a way, she had every right to do so. But at the same time, she *had* lost control and she knew it. She was better than that—that was why she was in this position, why she had been targeted by Dasaro in the first place. This was exactly what he wanted, and it angered her to no end that she had faltered.

She turned back to face the front of the car and wiped the sheen of sweat from her forehead. They continued the trip back to the garage in silence. There was still much that needed to be said, but now it was time for a break. And now that Dasaro knew they were coming for him, there was a lot of thinking and planning to do.

They pulled the vehicle into the shop alongside Kat's. She and Kade appeared on the stairs momentarily, watching from a cautious distance as Ziva and Aroska unloaded their equipment from the car. Ziva took the rifle to the workbench and leaned over it, feeling hot under their expectant gazes as they waited for an update.

It was Kat who spoke first. "What happened?"

Ziva ignored her, unsure what to say. She knew good and well that Kat was displeased with the way she'd been handling things, especially in Foda's case. Telling her Dasaro was still alive and no doubt headed back to Argall to kill her brother wouldn't go over well.

"In short, Nejdra Venn is dead, and Dasaro isn't," Aroska responded.

Ziva finally lifted her head to make eye contact. Kat's hands had curled into fists, but she remained in her place, her face set in stone.

"That's interesting," she said, slowly descending the remaining steps. She walked right past Aroska and angled toward Ziva, crossing her arms but continuing to keep her distance. "Do you think that was the best idea?"

"No," Ziva snapped, growing weary of the constant reminders of her mistake. She approached Kat and took up a similar stance. "But I can't very well change that now, can I?"

Kat drew in a breath and opened her mouth to speak, but she was silenced when Ziva lifted her hand and took another step forward. "Listen. I don't imagine you're happy with the approach I've taken on this, and believe it or not, neither am I. But whether we like it or not, I sent Dasaro a message and he read it loud and clear. He knows this isn't going to end until one of us is dead. He's going to be moving fast, but so will we. I promise you I won't let him touch your brother. Nobody else is going to die."

It struck her strange that Kat's face didn't soften at all after hearing those words. In fact, that same flicker of sadness Ziva had noticed before appeared briefly in her eyes, and she glanced down to the floor before nodding.

Ziva brought her hands to rest on her hips and gave Kat a bit of space. "Screw everything. Screw Dasaro and this damn conspiracy, and screw the exile law. It's time for us to fight back." She paused and looked around, briefly locking eyes with Kade, then Aroska, and finally Kat. "We're going home."

· 85 ·
HAPHEZIAN EMBASSY
CHAIAVIS

A s Dasaro stood there watching the local law enforcement officials secure the straps on Nejdra's body bag, he couldn't help but notice the trembling in his hands. He placed one on his hip and rubbed the other over his chin, praying no one else would notice. The hairs on the back of his neck had yet to settle back down, and Ziva's chilling words still echoed through his head: *"Do you know how long it takes a bariine round to travel eight hundred meters?"*

It had been nearly an hour since she'd shot his colleague, and during that hour, he'd felt more uneasy than he'd ever felt in his life. The realization that Ziva had been staring right at him for the duration of their conversation had hit him first, followed immediately by the unnerving idea that she could have just as easily killed *him*. Now he stood there obsessing over why she had chosen to shoot Nejdra instead. Was there something he was missing? The round she had used—or what was left of it, anyway—had indeed been partially composed of bariine alloy, a substance commonly found on Haphez and neighboring Fringe worlds. Surely she hadn't been using one of her own rifles; all her personal weapons had been confiscated immediately following her arrest. And yet she had still been able to make the shot. It was clear she had managed to catch up to him, judging by what she had revealed during the transmission, but now he feared she was actually a step ahead.

Dasaro shifted his attention from the body bag to the embassy doors when Kyron Hoxie emerged with a pair of investigators. "Nothing," he said, handing over a viewscreen displaying infrared views of every rooftop within eight hundred meters. "No signal from the comm, either. She's not stupid enough to leave it lying around."

A mistake Dasaro had already made when he'd continued to use the comm code he'd shared with Lieutenant Tarbic. That explained how they'd managed to track him to the embassy and contact him. Using Foda's communicator had been clever, indeed; the Cobian had no doubt been captured while searching for Kat Reilly, and Dasaro guessed he was dead now. He kicked himself for having answered the call so readily after Foda had failed to check in at the appointed time.

He lifted his eyes and gazed out at the surrounding buildings, mentally eliminating any that were too short or obscured by other structures. He paused to look at several towering buildings a bit farther away. "She was beyond eight hundred meters," he said, shaking his head. "Think about it. She'd want to be as far away as possible so she'd have plenty of time to escape again. She's a coward."

No, she's a crack shot, but saying otherwise still made him feel better. An eight-hundred-meter shot was child's play for a marksman like Ziva, and she was the type who could turn even the worst of weapons into effective killing machines merely by holding them.

It had always driven him mad how good she was. As her superior officer, he should have been proud to have someone so talented under his command. But the higher rank still didn't help the fact that she was better than him. He'd been the top dog in spec ops since she was still carrying around mock weapons at basic training, and suddenly she'd been bombarded with opportunities and job offers, all because she'd managed to kill some rogue Nosti. She'd gone straight into the special ops training track without graduating from—or even *completing*—the Junior Guard program.

One would have expected someone like that to be a cocky, mouthy little *shouka*, but that had never been the case with Ziva. In fact, she rarely spoke. She was always just *there*—he had to suppress a shudder—lurking, waiting to steal more opportunities from him. She was good and she knew it, but she never flaunted it. Dasaro often wished she would, just so he'd have a more legitimate reason for disliking her.

His hate went beyond petty jealousy, though. He was at the top of the food chain in special ops for a reason, so there was no point in being envious of Ziva's abilities. It had taken him years to finally be named lieutenant of the Alpha team, and after a mere nine months in that position, he'd been bumped up to captain to make way for Ziva and her team. In all reality, the promotion had seemed like more of a *demotion*, and he had fought for the chance to continue some field work. The director claimed the change was because spec ops needed someone younger, someone fresh, but that Dasaro was still invaluable and the agency couldn't afford to lose him. It had always struck him as a glorified way of sweeping him under the rug.

Okay, so maybe he was a little jealous, but only because he'd worked his whole life to get to where he was, and she'd simply been adopted into the program. The woman had skills, and he'd been totally honest in saying that she was the only real threat to his operations, which were the only thing that made him feel like he was in control anymore. It wasn't that others were incapable of catching on. It was just that, knowing full well that he despised her, Ziva tended to keep a closer eye on him than anyone else at HSP. She was bound to find out about Argall sooner or later, the reason she'd made a perfect candidate whenever he needed to arrange a distraction for the rest of the agency.

He suddenly became aware of Hoxie speaking. "...we check those other buildings?"

Dasaro shook his head and turned to face the other captain. "Sorry?"

Hoxie released an exasperated sigh and started over. "They say they're willing to extend the search radius and look again," he said, gesturing toward all the structures surrounding the landing platform. "If we check those other buildings, maybe we—"

"We'd be wasting our time," Dasaro finished for him. "Ziva is long gone by now, and now that she knows about Argall, she will no doubt try to launch some form of offensive. We need to make preparations to return to Haphez."

"She's got three people with her," Hoxie said, lifting an eyebrow. "How will they be any match for us?"

"They won't, but they can still talk. Nejdra was right—we can still tie everything up, but we have to hurry. Ziva will go straight to the director, but I think I know how to buy us some time."

"What should I tell Loric?"

Dasaro was quiet for a moment, contemplating the ultimatum they had finally reached. "Shut everything down," he said. "*Everything.*"

Hoxie reached for his communicator but stopped before he had removed it from his belt. He shook his head. "You're really prepared to kill all those people?"

"Keep your voice down," Dasaro growled, taking several quick steps away from the investigators. Hoxie reluctantly followed, and the conversation resumed. "We still have a chance to save ourselves here, but it will mean getting our hands dirty."

"They're not dirty already? HSP is going to find out what's going on."

"Time, Kyron!" Dasaro said, taking him by the shoulders. "The key is *time*. Erasing as much as possible will slow HSP down enough that we can get safely away. We'll be rich men, with the resources to hide and start new lives."

Hoxie set his jaw and shook his head again, making a show of securing his communicator to his belt. "This isn't what I signed up for. You promised us crystals at the beginning. You never said anything about wiping out an entire city."

Dasaro moved his hand down to rest on his holster and loomed over Hoxie, looking him squarely in the eye. "That's it then? After everything, you're going to just walk away?"

"What are you going to do, shoot me?" The former soldier remained unfazed. "Not here in front of all these people. Come on, Dasaro. Payvan's on to us, Nejdra's already dead. I think I'll take my chances and get out while I'm still breathing."

Dasaro stared him down a moment longer, but it was to no avail. He could see in the man's eyes that the decision was final. "Fine," he muttered, not wishing to make a scene with so many people around. He took a step back and gestured for Hoxie to be on his way.

The other captain nodded his thanks and took off at a brisk pace toward the embassy doors. He paused just outside and turned back for a moment. Dasaro saw him mouth the words 'I'm sorry,' and with that, he was gone.

The apprehension he'd felt over the past few days was nearly overwhelming. He'd been anxious after hearing of Ziva's escape, and even more so when he'd found out she was still alive. But this new wave of anxiety that washed over him trumped all the others. This was like a game of chess and his opponent had just put him in check. On top of that, he'd just lost the only two people he trusted to help him.

Angrier than ever, he pulled out his comm and opened a transmission to Emeri Arion. Trying to hide now was pointless, as there were plenty of witnesses who could place him there at the embassy. There was still a card he could play, a card that could potentially redeem the situation if he was lucky. However, he couldn't help but feel his luck was running out.

"Dasaro, Alpha 40824," he said in response to the automated prompt that would give him access to the director's personal line.

It seemed like an eternity before a gruff voice answered. "Captain! May I ask where you've been?"

Dasaro drew a deep breath and put a bit more distance between himself and the embassy officials, who were carrying Nejdra's corpse to the ship that would transport it back to Haphez. "Director, you have my sincerest apologies, but I think you'll be interested in what I have to say. I've found Payvan."

H earing those words shocked Skeet as much as they would have if he still thought Ziva was dead. There was total silence in the director's office for a moment as he, Zinni, Luko Zona, and Emeri all took turns throwing surprised glances at one another.

The call had come through as they'd been presenting some recent findings to the director, one of which was a surveillance recording from the Noro spaceport that showed Kade Shevin purchasing three intragalactic transport tickets. Since his wife and daughter were both accounted for, the only reasonable explanation they'd been able to conjure up was that Kade was in league with Ziva and Aroska and the three of them had escaped together. Where they had gone remained a mystery, but perhaps Dasaro could shed some light on that.

Emeri furrowed his eyebrows and tilted his head, playing the part of a confused man well. "What are you talking about? Lieutenant Payvan is dead."

"That's what I thought, too," Dasaro said. "But one of my people found footage of someone wearing the riding suit of the pilot who was found in the forest. I began to look into whether she could still be alive, and suddenly there was an attempt on my life. That answered my question well enough."

"Oh, please," Zinni muttered.

Emeri looked just as disgusted. "You're telling me Payvan is alive and that she tried to kill you?"

"That's why I left," Dasaro replied, "and why I couldn't tell anyone. If she knew we found that footage, she had to have somehow breached our system, and there was no telling what she'd do. If everyone was suddenly aware her death was staged, she would disappear for good. But if she thought she was still relatively safe, I thought she'd be more apt to slip up, increasing our chances of catching her once and for all."

"Is it possible that she staged her death because she's innocent? Is she defending herself?"

There was a suspiciously long hesitation on Dasaro's end, or at least it seemed long based on the simplicity of the question. Perhaps the director had moved too fast, though the conversation was making Skeet angry enough that he might have said the same thing.

"Director, Payvan killed Captain Venn."

Once again, the room fell dead silent. Skeet took a step forward, fighting away the nausea brought on by the doubt he suddenly felt. They had finally gotten close to proving Ziva innocent, and now, if Dasaro was telling the truth, she had just murdered another HSP agent. *She would have had her reasons*, he told himself.

Dasaro continued speaking as Emeri brought up the agency-wide alerts on his computer. Sure enough, there was a news flash with Nejdra's name on it, originating from the Haphezian embassy on Chaiavis. "She managed to track us here and she contacted me this afternoon, confirming my suspicion that she had somehow gotten into the system. She shot Venn and got away, and now Captain Hoxie has disappeared."

The director wiped his hand over his face and sighed. "What did she say when she contacted you?"

"She said she's not going to stop fighting. I believe she'll try to run again, and with your permission, I'd like to continue hunting her."

"By yourself?"

"Maybe it's better that way. I know how she operates, sir. I'm going to do what I can to put an end to all of this."

Emeri straightened his jacket and turned to face the rest of the group. "Permission granted, Captain, but I'll be expecting a thorough debrief every evening. The agency will do what it can to back you up, and I'll see to it that you have the Chaiavian embassy's full cooperation."

Zinni rushed forward the moment the transmission disconnected. "That was the biggest load of *sheyss* I've ever heard!"

"At ease, Officer Vax," Emeri said. "I don't believe a word of it, either, but how do you explain the fact that Captain Venn is dead?"

"We don't know the circumstances. She was in league with Dasaro anyway, so I say good riddance."

Skeet had to agree, especially after the way Nejdra had treated them in the interrogation room at the start of the investigation, but he placed a warning hand on Zinni's shoulder anyway. "What do you propose we do, sir?"

Luko Zona stepped forward. "If I may, I would suggest investigating Argall while Dasaro is still off-world. If any of the information I've found is accurate, we should find answers there."

"Fine," Emeri said. "Sergeant Duvo, prepare a recon operation. I want you to go in quiet—the galaxy only knows what we'll find there. You ship out tonight."

· 87 ·
KAT'S HIDEOUT
CHAIAVIS

Ziva poked her head out the door of the shop and was startled to find Aroska there, despite the fact that she'd been looking for him. He sat on the surface of the little balcony, leaning against the railing with his legs stuck through. They swung casually back and forth through mid-air as he lifted a govino stick to his lips and took a drag from it, staring vacantly ahead through the smoke as he exhaled. She looked out over the cityscape herself, wondering if he was looking at anything specific, but she found she couldn't see much at all; the sun was beginning to drop down behind the buildings, and it cast a bright orange light that glinted harshly off the structures and passing vehicles. Squinting, she looked away and blinked the spots out of her eyes before returning her attention to Aroska.

He didn't seem to realize she was there, so she took another step toward him and crossed her arms. "We need to talk."

He jumped, though he tried hard to cover it up, and flicked the govino stick over the edge of the balcony. "Fine," he said. "You caught me."

"That wasn't it."

"Well, if you want me to quit, I guess I've got to start sometime." Aroska sighed and looked up at her. "Now, what's so important that you're willing to come out here and initiate the conversation?"

"I think you know."

He scoffed. "Says the woman who was adamant that we not bring it up again."

"That's not it, either." Rather than argue further, she lowered herself down onto the balcony beside him, sliding her own legs through the railing. She looked down at her boots and then past them to the ground far below. The view was both nerve-wracking and relaxing. She felt almost as if she were floating, possibly the reason Aroska was enjoying it so much. She swore she would get him clean if it was the last thing she did.

He was watching her intently now, eyes filled with both fear and regret. *Yes...*he knew good and well what she wished to talk about. He fidgeted and looked back out into the glaring light, swallowing hard.

Ziva swallowed as well and drew a deep breath. "I want you to explain to me why you were going to kill yourself," she said. "I know it's not something you want to talk about, and I'm probably the last person you'd ever want to turn to for advice, but I know you need to let it out or it's going to eat you alive."

Aroska remained silent for a long time, staring into the distance and refusing to make eye contact. Unless it was her imagination, she saw his jaw tremble momentarily—she also saw the muscles in his face tighten as he tried to still it.

"You're probably going to think it's ridiculous," he finally said. "And please don't feel like it's your fault—that's the main reason I haven't wanted to say anything before." He sighed. "Nothing was the same after that day two months ago. When I left your house, I felt like I had nowhere to go. I'd found my teammates only to lose them again, the woman I thought I loved turned out to be a traitor, and once Solaris was gone, there was nothing left for me at HSP."

"I offered you that spec ops position and you—"

"—and I turned it down, I know. That's why I told you not to blame yourself for any of this." He ran his tongue over his lips and turned toward her for the first time since speaking. "After Solaris and the SCU were disbanded, the director offered me some paid time off, which I gladly accepted. I think it ended up being more detrimental than anything else, because the realization that everything had changed for good hit me before long, and I started not wanting to go back to work. When my leave was up, I started using accumulated vacation time, but things just got worse the longer I was away. I'd messed with govino back when I was working with Solaris, just to maintain a good rapport, you know? The bottle has been an issue since Soren died—Adin was trying to help me get better, and I was doing okay until he and his team left for a long-term mission. But...." He paused and shook his head. "But after Saun and Dakiti, I figured out those two things could help me forget all the *sheyss* going on around me. I knew I was destroying myself, but I couldn't stop."

Ziva nodded, surprised at how sorry she felt for him as she took in everything he said. Part of her was disgusted that he would have wasted so much time wallowing in self-pity, yet she could almost understand his reasoning. "So you figured you'd try something more efficient?"

He scoffed. "A harsh but entirely accurate way of putting it. I was miserable, I was sure I had nothing left to contribute, so I figured I'd end things before I had a chance to screw anything else up. It turns out I was sitting there in my bedroom that day, so wasted that I was seeing two guns in my hand. When I heard my front door open, I was so *angry* that someone was going to take away that means of escape. As soon as I realized it was you, I knew that you were there to save me, whether you realized it or not. You asked me the other night why I'm helping you—it's because you gave me a second chance when I was at the end of my rope. I guess you could say you were there for me in my time of need, though maybe not in a conventional way, so the least I can do is be there for you in return."

She raised an eyebrow and surveyed the passing traffic for a moment, wondering what the chances were that Dasaro was nearby. "If you want the truth, I think that's a little pathetic."

"Don't say I didn't warn you."

"I'm serious, Aroska. You have friends, family, people who care about you. Why didn't you get some help?"

"I don't know!" he snapped. "This is why I haven't wanted to talk about it—I *know* I messed up! I don't need you or anyone else to tell me what I should or shouldn't have done. Believe me, I'm well aware I'm incapable of doing anything right."

"That's not true," she said, any tenderness failing to break through the anger she suddenly felt toward him.

Neither of them said anything for a while, each allowing the other a moment to stew. Ziva shook her head and stared out into the blinding light. The man had nerve for even considering the possibility she blamed herself for his condition. *Then again...*she thought back to the day she'd stumbled into his house, to the things she'd pondered while cleaning up. Already it seemed like a lifetime ago. She'd wondered, hadn't she? She'd wondered if the mess he'd gotten himself into was somehow her fault.

No, the thought was absurd. He and *only* he was responsible for his actions, and he'd been plenty capable of fixing his own problems. But then, after Dakiti and what he'd done for her, shouldn't she have been looking out for him? She cursed both herself and Aroska under her breath and let her frustration out in the form of a sigh.

"Hey, you okay?"

She hesitated a moment before answering, unable to remember the last time anyone had bothered to ask her such a question. "I'm tired," she replied, fixing her gaze on some point in the distance and holding it there.

"Aren't we all," he said, sighing himself. She saw him turn toward her in her peripherals. "But after everything that's happened, there's got to be a little more to it than that. Maybe you're not great at giving advice, but I like to think I'm pretty good at it. What's up?"

Ziva forced a half-hearted scowl but didn't move otherwise. "Assuming there *was* something, why the hell do you think I'd ever tell you?"

"'Because I know you need to let it out or it's going to eat you alive'." He chuckled a bit then cleared his throat. "You can talk to me, you know."

She shook her head again and looked down at her feet, feeling rather numb. "I'm no good at talking."

"I know."

Several seconds of silence passed as Ziva struggled to organize her thoughts. The words came out sooner and easier than she had expected. "I should have been there for you, but I can't be there for everyone, you know? Just like I'm not there for Skeet and Zinni right now. For all I know, Dasaro could have killed them to get to me. Marshay, Ryon, Jada...I can't help but wonder if I made a mistake by leaving them all there while I'm running away to save my own skin."

"I wouldn't say you're 'running away'," Aroska said. "You're trying to get to higher ground, that's all. Besides, I think they can take care of themselves. They knew what they were signing up for when they took your side."

She drew her legs up against her. "That's the problem," she said. "They care about what happens to me, and I'll admit I care about what happens to them. But with the way I live and the things I have to do every day, I can't afford to care. The more people I care about, the more ways someone can hurt me, and the more I have to worry about. In my world, friends aren't assets—they end up being liabilities."

Aroska smirked. "I'd like to see the looks on Skeet and Zinni's faces when you tell them they're not assets."

"My point exactly—they *are*."

He took a deep breath and thoughtfully gazed out over the city. "I see where you're coming from, although I think your reasoning is flawed. Attachment is dangerous because it's not only emotionally compromising for you but could also put the other party in jeopardy. Am I right?"

She nodded.

"Did you ever stop and ask yourself what kind of person you'd be if you *didn't* care about anyone? What if nobody cared about you?"

She groaned. "Aroska...."

"I'm serious," he said. "You're one of the strongest people I know, braver and smarter than I could ever hope to be. Your life and career revolve around focusing on other people—targets, fellow agents, you name it—and in that sense, you might just be the most selfless person I've ever met. Devoting your energy to others is, by default, how you operate. But sooner or later, even *you* need someone to be there for you, and you're lucky to have people like that. What would happen if that weren't the case?"

Ziva was startled when a tear materialized from nowhere and ran down her cheek. "I don't want to see any of them suffer because of me."

"Then what do you plan to do? Stuff everyone you know into a bunker somewhere while you go off and fight all the battles? I doubt they'd be thrilled if you went and got yourself killed on their account."

He was completely right, and somehow that angered her. "I just...." She paused, realizing that she'd nearly been shouting, and lowered her voice. "I'm scared, all right? History is being made right here as the great Ziva Payvan admits she's afraid." She swallowed and watched a large transport as it drifted by. "Other times have been different, but this time Dasaro knows me, knows Skeet and Zinni. He knows how to get inside my head, and no amount of nostium or HSP training can change that or protect them. I feel, I don't know...helpless."

"Well, you're far from helpless," Aroska said, "and there's certainly nothing wrong with being afraid. I think you've spent way too much time making sure all your feelings stay bottled up inside you, and then they all come rushing out in the wrong way at the wrong time. Look at what happened with Foda! With everything you've been through, I don't think anyone would blame you if you showed a little emotion once in a while. Go ahead and cry. Maybe complain a little. I haven't heard one complaint from you since this all started."

"And what would I accomplish by crying and complaining?"

"Nothing, you're right. But you don't always have to be accomplishing something. Take a break—think of this as a mental vacation or something."

"If that wasn't the stupidest thing you've ever said, it was definitely a contender for second." She shot him an icy glare and shook her head. "No, at this point Dasaro won't hesitate to exploit any weakness I show. You say I'm brave? That just means *I'm* the only one who knows I'm afraid. I need to keep it that way."

He looked down at his feet and snorted. "I'd never thought of it like that."

She sighed again and raked her hand back through her hair. "I'd rather not discuss this anymore. I'm in danger of losing focus on what we're doing here."

Aroska nodded and edged toward her a bit, placing his arm around her shoulders. "Relax," he said, giving her a squeeze. "It sounds to me like the only thing you're in danger of is becoming a good person."

Ziva bristled but remained motionless, allowing him to hold her for a moment despite the fact that his touch felt like a sharp blade stabbing into her skin. It struck her that he was one of the very people he spoke of, one of the 'assets' who cared for her well-being and who would stick by her whether she liked it or not. How he could possibly feel that way after everything she'd put him through was beyond her.

"I'm not a good person," she muttered.

There was a brief hesitation before he formed a response, and when he did, it sounded forced. "Sure you are."

She turned to him and shook her head. "How can you possibly say that after seeing the things I do, after what I've done to you and your family?"

She was surprised when he tightened his grip on her shoulder rather than pull away. "Ziva, I'll be the first to admit that the things you do aren't always commendable. You'll always be the assassin who killed my brother—nothing can change that, and there are times I'd still like to put a bullet in your head because of it. But there's a lot more to you than I thought." He leaned forward, ensuring he had her undivided attention. "It's true that part of you is extremely dark, but there's a bigger picture here, and I think I'm starting to catch glimpses of it. You have a gift, this mind-blowing ability to kill, but along with that comes the ability to fight, to protect. I've seen that gift in action my fair share of times. Hell, without it, I wouldn't even be alive! Surely you can see that not everything you do is so damaging."

"'What I do' is my job, Aroska," Ziva retorted, shrugging his arm away. "I'm no hero! I solve problems, end of story. Whether or not I'm 'damaging' has nothing to do with it."

"Think what you want," he said, shaking his head. "You like to maintain this cold, heartless façade, but deep down, I know you've got good intentions."

She gnawed at the inside of her lip to keep from spitting out every foul word she could think of. "The road to hell is paved with good intentions."

He laughed out loud. "Okay, I give up," he sighed. "Now, you know what I think?"

"Hard to tell."

"I think you should take a break, maybe catch some shut-eye. You've had a rough day, and the galaxy only knows what the next few hours will bring. Go on—the rest of us can hold down the fort."

Ziva shook her head. "I can't, not now that Dasaro knows we're here. The second I let my guard down, he's going to show up. That's how it always works."

"I've also heard that a watched pot never boils."

Once again, he was right, and she hated him for it. "You're determined to win, aren't you?"

"I'm determined to see you through this. There's a difference."

She sat still for a moment, taking another long look at the sinking sun before rising stiffly to her feet and crossing her arms. Sleep wasn't an option, but the conversation was beyond over and she was all too eager to move on to something else. Preparations needed to be made for the trip home, and she wanted to know every possible detail about the mess they were getting themselves into. Perhaps she could occupy herself fashioning more ammunition for the rifle.

"For the record, I was way out of line earlier," Aroska said as she turned to go back inside. "With the way you were acting, I was afraid you'd go off and do something stupid, and to be perfectly honest, I was afraid we'd lose you. It was just the first thing that came to mind and—" he forced a sheepish chuckle "—that sort of thing usually works on women. But you're not an average woman, and that's not how I should have handled it."

Damn right, Ziva thought, though she remained silent. She hoped that was all it was—a strange, gut reaction and not an indication of some subconscious feeling. That was the last thing she needed to be worried about right now. But it was over and done. She'd punished him enough, and it appeared he was still punishing himself, which was just fine with her. He was lucky he'd caught her by surprise; otherwise, he still might have been unconscious on the floor. The thought drew her attention to the bruise she'd already given him, and she found herself massaging her own swollen knuckles.

"I'm sorry I hit you," she said.

Without a word, he looked up at her and gave her a single nod. It spoke more of acknowledgement than forgiveness, which was fine considering she wasn't sure how sincere her apology had been.

Feeling rather drained, she turned silently and slipped back into the shadows within the shop.

· 88 ·
CITY CENTER
ARGALL, HAPHEZ

The streets of Argall were eerily quiet at this hour. Everyone had been good about obeying the curfew the mercenaries had established, including Mag. Right now, he normally would have been asleep, exhausted after a long day on his feet and resting up for yet another one. But tonight, he was too wound up to sleep.

He had come up with a plan, one he honestly doubted would work. The only functioning comm grid in the city was the one at the police station, or what was left of it. It had been the mercs' first target upon arriving in Argall, and they'd made quick work of the officers stationed there. It could hardly have been considered a police station in the first place—two retired HSP officers and a handful of locals they'd hired as deputies weren't much, even for a town as small as Argall. Even if they'd been prepared for the mercs' arrival, they wouldn't have stood a chance.

Loric had set himself up in the station right off the bat, using the equipment there to not only jam and filter the rest of the city's communications but send his own private transmissions as well. As such, it was perhaps the most heavily guarded location in town, and anyone who had ever tried to enter unauthorized had been shot without question.

Mag knew the layout of the station well—he'd been there several times back in the day, and Loric had brought him in twice for questioning since the takeover. The building had sustained some damage during the attack and the mercs had done a bit of renovation, so he anticipated a few subtle differences: a missing wall here, a new door there. Regardless, he was confident he'd be able to navigate successfully once he broke in. And that was where things got tricky.

Mercifully, the mercs had disabled all the station's surveillance cams, as they could easily be monitored remotely by HSP or anyone else who ever caught on to their operations. All security work was done in person, but they had multiple sets of eyes working around the clock. Some form of distraction would be necessary in order to get inside, and Mag had been busy all afternoon preparing one.

Among the items he'd kept for himself while cleaning out his parents' house were a pair of old thermal grenades that were probably unsafe to even be handling. He'd mentally mapped out the city and selected two old houses near the police station that he knew to be empty. He didn't usually resort to violence—the initial rebellion against the mercenaries had been totally foreign to him—but as the old saying went, desperate times called for desperate measures. As much as he wanted to see Argall saved and rebuilt, he was willing to blow up a couple of buildings if it meant getting the job done. The end would justify the means.

He detached himself from the shadows in front of a store and stole across the street. Anyone caught out after curfew without a valid reason had usually been imprisoned, but he'd more likely be executed on the spot. Part of him didn't care anymore; he'd concluded the map must be hidden in a safe place far out of Loric's reach, so there was no longer any real need to protect it. And with his family dead, he didn't have much left to live for. He by no means *wanted* to die, but he certainly didn't have any qualms about it. There was a difference.

Regardless of what became of him, he decided he wasn't going down without a fight, the reason he'd finally chosen to take offensive action. The only way to alert anyone to the situation in Argall was to access that comm grid. If he got caught, at least the rest of the city would still have a chance to survive.

He rounded a corner and found himself within sight of the police station, the only building on the block still illuminated at this hour.

Security wasn't as tight at night since there were more patrols out enforcing the curfew, but the mercs who remained posted there were plenty vigilant. He could see three of them now—two stood at the front door, and another paced back and forth on the roof. A couple of explosions might not actually draw them away, but at least they'd have something else to look at while he made a move.

The first of the two houses on his list was right next door to the one Mag currently stood behind. The other was directly across the street from it. Initially, he'd toyed with targeting one on the far side of the police station, but it seemed like the mercs would be more likely to realize something was amiss. Besides, if by some miracle they were actually drawn away by the distraction, two explosions on the same side would allow him to get between them and the station, which somehow seemed desirable.

Keeping an eye out for sentries, he slipped around the back of the house and scaled the fence into the next yard. Many of the windows were already broken thanks to looters, saving him the trouble of trying to break one without attracting attention. He entered with ease and, after a brief survey of the empty space, proceeded to locate the home's old heating system. Enough gas probably remained to help intensify the explosion. He knelt and selected one of the thermal grenades, fixing it with a timer his brother had showed him how to make back during the original resistance. He set the timer for an hour just in case he ran into trouble planting the other charge, though he dreaded to think it would take that long.

The streets were still quiet when he exited through the back door. He'd discovered a sewer access hatch in the alley when he'd scoped out the area during the day, and unless he was mistaken, the tunnel led to an identical hatch in the adjacent alley, allowing him to cross the street undetected. He located the hatch and lifted it open, floored by the stench that wafted up into his face. Stifling a cough, he forced himself to climb down, carefully closing the lid behind him.

Mag stood there in the darkness for a moment, hand cupped over his nose, eyes smarting. If he had to guess, someone had come down here to hide, and for one reason or another, hadn't made it back out. He willed his feet to move forward and followed the tunnel to the end of the alley, wading through the half-meter of water that ran down the main sewer line under the street. Even in the darkness, the other access tunnel was easy to find, as all he needed to do was walk straight forward.

The hatch itself was another story. No amount of pushing or prodding could move the lid more than a fraction of a centimeter. He felt panic encroaching as he pictured something heavy sitting on top of it and blocking his escape, but after a moment of probing around, his fingers found a latch the maintenance crews had installed, probably to keep people like him out of the tunnels. The one on the other door must have been broken. He flipped the latch and pushed the lid open.

The exterior of the second house was nearly identical to the first one. This whole area, including the police station, dated back to the original establishment of Argall, when housing had been put up en masse to account for the hundreds of people migrating there to work. The looters had already hit this house as well, making a quiet entrance easy. He carefully worked his way through a broken window and slipped inside.

As he had expected, the layout of this house was identical to the other, only reversed. Finding the heating unit would be easy enough, at least once he navigated across the squeaky floor. He pulled up short, testing his footing, and was startled to find that the creaking didn't stop when he did.

The crackle of a comm unit, the exchange of a plasma cell—both sounds registered with Mag at once. He froze, expecting someone to rush around the corner and shoot him. But after close to a minute, nothing happened. A low voice spoke into the communicator, followed by more static and squeaking as a pair of boots paced back and forth across the floor.

"Everything's clear," the voice said.

As near as he could tell, the sentry was in the kitchen, stationed in front of the large window looking out over the street. It was clever on Loric's part, keeping extra men hidden in nearby buildings. What were they doing? Did they know Mag was coming? Not that it really mattered.

He'd already managed to outsmart them, regardless of whether he'd meant to, and even if they were looking for him, he doubted they'd be expecting the thermal grenades.

Well, planting the explosive directly on the heating unit was out. He retraced his steps, coming to a halt just inside the window he'd entered through. Even after giving himself an hour to get the job done, the thought of standing around wasting time still made him unbearably nervous. He slid the pack from his shoulder and searched his racing mind for options. It didn't take long to decide a single mercenary wasn't going to stop him from doing what he'd come to do.

He removed the second grenade and returned to the wall separating him from the kitchen. Taking the layout of the first house into consideration, the heating unit would be right on the other side. This flimsy wall would be no match for the grenade's power, and even if it somehow hampered the explosion a bit, it would still provide a reasonable—if not more realistic—distraction.

Once the device was in place and its timer synced with its counterpart, he retreated silently through the window and crept as close as he dared to the police station. The building was surrounded by a fair amount of open space, no doubt for security reasons, but if all went according to plan, he would be able to cross unnoticed while the mercs had their attention focused elsewhere.

The remaining minutes were some of the longest Mag had ever experienced, and he had to force himself to stop checking the time. He'd had plenty of experience over the past three years lying in wait for something or dreading the day Loric showed up at his house for one reason or another, so he would have thought he'd be an expert on the slow passage of time by now. The difference now was that he was essentially waiting for his own death. The cold truth was that he wasn't planning on surviving this encounter with the mercenaries. He'd told himself over and over that there was still a chance he'd escape undetected, but a small voice in the back of his head continually reminded him how slim that chance was.

The explosion in the first house was more than he could have hoped for, a brilliant fireball that billowed up into the sky and cast everything within half a kilometer in a bright yellow light. The other grenade went off a few seconds later as planned, bringing the house down with a muffled, dusty *boom*. The fireball came a moment later as a spark connected with the old heating unit. To someone who didn't know better, it looked as if the first explosion had set off a chain reaction via an underground gas line.

The mercs' reaction was priceless. The two stationed outside had dived to the ground and were just now crawling back to their feet. More poured out of the station, shouting and gesturing at the flames boiling up out of the demolished houses. Mag looked to where they were pointing and saw that one of the adjoining houses had also caught fire, and it would only be a matter of minutes before the heating unit went up and caused another explosion. He grinned, glad they'd all be pre-occupied for a while trying to keep the fires from reaching the station.

He began working his way toward the building, using a line of bushes for cover. With the dancing shadows caused by the flames, he doubted anyone would notice him creeping through the dark, but he wasn't interested in taking any chances. One of the mercs who'd been standing guard at the door had failed to recover the helmet he'd been wearing when he fell, so Mag scooped it up and darted inside.

As soon as he was through the doors, he turned and slipped into the dark space behind what had once been the station's front desk. He tugged the helmet down over his bleached blonde hair, the feature that perhaps made him the most recognizable. Hoping the subtle change in appearance would be enough to throw someone off at a glance, he rose to his feet and ducked down the nearest hallway.

The interior of the station hadn't changed as much as he'd feared. The hallway made an extra turn to account for some new walls, but otherwise, everything remained virtually unchanged. The place was even still equipped with the same security system. Mag guessed that ordering a new system and new equipment would have raised questions the mercs didn't want to answer. It was sickening, really, how much they'd left the same in order to avoid attracting attention. This was still Argall, the same place Mag and the other citizens had always known, and yet nobody had taken advantage of the familiarity to fight back.

The station's comm grid wasn't exactly in a room—the area was more of an open space surrounded by other rooms. As such, Mag only needed to get through one of those adjoining offices to access it. He was startled, however, to find the office door already open. He immediately stopped and listened, something he'd gotten into the habit of doing whenever something caught him off guard. The office was dark, but the comm room on the other side was fully illuminated—it appeared it was already in use.

Taking a deep breath and letting it out through his nose, he moved across the office and peered through the small window looking out into the comm area. Loric stood there in front of the control panel, speaking to one of the mercs while the life-size hologram of a man waited patiently on the projection pad. He was massive, with a shaved head and jet-black goatee. Somehow, Mag got the feeling he might be the one in charge of all this.

Bits of the conversation reached his ears through the open door. "We are *not* under attack," Loric growled. "If we were under attack, you'd know it."

"But sir!" the other mercenary said. "You don't think it's odd that both houses went up within seconds of each other?"

"Look around you. These places are falling apart. They were probably connected to the same gas line. Check the surrounding buildings if you're that worried, but get out there and get those fires put out before any more damage is done."

The man reluctantly turned and retreated. Mag sank back into the shadows, watching as he stomped through the office and disappeared without so much as a glance behind him. Everything was quiet for a moment before Loric resumed his conversation with the hologram.

"Is there a problem?" the strange man asked.

"Not at all," Loric replied, though he didn't seem convinced. "Just a disturbance, nothing more—my men are dealing with it now."

"I sincerely hope that's the case, because I've got enough trouble of my own. I don't need to deal with yours, too."

Mag watched through the window as Loric's eyes widened. "What happened?"

"I've run into a bit of a…snag," the hologram replied. "One should always be prepared for unforeseen circumstances, but this is more than we could have expected." He paused for several seconds as if the thought were painful. "Payvan is here, and she's coming after us again. She knows everything."

Now Loric fell silent. Mag wasn't sure who this Payvan woman was, but the thought that someone out there knew about the predicament in Argall sent a chill of relief through his body. It didn't necessarily mean help was coming right away, but judging by the conversation, Payvan was working to counter the mercenaries' actions, or at least those of their leader. Maybe she would slow them down enough for Mag to do something.

"What do we do?" Loric asked. It was the first time Mag had seen him so defeated.

The other man shrugged as if the answer was obvious. "I'll be there sometime tomorrow, but in the meantime, shut everything down. We still have some time, but we have to use it to save ourselves. The operation is over."

It was over? Once again, Mag felt sweet relief wash over him, but this time, he hesitated before allowing himself to get too excited. He wasn't sure what 'shutting everything down' entailed, but he didn't like the sound of it.

"You're sure?" Loric asked. His voice remained calm, but the shock was clear in his face.

"I am," the large man replied. "Take what you can and destroy the rest. There's no other choice." With that, the hologram flickered, and he was gone.

A hot tingle coursed through Mag's body, forcing beads of perspiration out onto his forehead. It was amazing how quickly a situation could turn sour—not five minutes earlier, he'd been praising his good luck, having not expected to successfully make it into the station. Now it seemed as though he was in potentially worse trouble than before.

Shut everything down. If it meant what he thought it meant, the scheduled massacre of Argall's citizens had just been moved up and now included the destruction of the mines and any surviving crystals.

He caught himself when he realized the chaos of such an act would allow him to escape the town undetected. Was he really considering running like a coward while the rest of his people were slaughtered? Of course, the only alternative was to stay and be slaughtered along with them. At least he might be able to take a few of the mercs with him that way. The issue was that there was no way to predict their method of attack. They could do anything from lining everyone up in front of a firing squad to dropping mining explosives on the city from the air.

Regardless of what they did, it would still require some measure of planning and organization, meaning help might still arrive in time if Mag managed to get a transmission out. He waited there in the dark office until Loric left the comm room. Then, not caring too much if someone caught him in the act, he approached the main control board and quickly tapped out a distinct distress code. Setting the signal to repeat on a loop, he sent the message out to anyone—anyone at all—who would listen.

· 89 ·
KAT'S HIDEOUT
CHAIAVIS

Night had long since fallen on Chaiavis, though with the overhead door open, the city lights lit up the shop's interior as if it were daytime. Ziva paused and examined the meager pile of items they'd gathered for the trip home: her rifle, the packs she and Aroska had brought, Kade's computer and satchel, the few weapons Kat had stashed around, and last but not least, the data pad containing the mysterious map. There was no way to know what exactly they'd find in Argall, but this was the extent to which they were capable of preparing.

According to Kat, Bosco had a ship they could use to travel. It was old but fast, and being able to take a direct route without stops would get them to Haphez as early as the following afternoon, Haphezian time. It was almost guaranteed that Dasaro would beat them there, but Ziva doubted he'd have much time to organize anything before they arrived.

She turned her attention from the car and wandered up the stairs, where she found Kat sitting on the cot that served as her bed. She held the data pad with her family's death records in her hands, though she didn't seem to be looking at it. Ziva tapped on the doorframe, and she jumped.

"You ready?"

Kat set the data pad down and rubbed her eyes. That sad look had returned to her face once again, worse than Ziva had ever seen it. "Yeah I..." She hesitated, overcome with another thought. "I need to talk to you."

Her tone made Ziva bristle; it spoke of complication, something that would give them one more thing to worry about when they already had so much on their plates. She found she couldn't quite suppress the nasty edge in her voice when she responded, "What is it?"

Unfazed by her harshness, Kat stood up and removed an object from the storage container beside her bed. "Have you ever heard of Ronan?"

"A person?"

Kat shrugged. "A person, a company, I'm not exactly sure." She beckoned for Ziva to come closer and shut the door behind her. "I had a friend from the embassy, Corey, who went missing late last year. He'd been in some trouble with the Niiosian Mob, so I thought maybe he was in the wind and just didn't want to tell anyone he was leaving. It was by pure chance that I bumped into him while working another job about six months ago." Her voice caught and she hesitated.

"Let me guess," Ziva said. "He'd been found by the Mob and needed your help getting away."

Kat recovered quickly. "No, nothing like that. He told me he'd been captured by some entity called Ronan, and that it had let him go and was tracking him as we spoke. He was practically feral, screaming at me to get away from him because he was sick and didn't want to hurt me." She managed a sad snort. "Naturally, I was too stubborn to listen. I finally got him to calm down, and he told me he'd been injected with something at the beginning of his captivity. Apparently, he'd felt fine until about two weeks before I saw him, when he'd suffered a major seizure. They let him go at that point. Ever since that day, he'd been getting these awful headaches. He said he thought there was something wrong with him neurologically, but other than the headaches, he was still functioning perfectly fine."

Ziva mulled the information over, unsure exactly how—or even *if*—it pertained to the current situation. "And he thought this had been caused by whatever he'd been injected with?"

"I guess so," Kat replied. "I asked why he didn't get some medical help, and he just kept repeating that it was too late, that nothing could be done now. And he was right, because…he died without warning a week later."

Ziva's brows slid together in response to the sudden twist. "Define 'without warning'."

Kat shook her head. "I don't know, he was acting normal, finally starting to calm down. Then there were about two days at the end where the headaches got excruciating. He started losing motor control—parts of his body would suddenly go numb. He cut himself pretty bad at one point and didn't even feel it, and it was all I could do to get the bleeding to stop. Then he was just gone."

Ziva was quiet for a moment, not wanting to sound insensitive but also not wanting to waste valuable time. "If you don't mind me asking, where are you going with all this?"

"No, no, of course," Kat said. "I mentioned I was stubborn, right? Well, I started looking for any information I could about Ronan, and I found the warehouse where Corey had been held. But he must have been right about those people watching him, because they found me as soon as I got there." She rolled up her jacket sleeve to reveal a large welt on her upper arm. "The injection site is still swollen to this day," she said, handing over the object she'd taken from the drawer. It was a syringe.

"*Sheyss*," Ziva muttered, mind racing as she tried to process what exactly Kat was saying. The syringe could almost be described as dainty—it was about the length of her index finger and maybe a quarter as thick. Tiny Standard printing adorned one side of the clear tube: RONAN 46-BETA.

She watched Kat for a moment. She couldn't recall ever seeing someone so impartial about the fact that they were dying, other than hardened capital criminals who'd been given a death sentence, but that was a different matter entirely. The sadness Kat had shown made more sense now—it had always manifested itself when the topic of conversation was saving, helping, rescuing. This young woman had dedicated her life to saving and helping, and she continued to do so even when she knew her time was so limited.

"How long does it take?" she asked, certain Kat understood what she meant.

"Corey was held for close to five months before the seizure," Kat replied, sitting back down. "After that, he lasted about three weeks." She stared down at the floor, swallowing hard. "Ziva, it's been almost *five* weeks since my seizure."

One blow after another, it seemed. It was a long time before Ziva managed to say anything, and when she did, it was the first thing that came to mind. "You mean you could die at any time." It was more of a statement than a question. "That's why you were so reluctant to help us."

Kat forced a sad smile and shrugged. "Yeah—I didn't want you to be relying on me for something, only to have me turn around and keel over."

"Why the hell didn't you go get some help?" Ziva cried, louder than she'd meant to. "You saw firsthand what happens! You could have stopped it!"

"Please keep your voice down!" Kat begged as the first signs of tears became visible in her eyes. "I don't want the others to know."

"Why not?"

"I don't want anyone to treat me differently. I've come this far, and I'm not about to let myself be sidelined now."

Ziva sighed. "Then why are you telling me? Why not just keep your mouth shut?"

"Because I need you to do something about it," Kat said. "You've got that syringe, and I'll give you all the data I was able to gather on Corey before he died. That was going to be Bosco's job, and now he's gone, too."

Ziva looked down at the object in her hand. The idea that such delicate things could bring about so much suffering and death never ceased to astonish her. "Are you in any pain?"

Kat shook her head. "The headaches sometimes get bad, but I've learned to deal with them. There's no sense in wasting the rest of my time dwelling on it and feeling sorry for myself. I've got to live my life while I still have it."

"Why didn't you get any help?" Ziva asked again, more quietly this time.

"I didn't want anyone else to get hurt. Whatever Ronan is, it felt threatened enough by me to track me to that warehouse. I'm just one person. Who knows how it would retaliate if the embassy or military found out."

That made sense, though Ziva was still disgusted by how she'd handled the situation, mostly because there was nothing anyone could do to fix it now.

"Is there anything I can do?" It was not a question she asked often.

"You can stay out of my way," Kat replied. Her words weren't harsh; rather, they were the final wishes of a dying woman, and they carried a commanding tone that compelled Ziva to honor them. "I'm not planning on coming back from Argall. I want to go out on my own terms, and I'm going to do whatever it takes to help those people... *whatever it takes*. I hope you can understand that."

As tempting as it was to ask if she was sure, Ziva resorted to a simple dip of her head. "If that's what you want."

"It is. Sometimes I think I've only lasted this long because I've been so determined to see this through." Kat handed Ziva her data pad. "All of Corey's information is on there."

Ziva pocketed the syringe and tucked the data pad up under her jacket. "Let's go home," she said, helping the girl to her feet. "And Kat, thanks for telling me about this."

· 90 ·
FOOTHILLS
ARGALL VALLEY, HAPHEZ

"This is too weird," Zinni muttered, sliding back down behind the large boulder she, Skeet, and Zona hid behind. "Everything looks so normal."

"After everything that's happened, I think it's safe to say nothing is ever as it seems," Zona said.

Skeet and Zinni each grunted in agreement. The three of them were silent for a moment as they contemplated the facts. They'd flown into the mountains under the cover of darkness, and, after leaving their ship a distance away, had hiked into the Argall area on foot. It was mid-morning now, and after multiple hours of climbing through the hills surrounding the town, they'd come across nothing of interest. The city was quiet, though at this distance, it was hard to tell whether anything unusual was going on.

"We should get closer," Zinni suggested.

The others agreed after a short pause. "We'll move south toward the loading docks," Skeet said. "If there's anything happening, maybe we'll be able to see it from there."

They mobilized again, moving slowly with their eyes fixed on the city and the surrounding airspace. Despite the relatively early hour and the crisp mountain air, the warmth of the sun beating down on the rocks made for a hot hike. By the time they made it to an open area where two roads converged, all three were soaked with sweat.

A single pile of rocks and charred wood sat in the center of the clearing. Upon closer inspection, it appeared to be a funeral pyre, and judging by the amount of ash that had settled into the cracks and crevices, it had seen a fair amount of use. Zinni stooped down and looked through the pile—there were no trinkets or jewelry, not like there'd been in the furnace room at Dakiti. There were no bones, either, telling her someone had taken the time to bury them elsewhere. This wasn't a disposal site; this was a legitimate cremation pyre.

"This feels wrong," she said. "Why wouldn't this be closer to the city?"

"Maybe this is some sort of sacred place," Skeet suggested. "The fact that it's secluded doesn't necessarily mean anything."

"I want to check in all the same. This is the first interesting thing we've found all morning, and it at least tells us quite a few people have died recently."

Skeet shrugged and pulled out the powerful HSP communicator they'd brought along. "If you insist," he said, keying in the code that would hail the director.

They stood there in silence, listening to the breeze as it whistled through the rocks. Zinni lifted a spotting scope to her eye, taking a long look at the little town resting in the valley below. The idea that it was the epicenter of all that had happened seemed absurd. She'd only been there once before, years ago, and it had struck her as the epitome of a small mountain town where the residents' lives all revolved around mining and everybody knew everybody else. If she remembered correctly, the city itself was quite beautiful, something she imagined seeing on an intragalactic holoprint with the words 'Greetings from Haphez!' scrawled across it. But that had been close to five years ago. If things were as bad as it sounded like they were, there was no telling what kind of shape the town or its inhabitants were in.

Zinni became aware of a presence beside her, and she turned to find Zona standing there with crossed arms, looking down over the city as well. "What do you think of all this?" she asked, returning her attention to the view through the scope.

"Even as small as Argall is, Dasaro would still need a fairly large force to control it the way he has," Zona replied. "He'd need enough men to continue the mining operations, or at least to keep the workers in check. They must have found some way to block communications, or we would have heard something by now."

Zinni shook her head. "You really think this has all been going on for three years without anyone knowing?"

"Yet another unanswered question," Zona sighed, "but one I intend to find an answer to."

Zinni nodded her agreement and turned back to find Skeet, suddenly stricken by how long it was taking him to check in with Emeri. She found him hunched over the communicator, his forehead divided into two equal halves by that crease that appeared whenever he was troubled.

"I'm not getting a signal," he said, aware he was currently the center of attention.

"What do you mean?" said Zinni and Zona simultaneously.

"I mean I've tried five times and I can't get anything to go through. The transmission keeps bouncing right back."

"You were able to check in when we first landed," Zona confirmed.

"Yeah, but..." Skeet shook his head as the comm failed again and looked around. "It's almost like there's some interference, something that didn't affect us earlier."

Zinni began to approach Skeet, but the glint of sunlight off something on the hill above them caught her attention. The realization that it was a rifle scope hit her just as a plasma bolt came sizzling past her head, burning through the space where she would have been standing had she not taken that small step.

"Down!" she screamed, yanking Zona to the ground with her as she dove behind the funeral pyre. Skeet slid in beside them in a cloud of dust.

Multiple sets of footsteps could be heard advancing up the road from the direction they'd come. A voice that sounded like it belonged to someone in charge rang out above the others: "Hold your fire!"

It seemed like an odd thing to say, considering the three of them had yet to take a shot, but it occurred to Zinni that the man hadn't been talking to them at all—he'd been addressing the sniper.

Skeet and Zona were on their feet in seconds, pistols drawn and trained on the newcomers. Zinni rose as well; a quick study of the group revealed an assortment of men and women, fifteen people total. They didn't appear to be in any form of uniform, but they all carried identical rifles bearing the same insignia. They were clearly organized on some level, but they certainly weren't HSP.

"Sergeant Duvo, Officer Vax, HSP operations, and Special Agent Zona, Royal Guard," Skeet shouted. "Lower your weapons immediately!"

"Do as he says!" the leader of the group ordered, dropping his rifle and lifting his hands. "My name is Remis. We're part of Tekele Private Security, based out of Seran. Are you the recon team responding to the distress code?"

Zinni and Skeet glanced at one another before shaking their heads. "This is a recon mission," Zinni replied, "but we don't know anything about a distress code."

They cautiously lowered their pistols as Remis approached, his hands held out in plain sight. "We intercepted it during the wee hours this morning," he explained. "It appeared to have originated from the main comm grid in Argall, but our reply transmission yielded no response and we lost the signal not long after that. We forwarded it to HSP, and your director said he'd make sure you received it. He told us we might find you up here."

"We must have left Headquarters right around the time you found it," Skeet said. "And we haven't received any messages—our communications are down. We don't know when exactly we lost them."

Remis almost looked relieved. "Then we're not the only ones. We lost contact with the other half of our team about two hours ago, about the time we moved farther down into the valley. They should be somewhere on the other side." He lifted a hand to shield his eyes from the sun and gazed out across the basin. "The interference is identical to what we saw after we tried to respond to the distress signal."

"You think there's something jamming communications in the area?" Skeet asked.

"It's possible. Trust me—I would have called my sniper off if possible. I'm terribly sorry about that. He must have thought you were with the mercenaries."

"Mercenaries?" Zona repeated.

"Part of the distress message mentioned Argall had been overrun by mercs. We don't know details, but it's got to be a sizable bunch in order to subdue the whole town. There aren't too many organized groups with those kinds of numbers around here, not since Solaris disbanded, so that narrows down the list."

That made sense. A large gang would be easy for Dasaro to control, most likely by bribing them with money. He'd be able to interact directly with their leader, minimizing the effort needed on his part and enabling him to conduct all this business with relative secrecy. "Do you have any idea who we're dealing with?" Zinni asked.

"If I had to make an educated guess, I'd say we're looking at a division of the Red Ring," Remis replied. "They're run by a man named Loric—used to be a sergeant in the Grand Army's 305th platoon before being dishonorably discharged. He...used to be a friend."

Zinni followed suit when Skeet and Zona finally holstered their weapons. "What makes you think it's him?"

"For starters, he'll do anything for money," Remis scoffed. "But he's also been off the radar for the past couple of years, making me wonder what he's been up to. He's got the manpower to handle something like this. I don't want to start jumping to conclusions, though. Regardless of who's running this circus, there are obviously people down there who are in trouble."

"He's right," Zona said. "We should continue on."

Skeet nodded toward Remis. "Sounds like you guys know more than we do about the situation. Mind if we join you?"

"We'd welcome it," the man replied, stepping forward to shake Skeet's hand. "According to your director, your team has some background information that could benefit us as well."

A sudden explosion rocked the ground, echoing off the surrounding hills and sending loose rocks tumbling down the incline. The entire group turned as a unit and watched as a fiery cloud billowed up from the edge of the compact little city. Even at this distance, the screams could be heard. Zinni scrambled to recover the spotting scope from where she'd dropped it and peered down at the scene below. The people were hardly more than bipedal shapes, but it was clear that they were running and the heat signatures from plasma weapons were unmistakable.

"The debrief will have to wait," she said, already on her way down the hill. "We need to get down there!"

CHAIAVIAN FREIGHTER *STEEL HAND*
HAPHEZIAN AIRSPACE

W hen Ziva walked back into the cockpit and found Kat with her face pressed against the front viewport, she couldn't help but smirk. The world of Haphez loomed ahead, a brown and green orb suspended against the black backdrop of space. It was a sight for sore eyes, even though they'd only been gone for a few days. She couldn't imagine what this moment might be like for Kat, especially in light of the things the girl had shared with her in confidence.

"I've only ever seen pictures," the young woman murmured, shifting her gaze to where the halo of light from the sun reflected off the waters of Haphez's single sea.

"Welcome home, Kat," Aroska said, grinning. "It's a beautiful place."

As they descended into the atmosphere, a cloud of apprehension about their return settled over Ziva. There was no telling what exactly the director—or the rest of the population, for that matter—knew in terms of the truth. For all she knew, there was still an execution order out on her, Aroska was wanted for aiding and abetting a fugitive, and Kade because he was a person of interest in the investigation. On top of all that, they were bringing a Defective with them. As comforting as it was to be home, she felt far from welcome.

They entered the airspace above downtown Noro and slid into place amid the mid-afternoon traffic. They reached her house in a matter of minutes and set the ship down in the small landing bay where the *Intrepid* usually docked. Her vessel had no doubt been impounded following her arrest, and she wondered briefly what it would take to get it back. She dreaded to think of what else HSP had taken—chances were they wouldn't have many supplies to choose from.

"I want to make this fast," she said as the four of them descended the boarding ramp. "We don't have time to stay and chat. Grab what you need, and we'll go."

They found the basement door to be locked, and after a bit of consideration, Ziva wasn't surprised. If Veya Shevin had done as she was told and had come here, Marshay and Ryon would have turned this place into a fortress. Feeling like a stranger in her own home, she led the group around to the front door and knocked.

They were greeted momentarily by Marshay, or more accurately, the barrel of a shotgun with Marshay behind it. The woman's jaw fell slack as she locked eyes with Ziva, and she immediately lowered the weapon.

"May we come in?" Ziva asked. She had no doubt it was a shock to see her there, maybe even to see her alive, but there was work to be done and not a lot of time to do it. Too impatient to be polite, she pushed her way inside with the others hot on her heels.

A shriek sounded from across the room the moment they cleared the doorway. The owner of that shrill voice was nothing but a blur as she streaked across the floor and latched onto Kade with a claw-like grip. It was all Shevin could do to catch Veya before she sent him staggering backward into the wall, holding her just as tightly as she held him. Kat and Aroska moved aside to give them some space and watched, amused, as the young couple laughed through their tears.

"I'm sorry," Kade kept repeating. "I'm sorry I left you."

Not feeling overly sentimental, Ziva crossed to the hall closet and opened the hidden compartment inside, cursing when she found the weapon locker open and empty, just as she'd feared. She turned and began to rush toward the guest room, narrowly avoiding a collision with Ryon as he emerged from his room. He looked perplexed when he noticed the new arrivals but recovered more quickly than Marshay had.

"Hello to you, too," he said.

Ziva had to give him credit for being so patient. It seemed that nothing she did surprised him anymore, not even showing up unexpected after being charged with murder, evading the authorities, and staging her own death. He could take one look at a situation and be ready to go with the flow, just as he was doing now upon recognizing the urgency in the air.

He gestured toward the open closet. "HSP took everything."

She slid her hands down to rest on her hips, taking this immediate misfortune as a sign that she should at least slow down and take a deep breath. She watched as Veya and Kade lifted their baby daughter from her carrier and showered her with kisses. She looked to Kat, who had somehow managed to maintain a spark in her eyes despite knowing this was a one-way trip. Aroska waited, weary but ready, and nodded her way when she looked to him. Since Veya was there, Marshay and Ryon had to have known she was alive, but they still regarded her as though they'd never expected to see her again. Even so, they were ready to offer their support.

"Not everything," she finally said. "They haven't taken our will to fight."

With any luck, HSP hadn't discovered The Loft, the hidden space within the ceiling of her bedroom. She entered and, relieved to find everything still intact, retrieved a medium-sized storage container. It didn't hold much—mostly ammunition and a couple of small pistols—but with some determination, a little bit could go a long way. And there was no shortage of determination around here.

A thought crossed her mind as she walked back through her demolished room. She still carried the syringe and data pad Kat had given her, so she took a moment to place them in the strongbox behind the hidden panel she'd told Aroska about. Now that someone knew about its location, she would have to find a new hiding place, but these items would be safe for now.

She returned to the kitchen and placed the box on the table. "Take what you can use," she instructed. Kat and Aroska began to cautiously paw through the collection.

She sighed and turned to face Marshay and Ryon once again. It was clear that they were trying hard to stay collected, but they were still having a hard time not staring. "Where are Skeet and Zinni?" she asked, trying to divert some of the attention away from herself.

It was Marshay who mustered up a response first. "They left in the middle of the night with Zona—wouldn't say where they were headed. They've been working themselves into the ground since they realized you were still alive."

So they *had* caught on to that little detail. Ziva silently thanked Veya for instilling some hope in her friends. She turned to the young couple and found that Kade had taken a sudden interest in the conversation.

"Wait, Zona?" he repeated.

Marshay nodded. "He's been here with them for the past couple of days, going over a copy of some files he said you stole."

A tingle of excitement shot down Ziva's spine. So Skeet and Zinni had seen Zona's files. Did that mean they knew about Argall and the truth behind her imprisonment on Cobi? Had they presented their findings to the director, thus proving Dasaro's involvement in the matter? Had they managed to find Tachi's killer? There were still too many questions that remained unanswered.

She turned and picked through the weapon box as well, selecting a projectile pistol, some spare ammo, and an old thermal grenade she'd picked up on a mission close to four years earlier. "Sorry to cut this visit short," she said, though in reality, she was eager to get moving again. "But we may not be in the clear just yet, and we've still got a lot to do."

While Marshay and Ryon nodded in understanding, Veya looked devastated. "You mean this isn't over?" she whimpered.

"Far from it," Kat said, sounding almost defensive as she fidgeted and glanced toward the door. "There's a lot more going on than a simple frame-up. People are dying!"

"Please, Kat!" Ziva said, halting the conversation before it could escalate. She hated to say the words because she doubted she could keep such a promise, but they slipped out anyway. "I swear we'll get there in time. Get your stuff and take it to the ship."

Kat and Aroska took up the items they'd selected, leaving the depleted box on the counter. The two of them made their way back out the door, leaving Ziva under the scrutiny of those who remained inside. Kade swallowed and squirmed, grasping his wife's hand. She'd had every intention of having him come along and see this mission through—they needed all the help they could get, after all. But in the split second she stood there studying him, she saw how tired he was, how afraid he was. He wasn't afraid for himself, though; he was afraid for his family. He was afraid because there was someone there waiting for him to come home every day. Ziva thought back to her conversation with Aroska on the balcony. She thought of Marshay and Ryon and how they loved her like a daughter but still understood what she had to do. They didn't like it, but they were aware of the way she and her team had to live in order to do their jobs. Not so with Veya. Kade had proven to be a good agent, but he was by no means spec ops. He wasn't cut out for this.

"Shevin," she said, making him jump. He gripped Veya's hand tighter, no doubt expecting the worst.

"Stay here and protect your family. Better yet, go to HSP where you'll be safe. They're probably going to take you into custody, but tell them I sent you and they'll listen to you in a heartbeat. Go to the director and tell him everything you know—*every single detail*. Ryon will make sure you get there safely."

"Got it," Kade said, releasing the breath he'd been holding. Then his face turned solemn. "You sure you'll be all right?"

It was an impossible question to answer with any shred of honesty. Ziva turned the thermal grenade over in her hand and nodded. "We'll be back."

· 92 ·

ABANDONED HOUSE

ARGALL, HAPHEZ

Mag ducked away from the window just as a hail of plasma fire pelted the front of the building. He reestablished his grip on his own pistol and checked the plasma cell for the umpteenth time, wondering how many more shots he could get off before the gun became useless. One thing was for sure—it wouldn't be enough.

He caught his breath and risked a look out the window. It didn't appear the mercenary who'd fired knew he was there—he'd been aiming for the two men who now lay dead in the street just outside. Surprisingly, they were the first people Mag had actually witnessed die all morning. He was sure there'd been more elsewhere in the city, but many had been spared the initial bloodbath thanks to the early warning message he'd sent out upon leaving the police station.

It hadn't taken the mercenaries long to realize communications were functional again. Loric had reset the jamming signal and the distress beacon had been disabled an hour or so before dawn. Escaping the police station undetected had taken a bit of doing, shortening the window of time for successful communication, but it had been adequate enough for Mag to send out transmissions to the few people in the city he still trusted, who in turn had forwarded the warning to others. By the time comms were disabled again, a good portion of the town knew about Loric's plan to shut everything down. All weapons had been confiscated upon the mercs' initial arrival so very few people had any means of defending themselves, but knowing was at least half the battle.

He slid back down to the floor and leaned against the wall, taking a moment to look around at the people he'd taken under his wing as he'd moved through the city. There were the two young men, apparently twin brothers, who couldn't have been more than twenty years old. Their eyes were wide, their faces stained with the soft gray dust that was so prevalent in the mines. Then there was the woman with the two small children, and the old man who was armed with a rifle he'd pried from the cold fingers of a dead mercenary. His haircut and the battle scars on his face told Mag he knew how to use it. He'd seen all of them around the town before, but he realized now that he didn't know any of their names. He'd spent so much time obsessing over the fact that everyone else had changed, not even bothering to think about the way he'd distanced himself from them. Worse yet, they all seemed to know who he was—he was practically the mascot of the mercs' occupation, after all. They sat there watching him, looking to him for leadership, and he had no idea what to do.

"It's going to be okay," was the only thing he could think of to say, though in reality he didn't know if it would be.

He wasn't sure if accessing the comm grid had helped or made things worse. Obviously, it was a good thing if the distress call had reached someone willing to respond, but it had also alerted Loric and his men to the fact that he knew about their plan. Granted, there was no way for them to know it had been *him* specifically, but that knowledge had still altered their plan of attack, in the most literal sense of the phrase. Nothing was planned, nothing was organized. The streets of Argall had been transformed into a chaotic warzone, and while the mercenaries' numbers were spread thin, there was still no way for the citizens to successfully fight back. They needed more firepower.

The door of the building burst open while Mag was still lost in thought. By the time he recovered enough to raise his pistol, it had been wrestled from him by powerful hands. Startled and at a loss, he resorted to raising his arms over his head and cowering in the corner.

"Nobody move!" shouted a tall, well-muscled man with wild orange hair, the apparent leader of the group who had entered.

"Let's see some hands!" cried a small woman who had come in behind him. Mag looked up to find her pointing his own pistol at him.

The rest of his little entourage did as they were told, and the old man grudgingly relinquished his rifle. Several more armed men and women crowded into the room, sealing the door behind them and successfully shutting out the noise and gunfire from outside. Mag studied the group past his quivering hands. The power and speed with which they moved told him they were professionals, but the realization that they weren't part of the mercenary gang hit him when the big orange-haired man spoke again.

"Is everyone okay in here?" he asked, motioning for the rest of his team to lower their weapons. His voice was gentler than Mag had expected.

The only responses were whimpers from the children and nods from the adults. The female agent flipped Mag's pistol over and offered it back to him. "You know how to handle this thing?" she asked. Her tone wasn't condescending—it was clear that she was entrusting him with the weapon. Her brilliant blue eyes were intense but kind.

"Listen," said the orange-haired man. "We're members of HSP and Tekele Private Security. I'm Sergeant Duvo, this is Officer Vax. We're here to help."

For a split second, Mag wasn't sure if he'd heard correctly. He'd expended so much energy convincing himself they were doomed—the idea that help had actually arrived was surreal. He sighed and covered his face with his hands, filled with a sense of hope for the first time in three years.

"My message got through," he breathed.

The man called Duvo snorted. "It's a bit of a long story," he said. "You can thank Remis here for picking up your signal. HSP is here for a different reason. Is it true you've been having some problems?"

"That's an understatement," Mag replied, allowing Officer Vax to help him to his feet. He gave them a rundown of what had transpired throughout the past three years, allowing the other refugees to comment and add details of their own. The mercenaries had taken control of Argall and the mining operations nearly three years earlier, killing a good portion of the town's population throughout the course of their operation. Their leader, Loric, had targeted him specifically because he supposedly had access to a map that would lead them to rich crystal growth. Desperate, he had risked a trip into the police station and managed to send a plea for help, only to learn of the mercs' plans to kill everyone and escape with the remaining crystals.

"I was right about Loric, then," muttered the man Duvo had addressed as Remis. "I'll take my team out and see if we can't whittle down the enemy numbers and pinpoint his location."

Mag watched as Remis and several others broke off from the group and headed back outside, moving up the street in a tight formation with rifles raised. The sheer chaos of the morning had already brought about a good deal of mercenary casualties, and now that help had come—despite the somewhat limited manpower—he had no doubt they would be able to form a successful resistance.

"What's your name, son?" asked the third HSP agent, an older man with streaks of gray running through his hair.

"Reilly," Mag replied, "Mag Reilly."

The agent turned to Duvo and Vax. "I recognize the name. A crystal farmer named Reilly was killed in one of several mining accidents a while back. The records are from around the same time Dasaro and Payvan started having problems."

"Well as you can imagine, there haven't actually been any 'accidents'," Mag scoffed. "They've slaughtered people like animals, even the ones who were cooperative." He hesitated. "Wait, what was that name you just said?"

All three agents exchanged glances. "Payvan?" Duvo said.

"I've heard that name! Last night in the police station, Loric was on comm with a man who said that Payvan was on to him, that she knew everything. That's why they're calling off the operation."

"Have you ever heard the name Diago Dasaro?" Vax asked.

Mag shook his head. "Not until you mentioned it a second ago. He's the man behind all this?"

They all nodded.

"He must have been the one talking to Loric, the one who gave the order to shut everything down. He was tall, bald, had a beard, talked like he knew Payvan personally—"

"That's him," Duvo cut him off. He looked to the older agent. "You were right about everything."

The other man grunted in agreement. "Did he say anything else?" he asked Mag.

Mag shrugged. "He said he would be here today, but I guess that's to be expected."

The way his words affected them was shocking. "Dasaro is *here*?" Vax exclaimed, followed by a string of expletives muttered under her breath.

Taking their reaction to the mere mention of Dasaro's name into consideration, Mag couldn't imagine what the man himself must be like. No, he took that back—he knew *exactly* what he was like. Anyone who ordered the execution of an entire town and did everything in his power to cover it up had obviously crawled straight out of hell. And now it appeared Argall's citizens weren't the only people he'd been terrorizing over the years.

"We can't worry about that," Duvo said in response to his colleague's outburst. "We've got to neutralize the threat for now, and then we can focus on him." He turned back to Mag. "We could use your help. Can your friends here handle themselves for a while?" He handed the rifle back to the old man, who gave an affirmative nod.

"I'll see what I can do," Mag replied. Then he addressed the civilians. "Lock the doors and move into the back room. Don't open the door for anyone but me."

"Let's get moving," Officer Vax said, still fired up after hearing of Dasaro's presence.

Mag adjusted his grip on his pistol and fell into position behind the three agents as they burst out into the street. Droplets of sweat had already formed on his forehead and his heart was racing, but he wasn't afraid—he was going to save Argall.

· 93 ·

CHAIAVIAN FREIGHTER *STEEL HAND*
ARGALL VALLEY, HAPHEZ

Ziva didn't take her eyes off the front viewport when Aroska returned to the cockpit and plopped down in the co-pilot's chair. "She's in the cargo hold," he said, speaking of Kat. "I told her we were about twenty minutes out and she said she'd be up here soon. Said she needed some time to herself. I can't say I blame her."

She said nothing. The knowledge that there was more to Kat's seclusion than apprehension about returning to her birthplace ate at her, but she had no intention of betraying the young woman's trust. She'd proven herself capable so far, and if her records were accurate, they'd be well aware if her mysterious disease began to manifest itself. Ziva was prepared to do what was necessary to put her out of her misery if the need arose.

"Want me to take over for a while?" Aroska asked, taking up the second set of controls before she could even respond.

She sighed and leaned back in her chair. "Sure," she muttered, removing her kytara from its harness to make herself more comfortable.

Aroska snorted. "I didn't think you'd bring that."

"Yeah, well, I'm sure Emeri's told half the galaxy I have it by now. There's not much point in hiding it anymore."

"As far as I know, he never said anything," Aroska said with a shrug. "But that's been a few days ago."

Ziva shook her head. "Why wouldn't he have said anything? That's the first thing he threatened me with when I first got taken into custody. Maybe I didn't actually kill Tachi, but now everyone's going to know about this. I'm not sure how I'm going to survive this round."

"Hey now, we'll think of something. You've survived up until now, and if there's anything you've taught the galaxy during this past week, it's that you're not going away." He was quiet for a moment before heaving a sigh. "How do you do it, anyway?"

Ziva watched through the clouds as the mountains flew by beneath them. "Do what?"

"Survive. You've seen more *sheyss* in your life than half of HSP put together, but you don't let it faze you. What motivates you to keep going?"

"What am I supposed to do, curl up in the corner and feel sorry for myself?"

"I'm serious."

"And so am I. Pushing and fighting is the only way to stay alive around here. I guess I don't know how to do anything else."

"But what about something totally debilitating? What about when you were captured by the Cobians? Sure, they've got rehab facilities like the one on Na that can get you back on your feet, but what would make you even *want* to come back to work after something like that?"

Ziva wondered if he was thinking of himself and how much he'd struggled after Dakiti. How strange her life must seem to him, clawing her way through each day despite the pain and suffering it often brought. She couldn't tell if he was jealous of her or ashamed that he hadn't lived up to that standard. Or maybe he just thought she was crazy.

"I didn't get to go to Na," she said quietly.

The Na Facility could most accurately be described as an intensive rehab center located at the military base on Haphez's only life-sustaining moon. It was run by the Grand Army, but they always admitted any agents HSP referred to them, probably because it wasn't very many. It was a rare privilege earned only by those the agency deemed irreplaceable; most agents, assuming they even survived their injuries, were forced to either recover on their own or seek employment elsewhere. The success rates for those who *did* manage to get admitted were off the charts. Not only did the facility provide medical care and rehabilitation, but it also focused on reconditioning patients so they could return to duty and perform at one hundred ten percent for their respective institutions.

"You're kidding," Aroska said.

"I guess HSP didn't think I mattered enough. We hadn't reached Alpha status yet, and of course everyone thought I had defied orders by going back into the compound. Recovering on my own was a punishment of sorts. HSP still paid for my medical care, but I don't think anyone ever expected me to come back to work." She scoffed. "Especially Dasaro."

Aroska lifted an eyebrow. "I guess my question still stands, more so in light of that. Why would you even come back?"

"At first, I think I just wanted to prove that I could. I got a lot of *sheyss* from the people who believed Dasaro's story, and I wanted to shut them up. But seriously, just try to picture me doing something other than this. Like I said, surviving is all I know how to do."

He chuckled. "Good point. Let's just survive another day, shall we?"

The cockpit fell silent for the remaining minutes of the flight. Kat appeared right on cue as they broke the crest of the mountains and descended into the Argall Valley, with Aroska bringing the ship into a sharp dive and gliding along at an altitude of mere meters.

Ziva wasn't sure what she'd expected to see upon their arrival, but the pillars of smoke curling up out of the city still made the hairs on her neck stand on end. She could see Kat's reflection in the front viewport—her face was as grim as it had been when she'd described her disease. This probably wasn't how she'd imagined her home.

There was a suspicious lack of activity on the ground as they brought the ship around and set it down on one of the landing pads at the loading area on the edge of town. Ziva slid the projectile pistol from its holster and tucked an extra mag into her pocket, opting to leave her kytara on board at least until she had a better idea of what they were dealing with. She moved into the cargo hold, her eyes taking in every detail of the landscape as the boarding ramp descended. The docks were devoid of any shipping containers or boxes—the nearest cover was a variety of outbuildings around the landing pads, probably storage sheds of some sort. She cautiously crept down the ramp, ready to sprint for cover at the slightest noise, but there still didn't seem to be anyone around.

"Dasaro's obviously got some sort of force here," Kat said. "I doubt they'll be in uniform—how will we tell them from the civilians?"

"I imagine they'll be shooting at us." Ziva stepped off the platform, keeping her eyes focused ahead. "We'll shoot back."

"And what if they're locals who think we're Dasaro's guys?" Aroska suggested.

As tempting as it was to say it didn't matter, she resorted to a wag of her head. "We'll worry about that when we actually see someone."

Gunfire could be heard somewhere ahead, though it was impossible to tell where exactly it originated and who was doing the shooting. Argall's layout was compact, even for a town with such a small population. A ten-minute walk brought them to a square that appeared to be the very center of the city, and still there were no signs of life. All doors appeared to be locked tight, and dead bodies littered the streets. Something gruesome had gone down here.

Movement in the corner of her eye caught her attention and she whirled, weapon trained on the door of one of the nearby shops. A face, that of a young man by the looks of it, ducked back down away from the shop's window when he saw she was looking. She bristled and signaled for Kat and Aroska to be wary, unsure whether the subject was a friend or foe. Either way, he was someone who could answer some questions.

The three of them moved to the door on light feet. It was locked as expected, so she gave it a couple of solid raps. "I know you're in there," she said, stepping to one side when she heard the *click* of some sort of weapon within. "Open the door."

When there was no response, she pounded her fist against the door again. "Open the door! Are you really planning on shooting a couple of HSP agents? Let me in or I'll let myself in!"

This time, there was a faint shuffling of feet crossing the floor, followed by some fiddling with the locking mechanism and a low hiss as the door slid open a short distance. Ziva slipped in through the opening with Kat and Aroska in tow, barely giving her eyes a chance to adjust to the darkness before taking the young man by the throat and pinning him to the wall.

"Where's Dasaro?" she hissed as Aroska relieved him of the rifle.

"Please," the boy stammered, tears streaking his dirt-stained face. "I don't know who that is. I'm just supposed to be protecting these people. I wasn't even supposed to open the door—"

She released him and turned to find several curious faces peering at them from another room: an old man, a woman, two little kids, and another young man identical to the one standing before her. These weren't Dasaro's thugs.

"You're late," the old man growled.

"Excuse me?" Aroska said.

"You said you're HSP," the boy said, rubbing his neck. "We already met some HSP agents. They've been here for hours. They told us to stay in here until everything was clear. We've been taking turns keeping watch."

Now it was Ziva's turn to do a double take. "You said HSP is already here?"

The whole group nodded in response. "Three agents and a large security team," replied the boy. "They've been past here several times, clearing out the mercenaries. Their leader is Sergeant Duvo."

While it was far from a complication, it was just one more unforeseen twist in this ongoing puzzle Ziva was trying to put together. She placed her hands on her hips and tapped her foot on the floor, shaking her head as she tried in vain to come up with an explanation.

"Who is he?" Kat asked.

"My second-in-command," she answered. She turned to Aroska. "What the hell is he doing here?"

He offered a perplexed shrug and turned his attention to the refugees. "How long since you last saw him?"

"An hour or so," the old man answered. "They've managed to coax some fight out of the locals. They've split into several groups and have spent the afternoon sweeping the city and cleaning house."

"Sounds like we missed the party," Kat said.

The thunder of approaching footsteps registered with Ziva just before the first plasma bolts began to fly outside. "Not quite!" she exclaimed, diving for the door controls and narrowly avoiding the streaks of scorching energy that made it through the opening. Plasma fire pelted the front of the building, and a small charge tore a hole in the wall, sending splinters and shards of glass flying inward.

Ziva raised her gun and put three rounds into the chest of the first man who entered. He fell backward into the path of another, who found himself on the receiving end of several repetitive shots from Kat's weapon. Neither of them appeared to be HSP, nor were they part of the security group judging by their mismatched attire and tattoos. Ziva dropped to the floor and rolled to avoid a spray of shrapnel as another frag grenade detonated. She rose up on one knee, squeezing off another couple of shots at the man who had thrown it.

"Leave them!" someone shouted as an old car screeched to a stop in front of the shop. "It's not worth it!" The remaining men outside piled into it, still firing as they went, and the vehicle tore away down the street. These were the mercenaries, and they were retreating.

Ziva slipped through the hole in the wall and went out after them, lowering her pistol when she realized it was far too late to do anything. She silently noted the color and model of the car, though she doubted it would matter, and stepped back into the building.

"They're hauling out of here," she said to no one in particular.

"Like we told you," said the boy, "your friends have done a good job clearing them out."

"Where are they now?" she asked.

"Last we saw, it looked like they were headed for the police station. Go straight up the street and take a right—you can't miss it."

"Okay, let's move." Ziva directed Kat and Aroska back outside, where the three of them broke into a slow jog in the direction the young man had indicated. Everything was dead silent now; even the distant gunfire had stopped, giving her the impression the retreating mercenaries had been the ones causing it.

"This is insane," Kat muttered.

Ziva was surprised by how much she cared about what the young woman was feeling right now. Maybe it was because she was glad to be home, too, but she already knew exactly what being home was like. To so many people, Haphez was a picture-perfect paradise, with gorgeous mountains and forests and cities and people. In many ways, that was still precisely what it was, but throughout her career, she'd had the opportunity to experience the underlying currents that flowed through those cities, the true nature of those people. Maybe Haphez wasn't always all it was made out to be, but this here in Argall? This *was* insane.

She slowed the group to a brisk walk as they approached the right turn that would lead them to their destination. Voices could be heard just around the corner ahead, though it was still impossible to know who they belonged to. If Skeet and his team had gone into the police station and were surrounded by the remaining mercs, they'd be severely outnumbered. Then again, that didn't make much sense, considering the mercs who had been retreating. But nothing had made much sense as of late.

They paused at the corner in the shade of the building and listened. The voices quieted suddenly, and shadows began darting to and fro as if their owners were taking cover. Then one approached.

That animal instinct flared up again, activated by the adrenaline surging through Ziva's veins with a force that was almost painful. Time slowed to about half speed; she could smell the blood, the sweaty bodies, the hot pistols, see the positions of the shadows and the movement reflected in the windows across the street. She adjusted the grip on her gun and drew a deep breath, stepping around the corner and expecting the worst.

The bright orange hair registered with her in less than a second, though her muscles were wound up so tight she found she couldn't lower her weapon right away. Looking into Skeet's eyes was what finally allowed her to relax. She holstered her pistol and lifted her hands when Zinni and two other armed men appeared at his side, but they stood down immediately when they saw he had done the same.

There was a long period of silence as her two teammates stared, wide-eyed, and the other men looked on in confusion. She understood that it must be strange seeing her here, considering how long she'd been out of the picture and the circumstances surrounding her disappearance, but then something else struck her. It was one thing to *hear* she was still alive, contrary to what they'd believed for almost two days, but it was something else entirely to *see* her in the flesh after such trauma. The looks on their faces told her they had wholeheartedly bought her little act at the relay station that day, regardless of what they'd learned since then.

"Looks like we missed out on all the fun," she said, stepping slowly toward them as if even the slightest movement would scare them away.

That finally coaxed half a grin onto Skeet's face, though it didn't remain there long. "Good to see you, Z," he said as though he were speaking to a ghost. His eyes shifted to Aroska, and Ziva realized his charade as her killer was what had really sold them.

An older man whose jacket bore the Royal Guard insignia appeared at Skeet's side. Ziva recognized him from the press conference on the day of her arrest: Luko Zona. "Please tell me agent Shevin is with you."

"He was," she replied. "In fact, he's one of the main reasons we even knew to come here, thanks to those files he was able to retrieve from your system. He stayed behind to look after his family and fill in the director."

"He left quite a mess at RG Headquarters."

"You have me to blame for that," she snapped. "In fact, you can thank me for it. If I hadn't shown up when I did, Kade would be dead, and those files would probably be in Dasaro's hands. Who knows what he would have done to cover his tracks."

"You were there?" Zinni asked.

"I was there. And I shot those men. No need to accuse Kade of that."

"Did you really kill Nejdra, too?" Skeet asked, a strange condemning tone in his voice that Ziva hadn't expected.

She was quiet for a moment. "I did. How did you even know about that?"

"Dasaro called the director and went off on some rant about how you tried to kill him, claiming that was why he left Haphez. He said you shot Nejdra, and that Hoxie had disappeared, and then he requested that he be allowed to continue pursuing you on his own."

"Likely so he could come here without anyone asking questions," Ziva muttered. "And anyhow, I don't know where Hoxie is. He was there at the embassy with the others. Have you seen any sign of Dasaro here?"

Finally, Skeet seemed to loosen up a bit. "All the remaining mercenaries are holed up in the police station," he said, leading them to an area farther up the street where several men were gathered around a stack of crates formulating a plan. "They've got all the doors barricaded except the front, but there are enough of them in there that they could pick us off without any trouble if we tried to go in that way. It's an effective choke point."

He caught the attention of one of the men and beckoned to him. "Lieutenant Ziva Payvan, meet Officer Remis of Tekele Private Security. We've joined forces with his team."

Ziva gave him an approving nod. "This is field ops Lieutenant Aroska Tarbic, and our new liaison from Chaiavis, Kat Reilly."

A voice, its owner currently unseen, spoke up before Skeet or Remis could respond. "Reilly?"

The two other agents with Remis stepped aside to let the speaker through. Once more, Ziva found herself rendered completely speechless. The man's hair was what caught her attention first, and then came the icy blue eyes and *gesh punti*. He looked to be in his mid to late thirties and had the weary features of someone who had suffered a great deal, but there was no mistaking that jaw line and those cheekbones. This man was a spitting image of Kat.

The entire group stopped what they were doing, just as shocked by what they were seeing as the two long-lost siblings were. Everyone moved aside to give them some space and looked on in fascination as they approached each other, eyeing one another as if they weren't quite sure if everything was real. They paused about an arm's length from each other and stood, just staring, for what felt like hours.

It was the man who finally broke the silence with a noise that sounded like a cross between a laugh and a sob. He reached out and placed his hand gently against Kat's face. "Hello, Kat. My name is Mag." Now he did laugh. "I guess I'm your brother."

Without another word, he pulled her into a solid embrace, and though she seemed timid at first, it wasn't long before she had just as tight a hold on him. For a while, it appeared she was laughing along with him, but as they turned in a slow circle and her face came into view, the tears came faster, and the fear became apparent. When she lifted her head and looked directly into Ziva's eyes, her thoughts were displayed clearly.

What am I going to do?

· 94 ·
City Center
Argall, Haphez

Skeet looked away from the police station when he sensed someone come up beside him. He turned and found Ziva standing there, just as she had been as they'd surveyed the guests at Tachi's palace. The gala seemed like a lifetime ago.

It was almost surreal seeing her right now. Even after finding out she was alive, he'd never expected to see her here of all places. In fact, he'd wondered if he'd see her again at all. If she'd done what she'd been taught to do, she would have disappeared to the farthest corner of the galaxy, never to be heard from again.

Then again, this was Lieutenant Ziva Payvan he was dealing with, the HSP special operations agent who was renowned for never doing exactly as she was taught. In all reality, he knew her well enough that he should have expected her to show up here. Maybe she was good at disappearing, but he'd also never known her to give up a fight. She'd come here to put an end to all this.

She didn't look at him when she spoke. "You're angry."

Was he? He certainly felt *something*, though he wasn't quite sure what it was yet. Sometimes, it seemed like she knew him better than he knew himself, so if she said he was angry, then he probably was, whether he realized it or not.

"I'm not mad, Ziva," he said anyway. "I'm just...." He turned for a moment and watched Mag Reilly conversing with his sister. "A lot of unexpected things have happened lately."

She stepped around in front of him and looked him squarely in the eye. "You understand why we did what we did, don't you? Why we pulled that stunt on the riverbank and left the planet?" She crossed her arms. "It was the only way to get ahead of Dasaro and figure out what was going on."

Just because he understood didn't mean he had to like it. "Of course I do," he replied, stealing a glance at Aroska, who was caught up in conversation with Zinni and Zona. *But I wish you could have come to us first.* "But I wish there was something more we could have done."

"It seems to me like you did plenty, considering you're here," Ziva said. "Obviously Zona's files had something to do with it. How did he fall in with you guys?"

"The director ordered us to bring him on board after Dasaro left. Argall wasn't much more than a hunch, but we figured we'd better get up here and check things out while the captain was out of the picture. It was all a routine recon mission until we bumped into Remis and his team, who were responding to a distress signal that had been sent by your friend's brother over there. Apparently, Dasaro's mercs have been jamming and filtering communications since they first got here, which is why we hadn't heard anything until now."

"Makes sense," Ziva said. "Kat said she hadn't ever been able to reach anyone here." She gestured toward the police station. "So they're all in there?"

Skeet nodded. "Remis knows the leader of these clowns, says he's not surprised they locked themselves in like this. According to Reilly, they'd been ordered to wipe out the whole city, but when the people decided to fight back, everything went to hell for them. That's about how it was when we got here."

"Any ideas on how we move forward?"

"Let's go find out." The two of them walked back over and joined the others, who by this time were engaged in a somewhat heated conversation.

"The front door won't work," Remis said. "We've already established that."

"Can we flush them out?" Aroska asked. "Put grenades in through the windows?"

"We're fresh out," Zona replied, massaging his temples.

"Comms are still down so calling for backup isn't an option right now," Zinni added.

Aroska shrugged. "Is there anything they want, anything we can give them that will give us a way in?"

Mag snorted. "Loric wants *me*. Even if I can't give him the crystals he wanted, he'd still jump at the opportunity to put a round through my head."

There was awkward silence for a moment during which nobody dared to make any suggestions. Skeet kicked himself when he realized he was actually considering using the man as bait. One look at Ziva told him she was thinking the same thing, though she kept her mouth shut as well.

Kat Reilly finally spoke up. "Is Dasaro in there?"

It struck Skeet as a rather odd question. "We found his ship earlier today, so if he's here in the city, then yeah, he's probably in there."

She studied the building for a minute and then stood up. "Before anyone says anything, I want you to hear me out. I've got an idea—I'll go in."

"Wait a minute—" Mag began.

"I said be quiet," Kat snapped. "You just got done telling me this Loric guy killed our family. Dasaro killed Bosco, and he was going to kill me. I want them both dead. This is my fight just as much as it is anyone else's."

Aroska crossed his arms. "You're not trained for anything like this."

"I've survived on my own on Chaiavis for the past seven years. I've got this handled."

"What's your plan, Kat?" Ziva asked, bringing her hands to rest on her hips.

To Skeet's surprise, a flicker of understanding flashed across her eyes. Tarbic was right, after all—Kat had no formal ops training, and he wondered why Ziva of all people wasn't protesting the idea of sending her in.

"It would be best if I don't say," the young woman replied. "I want to make this as realistic as possible, and the way you all react will be critical. We contact Loric, tell him Reilly wants to talk, Reilly wants to make a deal. He'll be expecting Mag, and he'll let me in." She moved to the edge of the group and stood, surveying the police station with her hands on her hips. "Split into two teams out here and surround the building. Once everything is in motion, you'll be able to enter through the side doors. You'll know when it's time to move."

Her brother placed a hand on her shoulder. "You're sure?"

"I know what I'm doing," she answered, turning around to look straight at Ziva. "Trust me."

Although Skeet got the feeling there was more going on than met the eye, it was the best plan anyone had come up with so far. "I'll see if I can raise Loric," he said.

· 95 ·
FORMER POLICE OUTPOST
ARGALL, HAPHEZ

K at hesitated for a moment outside the station door, straining to see inside. It was no use; the mercenaries had set all the windows to maximum tint, blocking all view of what—if anything—they were doing. Of course this bothered her, but she'd given up trying to see into the future once she realized she was sick. Her discomfort was something she would just have to fight through. This plan of hers was the only way to keep more innocent people, her brother in particular, from getting hurt.

"Reilly's coming in!" Sergeant Duvo called over the loudspeaker. They'd managed to wire a communicator into the city's emergency broadcast system, effectively capturing Loric's attention. After a bit of persuasion, he'd agreed to a meet, requesting that Mag wait by the front door and be escorted inside by his men.

There Kat stood in his place, listening intently to the sound of approaching footsteps inside. The door slid open just a crack, and she found herself staring down the barrel of a rifle. A confused face peered at her from the other end, and for a moment, she wondered if they would shoot her on the spot. But the man must have noticed the family resemblance, because he stepped aside and motioned for her to enter.

Several mercenaries converged on her the second the door shut behind her. She lifted her hands and looked each of them in the eye, determined not to reveal how terrified she really was. One of them approached to search her, so she tucked her hands into her pockets and spread her arms, opening her jacket to show that she was unarmed. He gave her a thorough pat-down anyway, removing her spare plasma cell and communicator even though they were both useless.

"Where's Loric?" she asked, holding her head high.

"This way," growled the man who'd searched her. He turned and began leading the group down the hall.

The interior of the station was dark, thanks in large part to all the tinted windows, but from what Kat could tell, it had once been a respectable little outpost. More armed men appeared at every turn, watching her from the shadows. She met each of their gazes, hoping to catch sight of Dasaro. If there were still this many survivors, she couldn't even imagine what kind of havoc they'd wreaked while they were at full force.

The mercs marched her into what appeared to be the only illuminated room in the station, and it was blindingly bright in comparison. A lone man whom she presumed to be Loric paced back and forth with his hands folded behind his back.

He didn't even look at her until she stood directly in front of him, and when he did, the shock was apparent in his face. "You're not Reilly," he said.

"Hello, Loric," she replied, reveling in the look he gave her when she addressed him by name. "And yes, I *am* Reilly. Kat Reilly. Word is you killed my family."

Loric smirked. "I haven't killed anyone who didn't have it coming, *Defekt*. If you're as much of a pest as the rest of your family, maybe I should kill you too and save myself the trouble of dealing with you." He shrugged and looked around at his men. "What's stopping me?"

Kat slid her hands back into her pockets and surveyed the room; there still didn't seem to be any sign of Dasaro. *Sheyss.* "I don't know. What's stopping you?"

That prompted a hearty chuckle from the man. "Oh! She's feisty for a *souhn Defekt*, just like...what is he, your brother?"

She said nothing.

"All right, I let you in here because you wanted to talk," he said, far too amused for Kat's taste. "I don't even know you. What could you possibly have to talk about?"

"I may not have been around here long, but I do know a couple of things," she said. "You've hurt my brother. Maybe I never knew them, but you killed my parents and siblings, and you made the rest of the world think it was an accident. On top of all that, you're working for Diago Dasaro, and he tried to hurt my friends. This may not mean anything to you, but I've made it my goal in life to *stop* people like you."

He laughed again, though Kat sensed she had struck a chord somewhere within him. "What do you want from me, *shouka*?"

His arrogance sickened her, especially since he knew full well that he and his men were screwed. She stared him down for several seconds, refusing to break eye contact. She couldn't recall the last time she'd been so angry, so passionate about something—when she'd realized she was dying, she'd done her best to steer clear of high-stress situations. She hadn't expected this encounter to feel so good.

"I'm giving you a choice here," she replied. "You and your men can get up and walk out that door right now, and nobody gets hurt."

"'And nobody gets hurt'?" he echoed. He snorted and shook his head. "There are fifty of us and one of you. Why should I be concerned?"

"You know as well as I do—there's a whole squad of agents outside ready to tear this place apart, including Ziva Payvan. It seems she's been giving your boss some trouble."

Loric closed the distance between them and loomed over her. "How about I just shoot you now?"

"That's not going to happen."

"You're in no position to decide what will or won't happen."

"I think I am."

Kat pulled the thermal grenade from her pocket and let it roll to the floor.

· 96 ·
CITY CENTER
ARGALL, HAPHEZ

Waiting was Ziva's job, whether she was behind the scope of her rifle or sitting in a parked car watching for a drop. But today in Argall, waiting felt different. It had been a long time since she'd felt this antsy. Perhaps it was because Kat had turned into such a wildcard in this game. She was more accustomed to waiting for something *specific* to happen or appear, and right now, there was no predicting what exactly Kat had up her sleeve. Just to be safe, she ejected the half-spent mag from her weapon and shoved her spare one in, chambering a round before lowering her arm back to her side.

She crouched behind the barricade they'd set up, accompanied by Skeet, Zinni, Aroska, and several Tekele agents. Remis had taken Zona and the remainder of his men around to the other side of the station just as Kat had instructed. The streets had once again fallen completely silent as every pair of eyes watched for the slightest movement and every pair of ears listened for the slightest sound.

Mag Reilly crouched beside her, continuously fidgeting and contributing to her anxiety. She'd never expected him to still be alive, much less present here. It was difficult to tell what exactly Kat thought of meeting him. At first, she'd seemed relieved, as if simply getting here and finding him meant she could live out her remaining days in peace, but then she'd gone ahead and volunteered herself for something that would practically have to be a suicide mission in order to work.

A suicide mission. Ziva's hand went to her belt, carefully probing the area where she'd attached that old thermal grenade. It was nowhere to be found. She searched her mind, conjuring up a memory of the slight tugging she'd felt as she'd shaken Kat's hand and wished her luck. She suddenly realized this was the young woman's way of going out on her own terms. She was doing whatever it took to help her people, just like she'd said.

"Damn it."

The building went up with such force that they were all knocked backwards, even with the barrier there. Ziva threw her arms up, shielding her head from burning debris as it rained down around them. With the roar of the blast combined with the crashing chunks of building and mercenary, the only things she could hear for close to a minute were her own heartbeat and Mag screaming.

A pair of hands, either Skeet's or Aroska's, took her arm and hauled her to her feet. "She took my grenade!" she sputtered, the sound of her voice muffled by the ringing in her ears.

Distant shouts could be heard as the other team made their way back through the massive cloud of dust and smoke. A couple of them sported cuts and bruises, but they were all accounted for and no one seemed to be severely injured. After a brief look around, it appeared her group had fared the same.

Everyone watched as Mag took several steps into the street and fell to his knees, staring through teary eyes into the burning rubble that contained his sister. Ziva couldn't comprehend how such a strong bond could have formed in the mere twenty minutes they'd known each other, but then it struck her that they'd known each other for a long time. Mag had, of course, known of Kat's existence since her birth, and Kat had devoted the remainder of her life to making sure her brother and home were saved. Finally getting a chance to meet had sealed the deal.

She followed him out into the street and stooped down beside him, taking a moment to survey the damage herself. "Look at me," she said, moving around to interrupt his view of the building. "Do you think she'd want you to do this?"

He looked at her, his tears mixing with the sweat already coating his face. "*Shouka*. How can you talk like that right now?"

She took him by the shoulders and pulled him into a standing position. "This is what she wanted."

"I doubt she wanted to die!"

"She was already dead!"

Ziva hadn't planned on sharing Kat's secret, and she'd never been one to blurt out information, but in this case, she felt the need to make everyone understand why the young woman had done what she'd done. She responded to the shocked looks around her with a brief rundown of what Kat had told her about the disease, not the specifics about Ronan and the syringe, but of how she'd never planned on leaving Argall, how she'd requested she be left to her own devices.

"I didn't realize what she meant when she said she wasn't going back to Chaiavis," Ziva said, not just to Mag. "I'll admit I wasn't expecting this. But don't you realize what she did? We may have had these guys cornered, but we were still outnumbered, and we would have lost people if we tried to go in. By going in there on her own, Kat spared the rest of us from getting hurt or killed. And by taking out the mercenaries at the source, she saved this whole town!"

Then she turned directly to Mag. "So be happy about that, and be proud of your sister."

For a long time, everyone merely stared at her, with Skeet and Zinni looking bewildered and Aroska looking disappointed. "She's right," he finally said to the others. "Kat put an end to this bloodshed. But why didn't you say anything?"

"She told me not to tell anyone because she didn't want to be treated differently," Ziva replied. "I know as well as you do that someone in her condition shouldn't have even been allowed to come here, but I wasn't going to tell her no. She'd spent the past three years of her life waiting for this, and if I were in her position, I would hope someone would respect my final wishes, too."

Skeet slowly approached Mag and gave him an understanding pat on the shoulder. "What your sister did was very brave. I'm not sure if I could have done the same."

That seemed to coax a bit of life into him. He gazed at the flames and caught a piece of ash as it drifted by. "I didn't even know her," he said.

"Well, I did," Ziva said, "and she wouldn't want you to stand around moping over her. She gave this town a second chance, and someone's got to take charge and start down that trail she blazed."

"You told me earlier you wanted to save this place," Skeet said. "Here's your chance."

Mag shrugged as if he didn't know what they could possibly expect from him. "They destroyed all our equipment and the crystals along with it. I wouldn't even know where to start."

"Aren't there more crystals you can harvest?" Zinni asked.

"They take time to mature. If you harvest them too early, they're not worth anything and you've just wasted an entire crop. Besides, there are people here who are starving, dying. We can't afford to wait for another harvest." Mag muttered something that sounded like a curse and wiped his hand over his eyes, mixing his tears with the soot and ash on his face. "What we need is that bloody map."

"You mentioned a map earlier," Skeet said. "What is it?"

"My father created a map that leads to a hidden vein of crystals," Mag explained. "He hid it before he died, and all the mercs thought I had it—that's why they targeted me. It's just a plain old data pad, but I've looked everywhere and haven't found it. The only thing I can think of is that my father sent it off-planet."

The pieces fell together in Ziva's mind as he spoke and she turned to Aroska, who was already looking her way with a grin on his face.

"I think we have it," he said.

That caught Mag's attention. "What?"

"Technically, Kat had it," Aroska went on, relaying the story she had told them about receiving the data pad from an unknown sender on Haphez. "She didn't know what it was, but she kept it anyway and still had it after all these years."

"Would your father have sent that map to her?" Ziva asked.

"I guess that makes sense," Mag replied, squinting as if he were deep in thought. "Knowing him, if he didn't leave it here, he would have entrusted it to someone elsewhere, someone nobody else would have suspected."

Ziva nodded. "And someone who didn't know what she was getting into. What Kat didn't know couldn't hurt her."

"Exactly!"

"That's got to be it, then," Aroska said, a twinkle of excitement in his amber eyes.

"It's in the ship," Ziva said. "I'll get it."

"Need a hand?" Skeet asked.

She turned and began to backpedal in the direction of the loading docks. "No. Get this fire put out and take any survivors into custody. Then we need to spread out throughout the city and bring everyone out of hiding. Now that the station is destroyed, comms should be back up. Keep your channels open and we'll rendezvous in the square in half an hour."

She took off at a steady jog, shielding her eyes against the late afternoon sun as a variety of HSP response ships came roaring into view. They angled toward the smoke rising from the ruins of the police station and began to circle the area, following a familiar landing procedure.

"Thank you, Shevin," she murmured.

Presently, she came to the square and turned down the street that would lead her straight to the landing pad. The shop where the twins and old man were hiding was still dark, but other faces were beginning to cautiously emerge from the shadows and some had even risked a few steps into the street to tend to the wounded. They watched, emotionless, as she passed.

She wasn't quite sure what to think of how everything had transpired. She couldn't help but be angry with Kat for not sharing her intentions, but at the same time, she completely understood her reasoning. Their goals had all been accomplished with minimal casualties— the mercs and their leaders were dead, and Argall was saved. She would have preferred that there be no casualties at all, but they were often a necessary evil in her world. *Sacrifice one to save many.*

The road gave way to the field containing the storage bunkers and landing platforms. Bosco's old ship waited ahead, boarding ramp still down. On top of preventing the execution of hundreds, they'd found the map and provided Mag Reilly with a means of rehabilitating the city without even meaning to. So rarely in this line of work did she actually get a chance to experience a happy ending. There were successful missions, sure, but their outcomes weren't always pleasant, per se. Dakiti was a prime example. They'd thwarted an attack on Haphez that could have potentially wiped out thousands, but in the process, they'd started a miniature war with the Sardons and good agents had been lost to the facility's sick experiments. This time, it seemed that everything had truly worked out for good.

Well, Tarbic, we've survived so far, she thought as she hauled herself up onto the landing pad.

The map was right where they'd left it, tucked into her backpack and wrapped in a rag for protection. She picked it up and examined it again, still unsure what the yellow lines represented. Even when she was back outside, a quick glance around the valley yielded nothing. Perhaps it was only meaningful to someone who knew Argall well. Mag would no doubt know how to interpret it, and she suddenly found herself looking forward to joining him on the expedition into the caves.

Preoccupied by the map, she made it halfway back across the landing pad before she noticed the figure standing in the field a short distance away. She looked up, startled to find herself staring down the barrel of a pistol...and even more surprised to see that the face on the other end belonged to Diago Dasaro.

Ziva froze. There wasn't time to wonder what he was doing there. The only thing that really mattered was that he hadn't been killed in the police station after all. She could see the muscles in his hands and forearm tighten just as Aroska's had at the relay station—he clearly wasn't in the mood for chit chat. *Shoot me, see what happens*, she thought. At this angle and distance, aiming for body mass was his best option, in which case any shots he fired would be absorbed by Jada's underlay. In turn, it would buy her enough time to move forward and squeeze off a couple shots of her own, enabling her to either put him down or find cover, whichever came first.

Time seemed to stop entirely as she let the data pad fall to the ground and brought her hand around to her own weapon. It had barely cleared the holster, however, when a sudden, sickening realization seized control of her mind. An image of the interrogation room flashed through her memory, and she could almost hear Dasaro himself speaking the words: "*You use a projectile pistol these days, don't you? ...Right, I carry one myself.*"

She had just enough time to draw a breath and begin to pivot. *Sheyss.*

No amount of anticipation could have prepared her for the sensation of his round ripping through the worthless underlay and into her abdomen. At first, it felt like someone had taken a war hammer to her gut, leaving her breathless and numb. Then came the centralized stabbing pain and the grotesque, warm dampness as she began to bleed. The impact sent the gun flying from her hand and it clattered to the ground several meters away. Stunned, she took a step backward to steady herself, locking her knees to ensure she maintained some shred of balance.

"Going somewhere?" Dasaro called, quickly ascending the short flight of steps up to the platform.

I've been shot was the only response Ziva could muster up, and even then, she couldn't bring herself to say it out loud. She'd made the mistake of not taking note of her surroundings before crossing the landing pad. The nearby outbuildings offered plenty of cover where Dasaro could lie in wait. She ran her tongue over her lips, which had become extremely dry. "What exactly do you think you're accomplishing here?" she got out. *Breathe. Need to breathe.* "Look around you, Diago. It's all over."

"It's not over until I say it's over," he snarled, taking an aggressive step toward her. "You took everything from me, and this doesn't end until I've returned the favor."

"I'd have thought you to be above petty revenge," she said, fighting away the faintness creeping through her head. How far away was her gun? "If I were you, I'd be trying to figure out a way to get out of here instead of wasting your time with me."

"Just shut up!" Dasaro screamed. He thrust his weapon at her, eyes crazed with hatred. He was going to pull the trigger again, and this time his sights were on her head.

Ziva commanded her body to move, telling herself that recovering her pistol was her only chance. But perhaps she had moved too quickly, or maybe locking her knees had been a mistake. The blood drained from her head, and her legs turned to liquid. She found herself once again falling blindly backward, body frozen just as it had been at the relay station. But this time, instead of a muddy riverbank, her head met the solid concrete landing pad. The resulting explosion in her brain was enough to drown out the pain of being shot, at least for a few seconds. She blinked and clawed at the landing pad's surface, unable to move and unable to orient herself.

Dasaro's shadow crossed over her face and she squinted up into the space above her, straining to see past the stars jumping around in her eyes. She gasped for the air that had escaped her upon impact and was rewarded with only a soft gurgling as blood rushed into her left lung. For a very brief moment, she thought she could feel something—the slug, a bone fragment, *something*—within her body, but it was barely noticeable when Dasaro's boot suddenly came down against the entry wound.

The ensuing pain was enough to snap her out of her dazed stupor. She gasped and pried at his foot, managing only a tiny breath past the foamy blood oozing into her mouth. She kicked wildly—or at least she thought she did. Her legs barely moved, and she had to settle with establishing a firm grip on his ankle.

"Maybe you were right," he said, his face becoming undefined as her vision swam. "Maybe it *is* over, at least for you. It's been a hell of a ride, but it has to end sometime."

She wasn't sure what triggered it—perhaps another memory of herself strung up in the Cobian prison, alone and helpless just as she was now—but she saw herself standing in Aroska's kitchen, admitting she wasn't invincible. The kitchen...her kytara! The dish she'd moved while hiding from Dasaro! In that moment of clarity, she remembered the gun she had been trying to reach only moments before, as well as the round that already waited in the firing chamber. How far was it... two, three meters? Although it was out of her grasp, it certainly wasn't out of her *reach*.

She coughed and turned her head, spitting a monstrous glob of bloody saliva onto the landing pad. She saw a blurry image of her pistol in the distance, and the knowledge that it could still be put to use caused her to inhale so forcefully she actually felt oxygen enter her lungs.

"Killing me won't solve your problems," she sputtered with that precious air.

"We'll see about that," Dasaro said.

Ziva mustered all the energy she could to fling her arm toward her gun. It was in her grasp a split second later, delivered to her by her own mind. She raised it above her head and took aim, conscious enough to revel in the look on Dasaro's face just before she pulled the trigger.

Hot blood sprayed her face, and she turned her head to avoid looking at the captain's brains as he fell forward onto her. Try as she might to get out of the way, the butt of his pistol still caught her forehead, sending another jolt through her skull and down her neck. His body settled beside her, with his legs and one arm still draped across her. She allowed her own gun to slip from her hand.

The subsequent silence was a relief for her pounding head, though it still throbbed enough to make her nauseous. She placed her palms flat against the landing pad and pushed as hard as she could, successfully sliding herself about half a meter thanks to the puddle of blood she lay in. She pushed again, crying out when the pain became excruciating, and managed to escape Dasaro's clutches once and for all. Three more pushes carried her an additional body length, but the extra effort sent a fresh stream of blood gushing from the wound.

She allowed herself to take a break, squinting upward at the clouds as they spun in a slow, hazy circle. She forced herself to continue breathing at a steady pace, despite the fact that it didn't feel like she was actually taking in any air. She tried lifting her legs to see if that was any more comfortable, but the effort only hurt worse, so she let them slide back down.

"Let's just survive another day, shall we?"

She was trying. She searched her mind for options, though it was nearly impossible to break through the cloud of seemingly random thoughts and intermittent periods of black nothingness. Nobody would be missing her for at least twenty minutes when she didn't show up at the rendezvous. Now that the mercs' jamming signal was offline, she could always try to raise someone on comm, but the razor-like shards poking her side where her communicator had been told her the device was no longer functional. She vaguely remembered hearing it shatter when she'd fallen.

Her eyes were watery, though whether it was sweat, tears, or her vision playing tricks on her, she wasn't sure. She didn't think she was crying—she couldn't breathe well enough to cry. But it was the only thing that made sense. She lifted a shaky hand and placed it over her wound.

Everything felt so much better when she shut her eyes.

· 97 ·
CITY CENTER
ARGALL, HAPHEZ

Aroska looked up from what he was doing when he heard the shot. At first, he thought it might have been one of the response ships, but when no other sound followed, he felt himself begin to sweat. It was impossible to tell where exactly it had come from—all he knew was that it was in the general direction Ziva had gone.

He handed a medipac to the woman he'd been helping and rose to his feet, staring down the street and listening. Without even realizing it, he had his communicator in his hand. "Skeet, did you hear a shot?"

"Sounds like it came from the west," the sergeant replied after several seconds.

"That's where Ziva went."

"Maybe she ran into another merc."

Something didn't feel right. "Probably. I'll go check it out."

He began walking, still bothered that Ziva hadn't told them about Kat. Everything had worked out okay in the end, but even though she'd been in her final days, he hated to see a friend die. Based on Ziva's behavior following the explosion, he imagined it must be commonplace for the spec ops agents to lose allies. He wasn't sure if he could ever handle that, but he was beginning to understand what she'd said about forming attachments when they'd talked on the balcony.

On the bright side, they'd actually found a use for that mysterious map. They may have lost Kat, but thanks to her, Argall could still be redeemed.

He lifted his communicator again and entered the code for the device Ziva had been using. When the transmission failed to connect, he tried again, still to no avail. "I'm not getting her on comm."

No sooner were the words out of his mouth than a second shot rang out. He heard Skeet curse and broke into a dead run, angling toward the field and docking area. When he caught sight of the two bodies on the landing pad, his heart skipped a beat. Even from a distance, he recognized that HSP riding jacket.

"Oh no, oh *sheyss*." He felt his breathing quicken. "I've got her! West landing platform—send medical!" He swore again and continued moving. "Skeet, you'd better get over here!"

· 98 ·
WEST DOCKS
ARGALL, HAPHEZ

She found herself standing in a vast expanse, a field that stretched as far as she could see in any direction. It was comprised of nothing but pale green grass, each blade a uniform length and perfectly straight. There was no sound when she walked—the grass bent under her boots, and the moment she lifted her foot, it turned brown and died.

There wasn't a single cloud in the sky above her, which was such a light shade of blue it seemed almost white. The sun was visible, but she couldn't feel its warmth. In fact, she was quite cold, freezing even. She noticed the sun was dropping lower in the sky, and as it did, the already-pale landscape continued to lose color. She could only stand there watching, wondering what would happen when it finally disappeared below the horizon.

A distorted, unfamiliar voice echoed across the field, startling her: "Ziva!"

She recognized that it was addressing her, but it sounded distant, somewhere behind her. She turned to locate the source, prepared to retrace her trail of footsteps, and ran headlong into a glass barrier she hadn't noticed before. The impact sent her reeling backward, dazed. She couldn't actually see it—there was no reflection from the sun, no line in the grass—but she could place her hand on it, feel its surface. The voice had come from beyond it.

As she stood there trying to wrap her head around it all, she realized the sun had paused in the sky when she'd heard the voice. It was just now beginning to drop again, more slowly than before but still at a steady pace. Somehow, she knew something bad would happen if she allowed it to disappear completely.

"Hello?" she called, pounding her fist against the glass. Neither action made any noise. The only thing she heard was the voice as it called out her name again.

"Ziva!"

The sun slowed its descent once more. This was good. She peered through the barrier, barely able to perceive a figure walking across the field in the distance. It was difficult to make out a face, but it appeared they were wearing the same clothes as she was. Was she looking at a copy of herself?

"Hello!" she screamed again, still unable to hear her own words. "Over here! Help me!"

The other person looked in her direction, smiled, and waved. "Ziva!" They beckoned for her to follow as they turned and began walking away in the direction from which she had come.

"No, no, no, no!" she said, feeling panic start to set in. She slammed both hands against the barrier. "Don't leave me!"

There, she'd heard herself! The sound frightened her at first, and it hadn't been as loud as she'd expected, but she'd done it nonetheless. Her words travelled forward and bounced off the barrier, sending a massive crack straight up the middle of it. The ground began to shake, and shattered glass rained down around her. A large crevice opened up where the base of the barrier had been, and try as she might to scramble away, she felt herself begin to fall.

The grass wasn't substantial enough to take hold of, and everything else she touched crumbled under her fingers. Just when she'd made the decision to stop fighting and let go, a hand appeared over the edge of the cliff and grabbed hold of hers with an iron grip. She couldn't see who the hand belonged to, but somehow this picture seemed familiar, and she knew she needed to hang on.

"I'm here, okay? I've got you." It was the same voice that had called to her earlier, clearer this time and much closer.

Ziva wasn't sure which was real—the grassy field with the barrier and the crevice, or the bright golden light she saw when she finally forced her eyelids apart. Her vision was still blurry, watery, with strange sparkling shapes floating around against the yellow background. As near as she could tell, she was looking straight up, covered in something warm and sticky. The only thing that remained constant, the only thing she could actually feel, was that hand that still held hers so tight. She reestablished her grip on it, clinging to it as if it were life itself.

She was vaguely aware of several different voices around her, some of which were shouting. Then came the sensation of something pressing firmly against her upper stomach. It hurt more than anything, but she was too numb to protest or do anything about it. Despite the pain, she somehow understood that this pressure—whatever it was—was meant to help her.

A face, hardly more than a blurry shadow, hovered over her for a moment. "She's still here," said the same voice that had comforted her a minute before.

Who's here? she thought.

"The medical transport is here," another voice said.

Someone must have gotten hurt.

"You hang on, Ziva. You hear me?"

She squeezed the hand even tighter, not daring to look down into the crevice for fear that she'd slip. "Okay."

"Did you hear that? She's still talking."

"Just get her onto the stretcher."

Ziva blinked, catching a brief glimpse of that face as it appeared above her again. It was Aroska, pressing a blood-stained palm against her ribcage. He disappeared after only a second, blocked from her view by a pair of bright red shield doors. Several sharp objects were jammed into her arm and some unseen force began to pry her hand away from the one she clutched. She grabbed at the grass, the cliff, anything she could hold on to, but it was no use. A high-pitched beeping filled her ears and she fell.

· 99 ·
HSP MEDICAL CENTER
NORO, HAPHEZ

Skeet snapped to attention when the door to the recovery ward hissed open for the umpteenth time, as did Zinni and Aroska. He tried to remind himself that he was sergeant of HSP's Alpha special operations team—the best of the best—but he was so physically, mentally, and emotionally exhausted that he couldn't help but let his guard down. Besides, it seemed that everything had finally quieted down; he didn't anticipate seeing much action for a while.

It was only another medical bot passing through, just as it had been the past six times; counting had kept him awake, at least for a while. He returned to his position against the wall and watched as Zinni continued massaging her forehead and Aroska buried his face in his arms where they were folded across his lap. They'd both resigned to the little cushioned bench against the opposite wall after standing and pacing for two hours. Skeet was determined to remain on his feet.

He couldn't help but think back to three years ago when they'd rescued Ziva from the Cobians. They'd been by her bedside rather than stuck outside the operating area, but the whole concept of waiting in a med center was still the same. Waiting right now was a relief compared to all the running around they'd done after leaving Argall. They'd started with a journey to the nearest trauma center in Seran, during which Ziva had apparently coded three times in the medical transport. Upon arrival, she had immediately been referred to their criminally understaffed intensive care unit. They'd kept her there long enough to stabilize her before shipping her off to the Severe Cases Center in Haphor, where they'd received a special circumstances message from Emeri ordering the SCC's best operating staff to accompany them back to HSP's med center in Noro. That was where they stood now, almost a full day later.

According to the medics aboard the transport, the only reason she'd even made it onto their ship was because Aroska had arrived in the nick of time and had managed to slow the bleeding. Skeet took a moment to just stare at him as he sat there, face hidden in the folds of his jacket sleeves. This was a man who had wanted nothing more than to see Ziva dead a mere two months earlier, and now it appeared he had come to care for her as much as Skeet or Zinni. Better yet, Ziva seemed to trust him to some extent, strange considering their rocky past. Gaining Ziva's trust was not something that could be done overnight— if Skeet recalled correctly, he'd said almost those exact words to Aroska during the Dakiti mission. And yet the man had somehow pulled it off.

The double doors down the hall slid open and Marshay and Ryon appeared, looking frazzled. Skeet had been in touch with them since leaving Argall, but they'd always been a step behind as Ziva was moved from place to place. Here they were, back where they'd started, having been almost to Haphor when they'd received the call to return to Noro.

"We're still waiting," Skeet said, shaking Ryon's hand and embracing Marshay. "The surgery should be over by now."

"Are they trying to kill her, moving her around like this?" the housekeeper said, teary-eyed but firm.

"She was stable the whole way over here," he assured them.

There really wasn't much else to say, given that they didn't know anything past what they'd seen for themselves. Ziva had been shot and had a gaping wound just beneath her left breast. Only the surgeons knew the full extent of the damage at this point.

Zinni and Aroska exchanged silent greetings with the newcomers, vacating their seats so they could rest. Everything was quiet once again, with Zinni resuming her pacing and Aroska taking up a stance similar to Skeet's across the hall.

Skeet just felt himself starting to doze again when the door opened for the seventh time. He almost didn't bother to look, but every time he heard that hiss, everything that had happened in the past day came flooding to memory and his eyes opened involuntarily. To his surprise—or maybe his horror—it was the doctor this time, immersed in the data pad he carried.

They were all on their feet in an instant, hovering before him with bated breath. It was difficult to tell what he was going to say based on his facial expression, making Skeet wonder if he even wanted to hear it.

"The surgery was a success," the man said, pausing while they all exhaled. "We've still got a lot of work to do, but she's expected to make a full recovery. She's starting to wake up now, so you all can go inside in just a minute. Please keep it brief—she's been through a lot. I'm going to get cleaned up and I'll be in shortly to talk to all of you."

· 100 ·
HSP MEDICAL CENTER
NORO, HAPHEZ

T he first thing Ziva noticed when her eyelids fluttered open
was the cold metal bracelet around her wrist. She didn't think
anything of it until she tried to lift her arm and found that a
chain restricted her movement to a few centimeters. A second bracelet
secured the chain to the metal rail bordering the mattress, effectively
rendering her immobile. After a couple of yanks for good measure, she
allowed her head to fall back against the pillow, too exhausted to care.

Her attention was drawn to the door when she sensed another
presence in the room. It turned out to be more than one—five, to be
exact. Her team stood in the doorway along with Aroska, Marshay, and
Ryon, looking at her in stunned silence. A guard who had been posted
there stepped aside to let them in, but they lingered there for a long
time, glancing at one another as if nobody was quite sure what to do. It
made her entirely uncomfortable.

"What are you all staring at?" she muttered, mustering all her
energy to sound as gruff as possible. It only made her wince—even
speaking was painful.

That seemed to snap them out of their stupor. They all came
crowding in at once, eyes still on her, faces grim. Skeet and Zinni took
up positions on her left, perching on the edge of the bed, while Aroska,
Marshay, and Ryon hovered on her right. Ryon reached down and took
up her cuffed hand, careful not to disturb the IV line held in place by
an adhesive strip.

"How do you feel, kiddo?"

Ziva coughed a bit, struggling to adjust her position. "I'm a little sore."

"I don't doubt it," said an unfamiliar voice.

Marshay and Aroska parted to make way for a doctor with graying hair who carried a data pad. His blue military uniform was visible under his crisp white lab coat, strange considering Ziva was fairly certain this was HSP's facility. "Ziva Payvan, you are a very lucky woman."

She forced a good-natured scoff. "I don't believe in luck."

"Well, maybe you should start." The doctor held his data pad up to a large viewscreen beside the bed, waving the information from the smaller device to the bigger one. "Captain Dasaro's bullet entered at an angle and passed just below your heart, nicking your liver and primary stomach," he explained, pointing toward one of the scan images on the screen. "Neither organ was completely penetrated, but we'll be keeping you under close observation for a while. Your left lung also collapsed thanks to a couple of broken ribs, but we were able to get it repaired. It should be functioning at one hundred percent capacity within a few weeks. Other than that, you suffered a nasty concussion when you fell, and there's still some swelling that needs to be dealt with. The remaining tissue damage is nothing that can't be fixed with a caura regimen and some rest. You'll be back on your feet in no time."

That was all good and well, but she was more concerned about what would become of her *after* all the caura and rest. The real question was whether HSP would take her back after all this. Maybe she was just tired, but the thought of having to recover on her own again was almost unbearable. Feeling panic encroaching, she opened her mouth to ask, but Skeet beat her to it.

"What does HSP think?" The same concern that she felt was apparent in his voice.

The doctor smiled, giving her the impression it wasn't the first time he'd heard such a question. "Director Arion has already authorized a ten-week session on Na," he replied, shifting his attention down to her. "I'll be personally overseeing your recovery. You leave the day after tomorrow."

Sighs of relief rose up throughout the group and Ziva closed her eyes. A second chance at the Na Facility was a rare privilege far too many agents had been denied, her included. The opportunity to recover there was an honor she had never dreamed of receiving. The rehab and conditioning were as brutal as HSP's elite training sessions, but nearly all those who were admitted had been able to return to work. She lifted her hand to rub her face, but the rattling chain was a stark reminder that she could not. "What about this?" she asked.

"You're technically still in custody," the doctor explained. "While the real killer is still at large, your involvement in Tachi's assassination has been waived thanks to the information that was uncovered regarding Captain Dasaro and Argall. But you did kill another HSP agent, and while it's clear she was in league with Dasaro, your charges can't be dropped until the proper evidence is brought forward, just like during a regular grace period. Unfortunately, the hearing can't take place until after your rehabilitation session is complete, so you'll be placed in military custody for the duration. As such, I'm sorry to say you won't be permitted to make contact with anyone outside the facility as you normally would during rehab. Do you understand everything I'm telling you?"

She nodded and then shrugged, giving the cuffs another yank. "I'm not going anywhere."

The doctor smiled again. "I'm sure you're not, Lieutenant. It's mostly a formality at this point. We're required by law to keep you under guard." He made a slight adjustment on one of the nearby monitors and checked the IV line running into her hand. "Again, I apologize for the inconvenience, but things already seem to be looking up for you as far as the case goes. Like I said, you're a lucky woman."

Ziva watched as he shut the viewscreen off and took up the data pad. Nodding respectfully toward the group, he turned and strode out of the room, his long white coat billowing behind him. She waited until he had disappeared before running her tongue over her dry lips and taking as deep a breath as the bandages around her abdomen would allow. "I really wish you all would stop staring at me," she said, closing her eyes to escape the pressure of their collective gaze.

The first signs of tears glistened in Marshay's eyes, but her voice didn't waver when she spoke. "We're just enjoying seeing you in one piece, my dear."

"I'm pretty happy to *be* in one piece." Ziva pulled herself into a more upright position, wincing against the fire that surged through her body as she did so. A throbbing ache engulfed her entire midsection, and she instinctively placed her free hand on her stomach in a futile attempt at alleviating some of the pain. She instantly regretted it when every member of her entourage gasped and leaned forward. How they expected to help, she had no idea.

She masked her genuine discomfort by sending them all a glare that did a sufficient job of keeping them at bay. "I don't need to be babysat, thank you."

Skeet laughed. "I'd better call ahead and warn the guys on Na about who they're dealing with. They don't know what they're in for." With that, his smile faded; the thought was obviously bittersweet. "You know Z, if you go to that facility, we won't hear from you for ten weeks. I think there's still a lot we need to talk about."

A familiar prickly sensation coursed through Ziva's nerves, aggravating the ache in her chest and abdomen. She doubted he and Zinni appreciated being left out of the loop the way they had, but they were no worse off than anyone else. On the other hand, they were her best friends—some of the few people in the galaxy she genuinely trusted—and she had still kept them in the dark. Indeed, there was much that needed to be discussed.

"I know," Ziva replied. "And we will, just not…now."

"Right *now*, I think you need to get some rest," Ryon said, taking up her hand again. "The last thing you need is all of us in your hair."

Though she couldn't have agreed more, part of her was still glad they had come to see her. "I'm sorry you all got dragged into this," she muttered.

"Don't be," Zinni said. "You did what needed to be done, and we weren't going to sit by doing nothing. There are some things you just can't handle on your own. That's when you need friends who can help you, whether you ask for it or not. We're here for you—don't you forget that."

The room fell silent for several long seconds before Marshay spoke. "I think we could all use some dinner," she said. Then she smiled and winked. "Don't worry, dear. I'll take good care of your crew."

There was a series of soft goodbyes murmured as everyone turned and began shuffling toward the door, bumping and weaving around each other in the same awkward manner in which they had entered. Ziva imagined seeing her alive was still taking some getting used to. She regretted having had to deceive them in such a way, but there hadn't been much other choice. Realistically, her actions had been far from self-centered. She didn't keep secrets because she didn't trust her friends—she did it to protect them. But now she wondered if they would ever trust *her* again.

Aroska, the person who knew more of her secrets than anyone else, was the only one who had said nothing for the duration of the visit. Ziva watched past drooping eyelids as he fell into position at the back of the line of people filing out the door. He seemed to have an odd cloud of emotions hanging about him, some mixture of sadness, relief, and sheer exhaustion. She didn't blame him—he'd dropped everything to follow her on what had turned out to be one crazy hyperspace trip. Even after he'd explained himself, Ziva still didn't feel like she fully understood his reasoning.

"Aroska," she murmured, catching him just as he reached the door.

He paused, startled by her voice, and sent her a questioning glance. He approached slowly when she beckoned, still moving in that same cautious manner. Ziva could sense a strange irrational fear emanating from him as he came to a stop beside the bed, hands shoved into his pockets. A confusing man, he was. In that respect, the two of them had a lot in common.

He lingered there for a moment before taking another step toward her and flashing a mischievous smile. "You really need to quit getting yourself shot."

She sent a half-hearted glare his way, unable to help but smirk herself. "You have no room to talk, considering you're the one who shot me last time," she said. "I thought we had decided it was your turn."

Aroska laughed and sat down beside her, nervously keeping his distance. "I can't help it if you want to go jump in front of bullets all the time." He looked down at her and nodded. "I'm glad you're okay."

"Thanks to you, I guess."

"So you remember?" He arched an eyebrow. "You seemed pretty out of it by the time I got up there. For a while, the only thing that told me you were even still with us was the death grip you had on my hand. I still can't feel my fingers." He winked.

"They look fine to me," she said, managing a brief eye roll. "Did Mag Reilly get his map?"

"We left it with Agent Zona. He stayed behind to make sure everything went smoothly. Word is they found that room of crystals. Argall is going to be okay."

"Where's my kytara?"

"I found it on Bosco's ship on the way back here. I'll put it away for you."

She was surprised she'd even remembered those details after all she'd been through, especially the kytara. The last thing she needed was for somebody to stumble across it by accident—she was in enough trouble as it was.

"Do you remember what you said to me?"

There was something odd in Aroska's tone of voice, the same sad quality Ziva had already noticed in his behavior. Curious, she looked up at him, eyebrows furrowed, and shook her head.

"I'd just made it to the landing pad, and I was sitting there trying to figure out what the hell to even do. For a minute, I thought you were already gone, but you looked up at me...and you told me not to leave you."

She tilted her head, eyes narrowed. "I think you're lying."

He broke out into a grin and shook his head. "Okay, I'll admit you were mumbling and I couldn't understand a thing, but it sounded like something along those lines." He pivoted around to face her fully. "I want you to know that I'm not *going* to leave you. You've turned out to be a good friend, and what Zinni said goes—I'm going to stick by you, for better or for worse."

"It'll most likely be worse, you know."

He shrugged. "Yeah, I figured."

She wasn't quite sure how to respond. "Well, I guess that's good, because I need to ask you for one more favor."

"Anything."

"If I'm gone, Skeet and Zinni are going to lose Alpha status because of the Rule of Three. I can't do that to them, not after how hard they've worked, and especially not after everything I've put them through. I need you to stay on board. Become the third member in my absence. You've got to help hold the team together or everything we've worked for will be for nothing."

He looked unsure. "The director's not going to let me just walk on."

"He will if I authorize it," Ziva said, "and I will. I can't order you to do this, but I'm *asking* you to—asking as that friend you were talking about." She paused and winced again as she drew a deep breath, surprised by the words she was about to say. "Please, Aroska, you're the only person I would ever trust enough to do something like this."

He hesitated for a long time, staring at the blank wall across the room. "Well," he began, "I'm flattered to finally be trusted by Ziva Payvan. I would be honored to join your team, Lieutenant."

She sighed and closed her eyes, feeling as though a massive amount of weight had just been lifted from her shoulders. Somehow her wounds no longer hurt quite so much. "Thank you," she murmured.

Aroska stood up, flexing his fingers again for show. "Well, I'd better catch up to the others—I wouldn't want to miss out on Marshay's cooking. Get some rest, and for what it's worth, enjoy your time on Na. The galaxy knows you could use the break."

He reached down and patted her on the top of the head. Even the simple touch was jarring, though she didn't dare admit it. "You're not so bad, Tarbic."

"I'm going to quote you on that sometime," Aroska said, dipping his head with a sheepish smile. "Take care of yourself, Ziva. It's been real."

"See you on the other side."

She watched as he turned and wandered out the door, standing up a little straighter than he had been before. Placing a hand on her abdomen once again, she carefully eased back down off the pillow and worked her way into a comfortable position. The room was completely silent now except for the gentle hum of the machines surrounding her bed, and she took a moment to bask in the peace and quiet. Then, settling her head down against the pillow, she closed her eyes and fell asleep.

NEXUS

SPECIAL THANKS...

...to Tanni, once again, for sticking with me over the past couple of years and being such a wonderful editor. You've sacrificed a lot of your free time and I thank you for that.

...to the rest of my awesome beta readers: Amanda, Brian, Brandy, Macey, Nola, and of course, my mom. I can only proofread on my own so many times, and fresh sets of eyes and open minds are invaluable when it comes to getting the job done.

...to any other friends, family members, and colleagues who have lent me your eyes or ears as I've brainstormed, researched, and edited. I'll say it again – the little things do count.

RONAN: ZIVA PAYVAN BOOK THREE

T he sound of the portable comm grid coming to life startled Skeet Duvo out of his thoughts. His long legs already dangled over the edge of the stiff little bunk he lay on, so he worked his way into a sitting position and planted his feet on the floor, standing bolt upright when he saw that the indicator light on the comm console blinked red.

He made it across the darkened room in two strides and hovered over the console for a moment, wide-eyed. A red message light meant only one thing: a transmission straight from Emeri Arion's office at the Haphezian Special Police's Noro Headquarters. And that in itself meant only one thing: bad news.

Skeet ran a hand through his spiky orange hair and drew in a deep breath before accepting the transmission. "Duvo, Alpha 40318," he said in response to the prompt preceding the message. A series of tones and static followed, odd for a call coming directly from Emeri. But instead of the director's gruff voice, he found himself listening to the eerie feminine voice of HSP's virtual intelligence.

"General distress. Agency-wide emergency protocols in effect. All agents currently dispatched to the field are ordered to cease communications immediately. Operate under Condition Black until further notice. Warning: for security purposes, do not attempt to establish contact with HSP or any affiliates during this time."

Condition Black. The team had conducted a mission under Condition Black once, Skeet recalled, but mainly for training purposes. They'd been allowed no contact with the agency, no contact with any other ops teams, no contact with *anyone* on Haphez, for that matter. Although it seemed like they were being hung out to dry, the protocol was in fact designed to protect agents. If the agency was somehow compromised, anyone in the field could remain anonymous and, theoretically, work independently to counter whatever force threatened

Headquarters. If Condition Black was in effect *now*, it could only mean—

"Does the user have any queries before this transmission terminates?"

Skeet drummed his fingers on the console. "What's the status of Noro Headquarters?"

"One moment...Noro Headquarters remains under Code Red lockdown following an attack on the Grand Army's Na Base. Casualties have been reported."

He felt his pulse spike at the mention of Na. "Nature of the attack?"

"Base officials have initially categorized the attack as type: chemical. No other information is available at this time."

"Find person: Ziva Payvan."

"Accessing personnel database...searching. Alert—status of person 'Ziva Payvan' not found. Please try again."

"*Sheyss*," he muttered, ruffling up his hair again. "No more questions. End transmission."

"Ending transmission. Warning: Condition Black protocols in effect. Please cease all communications immediately." The VI repeated itself twice more before the call went dead.

Skeet swore again and immediately began packing the communications equipment into its compact carrying cases. Everything in the room had been set up in a manner that allowed it to be torn down and stowed in a matter of minutes. Even on his own, he got the job done in no time. He held his pistol up to check the plasma charge, bristling a bit when the door of the room slid open. A quick glance revealed that the intruder was only Aroska Tarbic, and Skeet slid his finger away from where it had subconsciously come to rest above the weapon's trigger guard.

If the former field ops lieutenant was surprised to see the room empty and their supplies packed, he concealed it well. "Can I assume this is about the emergency code I just received from Headquarters?" he asked, holding up his own comm.

Skeet nodded and gave Aroska a quick rundown of what he knew, which, he regretted, wasn't much. "Sounds like the agency is secure for now. I'm sure they'll be on board with the investigation on Na."

Aroska was quiet for a moment as he checked his own pistol and slid his field pack over his shoulders. "Ziva's status?"

"Unknown," Skeet answered. "There...were casualties. But I'm sure she's fine. That base covers most of the moon—what are the chances she was even in the vicinity of the attack?" He forced a good-natured snort, trying to ignore the knot that had formed in his throat.

"We can't worry about that now," Aroska said, brow wrinkled as if it pained him to speak the words. He held up the data pad he'd been carrying when he entered the room. "We may have a lead, and you know as well as I do that we're running short on time." He offered the pad when Skeet reached for it. "Emissions signatures from a ship matching our target were picked up by a science team on Bectin. They said it was headed farther out into the Fringe, toward Aubin or Plaunus."

Skeet handed the data pad back and gathered up some of the cases he'd packed. "Then what are we waiting for? Let's get moving."

Like what you read? Tell someone about it!
Taking the time to leave an honest review is immeasurably helpful
for any author, new or established. Your opinion helps other
people make informed decisions about their reading options and
allows the book to reach its target audience.

Your ratings and reviews are greatly appreciated!

About The Author

EJ Fisch is a long-time action junkie and fan of the science fiction genre. She'll readily admit that she has a vivid imagination, which can be both a blessing and a curse. She has been writing as a hobby since junior high and began publishing in the
spring of 2014.

When she's not busy writing or working her day job as a data analyst in the medical field, she enjoys listening to music, working on concept art, reading, gaming, and spending time with her animals. She currently resides in southern Oregon.

Nexus is her second novel, Book 2 in the Ziva Payvan series.

Find EJ Fisch on your favorite social media site!

Keep up with news, catch sneak peeks, and more at:
www.ejfisch.com

Questions? Comments? Use the resources above or email at:
ej@ejfisch.com

Your thoughts about the characters and storylines are always welcome and appreciated!

www.ingramcontent.com/pod-product-compliance
Lightning Source LLC
Chambersburg PA
CBHW051535250626
47157CB00001B/58